Sandy started making funny little noises in her throat. They all turned to look at her. She was on her knees by the fire, pointing into the air.

The Ouija board had levitated off the ground about five feet and was hovering, trembling slightly. The planchette was balanced on the board. It settled slowly back to the ground and began vibrating, the planchette bouncing on the board, but never slipping off.

"This is just too weird," Hillary said. "And I don't like it."

Paul laughed at her and walked to the board, picked it up, and moved closer to the fire. He knelt down and spelled out: What is going on?

With Paul's fingers resting lightly on the planchette, the three-cornered wooden device spelled out: Death.

Paul moved the planchette, spelling out: Whose death?

All of you was the reply.

THRILLERS BY WILLIAM W. JOHNSTONE

THE DEVIL'S CAT (2091, $3.95)

The town was alive with all kinds of cats. Black, white, fat, scrawny. They lived in the streets, in backyards, in the swamps of Becancour. Sam, Nydia, and Little Sam had never seen so many cats. The cats' eyes were glowing slits as they watched the newcomers. The town was ripe with evil. It seemed to waft in from the swamps with the hot, fetid breeze and breed in the minds of Becancour's citizens. Soon Sam, Nydia, and Little Sam would battle the forces of darkness. Standing alone against the ultimate predator—The Devil's Cat.

THE DEVIL'S HEART (2110, $3.95)

Now it was summer again in Whitfield. The town was peaceful, quiet, and unprepared for the atrocities to come. Eternal life, everlasting youth, an orgy that would span time—that was what the Lord of Darkness was promising the coven members in return for their pledge of love. The few who had fought against his hideous powers before, believed it could never happen again. Then the hot wind began to blow—as black as evil as The Devil's Heart.

THE DEVIL'S TOUCH (2111, $3.95)

Once the carnage begins, there's no time for anything but terror. Hollow-eyed, hungry corpses rise from unearthly tombs to gorge themselves on living flesh and spawn a new generation of restless Undead. The demons of Hell cavort with Satan's unholy disciples in blood-soaked rituals and fevered orgies. The Balons have faced the red, glowing eyes of the Master before, and they know what must be done. But there can be no salvation for those marked by The Devil's Touch.

Available wherever paperbacks are sold, or order direct from the Publisher. Send cover price plus 50¢ per copy for mailing and handling to Zebra Books, Dept. 3120, 475 Park Avenue South, New York, N.Y. 10016. Residents of New York, New Jersey and Pennsylvania must include sales tax. DO NOT SEND CASH.

DARKLY THE THUNDER

THUNDER

WILLIAM W. JOHNSTONE

ZEBRA BOOKS
KENSINGTON PUBLISHING CORP.

ZEBRA BOOKS

are published by

Kensington Publishing Corp.
475 Park Avenue South
New York, NY 10016

First printing: September, 1990

Printed in the United States of America

We are spinning our own fates, good or evil, and never to be undone. Every smallest stroke of virtue or of vice leaves its never so little scar . . . Nothing we ever do is, in strict scientific liternalness, wiped out.

William James

Book One

Chapter One

Early afternoon.

He was awakened from a restless nap by the rumbling of thunder. He lay on the couch in the silent house and listened to the distant grumbling. It seemed to hold an ominous note. And he knew that was not just his imagination.

He couldn't explain how he knew.

The thunder brought back memories; memories that the retired head of State Police had never been able to push completely out of his mind.

But dear God in heaven, how he had tried to forget that bloody, awful night so many years ago.

"I'm not going far!" Sand had pushed the words past his bloody lips. "I'll be back, Al."

Those were some of the last few words the young man had spoken.

"You don't know it, Al," Sand had said. "You can't see it. But I can. You'll need me someday."

Then the thunder began, and the young man had slipped into some sort of language that sounded to Al Watts like Gaelic.

Alvin S. Watts rose from the couch and rubbed his face with his hands. "Get out of my head, Sand," he muttered. "Get out of my head!"

In the distance, the thunder rumbled.

Watts suddenly shivered, as if something cold and slimy and . . . evil had slithered across his flesh.

Watts knew no rain would accompany the thunder. It never did. And he also knew that few people ever heard the rumbling.

Or if they did, they wouldn't admit it.

The rumbling of thunder—dark thunder, was how Al thought of it—had started thirty years back, almost to the day. And Watts had finally figured out that the only way to stop it was to go to the old deserted mining town and face the invisible rumblings. Acknowledge that he felt their presence, believed that it was real and not just in his mind. And the thunder would cease. He had to acknowledge, silently, that he was listening to some sort of message from Sand and Joey and Morg and the others.

Al had always felt compelled to warn any tourists he found there that they were in danger.

They usually left pretty quickly, as if he were the danger.

The thunder rumbled.

"Not again, Sand. I'm an old man. Leave me alone, Sand. Go away!" Watts shivered. "Jesus," he muttered, "I'm talking to a person that's been dead for thirty years."

And who talks to me, he thought. In a way.

Watts walked the den of the house. A sixty-five-year-old man who had spent forty years behind a badge. His wife had died two years back. He had never accepted her death in his mind. She had been, and still was, too much a part of him. The rock he had always leaned on for support.

Especially after that bloody night on Thunder Mountain.

His children were all grown up and had moved away. Now he rattled around alone in the big house on the quiet street of the peaceful town.

And talked to dead people. One dead person in particular.

"Damnit, Sand! Don't you know I cried like a baby at your funeral?"

The thunder rumbled. Watts listened carefully. He was sure it held a different note than ever before.

"All right, Sand," he finally said, a weary note of resignation and acceptance in his voice. "What do you want?"

She was sitting in her car at one of the local drive-ins, listening to her radio, and eating a hamburger and fries, and sipping at her Coke. Suddenly, Carol felt like she was being watched.

She looked around her. The place wasn't very busy, and she couldn't detect anyone looking at her.

She shrugged it off and turned her radio up louder. Then she felt something touch her leg, under her jeans. She jerked, spilling part of her soft drink down the front of her blouse. She wiped at the spill with a napkin, set the soft drink on the window tray, then looked at the floorboards, and felt her leg. Nothing. She sighed and took another bite of burger.

The carload of kids parked next to her pulled out, the teenagers waving and calling to her that they'd see her later that evening, at the movies. There was a real good horror movie showing.

Carol hollered back at them and felt better.

She looked around her. The place was deserted. Emptied of other cars and people. The cook and the two girls who worked the outside were inside, listening to the jukebox. And it was turned up loud.

Carol suddenly experienced a horrible, searing pain in her right ankle. She opened her mouth to scream, but the pain was so intense, she felt herself sliding into sudden darkness, unable to push the scream out of her throat.

White-hot pain brought her out of her near-faint and into a world of intense agony. She felt herself being pulled down, out of the seat, onto the floor of the car, to be wedged between the steering column and the floorboards. The bones in her other leg broke under the strain, and she shrieked in agony.

But no one heard her.

The half-eaten hamburger was jammed into her mouth,

11

stilling her screaming. A slice of onion hung out of her mouth.

No one heard the tearing sounds coming from the interior of the car. The sounds of flesh ripping, of bones breaking.

Willowdale, Colorado sat nestled in a large valley in the Rockies. It was surrounded by several farms and ranches; the farms and ranches were surrounded by towering, snow-capped mountains. Sometimes in the winter, the town would be cut off from the outside for several days at a stretch. As long as it didn't last too long, most of the people of the town didn't mind all that much. It was kind of peaceful in Willowdale when that occurred.

There were two paved roads leading into the valley, a state highway and a county road. Half a dozen dirt and gravel roads wound down from the various passes in the high mountains.

About seven miles from town, high up in the mountains, there was a ghost town. One would be hard-pressed to get any of Willowdale's residents to talk about it. They weren't afraid of the town, they just didn't want a lot of nosy tourists coming through. One could find the town on any map dated before 1920. Not on any map since then. Most of the people under sixty in the state didn't even know it existed. A few tourists came through each year to gawk at the silent ruins, and that was it.

It had been a roaring boomtown. A gold rush town. It was called Thunder.

Even back in the fifties, no one went to Thunder. Except for Sand, and those that followed the young man in their noisy hot rods and custom cars.

But everyone with any sense knew that Sand was a rebel without much of a cause. And those that followed him were a bunch of malcontents.

What really happened was, so the stories go, one day back around 1889—no one is really sure of the date—the people in Thunder just disappeared. Without a trace. Just flat-out vanished from the face of the earth. And there had been, give or take a few, five hundred people in the town of Thunder.

Gone.

Some reports stated that the town looked like a slaughterhouse, with blood splattered everywhere, along with guts and brains and slick, shiny bones and staring eyeballs.

Some people blamed it on the Indians. But no one really believed that.

Other reports say there wasn't anything left of any human being. It was as if they all, as of one mind, got up and vanished.

No one ever knew the truth. To date.

But a lot of folks were about to learn the truth. Some of them to be enlightened only briefly. Others would linger longer. To share the horror.

Willowdale had no police department. All that law business had been contracted out to the county sheriff's department. And a very puzzled Gordie Rivera and his chief deputy, Lee Evans, were studying the carnage at the drive-in.

"Jesus Christ, Gordie!" Lee finally whispered. "What the hell happened here?"

The drive-in had been ordered closed, and the area was sealed off with wide orange tape: SHERIFF'S DEPARTMENT—CRIME SCENE—DO NOT CROSS.

Gordie looked at his chief deputy. "We got a head, several yards of guts tied around the rearview mirror—somebody's idea of a very sick joke, like the hands on the steering wheel—and several gallons of blood. Now where is the body?"

Lee opened the right side door. Something slick and white and shiny dropped to the asphalt. He squatted down. "Gordie, come around here and look at this, will

13

you?"

Gordie looked and knelt down, poking at the bone with the tip of a ballpoint pen. "It's a bone. Part of a rib bone." He felt silly after saying it. Anybody could tell it was a bone, for Christ's sake!

"But whose bone is it?" Lee whispered.

"Why are you whispering, Lee?"

"I don't know. I just feel sort of, well, icky."

"Icky? What the hell kind of explanation is that?"

"Damnit, Gordie, it's spooky, too."

Gordie shook his head and looked at the sloppy mess inside the car. "Nobody could have done this without the kids in there"—he cut his eyes to the drive-in building—"seeing it. Surely the girl must have screamed. Nothing makes any sense about this."

Both men looked up as a car pulled over to the side of the street, across from the drive-in, and stopped. Al Watts looked at the lawmen from behind the wheel of his car.

Gordie waved him over, and the men shook hands.

"What'd you got, Gordie?" Watts asked. Then he looked at the dashboard. He did not change expression. Forty years behind a badge means that a person has seen just about everything horrible that can befall a human being. Only his eyes showed any emotion. "Carol Ann Russell."

"What's left of her," Gordie added.

"I can see what happened," Watts said. "How and why, Gordie?"

Neither current lawman was at all resentful of the ex-state cop's presence. The ex-head of state police was known statewide as probably one of the finest investigators ever to pin on a badge. And he never lost his cool.

"We don't know, Al," Gordie admitted.

Watts didn't have to ask if they'd dusted for prints. He could see they had. He could see the camera bag, and knew they'd taken pictures. Gordie was a professional cop; not just someone elected in a popularity contest. Watts moved around the car, to the driver's side, and looked in.

14

He'd seen worse. He circled the car and rejoined the men.

"Surely somebody heard something. Unless someone jammed that hamburger in her mouth to prevent her yelling."

"If she screamed, no one heard it. And no one saw anything. It's puzzling, Al."

In the distance, thunder rumbled. Lee appeared not to notice. Gordie and Al looked at one another. Only in his mid-thirties, Gordie was not old enough to remember Sand; did not know much about the old case. But ever since he'd taken office as sheriff, he'd heard the strange thunder.

He'd always wanted to ask Watts, if he was alone in hearing the rare rumblings.

Now he knew he wasn't.

A man from the coroner's office—in the case of Willowdale, a local undertaker—pulled up. The young man looked at the head on the dash and the hands on the wheel and closed his eyes for a moment. He opened his eyes and glanced at the sheriff. "You have all your pictures and prints, Sheriff?"

"Yes. Bag it."

The head, guts, and bones were dropped in rubber bags.

"Put it all in a cooler and seal it, Mark," Gordie instructed.

A wrecker pulled up, and the driver was instructed to tow the car to the department's impound area.

"You going to call in the state, Gordie?" Watts asked.

"Probably. You want some coffee, Al?"

"Sounds good. I'll follow you to the office."

Thunder rumbled in the distance.

The students from the university, on their spring break, parked their cars and got out, looking at what was left of the old mining town of Thunder. On their way up the winding mountain road, all had seen the barren, odd-

15

looking circle on the plateau below them.

Nothing grew there. Nothing at all.

"That's weird," a girl said.

"All this area is supposed to be haunted, or something," a young man told her, doing his best to look spooky. He almost pulled it off.

"I didn't know this old ghost town was even here," another girl said.

Not too far from where the group stood in the silent town, a wolf howled, the call wavering in the afternoon air. The call touched them; seemed to contain a note of warning.

"I didn't think there were any wolves left in this part of the state," a young man said.

"These aren't pure wolf," the college student who had organized this foray explained. Paul Morris had been born and reared in the valley. And he had always heard the thunder. "These are mixed breeds. Hybrids. Wolf/husky, wolf/shepherd."

"Why is this place supposed to be haunted?" Sandy Dennis asked.

"I'll tell you," Paul grinned mysteriously. "Later. Like tonight."

"Oh, wow!" Sandy rolled her eyes. "We're going to hear ghost stories, gang."

"Was somebody murdered up here?" Leon Meeks asked. A law major.

"So the stories go. Let's get the tents set up and build a fire. Bos, you and Hillary gather up the firewood; and try to get a bunch of it. The nights get really cold this high up. Then we'll fix supper and talk. I . . ." he paused, a funny look on his face. "I only know part of the story. It's just . . . well, nobody in the valley wants to talk about it."

"I love it!" Lynn Stillmore grinned. "I love ghost stories in the night. Especially when we've got lots of wine to drink. Did you remember to bring the Ouija board, Doyle?"

Doyle remembered.

16

"This is going to be fun!" Pat Irwin said. She paused, cocking her head to one side, frowning. "Did any of you just hear someone chuckling—kind of a deep voice?"

"Yeah," Leon said. "As a matter of fact, I did."

Faint singing drifted to them. "Do bop de do bop de do bop, de do."

Coffee poured and the men seated, Gordie said, "Gomez finally got around to telling me, yesterday, about a missing cowboy of his. Of course, that's not unusual. Last week, Lowman had a man disappear and never come back. Several ranchers and farmers have told me that their dogs just flat refuse to leave the house at night. Just simply refuse to leave the porch. They whine and whimper, until someone lets them inside."

"What are you saying, Gordie? A bear on the prowl? No bear did that to Carol Ann."

"Cowboys have a habit of drifting, Al. No damn grizzly wandered up to that drive-in and tore that girl apart. No grizzly tied that goddamn bow of guts on the mirror, and placed her hands on the wheel perfectly at ten and two. With that much blood loss, Carol Ann was ripped apart. There are bits of flesh all over the car, which indicates to me that she was eaten right there at that drive-in."

Watts grimaced at the thought. "Which leads us . . . ?" He let it trail off.

Gordie smiled at the us. The old warhoss wasn't about to be excluded from this case, and Gordie—no publicity hound, and with not an ounce of professional jealousy in him—welcomed his help. "I don't know, Al. Yet. Al? What's with this thunder that only a few of us seem to notice?"

Watts's eyes were bright and sharp and alert. "You think some distant thunder has anything to do with cowboys disappearing and Carol Ann's death?"

"Do you?" the sheriff tossed it back to him.

Watts shrugged his still muscular shoulders. He looked

17

and acted more like fifty than sixty-five. "I'll reserve comment on that for a time. Have you notified Carol's parents?"

"They're out of town. Visiting relatives somewhere. We haven't been able to locate them."

"The press?"

"Just our little paper. And I haven't exactly leveled with them. That's the main reason why the drive-in was cordoned off and closed."

"The car hops? Or whatever the hell they're called now."

Gordie laughed. "That dates you, Al. Yeah, I think I put the fear of the law in them. But it'll eventually leak out; you know that."

Watts nodded and met the sheriff's eyes. "You believe in the supernatural?"

"I believe in God and Satan and the hereafter."

"That isn't exactly what I meant."

"You mean like spooks and hobgoblins and werewolves and things like that?"

"No."

"Then what the hell do you mean, and what are you getting at, Al?"

Watts rose from his chair and walked to a window. Getting dark. "More and more thunder occurring. It's like . . . he's trying to tell us something."

"Who?"

"Sand."

"Sand?"

"Long story, Gordie."

"I got the time."

"Maybe you're right."

"About what?"

"Maybe it is time."

Gordie shifted in his chair. "This conversation is getting just a little strange, Al. I've got a dead girl foremost on my mind."

"You're the one who asked about the thunder, Gordie."

"Who is Sand?"

18

"A young man I killed thirty years ago. Almost to the day."

"I was five years old," Gordie said drily.

"If I remember correctly, Sand was twenty-one. Right after his death, I started hearing the thunder." Watts moved toward the door. "Let's see what this night brings, Gordie. Then we'll talk."

Without another word, Watts opened the door and walked outside. He looked up at the sounds of distant thunder.

The sheriff called for an inside deputy. "Dig through the files, Mack. See what you can find on somebody named Sand. It might be interesting reading."

"Sand was his nickname, Sheriff," the old deputy said. "You're from Logantown; you wouldn't have any reason to know anything about the Saunders boy."

"You know the story?"

"Oh, yeah. There's still a few of us around who remember what went on."

"Get some coffee and have a seat, Mack. Talk to me. Who was he? We don't have any Saunders in this valley. Not to my knowledge, anyway."

"The family moved away shortly after the boy was killed. I don't know where they went. Sand said he'd be back. Told Captain Watts that right before he died. I know; I was there."

"Where is there?"

"On that flat just below the ghost town."

That's the direction the thunder seems to be coming from, Gordie thought. Oh, come on! he silently berated himself. Next thing you know, you'll start looking under the bed at night.

"And Sand said something else, too," Mack broke into his thoughts. "He said that we couldn't see . . . something. He never did say what it was. But he said he could see it. And someday we'd need him. I'm gonna admit something to you, Sheriff: I felt, that night, standing over that broken, bloody, dying, but still unforgiving young

19

man, I felt like, well, that his soul didn't really leave. Me and Watts talked about it—just one time. We never spoke of it again. But we both saw misty shapes all around us that night. You see, a lot of Sand's friends—and his wife—had been killed before Sand got killed. I ain't never been back to that mountain. Never. And I'm not goin' back, either."

Some invisible *thing*, slimy and greasy and fear-producing, crawled lightly over Sheriff Gordie Rivera's flesh. He looked down at his hands. They were trembling.

The sky rumbled with thunder.

Chapter Two

That evening.

He was sitting in the Roxanne Theater, watching the previews of coming attractions, when he suddenly jumped up and began screaming that he couldn't stand the pain. Holding his head, he ran down the aisle, his screaming almost drowning out the sounds of dialogue from the huge lips on the screen. He jumped up on the stage, just as the theater manager was yelling for someone to turn on the house lights. The lights popped on, flooding the stage with brightness.

Then the young man's head exploded.

The little kids sitting on the front row were showered and splattered with blood and brains; eyeballs rolled around on the dusty floor of the stage, and then silently slipped off, to land with a soft plop on the floor of the building.

Later, some would swear they heard someone humming some do-bop stuff. Fifties music.

"Do bop de do bop de do bop, de do."

Those seated around the front went into a blind panic, screaming and yelling and running away. Some of them were injured, trampled in their terror-stricken rush to get out, to get away from the awfulness.

The sheriff's department was called.

Sitting in his den, the lights turned down low, listening to a scanner, Watts got out of his chair and slipped on a light windbreaker. He was reaching for a pistol, when a voice popped into his head.

"That won't do you any good."

Watts felt the strength leave his legs. Afraid he might collapse, he leaned against a wall for support, waiting for the shock to leave him. He knew that voice well. Sand.

When he was sure his legs would once more function, Watts walked out of the house to his car. He left his pistol on the table by the scanner.

He arrived at the Roxanne Theater just a few seconds behind Sheriff Rivera.

"Don't ask," Gordie said. "I don't know what's going on."

"Then we'll find out together."

Gordie ordered some of his people to start working the crowds that were milling around the outside. Try to find out something.

"Somebody must have blowed his head off with a shot-gun!" the theater manager said. "Goddamn, it was awful. I never seen anything like it."

Both Gordie and Watts had seen enough shotgun deaths to discount the manager's theory almost immediately. At point-blank range, brains and blood and bone and teeth and eyeballs might splatter left and right, certainly following the rearward path of the blast. They would not splatter all to the front, certainly not in a neat semicircle.

Gordie ordered the theater closed for the night.

"Do bop de do bop de do bop, de do!" the singing sprang out of the cavernous interior.

"Turn off that damn music," Gordie ordered.

"There's nothing on," the manager said.

The law personnel exchanged curious looks. Watts said, "The head had to have exploded from the inside."

"You know what you're saying is virtually impossible, don't you?"

Watts shrugged.

Pictures were taken of the headless body, and the body was bagged and hauled off.

"It started out to be such a pretty spring," Deputy Jane

22

Owens said.

"It's going to get worse," the voice sprang hollow and eerie from the air.

Jane jumped about a foot off the floor and looked around her. "Who said that?"

Gordie looked at Watts. "Don't tell me. Let me guess. Sand."

"Yeah. In spirit, if not in the flesh."

The night was cold and the fire was crackling. The group of college students sat just a few yards from the beginning of the old ghost town's main street, lined with crumbling buildings, built of stone and mortar and wood. Leon produced a bottle of booze. It was quickly consumed, the wine warming them. The Ouija board was brought out and set up.

"Tell us about that huge circle down below us," Sandy said, turning to Paul Morris. "That's a weird-looking thing."

"It's where then-captain Al Watts killed a young man named Saunders. Everybody called him Sand."

"Who is Captain Watts?" Hillary asked.

"He retired as head of the state police. I've known him all my life," Paul said.

"You knew this Saunders person?" Bos asked, producing another jug of wine.

"Oh, no. I wasn't even born when he died. It happened thirty years ago."

"Back in the marvelous fifties," Lynn said wistfully. "I wish I'd lived back then."

"Jesus, Lynn," Doyle said, giving her a strange look. "Why?"

"Because everything was so laid-back and cool and easy, that's why."

Nobody had anything to add to that, for none among them really knew anything about the fifties, except for the bullshit that Hollywood has produced, with not one film

23

in a hundred portraying that time period accurately.

They drank more wine; all were getting a slight buzz on. Doyle said, "Let's get the Ouija board."

But when he went to get it, it was not where he had put it.

"Come on, people! Where'd you hide it?"

Sandy started making little funny noises in her throat. They all turned to look at her. She was on her knees by the fire, pointing into the air.

The Ouija board had levitated off the ground, about five feet, and was hovering, trembling slightly. The planchette was balanced on the board.

"Holy shit!" Pat said, and took a slug of wine from another bottle.

The Ouija board settled slowly back to the ground.

"Ask it a question," Leon suggested.

"*You* ask it a question!" Doyle said.

"Oh, come on!" Leon laughed at the group. "It was a wind gust, that's all. None of you people believe in that spook crap, do you?"

The Ouija board began vibrating on the ground, the planchette bouncing around on the board, but never slipping off.

"This is just too weird," Hillary said. "And I don't like it."

Paul laughed at her, and walked to the board and picked it up, moving closer to the fire. He knelt down and spelled out: What is going on?

With Paul's fingers resting lightly on the planchette, the three-cornered wooden device spelled out: Death.

Paul moved the planchette, spelling out: Whose death?

All of you was the reply.

Hillary scrambled to her feet. "I'm getting out of here!"

Bos pulled her back down to the ground. "Don't be a jerk. This is just a game, Hillary. Paul is just trying to scare us, that's all."

Only Paul knew that wasn't true. But he couldn't resist just one more try at the mysterious board. He spelled out:

24

Why us?

The planchette moved: Why not, asshole!

Paul jerked his fingers away.

Lynn frowned at him from across the fire. "This isn't one bit funny, Paul."

DO BOP DE DO BOP DE DO BOP, DE DO.

"Now what?" Leon asked, looking around him, trying to pinpoint the source of the singing.

"Now this," Paul said. He picked up the Ouija board and threw it into the fire.

The board and planchette popped out of the flames, unsinged.

"Now, damnit!" Paul yelled. "You all try to blame that on me." He pointed at the board.

The others could but sit or stand in silence and stare.

The board spelled out: Play with me! Play with me!

"Doyle," Pat said, forcing a calmness into her voice that she did not feel. "I want to get out of this place, and I mean like right now!"

The board spelled out: Stupid cunt!

"Screw you!" Pat screamed at the board.

Chuckling, deep and dark-tinged, sprang out of the rotting and crumbling and boarded-up buildings of the old town.

"That's it!" Paul said. "Come on, gang. We're getting the hell out of here."

No one argued with that.

Only problem was, none of the cars would start.

"I've got a bad feeling about this," Leon said.

"You're not alone," Hillary assured him.

"I'm for walking out," Bos said.

A voice sprang out of the darkened town. IT'S PARTY TIME. Then it sang, TURN YOUR RADIOS ON, TURN THE VOLUME UP. WHEN YOU GET TIRED OF DANCING, YOU CAN ALWAYS FUCK!

"Paul," Hillary said, disgust in her voice, "this is a very sick joke."

"I got news for all of you people," Paul said. "I don't

25

know what the hell is going on around here. I don't have anything to do with any of this."

"I believe you, Paul," Sandy said. "I just wish I knew what was going on."

TURN ON YOUR GODDAMNED RADIOS! the voice screamed from the darkness.

Feeling somewhat like a fool, but not knowing what else to do, Leon turned toward the town. "How can we turn on the radios, if the cars are as dead as a hammer?"

OH, YE OF LITTLE FAITH, the voice crooned soothingly.

"Well, let's try it," Paul said. He walked back to his car and clicked on the radio. Music from the fifties filled the air. Patti Page singing "Doggie in the Window."

Arf-arf.

The radios in the other car and van were tried. Same results. No matter how the dial was spun, or what button was pushed, the same music played on all.

"Now maybe one of you would like to tell me just how I could manage to do that?" Paul challenged, still irritated about his friends blaming him.

"No one's blaming you anymore, Paul," Bos said. "Back off some. Hell, we're all in this together."

"That's right, Paul," Hillary said. "Cool down. I think we're all going to have to work together before this—"

BOOGIE! BOOGIE! BOOGIE! the voice yelled.

The rhythmic sounds of Bo Diddley filled the cool night.

The voice laughed.

"It's gonna be a long night," Bos said.

In his office, Sheriff Rivera picked up the phone, stuck it to his ear, and started to punch out the number. His finger stopped when a deep voice said, WHAT DO YOU WANT NOW, YOU STUPID SPIC?

Gordie held the phone away from him and looked at it as if he were seeing it for the first time.

26

"What's the matter?" Watts asked.

"Goddamn thing just called me a stupid spic."

Watts stared at him for a moment. "It wasn't Sand. Sand never used racist language."

Gordie shook his head in exasperation. "Al, have you lost your mind? Dead people don't talk on the damn phone."

"Don't bet on it." He took the phone from Gordie. "Who were you going to call?"

"State police.

Watts punched out the number and stuck the phone to his ear.

STUPID OLD COPPER!

Without hesitation, Watts asked, "Who is this? What kind of sick game are you playing?"

DO BOP DE DO BOP DE DO BOP, DE DO.

Watts held the phone out so Gordie could hear the singing.

"I grew up with the Beatles and the Stones and the Supremes, Al. That's some kind of fifties' stuff, isn't it?"

"Yeah. Do-bop."

The singing stopped, and Watts again punched out the number to the state police HQ nearest to Willowdale. It was answered promptly.

"This is Al Watts over in Willowdale. Let me speak to the watch commander, please."

"Al? Lieutenant James here. What's the problem? I know you must have one, 'cause you damn sure never call to let us know how you're getting on."

"I promise to do better, Shel. Look, we, ah, have a situation here in Willowdale, and we—the sheriff and I— would like to keep a press lid on it for as long as possible. And I would really rather not discuss too much of it on the horn."

"Just sketch for me, Al. Give me something."

"Two rather bizarre homicides do?"

"Sure will. I'll—"

THIS LITTLE PIGGY WENT TO MARKET, AND

27

ANY PIGGIES WHO STICK THEIR SNOUTS IN
HERE WILL END UP AS PORK CHOPS AND CHIT-
TERLINGS.

"What the hell was that?" Lieutenant James shouted.

"Part of the problem."

"You been having many phone disruptions by some
nut, Al?"

SCREW YOU, COPPER!

The watch commander contained his temper. Barely.
"I'll roll a team as quickly as possible, Al."

"Thank you, Lieutenant. I—"

The phone went dead.

"Troops coming in?" Gordie asked.

"Yes. For whatever good they'll be." He handed the receiver back to the sheriff. "Line's dead."

Gordie listened, nodded his head in agreement. "Like a
hammer. Judy!" he called. "Check your phones, please."

A few seconds later the dispatcher buzzed him. "They're
working, Sheriff."

Gordie jerked up the phone on his desk. It hummed in
his ear. He replaced the phone and shook his head. "I
don't understand any of this, Al. I can't get a fix in my
head on what we're dealing with."

"You want a guess from me? Something from off the
top of my head?"

"Why not."

"I think we're dealing with . . . well, something beyond
our realm of understanding."

Gordie blinked and stared at the man for a moment. He
sighed and drummed his fingertips on the desk. "Ghosts?"
he asked softly.

"No. Well, in a sense, yes."

Gordie fixed him with a jaundiced look.

"Let me explain that."

"Please do."

"Sand is dead. But Sand's . . . soul, I guess, did not
leave this area."

Gordie groaned softly.

28

"So in that respect, yes, we have ghosts."

"Wonderful," Gordie said.

"But we also have something much more hideous. Something . . . evil."

"The devil, Al?"

"I don't know. Maybe. It's possible. A spawn of the devil, perhaps. Maybe it's something from space. Whatever it is, it knows everything we're doing. All the time."

"All right, Al. All right. Let's play with this . . . theory of yours for a moment. Not that I buy a damn word of it," he quickly added. "Do you think this Sand person has anything to do with the deaths?"

"Absolutely not. Sand was not a bad person. Not in the life . . . not when he was alive. He was the type of person who would stop by the side of the road to help an animal that'd been run over. He wouldn't pass a stranded motorist. Sand was a nice guy, who was born out of his time frame."

"You really believe that, Al?"

"Yes, I do, Gordie. Carl Lee—Sand married his daughter, Robin—thought the world of the boy. And you'd be hard-pressed to find anyone, even now, who would speak ill of Carl. Sand went off the deep end, after Robin was killed. That's when the killing started."

"Mack briefed me earlier. Sand really raised some hell that night, didn't he?"

"He and Mack. Yes." Watts met the sheriff's eyes. "Those punks they wasted got exactly what was coming to them."

Gordie grunted. "That is a very interesting thing for a cop to say, Al."

"Just seconds before he died, Sand told me—Hack was there, he heard it—about something he could see and we couldn't. And that we'd need his help someday."

"And you really believe that he saw something; you think that what he saw is what's causing the deaths in town? And you think it's some afterlife form of evil?"

"Yes, I do, Gordie. And knowing Sand as I do—did—

29

and Morg and Joey, too, I think they've been fighting this thing, perhaps helping to contain it. Whatever it is."

Gordie looked disgusted for a moment. He slammed his hand down on the desktop. "Aw, shit, Al!" he yelled. Outside the office, in the open dispatch area, Judy looked up at the shout. "We've got a damn nut working this area. Killing people. And I don't think those cowboys just wandered off. I think they're dead, and I think this nut killed them. This guy—or gal—is disrupting phone service. How? I don't know. Computers, maybe. But one thing I don't want to hear, is some off-the-wall crap about dead folks coming back from the grave."

Judy's screaming brought both men out of their chairs and running out of the office. Judy was standing, her .357 Mag in her hands in a double grip, the muzzle pointed at the window.

"What happened, Judy?"

"Something at the window. A . . . creature of some sort. It wasn't human, Sheriff. But it wasn't any kind of animal that I've ever seen. I don't know what the hell it was—is. I know that I've never seen anything like it before."

That deep, well-hollow voice began singing lines from *The Purple People Eater.* Then, after a chuckle, silence.

Judy holstered her pistol, then looked first at Watts, then at Gordie. "What in the name of God is going on around here?"

All phone lines coming into the office began buzzing and blinking and ringing.

Judy answered one, listening for a few seconds. Her face hardened, and she slammed the phone down. She punched another line-button and listened. Her face registered the same shock and disgust as before.

She held the phone away from her and yelled, "You lousy perverted creep!"

"Steady, Judy," Gordie said, taking the phone from her and listening.

I'LL HUMP YOUR EYEBALLS OUT, BITCH. THEN

30

Gordie broke the connection. But it wouldn't break. The voice kept speaking filth, sprewing it out over the disconnection.

The sheriff finally tossed the phone on the desk and walked away from it. He stopped and turned around, pointing at the phone. "That is impossible. I broke the connection. That cannot be happening."

"But obviously, it is," Watts said, sitting down on a corner of the desk. "You ready to start talking about ways to deal with something neither of us understand?"

BOO! the voice came from behind them.

The three of them looked up and around. Gordie almost fell down as he tried to avoid a pair of wet, bloody-slick eyes that hovered in front of him, at eye-level with the sheriff.

"Get away from me!" he yelled.

The eyes shifted, staring at Watts. Watts stared back. The eyes once more shifted, moving through the air toward Judy. The eyes were now joined by a pair of bloody lips.

KISS ME, BABY! the lips moved, making smacking sounds.

Judy jerked out her Mag and jacked the hammer back. "I'll blow your shit away!" she shouted.

The eyes and lips suddenly dipped and darted as a pair of bloody hands joined them. The hands separated, one hand darting down to grab Gordie's crotch, the other hand clamping onto Judy's breast. The lips were on Judy's face, kissing and sucking, leaving bloodstains on her face.

Both Judy and the sheriff hollered, in pain and shock and fright.

Watts jumped up and grabbed one of the hands.

It vanished under his touch.

He looked around. The hand that had been fondling Judy's breast was gone. But there were bloodstains on her shirt and face, on Gordie's crotch, and on Watts's hands where he'd grabbed the hand.

The eyes and lips had disappeared.

"What the hell . . . ?" Gordie said.

AH, SWEET MYSTERY OF LIFE! DO BOP DE DO BOP DE DO BOP, DE DO.

When the college kids camped near the old ghost town of Thunder awakened, the sun was shining, and it was a beautiful day, clear and crisp. Paul was the first one out of his blankets. He built a fire and put the coffee pot on. He laid strips of bacon in a skillet and placed the skillet on the wire rack over the rock-encirled fire. Then, on impulse, not totally convinced that what had taken place the night before had been real, he walked over to the line of vehicles. They all started. He turned on the radios and began punching buttons. Various stations. He could not find any fifties music at all.

He returned to the campsite and woke up his friends. They gathered around the vehicles, listening.

"Then it was a dream?" Leon questioned. "It didn't happen?"

"I don't know," Hillary said. "It sure seemed real to me."

"Me, too," Bos said.

"Let's fix some breakfast," Doyle suggested. "And then let's get the hell gone from this place."

That sounded like a fine idea.

They gathered around the fire, warming their hands and waiting for the coffee to boil. Just as they were pouring the hot coffee, all the radios in the vehicles came on.

Rock Around The Clock, from back in the fifties.

Watts finished his breakfast and rinsed out his plate, then put it in the dishwasher. He slipped into a shoulder holster rig and checked the loads in his snub-nosed .357. Watts had slept deeply and surprisingly well. He felt refreshed. He also felt excited for the first time in a long time—since his retirement. He felt like an old firehouse dog who'd just jumped on the fire truck for a ride to another three-alarmer. He turned at the ringing of the phone and picked up the receiver.

STUPID OLD COPPER!

He slowly replaced the receiver into the cradle and headed for the door.

Sheriff Gordie Rivera sat in his car for a moment. He looked at the radio, puzzled by the music. He could not find anything except for one station that played all fifties music, and he'd never picked up that particular station before.

He stopped fooling with the car radio and picked up the mike to his unit radio. "Blanco County One to headquarters."

WHAT DO YOU WANT, ASSHOLE! the voice sprang out of his speaker.

Gordie tossed the mike to the seat beside him. He had made up his mind during the often-restless and sleepless night, that this entire thing was the work of a nut. Nothing supernatural about it.

And he wasn't going to dignify that nutty craphead with a reply.

HEY, GREASER, I'M TALKING TO YOU.

Gordie's good intentions went flying out the window. He grabbed up the mike and keyed it. "Listen, you jerk. I'm gonna put your butt so far back in jail, somebody is going to have to pump light to you. Now what do you have to say about that?"

The voice started singing *Jailhouse Rock*.

"You miserable . . ." Gordie choked back the rest of his remark, which was to have been laced with some very personal comments about the ancestral quality of the voice's lineage.

Gordie turned off the sheriff's department radio and backed out of the drive.

33

"You got traffic for us, Sheriff?" dispatch asked, the words coming out of a dead speaker.

Wearily, Gordie picked up the mike. "Yeah, headquarters, I have traffic."

No response.

"You copy, headquarters?" Gordie asked.

YOU DUMBASS! YOU HAVE TO TURN THE RADIO ON!

Chapter Three

"It's the reporter," the man said. "It's time, honey."

Their eyes met. "How much time do we have?" she asked.

"I don't know. Enough, I hope."

She returned to the stove. It felt so strange, cooking again.

But Robin had to eat.

"Is anybody going to answer the door?" a teenage girl asked, walking into the kitchen.

"Yes," her father said, but there was reluctance in his voice. He hoped that he could pull this off. He had to make this reporter believe.

Exasperated, the girl plopped down in a chair. "Mother, why won't anybody in this family ever talk about Uncle Sand? It's stupid!" She brushed back a lock of raven hair from her forehead, her dark eyes moving from man to woman as the knocking on the door came again.

She has changed, the mother thought, looking at her daughter through loving eyes. All grown up now. And looks so very much like her namesake.

"Sand didn't do anything wrong," the man defended the mysterious Sand. "Those punks had it coming. All of them." He balled big hands into big fists.

His wife noticed and thought: After all these years, and the emotion is still within him.

And the sorrow still within me, she finished it.

"Now somebody wants to write a book about Sand, and make a movie about his life." He snorted and then smiled, the smile was a bit savage, a lot more knowing, and a bit scornful.

"We started it, Richard," his wife said. "So now let's get it done."

A woman's voice spoke from the open window by the breakfast nook. "I really hate to be a pest."

"Then why are you a reporter?" the man asked, but it was said with a smile.

The young woman standing on a box outside the window laughed. A nice laugh. Not like some of those reporters who used to come around.

"Come on in," Richard said. "Have a cup of coffee. I don't believe I've ever talked with a big city reporter." He fibbed about that, having talked with a lot of reporters where he'd been first sent some years back. He hoped the fib would go unnoticed by those who kept such records.

His words sounded rather hollow to the young woman. A deep, rather odd sound to them. She shrugged that away, stepped off the box, and walked around to the back door, stepping into the kitchen.

The teenager wriggled with excitement. A book and a movie about Uncle Sand. Wow! The local legend. A hero to some, an outlaw to others. But a legend that few would ever talk about.

And the girl could never understand that.

"I'm Sunny Lockwood," the young woman introduced herself.

"Richard and Linda Jennings. Our daughter, Robin." He looked at Robin, the love shining in his eyes. Richard had been dreading making contact, but knew it had to be. The Fury was loose. And if it was to be stopped, it had to be in this time frame.

Richard did not really fear the Fury. The thing could not destroy him, or any with him. But if Sand didn't

36

like this young woman; didn't believe she would tell the truth—it would all be for naught. For if the growing Fury was to be stopped, the townspeople had to have Sand's help. For no one could stop it without help from the other side of life.

But the truth—the truth from Sand's mind, and only he knew the truth—had to be told.

That the truth would set you free was a lot more than mere words to Richard and Linda and several others. When one took into consideration where they'd been existing for some time.

Around them, for some distance around them, time ceased its passage, allowing just a tiny part of the universe to settle stationary.

Sunny felt a falling sensation. She grabbed at the corner of the table to steady herself. She blinked. The sensation passed.

Jesus! she thought. Earthquake?

Then she could not remember anything about the odd sensation.

Richard closed his eyes for a moment. Time and strength and truth, he prayed. Please? Amen.

He opened his eyes to find Sunny looking at him. "Some breakfast?" he asked her. "Robin must eat to sustain herself." Watch yourself, Ace, he cautioned his mind. Remember where you are . . . and what you are.

Talks funny, Sunny thought. "Some coffee would be very nice, thank you."

"I'll get it," Robin volunteered.

"No!" the father's words were sharp. He smiled at his daughter and said, "You . . . can't, baby. This time will be on us. You just relax."

"You mean I don't have to do dishes?"

"That's right, baby."

"You got a deal, Pop."

Sunny looked down. A steaming cup of coffee was on the table in front of her. Who put it there? She could swear that no one in the room had moved.

She sighed. "Lots of excitement in town yesterday and last night. But I guess you all heard about it."

"In a manner of speaking," Richard said. He looked at Robin.

The girl closed her eyes, then slowly opened them.

"Did you hear about it, Robin?" Sunny asked.

"Hear about what?"

"Those gruesome murders."

"What murders?"

Sunny began to wonder if she'd wandered in through the back door of a nut house.

Then she couldn't remember what she'd been talking about.

Something cold touched the young woman; something the hot coffee could not warm. She shuddered.

"We're too close," Linda said.

"Can't be helped," her husband told her. "We're running out of time."

There was a roaring in Sunny's ears. She could see the lips of Richard and Linda moving, but she could not hear the words.

Then the roaring abated, and she could not remember ever experiencing it.

"I got into town yesterday, Mr. Jennings," Sunny said, "and went to the local newspaper to go through their morgue. But all the stories concerning Sand were gone. I found that really odd." She stopped when she noticed the word morgue had brought Richard's head up, his eyes changing to a very strange color . . . and so cold-looking. She was suddenly uncomfortable under his cold gaze. "I'm sorry. Morgue is newspaper jargon for . . ."

"I know," the man said, a gentleness to his voice. "It's just that we," he indicated his wife, "have a very close friend named Morg. M-O-R-G. He was killed the same night Sand got his ticket punched."

Sunny let that register. She blinked. "You *have* a

friend named Morg who is *dead?*"

Richard smiled. "Why don't we all go into the den? We'll be much more comfortable there. We must talk about Sand. We're wasting time."

"I'll bring the coffee pot," Robin said.

"No!" her father told her. "You . . . can't. Remember our deal, honey."

Sunny sighed, thinking: Weird family.

"Nice-looking town," Major Claude Jackson said. "Friendly-looking place."

"I wonder if they'll remain friendly, when they learn why we're here?" Capt. John Hishon asked.

Three officers rode in the lead van. Three sergeants in the van behind them.

"I don't see why they shouldn't." Lt. Kathy Smith said. "It's going to mean big bucks in their pockets when this is set up."

Major Jackson shrugged and put the van in gear, pulling away from the shoulder of the road and onto the main highway. "You never know how civilians are going to react to the military. Especially when they learn the base—however small—will be used for the rough training of special warfare troops. We'll just have to play it by ear."

Since government vehicles don't normally come equipped with personal radios, Sgt. Keith Preston had brought his own, complete with ear plug.

Sgt. Janet Dixon noticed Keith's frown. "What's the matter, Keith?"

The nineteen-year-old buck sergeant looked at her and smiled. "I just lost all my stations except for one. And all it plays is crap out of the fifties."

"Watch it, buddy," Sgt. Maj. Gary Christensen said jokingly. "You're talking about my music now."

"You can sure have it, Sergeant Major."

Keith listened for a moment, his face a study as he changed expression several times.

"What's the matter now?" Janet asked.

"Jesus, Janet. This guy's voice is spooky. And the crap he's laying down is wild. Here," he jerked the jack out of the radio, allowing the sound to come through the speaker. "Listen."

Raw, undiluted sewer filth came spewing out of the speaker, embarrassing the men and shocking Janet.

"That's a radio station?" she asked, disbelief in the question.

YEAH, YOU DUMB ARMY WHORE. the voice sprang from the radio. WHAT DO YOU DO, SCREW THE TROOPS?

Janet's mouth dropped open.

YOU WANT A DICK SHOVED IN THERE?

Janet closed her mouth.

"Turn that crap off, Keith," Gary ordered. "And keep it off."

"Yes, Sergeant Major." He turned the radio off.

"Was that a tape, Keith?" Janet asked, finding her voice.

"No. Look." He opened the cassette compartment. It was empty.

The lead van pulled over, and Gary pulled in behind it. Major Jackson ran back to the van. "Have you people been listening to a radio?"

"Right," Gary said. "I never heard anything like that before."

"Same with us. That can't be a licensed station. Has to be someone with a sick sense of humor."

Janet looked around at the outskirts of the town. "I don't know whether I like this place or not."

Norris and Bergman, the state police team sent in to assist, sat in Gordie's office and listened. They had

40

viewed the remains of the two victims, both agreeing it was shaping up to be a very strange case.

Now, all of a sudden, it was going from strange to really wild.

Norris clicked off his tape recorder and looked at Sheriff Rivera and Watts. "Now, guys . . . come on! Floating eyeballs? Detached hands? Bloody lips? Monsters in the night? You people haven't gotten into your evidence room and been smoking left-handed cigarettes, have you?"

Gordie tossed his crotch-bloody trousers on the desk. Judy's bloody shirt followed that.

"I've had Dr. Anderson up since before dawn, comparing blood from the victims against blood scrapings from that clothing. It's a match. One victim now has no hands, the other no eyes or lips. The assistant coroner checked the coolers this morning." Gordie stared at the state men. "Last night, I had made up my mind that it was nothing supernatural. Had to be the work of a madman. Or madwoman. Person. Whatever. But sounds do not emanate from a dead radio. And I just had my radio checked out."

"Could have been a skip. Good time of year for it," Bergman offered.

"No," Watts said. Up to this point, except for corroborating Gordie's story, he had remained silent. This was Gordie's show. Watts was just a civilian. Technically.

"You have a theory, Colonel?" Norris asked. It was a bit difficult to address Watts by any other title, even if he was retired.

Watts spoke for five minutes without pausing except for breath. He took it from the beginning. Sand. The killing of Sand. The thunder. The whole bag, from thirty years back to the present.

Norris and Bergman stared as if Watts had taken leave of his senses. The phone rang. Gordie picked it up; his unlisted private number. He listened, smiled grimly, then

41

handed the phone to Bergman. "It's for you."

Bergman stuck the phone to his ear. "Bergman."

HEY, JEW-BOY! I'M GONNA NAIL YOU UP BY YOUR PECKER AND STICK YOUR YARMULKE UP YOUR TUSHIE!

Bergman was speechless. He opened his mouth to speak. Nothing came out.

DO BOP DE DO BOP DE DO BOP, DE DO.

The singing faded.

Bergman cleared his throat. "How . . . did he know my name? How did he know I was even in town? And Bergman is not necessarily a Jewish name. How?"

"It seems to know everything," Watts said. "And it seems to be everywhere. But something that we've been missing, or avoiding, came to me last evening."

All looked at him.

"What does it want?"

Angel Ingram and her brother, Howie, sat on the curb, waiting for the school bus. The kids, ages ten and eleven, looked up and down the street, wondering why the other kids had not shown up. It was almost time for the bus to arrive.

But unless the other kids hurried up, it looked as though they were going to be the only ones getting on.

"This is weird," Angel said. "I guess I'm going to have to apologize to you. So I'm sorry. Big deal. You were right."

"You feel it now, Angel?"

She sighed as only a ten-year-old can. "No, Howie, I don't. But if you say *you* do, I believe you."

"Thank you. It's rather hard to explain. It's just a . . . feeling, you know?"

"What sort of feeling, Howie?"

"Just odd, that's all. A feeling of impending doom, perhaps."

"Howie, would you like to say that in English, please?"

"Something bad is going to happen."

"I still don't know what you mean."

"I have elucidated to the best of my ability, Angel."

She laughed at him. Even though she was a year younger, Angel was always looking after her brother—the smart one. The brilliant one. The eleven-year-old who was taking high school and college courses. But Howie sometimes didn't keep up with things like other eleven-year-old kids. Howie didn't give a flip about sports—which was all right with Angel, she thought them sort of dumb herself—but Howie didn't even like to be around kids his own age. He was just too damn smart; even though he tried to talk like your average eleven-year-old, he just couldn't pull it off most of the time. The funny thing was, with Angel, he could.

When he wanted to.

But the other kids didn't like him. They shunned Howie and made fun of him. And Angel, who was no dummy herself, knew a lot of that ribbing had to have originated in the kids' homes, from stupid parents with misguided values.

"Here comes the bus."

"Nobody on it."

Angel looked around. Front doors were opening, and the kids were pouring out of the homes in the subdivision. She was curious about that, for usually the kids all gathered at the curb, talking and bitching about school.

'Course, Howie never bitched about school. Except when he caught a teacher in a mistake. Which didn't endear him to the few sloppy teachers. Howie liked school.

"Something is wrong with them," Howie said, observing the mass of kids.

Angel looked. "They seem fine to me."

"Look again. They're all moving as though they've been automatized."

43

"Say what?" the pretty and petite honey-blonde asked her tow-headed big brother with two left feet.

"Zombies, Angel." He grinned, the kid in him surfacing briefly. "Doom doom de doom doom de doom doom doom," he hummed a very bad version of the funeral march.

"You want to knock that off, Howie?" Angel looked. But her brother was right. The kids were moving funny. She stood up. "Come on. We'll miss the bus."

"We should be so lucky."

"Your home is lovely, Mrs. Jennings," Sunny said, as she sat down in the den. The home was lovely, but there was a very faint odor of charred wood in the house, and she found that odd. And a very slight musty smell. There was another sort of floral smell that she couldn't quite pin down. Then it came to her: that sweet fragrance was the smell of flowers. The smell of a funeral home, with the casket open and flowers all around it.

This just gets weirder and weirder, she thought.

"Please call me Linda," Mrs. Jennings said with smile.

Sunny nodded and placed a cassette recorder on a coffee table. She glanced at Richard. "Do you mind if I record all this? It's so much easier than taking notes."

"No. I don't mind at all. But there are others who might. If nothing comes out, I'll apologize in advance for that."

Sunny stared at him briefly. What others might object? She wondered if Richard might have a drinking problem? Was he hitting the sauce this early in the morning?

Richard said, "Sand wants the truth told, Sunny. The truth."

"Sand wants? . . ." She closed her mouth. Humor him, she thought. Just . . . humor him. "Sand has been dead for thirty years, Mr. Jennings. But I assure you,

44

the truth will be told."

"Or nothing at all will be told, Sunny. Because no one will be here to tell it." He knew it was wrong of him to say that; and knew those who kept the records would know it was no slip on his part. But right or wrong, Richard—as he was aware of his wife's sharp glance at him—had concluded that Sunny Lockwood had to know at least a part of what faced her.

Sunny leaned back. "Mr. Jennings, what in the hell are you talking about?"

Richard and his wife both laughed. Robin seemed to be dozing. Richard said, "I mean, Sunny, that things are not quite as they seem here. If you stay, you could be in very serious danger. Now listen to me, young woman: I'm taking a chance just by telling you this much. Look at Robin, Sunny."

Sunny looked. The girl's eyes were closed. My God, was she asleep?

"No," Linda broke into her thoughts. "She is not asleep as you know it. Our daughter is just . . . well, *away* for a time."

Her husband said, "She has to be protected for she is our flesh and blood, and much more vulnerable than you. And, I'll admit, much more valuable."

Sunny tried a laugh. It came out more like a very nervous giggle. "You're . . . deliberately trying to scare me. I was warned that you hated reporters."

"It would be very difficult for me to hate, Sunny. I am limited to strong dislike. But even . . . before, I didn't hate reporters. I just didn't like the way many of your colleagues twisted words to suit their own gains. Sunny, be very sure you want to do this. There is still time for you to leave. But not very much time."

Sunny rose from her seat to pace the den. That damn sweet smell was annoying. She glanced at Robin. The teenager was still out of it. If she wasn't asleep, then what the hell was she? Her eyes were sure closed.

45

Thunder rumbled in the distance. Sunny looked out the window—and for a moment, she could see nothing—and became frightened. She did not see Richard lift a hand. All of a sudden, the landscape came into her view. The day was clear and cool and lovely.

She didn't understand the thunder.

Yet.

She sat back down. "Why am I in danger, Mr. Jennings?"

She felt his eyes, those strange eyes, boring into her, almost as if he was seeing into her thoughts. She mentally shrugged that off as impossible. "I can protect you, Sunny, only as long as you remain here, with us, in this house. That's why Robin is here, and not in school. Even we are permitted some . . . well, call it latitude. But once you leave our presence, if you do decide to leave, to return to your motel, I cannot help you."

She shook her head. "I've covered stories in Lebanon, Central America, Northern Ireland, and in Africa. Are you comparing Willowdale, Colorado with those places?"

"Get out, Miss Lockwood," Richard ordered. "Take your tape recorder and leave here. You have no idea what you're facing."

"No. You invited me here, remember?"

Both Richard and Linda Jennings laughed softly at that, Richard saying, "Did we, Sunny? You're sure of that? Oh, I have no doubt that you were invited, but it wasn't us who did the inviting."

She waved that away. She had the letter from them. At least a letter that was signed by Richard Jennings. Why was the man smiling so? It was infuriating. "Tell me what's going on, Mr. Jennings."

"I've told you as much as I can, Sunny. The rest is up to you."

"To stay or to leave?"

"Yes."

46

"I'm staying."

Richard sighed. "Very well. May God have mercy on your soul."

The thunder rolled in heavy cadence.

Chapter Four

Detective Norris got up and walked to a window. "What is with this thunder? There isn't a cloud in the sky." He stopped, turning around to look at Watts. "The thunder? . . . That's what you just told us about, right?"

"Yes. And now you're hearing it."

"Which means?"

"I don't know."

The sheriff's intercom buzzed. "Some soldiers out front to see you, Sheriff."

"Soldiers?"

"Yes, Sheriff. Half a dozen of them. They said they sent a letter several months ago, requesting a meeting with you and the mayor and the city council."

"Ahhh . . . yeah!" Gordie pawed through a basket. "Here it is, Sarah. Sure, why not? It can't get any more confusing. Send them in, please."

"You want us to stay?" Bergman asked.

"Why not? This probably won't take long."

With six more people, the room was too small. Gordie suggested they move to the coffee room, where there were more tables and chairs.

"I apologize for the mayor and the city council not being here, Major," Gordie said. "I can't imagine all of us forgetting about the meeting. However, speaking strictly for my office, things have been, well, a little weird around here the last couple of days."

"Weirder than your funky, filthy radio station?" Lt. Smith asked. She was still somewhat irritated about that.

"We don't have a radio station, ma'am. We had one, but it went out of business about five years ago. What radio station have you been listening to?"

"K-U-N-T," Sgt. Preston said.

Norris choked on his coffee and went into spasms of coughing at that.

"Are you serious?" Watts asked.

"That's what that deep-voiced announcer said," Capt. Hishon told him. "But I'm here to tell you all: that was filth coming out of those speakers."

Gordie glanced at Watts. The man arched one eyebrow in a knowing reply.

Maj. Jackson didn't miss the furtive glance or the arched eyebrow. He wondered what was going on.

Gordie picked up the phone and punched out the mayor's office number, silently praying that the phone was working, and that damnable voice would not choose this time to start some crap. The town was not large enough to afford a full-time mayor, but Mason Adams was semiretired, so he spent most of his time in the office.

Nell, the mayor's part-time secretary, answered. Gordie identified himself.

"Hi, baby!" Nell yelled into his ear. "How's it hangin' today, Gordie?"

Gordie placed the phone on his desk and stared at it. Nell Upshaw was in her mid-fifties, married to the Methodist minister, and about as straightlaced as an old corset. She was vice president of the local chapter of Citizens for the Return of Acceptable Programming. CRAP. Nell didn't like anything on TV. Not even the news.

Watts looked at Gordie's expression. "What's wrong?"

"Nell Upshaw. She just called me baby. Asked me how it was hangin' today."

The chief deputy's mouth dropped open at that.

Gordie picked up the phone. "Ah . . . Nell, is the mayor around?"

"Around? That son of a bitch is so round he looks like a blimp with legs. Can you imagine him humpin' his old lady? What a sight! Naw. I ain't seen the old goat today."

"Ah . . ." Gordie wiped away sudden sweat on his forehead. "Nell, tell Mason I called, okay?"

"Sure, baby. Come around sometime. I got a bottle stashed in the desk." She hung up.

Gordie related the conversation, forgetting, momentarily, the military personnel.

Gordie rubbed his graying temples with his fingertips. "Two murders in one day, strange voices on the radio and on the phones, now this. What else is going to happen?"

"Don't forget the eyes, hands, and lips," Watts said.

The military looked at one another.

"And the monster that Judy saw," Lee said.

"I knew I wasn't going to like this town," Janet said.

ROCK A BYE, BABY, ON THE MOUNTAIN TOP,
WHEN THE WIND BLOWS, THE JAILHOUSE WILL ROCK.
WHEN THE TIME COMES, AND IT WON'T BE LONG,
DOWN WILL COME GREASEBALL, OLD PIG, AND TOWN.
DO BOP DE DO BOP DE DO BOP, DE DO.

50

"Let's go home, Angel," Howie said, taking her hand.

"Howie!" She pulled away. "Don't be dumb. This isn't like you. We can't just walk out of school."

He grabbed her hand again and jerked her along. "Now, Angel. Right now. Move. I mean it."

"All right, Howie. All right!" She walked along with him. "Where are we going?"

"I don't know. Just away from this place."

"You're weird, Howie. And you're beginning to scare me, you know that?"

"I hope so, Angel. I really do. Something is wrong around here."

"I can just see mother buying that excuse. Your butt is beat when daddy gets home."

"I'll take that chance."

The kids walked slowly toward the main part of town, about a mile from the school complex, grades one through twelve. Three huge new buildings.

Howie started to tell her that lately daddy had been acting just as strangely as many of the kids. He decided to let that slide.

"The other kids giving you a bad time of it, Howie?"

"What? Oh . . . no. No more than usual. I really don't pay that much attention to it, Angel. It used to bother me a lot more than it does now."

"Howie, I'm going to punch you out, if you don't level with me about what you think is going on. And I mean that."

"Angel, I am usually very articulate, as you know." She rolled her blue eyes at his language. "As well as quite precise in any explanations—"

"Yeah, Howie. Right. You're a regular walking dictionary. But not with me. So how about dropping the

51

professor bit?"

"It's very difficult playing a double role, Angel."

She smiled, and her attitude softened toward her brother. "Be what you are, Howie. It's wrong trying to please others. And I've been wrong in egging you on to do that."

"It might not make any difference, Angel. Not now. And I'm not trying to scare you. I'm just trying to find some way to explain my feelings."

"Well, my best friend Cindy is acting real cold toward me. That's been going on for a couple of days. I think she's now my ex-best friend. Is it things like that, what you're trying to tell me?"

"Yes. Precisely. There have been subtle shifts in attitudes and demeanor among many people . . ."

"People are acting weird, right?"

"That's what I said, Angel. And I have been seeing more and more evidence of it over the past few days. Now you think about that."

She thought. Screwing her face up into an ugly, deformed mask and letting her tongue hang out, knowing how that irritated her brother. Angel was known as the class clown for good reason.

Howie glanced at her and sighed. "Enough, Angel. Be serious."

"Howie, so people have been acting funky . . . big deal. Maybe it's the moon or something. It doesn't mean that werewolves are prowling the town."

"Two people were gruesomely murdered yesterday."

She moved a little closer to her brother with that reminder. "You do have a way with words, Howie." Then she noticed the direction they were taking. "The sheriff's department? Oh, come on, Howie! This is gettin' too much, don't you think?"

"Let's just say, I think I probably know something that you don't about this matter," he said mysteriously.

She knew from experience that she wasn't going to get much more out of him. "Okay, Howie. Right. Well, since we're going to get our butts beat for skipping school, do we have time for a milk shake before we meet with the cops?"

"No."

"Why doesn't that surprise me?" She shifted her gaze and gasped. "Howie!" She gripped his arm. "Look at Mr. Hubbard over there."

Howie looked at the man standing in the doorway of his hardware store.

Hubbard had unzipped his trousers and was exposing his penis to them. He grinned and called out, "You wanna come play with this, Angel?"

The kids broke into a run, heading for the sheriff's department building.

They ran into the building and up to the desk. Old Mack grinned at them. "Now, why aren't you kids in school?"

"We wanna see the sheriff!" Angel blurted. "Old Man Hubbard just shook his pecker at me!"

Mack swallowed his chewing tobacco.

"They won't start," Paul told the young women. "The gauges show the batteries at full charge. The radios play—that same weird station—but we can't crank the engines."

"I'm packing up and getting away from this crazy place," Lynn said.

The other girls agreed with that, loudly.

Hillary turned around and felt a hand slip between her legs, rubbing her crotch. She whirled and took a wild swing at Bos.

"Goddamn you!" she screamed, missing with her swing.

53

Bos caught her arms and held on. "Damnit, Hillary, now stop. What's wrong with you?"

"I don't like you trying to feel me up!" She struggled to free herself from his hands.

Bos shoved her away. She stumbled and almost fell down. "Feel you up? I didn't put a hand on you."

Paul stepped between them and looked at Hillary. "Nobody touched you, Hillary. And that's the truth." Paul jumped and yelled as a hard finger goosed him in the butt. "What the hell!"

"What happened?" Sandy asked, fear on her face.

"Somebody just goosed me."

Leon suddenly found himself flat on his back, on the ground, his jeans and underwear down around his ankles. He struggled to pull them back up, embarrassed by his nakedness.

Lynn's shirt was abruptly ripped open, her bra torn from her, exposing her breasts. She screamed and tried to pull together her ruined shirt.

WHAT A SET OF KNOCKERS!

The invisibly embattled little group looked wildly around them, fear touching them all.

Leon was still struggling to pull up his jeans and underwear. Everytime he managed to cover his nakedness, the clothing was jerked back down around his ankles. He rolled on the ground, fighting the unseen hands.

Paul ran to help his friend. A blow to the back knocked him sprawling, driving the breath from him.

Pat was tossed to the ground, her jeans torn from her, bruising and cutting her flesh with the savage jerk. She screamed in pain. Leon was picked up and dropped down on top of her.

POP IT TO HER, LEON!

"Somebody help us!" Leon cried, blind panic and fear in his voice.

EVERY PARTY HAS A POOPER, THAT'S WHY
WE INVITED YOU, PARTY POOPER, PARTY
POOPER!

They could all feel whatever it was surrounding
them, leave. Leon rolled from Pat and lay face down
on the ground. He was very close to hysteria, his chest
heaving and his flesh clammy to the touch. He was
trembling.

Sandy ran to help Pat, and Bos went to Leon, helping him pull up his clothes and get to his feet. Paul
was groaning as he rose unsteadily to his feet.

"Get the canteens," Paul finally managed to say.
"Leave everything else. We've got to get out of here."

"What if that *thing* won't let us?" Hillary asked.
"Whatever it is."

"We won't know until we try," Paul said grimly.
"Let's go."

Sunny cut her eyes to Robin. "Robin? That was
Sand's? . . ."

"Wife," Richard said. "My wife's older sister.
Daughter of Carl and Flora Lee."

"Your parents?" Sunny asked the woman.

"My father died in prison a few years ago. Death
freed him. He's much happier now."

The eyes of the women met, held. A beautiful
woman, Sunny thought. Just a touch of gray in her
dark hair. "Your mother?"

"Insane. Confined to a nursing home . . . if that is
what one wishes to call that dismal place. But all
signs point to her ordeal soon being over."

Sunny didn't pursue that last bit. She waited.

"My mother was driven insane by the events prior to
and just after Sand's death."

"I heard the country western song about Sand sev-

55

eral years ago," Sunny said.

Richard smiled. "Yes, we know."

How? Sunny wanted to ask. She didn't. "A friend of mine, a few years older, was in Vietnam. He worked with a correspondent named Dan Thompson. Dan used to live here in Willowdale."

"Yes. Little Dan," Richard said. "He used to run with us. He's dead."

"The State Department still has him listed as missing," Sunny corrected.

"He's dead," Richard said flatly.

Sunny fought back a slight feeling of irritation. The man's know-it-all attitude was beginning to get next to her. "Whatever, Mr. Jennings. Anyway, Dan used to tell my friend about a young man called Sand. Dan said that Sand was the greatest guy in the whole world. Said he was going to write a book about him; tell the true story about what happened. And why. Ever since I heard that, it's been on my mind. I was glad to receive that letter from you."

"Think nothing of it," Richard said drily.

Robin suddenly opened her eyes and sat up straight. "Daddy? Why don't you show Miss Lockwood that old car you keep out in the shed? It has something to do with all this, doesn't it?"

Sunny looked at the father. The man's face changed. Sunny could not name the emotion.

"Yes, baby. It has a lot to do with it."

"I'd like to see that car, Mr. Jennings." Sunny punched off the recorder.

Richard nodded. "All right. That can be . . . arranged without too much difficulty. Come on." He rose from his chair. It was the most graceful and fluid movement Sunny had ever witnessed.

He escorted her out the back door. But he did not touch her.

56

"What song, mother?" Robin asked.

"It was never played in this part of the state."

"Do you have the record?"

She smiled. "Not anymore. It was destroyed in a fire. But I can probably arrange to get you a copy.

The doors to the shed were unlocked and opened. Sunny sucked in her breath at the sight.

The car was classic. A 1950 model Mercury two-door. Chopped and channeled, lowering blocks in the rear. The interior was rolled and pleated leather. White leather. The exterior of the car had been painted a deep blue, and done so with expert hands.

It was beautiful, and Sunny said as much.

"Yes, it was, Sunny," Richard agreed.

Was? "Your car, Mr. Jennings?"

"No. It belonged to Sand. He was driving it the night he got killed. Long time ago. Drove it up the side of Thunder Mountain as far as he could push it; car shot all to hell and back."

"You restored it?"

Richard smiled. "No. Get in and turn on the radio, Sunny."

Somebody sure restored it, Sunny thought, as she opened the door and slid in behind the wheel. She turned on the radio. Fifties music poured from the rear-mounted hi-fi speakers. She looked out at Richard. He was still smiling at her. She clicked off the radio, not understanding what was taking place. She felt sure he was trying to tell her something. But what?

"Do you drive it much, Mr. Jennings?"

A strange light sprang into his eyes. "That would be, ah . . . difficult, at best."

She walked out of the shed to stand beside him. Even outside, she could still smell that odd odor of charred wood and the sweet smell of flowers, all mingled in with the odor that all funeral homes seem to have.

"So many people dead," Richard said, his voice no more than a whisper. "And many, many more to die before this is all over."

"Before what is over? I don't understand."

"You will."

Richard closed the doors and locked them. Sunny noticed the hasp and lock were very old and terribly rusty. She wondered about that.

She reached out and touched his arm.

She felt as though she had time-traveled, and her senses had not yet caught up with her. One instant they had been standing outside by the shed, now they were sitting in the house, back in the den, and Sunny, for the first time, was really frightened.

"Don't touch me, Sunny," Richard told her. "Me or Linda. You were lucky this time. The next time, you might not fare as well."

"What the hell happened?" Sunny almost shouted the question.

Richard ignored that. "Let's get on with the interview, Sunny. I don't know how much time we have left."

"Lee," Gordie told his chief deputy, "send a deputy down to Hubbard's store and find out what the hell is wrong with him." He looked at the kids. "Howard and Carly Ingram's kids, right?"

"Yes, sir," they both said. Like many kids their age, cops frightened them. The guns and the creaking leather and the Mace holders and the handcuffs, all combined with the TV and movie bullshit to give kids a bad image of cops.

"How come you kids aren't in school? You playing

58

hooky?"

"Don't blame her," Howie said, stepping closer to shield his sister—a move that escaped no one's attention. "Blame me. Actually I like school, but I made her leave and come with me, because of what I perceive to be impending trouble in this community."

Bergman looked at Howie and winked and smiled. "You're really a midget, right? You're not a kid. I got a sixteen-year-old that can't speak English yet—at least not where I can understand it."

Howie returned the plainclothes cop's smile. "I'm very advanced for my ten years."

"So I've been told," Sheriff Rivera said, not trying to hide his smile. It was nice to have something to smile about. "What sort of trouble are you talking about, son?"

"It's very difficult to explain, Sheriff. But I shall try my best. For the last few days, I have been experiencing a very subtle change taking place in this town. The people are behaving, well, oddly."

"Gordie," Watts said, motioning for Gordie to step away from the kids. "Out of the mouths of babes and all that."

"That is one brilliant kid. Yeah. I see what you mean. I know from personal experience that kids are very quick to pick up on things. What do you know about the Ingram kids?"

"The girl is plenty smart, but Howie's I.Q. is astronomical. Speaks two or three languages. Can make a computer do the diddy wa diddy. And a college professor would be hard-pressed to throw a math question at him that Howie couldn't work. And that's just touching the tip of his brainpower."

"And the boy is probably shunned by his peers."

"Sure. But that comes from the home, Gordie. From stupid parents who place more value on sports than on

59

brilliance. I whipped a coach's ass years ago, when he made some dick-headed remark because my youngest kid left sports to spend more time with studies."

Gordie grinned. "I'm just finding out all sorts of things about you, aren't I, you feisty old bastard!"

Watts laughed softly. "That's why I liked Sand so much. Damn, but that boy was brilliant. Such a waste."

"But what did he do with that brilliance, Al? He was a rebel, and that's all."

"Oh, no, Gordie. He was much more than that. As to what he's doing with it . . . he just might be working to get our asses out of a very bad crack."

"You still cling to that theory of yours, don't you, Al?"

"You bet."

"What am I going to do with all these military people? What would you do with them, Al?"

"Keep them around. Bed them down at the best motel in town, compliments of the town. The meeting was okay'd and nobody from the town or county showed up. We owe them something. Besides, if things get tight, I want them on our side."

SPEAKING OF WHAT PEOPLE WANT! the voice boomed. I WANT A PIECE OF THAT PRETTY LITTLE GIRL.

Bergman stepped over and pulled Angel close to him. "Easy, honey. It's all right."

Angel didn't buy that for one second, but she felt better with his arm around her shoulders.

The military people looked at each other, all with questions in their eyes. They remained silent.

Howie cocked his head to one side and waited for the voice to speak again.

THANK HEAVENS, FOR LITTLE GIRLS, the voice sang.

60

Howie listened as the voice sang. It was not unpleasant; not a monotone. And the melody was just about right. Howie enjoyed show tunes and serious music.

"Ignore it," Gordie told his deputies. "Go on about your duties."

The singing stopped. Maj. Jackson yelped and jumped as what appeared to be an invisible finger gave him a sharp goose in the butt.

Both Lt. Smith and Sgt. Dixon began slapping at invisible hands that roamed over their bodies, touching and squeezing.

The sheriff's secretary, Sarah, began screaming as her clothes were ripped from her, leaving her in only bra and pantyhose. When Deputy Alan Hibler ran to cover her with a coat he'd grabbed from a rack, something clobbered him on the jaw and knocked him to the floor.

DO BOP DE DO BOP DE DO BOP, DE DO.

The room fell silent.

The men and women and kids stood numbed by it all. Hibler struggled to his boots, helped up by the half-naked Sarah, who suddenly realized a lot was exposed that shouldn't be, and ran toward the ladies room, clutching the coat that Alan had received a sock on the jaw for.

"What the hell was that?" Major Jackson broke the silence.

"Whatever it was," Howie said, "the voice is not real. Not a human voice. It is electronically produced."

Sgt. Maj. Christensen said, "What do you mean, son?"

"It's like a computer voice, sir. But a highly refined one. Like a voice out of a game. Not natural. It's very good, but still not human. Not God-given."

HOLY, HOLY, HOLY! the voice sang. LORD GOD

61

ALMIGHTY. That was followed by the sound of a long fart.

Kathy Smith and John Hishon both crossed themselves, as did Gordie.

YOU'RE A SMART-ASSED LITTLE PUNK, AREN'T YOU, HOWIE BABY?

Howie did not choose to reply.

ANSWER ME, YOU LITTLE SHIT-HEAD.

"You're not real," Howie said.

NOT REAL? THEN EXPLAIN THIS.

Howie was knocked to the floor, one side of his face red and swelling, a trickle of blood leaked out of one corner of his mouth.

Angel ran to him and knelt down. She glared up at empty space. "Pick on someone your own size, you creep!" she yelled.

THE NEXT TIME, BITCH, HUBBARD WON'T JUST SHAKE IT AT YOU.

"What do you want?" Watts asked, his voice strong and firm.

HOW INTERESTING! NOT: WHAT ARE YOU? NOT: WHERE DID YOU COME FROM? JUST: WHAT DO YOU WANT?

"It's a fair question."

PERHAPS.

"Did you kill Carol Ann and the Branson boy?"

THE GIRL WAS DELICIOUS.

"Why them?"

WHY NOT, OLD COPPER?

Howie was listening intently.

"All right. I'll ask. Who are you?"

I THOUGHT YOU'D NEVER ASK.

Silence.

"Are you going to answer the question?"

The voice sang a few lines from the song *Too Old To Cut The Mustard Anymore,* then dedicated it to Al

Watts.

All felt the following silence. Whatever it was, it was gone.

"What in the hell *is* that thing?" Norris asked.

A deputy pushed over the front door and shoved in a redfaced Hubbard. His face turned even redder when he spotted Angel, glaring at him. Gordie had to stifle a laugh when the pretty little girl popped him the bird.

"You're a dirty old man!" Angel yelled at him.

"Take Angel into my office," Gordie told Lee. "And her brother. See if Howie needs medical attention."

The kids gone, Gordie faced the hardware man. "Angel says you exposed yourself to her."

"That's a vicious lie, Sheriff."

"Then why did your face turn red, when you spotted her in here?"

"I want my lawyer!"

"All right, Hubbard," Gordie said with a smile. He turned to Mack, who had recovered from swallowing his chewing tobacco. "Contact social services. Have them send a female over here. Alan, read Mr. Hubbard his rights and then lock him up."

"Wait a minute!" Hubbard hollered. "I can explain what happened."

"Please do," Gordie said.

"I'd just gone to the bathroom. I forgot to zip up my pants. That's all there is to it."

Judy had entered the office. She looked at the man with open disgust in her eyes. "You always walk around the store in the middle of the day with your dick hanging out?"

Hubbard began cursing and screaming insanely. He charged Judy, shouting that he was going to kill her. Judy sidestepped and tripped Hubbard, sending him tumbling to the floor. She pulled a leather slapper out of her back pocket and popped the man on the noggin. Hubbard went to sleep.

"Toss him in a cell," Gordie ordered. "Charge him with disturbing the peace, assaulting a peace officer, threatening a peace officer, indecent behavior with a juvenile, and anything else you can think of."

Watts rubbed the side of his face with a finger. "I've known Hubbard for forty years. I've never seen him behave like this."

Before anyone could offer any opinions as to the hardware man's bizarre behavior, Maj. Jackson said, "What in the name of God is producing that voice?"

Gordie cut his eyes to the man. "We don't know. Still want to stay in this town?"

"We're under orders to put the finishing touches on a training base not far from here. The government has spent a lot of money in this area, as you well know. We'll just go on up to the base. We have MREs to last us a week. More supplies will be brought in if we need them."

"I think not," Gordie said coolly.

"Then you'd better have one hell of a good reason for detaining us, Sheriff."

"You think you're immune from civilian law; is that it?"

"You know better than that, Sheriff. But we are acting under orders from the government, and we all have high security clearances. If you're going to detain us, I want the charges all spelled out, nice and legal."

Gordie smiled. "You have a radio with you, Major? Shortwave, perhaps?"

"Whether I do, or not, is certainly none of your business, Sheriff."

"I just made it my business, Major Jackson. You want it spelled out? Okay. I've got two murders on my hands. I have some *thing* in this town that is making

64

people and electronic equipment act nuts. Whatever it is just goosed you in the butt about five minutes ago, and did some titty-squeezing with your lieutenant and your sergeant. You saw it slap a boy down, rip the clothes off a lady, and knock one of my deputies to the floor. What I don't need at this time, Major, is a lot of press types in here. You get my point?"

"You can't detain us, Sheriff; not with our credentials. But we might be of assistance if we stayed here."

Gordie walked to a window and looked out onto a side street. The view was somewhat less than awe-inspiring. With his back to the military people, he said, "You didn't offer to stay."

Maj. Jackson thought about that for a few seconds, then smiled. "Sheriff Rivera, would you like for me and my people to stay here in town so that we might possibly be of some assistance to you and your people in the event of further trouble?"

Gordie laughed and turned around. "Isn't there some sort of federal law about active troops getting involved in local civilian matters without prior government approval?"

"Yes. But if we are attacked, we certainly have the right to defend ourselves."

"That's good to know. I don't suppose any of you came armed?"

"Sidearms."

"Lemmie out of this son of a bitch!" Hubbard screamed from the drunk tank just up the hall.

He was ignored.

"I would like for all of us to be brought fully up to date, Sheriff," Jackson requested.

"Of course."

"I have a question, Sheriff," Kathy said.

"Ask."

"Why don't you just call in the highway patrol, or

ask the governor to send in the national guard?"

"I can answer that," Howie spoke from the doorway. He was holding a wet cloth to the side of his face. The swelling appeared to be going down.

All turned to face the small boy.

"Go ahead, Howie," Gordie said.

"The sheriff doesn't want to involve any more people than he absolutely has to. He doesn't want to risk any more lives. He isn't sure that any of us are going to live through whatever it is that is menacing us. And he isn't at all certain that . . . that, whatever it is, call it a thing, would allow any of us to leave this area."

"Is that it, Sheriff?"

"That about sums it up," Gordie said with a sigh. He looked at Howie. "You're a very smart boy, Howie. I have a hunch that you know, or think you know, more about this thing, as you call it, than you're letting on. Am I correct?"

"Yes, sir. I think so."

"Want to share it with us?"

"Of course. Just as soon as I get it worked out in my head."

Country and western music suddenly filled the room, the music heavy with guitars and drums.

"He came rollin' out of Monte Rio, with blood
    stains on his hands.
"Crazy Morg was with him, as they screamed
    across the land.
"With their future all behind them, they threw
    their fates to the wind.

"Sand, good-bye, Sand."
I HATE THAT GODDAMNED SONG! TURN IT OFF!

66

"Screw you," another voice was added.

Watts had to lean against the table for support. The second voice belonged to Sand.

Chapter Five

"Mr. Jennings, you used to be called Ace, were you not?"

Richard laughed that strange, hollow laugh. "Yeah, I did. A long time back."

"And you were friends with Sand? You were a part of that . . . club?"

"Yeah. From the beginning to the end. The Pack. That's what the city police hung on us. It stuck. Willowdale doesn't have a city police department anymore. The sheriff's department handles all that now."

"The pack? From wolf pack?"

"Probably. They hung it on us after a bad fight."

"With whom?"

"A bunch of college boys—rich kids—from over the pass. A town called Monte Rio."

"The resort town?"

"That's the one."

"Can we skip ahead, Mr. Jennings? Hit the high spots?"

"Just like a reporter, Sunny. You don't want to know the whole story. You don't want to know why somebody did something. All you want is the gory part of the story."

Sunny chuckled with no small amount of irony. Trouble was, he was right. "All right, Mr. Jennings. I can take all the time in the world to get this done. We'll do it your way."

"Time is something we don't have much of. But we can get it down, I think. But we'll do it Sand's way, Sunny."

She shook her head and said wearily, "Whatever, Mr. Jennings. May I use your bathroom?"

"Sure." He pointed. "One right down that hall."

After using the toilet, she washed her hands and face. She noticed several magazines and a newspaper on a stand by the commode. She picked them up. Everything was old, dated 1979. She looked in the medicine cabinet. All the prescription medicines were years out of date. She closed the mirrored cabinet door and stared for a long terrifying moment. She had to cling to the vanity to keep from passing out. Bite her lips to keep from screaming.

She had no reflection in the mirror.

The college kids smelled it, before they saw it. Then they rounded a curve in the gravel road and came face to face with the source of the horrible odor.

Piles of dead cattle and sheep. The stinking mound was completely blocking the road. The animals had been torn apart, heads and legs and entrails tossed in all directions. Sandy turned her head and vomited.

Paul took a deep breath and instantly regretted it. He said, "We're going to have to climb over the animals, people. It's the only way out."

"You've got to be kidding!" Bos protested.

Paul fixed him with a hard look, and then gave them all a hard choice. "It's either that or we go back to the ghost town and wait until help comes."

With a grim look on her face, Sandy wiped her mouth, took a drink of water from her canteen, and moved toward the mound of stinking death. Slowly, the others followed.

The wild shrieking brought them all to the feet, running toward the drunk tank. Gordie yelled for someone to get the kids out of this section of the building, and not to leave them alone.

He slid to a halt on the concrete floor and stared in horror at the sight before him.

Hubbard was being squeezed against the bars; already the bars had crushed his shoulders and hips, the bones breaking and sticking out, the blood squirting. The front of his head was being slowly crushed, the skull indenting. His screaming ceased as his brains oozed out of his mouth and ears and nose. Broken teeth fell from his mouth and clicked wetly on the floor.

The broken and crushed remains of Hubbard the hardware man slopped to the cell floor.

FOR EVERY EVIL UNDER THE SUN
THERE IS A REMEDY OR THERE IS NONE
IF THERE BE ONE, TRY AND FIND IT
IF THERE BE NONE, NEVER MIND IT.

The voice howled with laughter.

ISN'T THIS FUN? THIS IS MORE FUN THAN DANCING ON SOMEONE'S BLUE SUEDE SHOES.

Gordie leaned against the brain- and blood-splattered wall opposite the death cell. He felt the ooze of gore through his shirt and pulled away from the wall.

Maj. Jackson looked at the gory mess in the drunk tank and lifted his eyes to the sheriff. "You want to try to evac the town?"

"Let's try it."

DON'T.

"How do you propose to stop us?" Jackson asked, feeling sort of silly talking to the air.

EASILY, TOY SOLDIER.

"I don't think you're that powerful," Gordie said.

THEN GO TO YOUR OFFICE AND LOOK OUT THE WINDOW TO THE STREET, GREASEBALL.

"What are you going to do?"

HAVE FUN.

Jackson caught Gordie's eyes and shrugged. "Do we have a choice?"

"I guess not."

FOR ONCE, YOU'RE RIGHT.

Gordie walked into the big room that housed the waiting area, up to the circular desk that housed dispatch. He looked at Mack. The old deputy was scared, but holding on.

"Mack, go to our tach frequency and advise all units to start setting evacuation routes and procedures. Alert civil defense. Notify the school and the fire department. Get the principal up here to the office right now."

"Yes, sir."

Dark, evil chuckling filled the big room. DO YOU LIKE SURPRISES, BURRO-BRAIN?

Gordie looked around him and waited.

LET'S BOOGIE, BABIES!

A series of explosions rocked the town, followed by booming laughter. All the phone lines lit up. When the callers were calmed—as best the deputies could—units were dispatched to the various scenes of destruction. Gordie rubbed his face with his hands when all units reported back by radio.

"A grain elevator blew up just south of town. An eighteen-wheeler loaded with food was blown off the state road north of town. Here in town, to the east, Adamson's little store no longer exists. West of here, William's service station exploded. Deputies and firemen are looking through the debris now, for survivors. And bodies," he added.

AS THE DAYS GROW LONGER,

71

THE STORMS GROW STRONGER.

The wild laughter that followed the children's rhyme gradually faded.

"Showing us that it can do just about anything it wants to do," Watts said.

"And warning us, I suppose," Jackson added, "not to try any evacuation."

Gordie picked up his cowboy hat. "Let's go see the damage. Then we've got to have some sort of town meeting. Lee, see if you can get in touch with the mayor."

"Yes, sir."

"What in God's name are you going to tell them without putting everybody into a blind panic?" Captain Hishon asked.

"I don't know," Gordie admitted.

"And after you do tell them?" Watts asked.

"I don't know that either. Hell, I don't even know what it is we're fighting."

He turned and walked out the door.

"I've done some brushing up on hot rod jargon of the 1950s," Sunny said, attempting to put a calmness in her voice that she certainly did not feel. She was shaky from her experience in the bathroom, but was trying very hard to convince herself that Richard, for whatever reason, was playing tricks, mind games, trying to scare her away. "Were you people outlaws?"

"Absolutely not," Richard stated. "There was not a criminal in the bunch. We never had any serious trouble with the law until about a year before the bottom dropped out. But when it did drop, all hell broke loose."

He laughed at that, and Linda smiled. Sunny did not see one bit of humor in it. But she was getting some clues, and prayed that she was wrong.

72

"Sand is the best friend I ever had in either world. I love him like a brother, and always will."

I'm not believing this! Sunny's mind was working furiously. It's a trick.

"Perhaps telling is too slow," Richard said. "Maybe you should see for yourself."

"What kind of game are you playing, Mr. Jennings?"

"No game. Relax."

Sunny experienced a heavy sensation; she thought it must be like jet fighter pilots feel. Several G's. The smell, that sickly-sweet funeral-home odor became stronger. She tried to fight the feeling of motion, or travel. In her mind, she hoped, the room began to tilt. She suddenly felt as if her inner clock had stopped, and then been reversed.

"Do not be afraid," a voice entered her head. The voice was not Richard's. "No harm will come to you. I am the Force."

Thunder cracked.

It didn't take long for Gordie and his people to get the picture. Whatever they were facing had enormous power. Power enough to strike at all corners of the town simultaneously. And there wasn't enough left of whoever got in its way to body-bag.

Dr. Craig Anderson shoved his way through the crowds—and they were curiously silent and well-behaved—and walked up to Gordie.

"Nothing," the doctor said. "There isn't enough left of the bodies to make a positive I.D. on any of them. Oh, before I forget." He lowered his voice to a whisper. "The hands and eyes and lips have now returned to the coolers."

The doctor's eyes held a dozen questions. But he kept them to himself. Gordie knew he was waiting until they could speak privately.

"How many dead, Doctor?" Watts asked.

"Hard to tell, Colonel. Mr. and Mrs. Adamson, for sure. They were in the store, as usual. Maybe a couple of customers. Two men for sure at the grain elevator. Dr. Shriver is working over there. The truck driver and his helper are scattered all over the place. One man for sure at the service station. But taking into account the savagery of the initial implosion, there will probably be more."

"Implosions, Craig?" Watts asked.

"Yes. Everything initially blew inward. Witnesses say the truck, the entire rig, was just sucked inward, and then scattered like a tornado hit it. The truck driver and helper were literally crushed like tomatoes, and then flung out with the bits and pieces of the rig."

"An implosion and explosion?" Gordie asked.

"I would say so, yes."

A man grabbed Gordie's arm and jerked him around. "We elected you sheriff, Gordie. You gotta do something." The man's eyes were wild. "What are you goin' to do?"

Gordie evaded that. "Go home, sir. Stay in your home." Gordie pried the man's fingers from his arm. "I've ordered school dismissed for the remainder of the week. Keep your kids inside as much as possible. Don't let them out of your sight."

A deputy walked up to Gordie and whispered, "The principal over at the high school said—when we informed him that it would be best if school was dismissed—and I quote, 'It don't make me a good goddamn if I ever see any of these little shitters again. Fuck 'em all.' "

Gordie stared at him. "Principal McVay said that?"

"Word for word."

"It's a madman loose, isn't it, Sheriff?" a woman hollered.

"Quite possible, ma'am. Now let's break this crowd

74

up, and you all go home, please."

They all noticed that the majority of the crowd all turned as of one mind and walked off. Only a few chose to linger and rubberneck at the carnage. The deputies shooed them away from the scene of destruction.

"Strange behavior," Dr. Anderson observed. "Very strange. Only a few showed any emotion at all. Only a few cases of excitement. No hysteria at all." He looked squarely at Gordie. "When do we talk, Sheriff?"

"Right now. At my office."

Anderson's coffee remained untouched on the table. He had listened carefully, his facial expression clearly mirroring his disbelief, as the men and women told their stories.

Then Gordie took him into the cell block that housed the drunk tanks. Lee lifted the blood-soaked blanket that covered the crushed and mangled body of Hubbard. Craig had already noticed the blood- and brain-splattered walls.

The doctor opened his mouth several times to speak. Each time he closed it silently. Finally he sighed and shook his head.

Gordie waved them out of the cell block and back into the main room.

"All right," the doctor said, facing the group of men and women. "For the sake of argument, I'll accept everything you have told me as truth. Now then, what is this thing?"

"We don't know," Gordie said.

"What does it want?"

"We don't know that either. And yes, we have asked it. It answers in nursery rhymes and riddles and singing." All songs that are at least thirty years old, that thought suddenly come to Gordie. That's got to mean

75

something. But what?

Clearly, the doctor thought the sheriff was nuts.

Although he didn't say it, his eyes spoke loudly enough.

Watts picked up on the man's feelings. "If it was just one or two of us who heard it, Craig, you'd be right in thinking us a bit loony. But we've all heard the thing."

Mack called out, "Sheriff, Blanco Five reports a group of young people, college age, coming down on the ghost town road. They're about a mile from Ed's cafe. Four boys and four girls. They're all bloody as a butcher and pretty well shook up. He's requesting two more units to help bring them in."

"All right, roll them. Bring the kids here. How'd they get bloody? An accident?"

"No." Mack chose his words carefully, in this day of scanners and people listening to every word the cops say. "The same thing that's been giving us a little trouble."

"That's interesting."

"Now what?" Judy asked.

"We'll soon find out." Gordie turned to his chief deputy. "Lee, get that meeting with the mayor and city council set up. Right now. I want them here in ten minutes. Go." He turned to Dr. Anderson. "You stay for this, too, Craig. You can check out the young people as we bring them in."

"All right. I'll get my bag out of the car, and call for a nurse to meet me here."

OH, GOODY! MORE PUSSY ON THE WAY.

That stopped the doctor cold. He looked back at Gordie. The sheriff spread his hands in an I-told-you-so gesture.

Gordie looked around for Howie and Angel. He found them sitting together in a corner of the room. He smiled at Angel and winked at Howie.

They both grinned at him.

I DO HOPE THE DOCTOR IS CALLING FOR THAT GOOD-LOOKING NURSE AND NOT THAT OLD BAT. HE'S GOT ONE OVER THERE THAT WOULD STOP A P-38 IN A POWER DIVE.

Howie jerked his head up at that, his eyes narrowing. Gordie watched the boy, wondering why the sudden interest.

DID YOU LIKE MY LITTLE SURPRISE, GREASEBALL?

"If you're speaking of the destruction, yes, it got my attention."

GOOD. THEN I TRUST YOU WILL DO NOTHING MORE ABOUT YOUR ABSURD PLAN TO EVACUATE THE TOWN?

"We have no plans to do so at the moment."

GOOD. VERY GOOD. WELL, TA-TA, ALL. I MUST BE OFF TO SPREAD MORE GOOD CHEER.

Craig sat down heavily in a chair. His tanned face was shiny with sweat. When he spoke, his voice was shaky. "Any chance that it's being done by human hands? You know what I mean."

"I think you know the answer to that as well as I do, Craig."

"Yeah. Unfortunately, I do."

"Cars coming in with the kids, Sheriff," Mack said, standing up behind the console. "They look like they've had a bad time of it."

"Take their statements, Rich." He walked over to Howie and Angel. "Howie, you seemed awfully interested in what the voice had to say."

"Oh, not really," the boy said with a smile. He held up a piece of paper. He had written: Nothing important to be said aloud, Sheriff.

Gordie grinned and patted the boy on the shoulder. He took the note and handed it to Watts, who read it, shook his head in agreement, and began passing it

77

around.

The others read the note and grinned at Howie.

"Now he's a star," Angel said. "I always knew you'd make it, Howie. Just remember me when you're rich and famous."

Gordie laughed and then sobered as he looked at the gang of young men and women walking wearily through the front door. They did indeed appear to have had a rough time of it. He checked his watch, wishing the mayor and the town council would get their butts in gear.

Events were flying past Sunny's eyes so fast she could hardly catalog them in her mind. She did not know whether she was actually, physically, going backward in time, or whether it was all in her mind. She suspected the latter.

Time — or whatever it was — slowed.

She saw a football game in progress. She watched a tall, rugged-looking and handsome young man remove his helmet and stand in the middle of the snowy playing field as play was stopped. Someone was hurt on the field.

There was a look of disgust on the young man's face.

The old-fashioned — to her — scoreboard read: Willowdale 49, Monte Rio 7. The locals had given the other side a real pasting. A band was playing "Twelfth Street Rag" as the cheerleaders danced and waved their pompoms.

One cheerleader in particular held Sunny's attention. It was Robin. She looked closer. It was Robin, but not Richard and Linda's Robin. This was the original.

Sunny felt slightly sick at her stomach. Had she actually traveled thirty years back in time?

The handsome and well-built football player walked

off the field, ignoring the shouts from his coach. The young man's hair was very thick, and worn much longer than the 1950s dictated.

Sunny got the accurate impression that this young man didn't give a damn what style demanded. It had to be Sand.

She was suddenly so close to the young man that she felt she could reach out and touch him. And as a woman, she certainly would do that, if she could.

Sunny was embarrassed by her sexual thoughts. The young man turned his head to seemingly look straight at her. He had very pale gray eyes.

At the sidelines, he was met by a stocky, good-looking young man.

Joey, Sunny thought, and wondered how she knew that.

"Last game, Sand," Joey said.

"Yeah, and I'm glad of it."

"Did all your bruises and contusions accomplish what you thought they would?"

Sand smiled. "You know they didn't."

"Ah, well. Perhaps Blasco Ibañez was right."

"Yeah. The real beast is in the stands. I'm going to shower and get out of this clown suit. I'll see you later."

"Andrews!" the coach hollered. "Get your butt in there."

"How can Sand just walk off, Coach? It's his last game. He scored six of the seven touchdowns."

"Who the hell knows why Sand does anything. Move!"

Sunny smiled as a slender young man stopped Sand. She had seen his picture in California. Dan Thompson.

"Great game, Sand."

"Thanks, Dan."

Hero worship if there ever was a case of it, Sunny thought.

She looked at the date on a program that had been tossed to the ground. November, 1957.

Events began unraveling so fast she could not keep up with them. Once she picked out Sand's Mercury; just like she had seen it in the Jennings' shed. Then there was Sand, in street clothes: jeans, boots, black leather jacket. She had to smile for somehow she knew he wore it just to irritate other people.

Custom cars were parked around the Mercury. Thirty-four and '36 model street rods, all the way up to '49 and '50 model Fords, Mercurys, and Olds, all chrome and customized.

A man and woman walked by. Sand spoke. The woman smiled, and the man gave him a dirty look.

Sand laughed at him.

The scene shifted. The den of a home. A very angry man stood pointing a finger at Sand. "As long as you're in this house, you'll do as I say, young man. Jesus, why can't you be more like your brother, Harry? You'll never amount to a hill of beans."

Sunny opened her eyes. She was back in her chair, looking at Richard Jennings. She cleared her dry throat. She had a slight headache. "I don't know what happened, Mr. Jennings. I don't know if this is some sort of trick or not. But I'll play your game. Who or what is the Force?"

"You. Me. All things in all people. Old loves, old fears. Old hates, and everything good and bad. Part of the Force is present in all of us. It becomes very vocal when death is imminent. The Force is the Fury's nemesis. They are longtime enemies. The Force is the God of retributive justice—vengeance."

"Then . . . that isn't just mythology?"

"No. The Force is very real. And very close to us right now."

"As is Sand."

"Yes."

80

"How much of what you're telling me is truth, and how much is pure crap, Mr. Jennings?"

Thunder cracked so loudly, it rattled the windows in the house.

Chapter Six

"What in the hell do you mean: you can't evacuate the town?" Mayor Adams yelled at Gordie. "What the hell are these soldier boys—and girls—doing here then? Didn't you call for them?"

Gordie tossed the months-old letter on the table. "That's why they're here."

The mayor grabbed up the letter and scanned it. "Well, I'll be damned! I remember this. 'Deed, I do. Nell forgot to remind me of it."

"Have you spoken with your secretary today?" Gordie asked.

"Eh? Ah, yes. Briefly. I called her. Acted like she was drunk or something. 'Course, that's ridiculous. The woman doesn't drink. Stop changing the subject, Sheriff." He turned to the chief deputy. "And why aren't you dressed out, Lee? You have gym in ten minutes. You'd better get cracking, young man."

"Yeah," Councilman Fulbright said. "And it's my turn to pitch."

"It is not!" Councilman Brady shouted. "You get to pitch all the time. You're just a big fatso, fatso! Tubby Toby, that's you!"

"I'm gonna tell Mr. Emerson that I seen you all peekin' into the girls' dressing room!" Councilwoman Edith Wilson yelled.

DO BOP DE DO BOP DE DO BOP, DE DO.

Neither the mayor nor any of the squabbling city council members showed any signs of hearing the singing.

Shaking his head, Gordie motioned for the others to follow him out of the county courtroom. He shut the door behind him and looked at Al Watts.

"I'll tell Sand on you, you big bully!" could be heard from the other room.

"Toby Fulbright," Al said. "Sand used to take up for him at school."

"Tubby Toby! Tubby Toby!"

Capt. Hishon said, "Sand? Why does that name ring a bell?"

"Ten years or so back, there was a record out called *Good-bye Sand.*"

Hishon snapped his fingers. Anything to get their minds off this damn crazy town. "I remember that. It was a hit. Sand is from here?"

"Right here," the sheriff said.

"What happened to Sand?"

Watts had started to walk away. He stopped and turned around. "I killed him. Thirty fucking years ago!"

Hishon grimaced. "Sorry, Mr. Watts."

"For what? You didn't do anything."

Gordie said, "What about the college kids?"

"They're all right," Hishon said. "Scared, bruised up some. That . . . thing really gave them a good working over. Mentally and physically. Sheriff, ah, what are we going to do?"

"First thing we're going to do is get the Ingram kids back home. See to that, will you, Judy?"

She nodded.

"Then we're going to seal off the town. We don't let anyone in here, for any reason. Pass the word, Lee, and get cracking on that." He smiled. "After you get through with gym, that is."

Lee grimaced and walked away.

Gordie looked up. "Does my sealing off the town meet with your approval?"

I'M SO GLAD YOU'RE INCLUDING ME IN YOUR DECISION-MAKING, RIVIERA.

"Rivera!"

WHATEVER. OH, GO AHEAD AND SEAL IT OFF. NOBODY EVER COMES IN HERE ANYWAY. IT'S SUCH A DUMP.

Gordie took a chance. He winked at Watts, and said, "Sand didn't think so."

The voice screamed in rage, and Gordie was picked up and thrown across the hallway, to crash against a wall. Stunned, he slumped to the floor.

NEVER, EVER, MENTION THAT VILE ARROGANT UPSTART TO ME AGAIN. NOT EVER AGAIN, SPIC. YOU UNDERSTAND THAT?

Gordie got to his knees, crawled to his boots. "I get the message. Ah, do you have a name?"

YES. BUT AS FAR AS YOU ARE CONCERNED, YOU MAY ADDRESS ME AS . . . YOUR MAJESTY.

Gordie rolled his eyes. "Wonderful. Fine. Your majesty. At the risk of getting tossed around again . . . what do you have against the, ah, person I just mentioned?"

The hallway pulsed with invisible anger. HE HAS FOUND A FRIEND. A . . . SOMEONE I DESPISE. THEY CONSPIRE AGAINST ME. THEY INTERFERE.

The pulsing ceased before Gordie could ask anything else. Majesty was gone. Gordie brushed himself off. His elbow hurt and he rubbed it, stretching his stocky frame and groaning as he discovered new bruises from his impact with the wall.

"You took a chance, Gordie," Watts said.

"But I found out something we didn't know for sure."

"That Sand is fighting this thing?" Watts said.

"Yes."

"But who is his friend?" Jackson asked. "This conspirator that thing spoke of?"

The door to the courtroom opened and a very red-faced and angry mayor stalked out, followed by the city council. "I demand to know why you left us in there, Sheriff!"

Gordie just looked at him briefly, and walked outside.

84

He needed some air.

The sheriff drove through town, window down, his sore elbow hanging out. The cool fresh air felt good. Then he realized that he had not given any further orders for sealing off the town.

He radioed in and told dispatch that no one—absolutely no one—was to be allowed inside the city limits.

Damnest location he'd ever seen for a county seat. One of the smallest towns in the county, and surely the hardest to get to. Especially when it snowed.

So there is life after death. There really is. And somewhere . . . out there—Gordie cut his eyes to the sky—a man who has been dead for thirty years is fighting some sort of being. Some sort of . . . Gordie didn't know what to call it; didn't know what it was. A creature, a monster. Whatever.

"What does it want?" he muttered. "And why did it pick this town?"

And what the hell am I going to do? he silently questioned.

The press must not get wind of this. They will eventually, but, Lord, give me a little time before they fall in on us. I don't have enough people to handle a major crowd. Crowd! If news of what is happening ever leaked out, it wouldn't be a crowd . . . it would be a mob!

Maybe that's what *it* wants. But why?

Driving the deserted streets, he muttered, "People sure took my orders to heart. Nothing and nobody is moving."

Something struck the side of his car hard. Gordie braked and got out. A gaggle of Willowdale's hard-core punks stood by the curb, laughing and drinking whiskey. Gordie knew them all by name. High school dropouts, thieves, and minor dope-pushers. He looked at the side of his car and cussed under his breath. A dent in the rear quarter panel. The thrown brick that put it there lay in the street.

85

Gordie picked up the brick with his left hand and walked up to the group of young men. "Who threw it and why?"

A big gangly young man laughed and said, "Fuck you, pig!"

Gordie grinned at the would-be tough boy. Then a thought came to him: there was a good possibility that none of them would come out of this mess alive. So to hell with social workers and sob-sister bleeding hearts and mumbling judges and out-of-touch-with-reality shrinks.

Gordie knocked the big punk on his ass.

The others sprang at him. One fell as Gordie swung the brick and hit him smack in the mouth, pulping his lips and knocking out teeth. Another went down as Gordie kicked him in the balls, going down puking and gagging on it.

The melee ended when Gordie stuck the muzzle of his pistol, the hammer jacked back, into a young man's mouth. "Freeze as still as ice, asshole!"

He froze.

Gordie removed the muzzle from the punk's mouth and said, "Out in the middle of the street—all of you! And lay flat on your bellies." He glanced down at the thug he'd flattened with his fist. "You drag the crud with the busted balls. Do it!"

When they were all spread-eagled on the pavement, Gordie called in.

In less than two minutes, two units showed up. One of them driven by Lee Evans.

"You remember these crap-heads, Lee?"

"Unfortunately, yes."

"Don't they live around here?"

Lee pointed out the houses.

Gordie told the other deputies, "Take them to jail and lock them up. Have a guard outside the cells at all times. Keep Hubbard in mind."

They got the message.

"Come on, Lee. I want to talk with some parents."

86

One of the young thugs laughed and said, "Good luck, pig."

"Whatever that means," Lee muttered. "And I hope it doesn't mean what I think it does."

"I heard that."

They knocked on the doors of five houses and got no response from any of them. Gordie checked his watch. Almost five. Somebody should be home. He tried the doorknob of the fifth house. Unlocked. With a glance at Lee, he turned the knob and pushed open the door.

The odor hit them hard. Both of them had smelled it many times in their careers. Death. Stinking, bloated, maggot-covered bodies were the only thing that would produce such an odor.

And dead rotting animals have a different odor than dead rotting humans.

"Damn!" Lee said, pointing to the body.

A naked girl was lying on the living room floor, bloated in death.

They quickly searched the house. No more bodies. Gordie motioned Lee outside, and both men left quickly. That smell will get to you in a hurry. And it lingers on one's clothing.

"Let's check the other houses, and get it over with, Lee."

All they had to do was open the front doors and take a whiff. A short one.

"All right," Gordie said. "It's coming to a head, I think. Get some people out here, including Dr. Anderson and Watts. And tell the coroner to bring lots of body bags."

"Beaten to death, tortured," Bergman said, looking at Watts. The retired cop nodded his head in agreement. "All of them. Three or four days ago, I'd guess." He pointed to the dried blood on the girl's buttocks. "Raped for sure, probably sodomized."

They moved on to another house. An entire family:

man, woman, girl, boy. All had been tortured. The woman's head was missing.

"The teenage girl you found lived here," Watts said. "She was going steady—or whatever they call it now—with one of the punks you locked up. She was a pretty good kid, but had lousy taste in men."

The other homes were simply a repeat of the first two: stinking death houses filled with mutilated bodies.

BIRDS OF A FEATHER WILL FLOCK
   TOGETHER,
SO WILL PIGS AND SWINE.
DOGS AND CATS WILL HAVE THEIR
   CHOICE,
AND SO WILL I HAVE MINE.

"Are you responsible for all this?" Gordie asked the voice.

HEAVENS NO.

"But you knew it was going on?"

CERTAINLY.

"So the boys I arrested did it?"

I AIN'T NO STOOLIE, COPPER.

The heavy laughter rocked the dying afternoon, then gradually faded.

"Bastard," Gordie said.

"You know what I think, Gordie?" Bergman said.

The sheriff looked at him.

"I think that creature is planning on killing us all. One by one, taking his, or her, or its, own sweet time in doing it."

"Yes," Gordie said, adding for the voice's benefit, hoping to buy a little more time. "And we're powerless to do anything about it."

DO BOP DE DO BOP DE DO BOP, DE DO, came the dark reply.

* * *

Sunny had accepted the fact that she was involved in some sort of supernatural happening. There was simply no other suitable explanation. Logical was totally out the window. What she didn't know was how deeply she was involved.

She wasn't far from finding out.

With a sigh and a deep breath to try to calm shaky nerves, she forced herself to once more fall back into her role as writer/reporter. "Sand was a rebel?" she asked. She was becoming accustomed to the sweet funeral-home smell in the house. Some sort of disagreeable room deodorizer, she guessed. The charred wood odor puzzled her.

"To a degree," Richard said. "He didn't like unfairness. His father was always throwing his brother, Harry, up to him, and telling Sand that he, Sand, would never amount to a hill of beans. And Harry was a total jerk."

"I . . . saw the older man tell him that. Tell me about Harry."

"Harry was a coward, a tattletale, a twerp. He ran with the rich, snobby crew over at Monte Rio. Sand's dad was always telling Harry that his brother, Sand, was a shame and a disgrace to the family. He thought Harry was the perfect son."

"Then it would be an understatement to say that Sand and his father did not get along."

"That's putting it mildly." Richard glanced out the window. "It's growing late, Sunny. Did you bring along a change of clothing?"

"Why . . . no. I guess I'll go on back to the motel."

Husband and wife exchanged glances as thunder cracked sharply. Sunny noticed that both the man and woman seemed to be listening for something more than the thunder. A message, perhaps? But what kind of a message could the thunder contain?

"You'll be safe for this night," Richard told her. "But when you come back in the morning, and make it early, bring a change of clothing and some toilet articles."

"Yes," Sunny's reply was drily given. "I noticed that most of the articles in the bathroom were years out of date."

"We wondered if you'd notice." He looked at Robin. The girl was stretched out on the couch and appeared to be sound asleep. "When the house was . . . well, reconstructed, so to speak, nothing could be changed. It is not permitted. Although I don't believe you're quite ready to understand that."

"Mr. Jennings, I don't understand anything about you or this place, or your wife, or where I went flying this afternoon."

Robin sat up on the couch. "Flying?" she laughed. "What have you been smoking, Sunny?"

Gordie stopped by the Ingram house. He was met by a grimfaced father.

"Sheriff Rivera. You want to tell me what in the hell is going on in this town?"

Gordie sidestepped that. "How are the kids?"

"Fine. Angel is watching television, and Howie is in his room, working with his computer." He stepped out onto the stoop and closed the door behind him. "When I left my business this afternoon, I was told by a deputy that no one is allowed to leave town. Is that correct, Sheriff?"

"That is correct, Mister Ingram."

"Next question is why?"

"You know, of course, about the murders and the explosions?"

"I'd have to be any idiot not to."

"Mister Ingram, keep your wife and children inside this evening. Warn them not to go outside tomorrow. It would probably be best if you did not open for business until further notice."

"Is that an order?"

"No."

"That's good. Because I intend to open for business as

90

usual." The men locked glances. "All right, Sheriff. I suppose you have your reasons for behaving in this totalitarian manner. Howie and Angel think you're a really neat guy. Personally, I can't see it." He turned his back on the sheriff and walked back into the house, slamming the door behind him.

Gordie grimaced and muttered, "Well, at least he didn't ask me why I wasn't dressed for gym."

He drove to all six checkpoints leading into and out of the town. He was stalling on going home and knew it. All checkpoints were manned, and his personnel was stretched thin. About a third of his people had not shown up for work on the first shift. He didn't want to think about where they might be, or what had happened to them.

He thought he knew.

He decided not to go home. Pam was probably still over at a girlfriend's house, moaning the blues about their crumbling marriage.

Either that or screwing somebody.

Gordie went back to the office.

"What do the punks have to say?" he asked Lee.

"Oh, they're having a big time locked down. Singing and laughing and cussing us—mostly you."

"Who's watching them?"

"Bob."

"How many of the second shift went 10-8?"

"About half of them."

"The military people?"

"Went back to the motel to clean up. Said they'd all be right back. I'm glad they showed up, Gordie. Couple of them are Special Forces types. Airborne rangers. I believe they'll stand solid—all of them."

SPECIAL FORCES! BAH! WHAT A BUNCH OF SISSIES. RADIO ANNOUNCERS AND QUEERS.

Gordie and Lee exchanged glances, Gordie thinking: It doesn't know about Special Forces. It's confusing Special Forces with the old World War Two unit called Special Services. That's why Howie looked so funny when it made

91

the comment about a P-38—a World War Two plane. The thing knows nothing from about nineteen-fifty-eight to this point.

WHY ARE YOU SO QUIET, GREASER?

"I'm trying to figure out a way to destroy you, you big-mouthed glob of whatever."

Wild laughter ripped the late afternoon, booming throughout the office. YOU ARE A BALLSY BASTARD FOR A SPIC, RIVERA.

"Actually, I'm only half-Spanish, but very proud of it. My mother was Irish."

IRISH! the tone was contemptuous. WHY THOSE SILLY FOOLS HAVE BEEN FIGHTING EACH OTHER FOR CENTURIES, AND DON'T EVEN KNOW WHY THEY'RE STILL FIGHTING.

Gordie ignored the voice and walked to his office, closing the door.

The voice followed him. I SUPPOSE YOU'RE GOING TO TELL ME THAT YOU WERE IN SOME SUPER-DUPER MILITARY UNIT, EH, GREASEBALL?

Gordie leaned back in his chair. "I was a groundpound-ing grunt in Vietnam. An eighteen-year-old infantryman."

SO THIS COUNTRY REALLY DID GO IN AFTER THE FROGS GOT THEIR SILLY ASSES KICKED OVER THERE, EH? HOW ABOUT THAT. WELL, IF THIS CESSPOOL YOU CALL AMERICA HAD KEPT ITS AGREEMENTS WITH HO CHI MINH, THERE WOULD NEVER HAVE BEEN A WAR, AND VIET-NAM WOULD HAVE BEEN ONE OF YOUR BETTER ALLIES. DID YOU KNOW ALL THAT, DANNY-ME-BOY?

"No, I didn't."

IT'S TRUE. I WAS THERE.

"Thanks for the history lesson."

YOU'RE WELCOME. I HATE TO SEE SOMEONE DIE IGNORANT. DID YOU KNOW YOUR WIFE, PRETTY PAM, IS SCREWING SOMEONE RIGHT NOW?

Gordie didn't know. But the news didn't come as any great surprise. Her affairs were known countywide.

WHEN YOU SEE HER, GIVE HER A GREAT BIG JUICY FRENCH KISS. THEN YOU'LL KNOW HOW CHUCKIE-BABY'S DICK TASTES!

Howling with laughter, the voice faded away.

Not a soul kiss, not openmouthed, but French. You have a thirty-year-old weak spot, Voice. If I can just figure how to use that against you.

Gordie couldn't even dredge up the oftentimes-soothing emotion of anger toward his wife. He didn't feel anything for her except contempt. They had slept in separate bedrooms for over two years.

The sheriff easily pushed his wife out of his thoughts. He listened for a moment. Something was wrong. Then he realized what it was: the singing and laughing from the cell block where the punks were housed had stopped.

He stepped out of his office and walked to the door leading to the basement cell block. The smell hit him hard. Steeling himself, he walked down the steps to the cells and stood for a moment, fighting back a sudden rush of nausea.

Deputy Bob MacGregor was spread all over the cell block. His head had been placed on a bunk in an empty cell. The mouth was open in a silent scream, the eyes wide and pain-filled. His guts were twisted around the bars. The walls were splattered with blood.

"Lee!" Gordie called.

The chief deputy paled at the sight. "I was out front talking with that Ricky-what's-his-name. The one that goes with Robin Jennings. He can't find her. Says he's looked all over town. Jesus, Gordie, I didn't hear a thing from back here."

"Nor did I. The voice was giving me a history lesson when it happened. Obviously, it can split itself. But I have another question."

Lee looked at him.

"How in the hell did the punks get gone?"

93

When Sunny left the Jennings' house, she felt a myriad of emotions. She felt both depression and elation, a sense of excitement and of physical exhaustion. She could not understand the latter.

She could not understand any of her emotions.

As she backed her rented car out of the drive, she once more experienced that odd sensation of feeling the earth shift—although she knew it was all in her mind.

She hoped.

As she drove back to her motel, the best of the two in town—the hotel was about a hundred years old and in pretty sad shape—she noticed how deserted the town was. Then she saw several men standing on a corner.

One of them gave her the finger, and another one rubbed his crotch and grinned at her. The third one called out some very obscene things he'd like to do to her.

Her face red and her jaw set in anger, Sunny drove on. "This is the weirdest damned town I have ever been in," she muttered.

Passing an intersection, she saw, far down the way, a police car blocking the street. On impulse, she braked, backed up, and drove to the blockade, intending to tell the officer about the rude behavior of some of the town's citizens.

That went out the window as the deputy raised his hand, indicating that she stop. She stopped, lowered her window, and waited as the deputy walked up. "What's the problem, officer?"

"No one is allowed out of town, Miss." He studied her for a moment. "You're not from around here, are you?"

"Ah . . . no. I'm not. What do you mean, no one is allowed out of town? What's happened?"

"Sheriff's orders, ma'am. No one is allowed in or out of Willowdale."

Sunny instantly smelled a story. "What's happened, officer?"

The deputy stared at her. She noticed how tired he looked. "Where have you been all day, ma'am?"

"Why . . . visiting here in town."

"You don't know about the explosions and deaths?"

"I am aware of the murders yesterday."

The deputy shook his head. "No, ma'am. I'm talking about the . . . incidents that occurred today."

"I don't know anything about them. I've been interviewing some people on a story I'm doing. I'm a writer."

"I . . . see. I guess. And you really didn't hear the explosions?"

"No. Nothing. And neither did any of the people I was interviewing."

"Strange," the deputy muttered. "Where are you staying, Miss?"

"At the newest and nicest of the motels."

"Who are you interviewing for this story?"

Sunny was growing tired of the questioning. "Am I under arrest?"

That brought a smile to his face. "No, ma'am. You are not under arrest. I'm just curious as to where you've been. You see, the whole town was rocked by the explosions. Everybody in town poured out into the streets. Well, almost everybody—you didn't."

Her anger faded. His questions were legitimate and deserved an answer. "I spent the entire day at the Jennings' home, interviewing Richard and Linda Jennings. Their daughter Robin was also present."

The deputy stared at her. "Jesus!" he whispered. He closed his eyes and shuddered.

"Are you all right?" Sunny asked.

"Oh. Yeah. I'm fine. Been a long day is all. Ma'am, would you mind waiting here for a moment—please?"

Sunny was really looking forward to a hot bath and something to eat. And she wanted desperately to go over the tapes. She sighed. "Deputy, if you tell me to wait, I'll wait."

"Thank you, ma'am. It won't take long, I promise you.

Couple of minutes. And, ma'am," he smiled, "you are not in any kind of trouble."

Sunny sat in her car for much longer than a couple of minutes. She grew impatient and got out to stretch her legs. It was almost completely dark when another car pulled up. She watched as a stocky, rather handsome man got out and walked up to her.

He smiled. "I'm Sheriff Gordie Rivera, ma'am. And I apologize for this inconvenience, and thank you for waiting. We're talking with all strangers in town, and thought we'd spoken to them all. May I see some identification, please?"

Slightly miffed, Sunny dug in her purse, found her wallet, and held out the clear plastic case to the sheriff.

"Take it out of the wallet, please?"

She complied and waited, watching his face as he inspected the license. She expected him to say something coplike . . . "Let's run it," . . . or something like that. They always do in the movies.

He handed the license back to her. "Sunny Lockwood. And you have been interviewing Richard and Linda Jennings all day, is that correct?"

"Yes." What about, Miss Lockwood?"

"That, Sheriff, is none of your business." She braced for a hassle.

She got another smile. "You're right. It isn't. But I can ask you where you're staying."

"I told the deputy."

"Tell me."

"I believe it's called the Lodgepole Inn."

"That's right. Thank you, Miss Lockwood."

"I'm free to go?"

"Certainly. And I'm sorry for any inconvenience we might have caused you."

She looked at him. He was a handsome man. And, like the deputy, he looked tired. "Sheriff, we talked about a local—well, rebel, outlaw—I don't know yet just how to describe him. His name, his nickname, is, was—Sand."

"Saunders. Yes. I'm familiar with the case. And what did you learn about Sand, Miss Lockwood? And you do not have to answer that question."

"Not very much, Sheriff. We just got into the interview. What do you know about him?"

Gordie shrugged his shoulders. "I was about five years old when all that went down. I'm not from the area originally. Perhaps you should talk with Al Watts. He's retired head of the Colorado State Patrol. He's the man who killed Sand."

"Yes. Yes, I would very much like to speak with Mr. Watts. Where can I find him?"

"I can have him in my office in about an hour. I imagine you would like to freshen up a bit. It's probably been a rather trying day for you."

That last bit was spoken very drily, and Sunny picked up on it, wondering about it. "Yes. It has been. And I would like to freshen up. That's very considerate of you, Sheriff Rivera."

Gordie explained how to get to his office and stood watching as Sunny drove off.

The deputy walked up. "Ah . . . Sheriff?"

"I know, Sid. I know. It just keeps getting stranger and stranger."

Chapter Seven

Watts almost spilled his freshly poured coffee. "She's been doing *what?*"

The retired cop had been waiting at the sheriff's department when Gordie returned.

"Interviewing Richard and Linda Jennings," Gordie told him. "About Sand."

"That's impossible!" Watts yelled.

"I'm just telling you what she told me. And she was very sincere about it."

The military was out, voluntarily, helping to beef up the roadblocks. The college students were housed at a motel. The office was quiet, with only a dispatcher, Norris and Bergman, and Lee Evans joining Gordie and Watts.

Norris and Bergman didn't understand the fuss Watts was kicking up about the interview. Bergman said, "You know what bothers *me?* The phones still work; the teletype is fully operational. It's like this . . . *thing* knows we can't beat it, so what the hell!"

Gordie glanced at Watts. "We'll see what happens tonight, and then I'll make up my mind about calling in more personnel and phoning the governor."

Watts grimaced at the thought of calling Gov. Siatos. Watts disliked the man intensely.

"Colonel," Norris said. "Before this reporter gets here. What about Sand?"

Watts was reflective for a moment. "The system failed. Justice did not prevail in our courts. Those turd-heads from over Monte Rio got away—for a time, a short time—

98

with murder. They killed Joey and Tuddie, they killed Boom Boom, and then they finally killed Sand's wife. The whole scummy crew of them lied to protect each other. I'm not going to defend what Sand and Morg did—certainly not—but I can sure understand it."

"Boom Boom?" Bergman asked.

Watts chuckled in remembrance. "Boom Boom Dobrinski. Ramrodded an all-girl motorcycle club a couple of counties over. She was wild, I'll tell you that for sure. Wild, but not a mean person. You see, people, after the trouble started, several custom-car clubs, hot-rodders, and several motorcycle clubs all banded together under Sand's leadership—"

"So it wasn't just a few rich kids from Monte Rio after Sand's butt?" Norris asked.

"Oh, no. Those crapheads at Monte Rio got several fraternity houses involved for about a year. *Some* members of certain frat houses," he amended that. "It was open warfare whenever the two factions met. Which was often. The governor at that time—whose main base of support, financially speaking, came from the wealthy—unofficially declared war on Sand and the others. A lot of city and county cops around the state rousted Sand and those who chose to follow him. I am proud to say that the state patrol took no part in any rousting . . . that I am aware of," he added.

Bergman sighed. "People, I am not a practicing Jew. I don't know whether there is a heaven or a hell. I like to think there is a better place after this one. Point I'm trying to make . . . where did this creature we're facing come from? And where, in God's scheme of things, is Sand?"

His partner looked at him. "You mean, is he in heaven, or hell?"

"Yeah."

"Maybe he didn't make it to either place," Lee said. "Personally, I think there are levels of heaven and hell."

"I'll go along with that," Gordie said. "And I'm not a Catholic either."

Watts agreed. "With Sand, I'd have to opt for Valhalla. His grandfather, on his mother's side, was an emigrant from Norway. And Sand believed very strongly in Valhalla."

Gordie said, "The voice said that Sand and his friend interfered — interferes actually." He felt reasonably sure the voice was listening. "Would that be like Sand?"

Watts smiled, and the smile was soft. "Oh, yes." All had gotten the impression that Watts had genuinely liked Sand. "Sand hated a bully. He'd go out of his way to hunt one up and stomp the piss out of him. And if that sounds like a contradiction in terms, it is. You all must understand that Sand was one hell of a young man. Extremely powerful physically and extremely intelligent. Brilliant. He was a walking contradiction. He respected brains much more than brawn. He and Joey had I.Q.'s that went right through the ceiling. Highest ever tested — to date — here in Willowdale. And yet," his voice dropped to a whisper, "they did nothing with all that brilliance. Except die needlessly, foolishly. Rebels fighting the system, both of them knowing they could never win."

SAND IS A MEDDLING, IDEALISTIC FOOL.

Watts looked up. There was no fear in him. He had never backed up for anybody or anything in his life, and he wasn't going to start now. "And you're afraid of him, aren't you?"

The voice howled with wild rage. It screamed in a language that none in the room could understand. A table was picked up and hurled across the room, shattering against a wall. The building actually shook under the powerful wrath of the being.

Hard-breathing pulsated, the rage touching them all in its fury.

I HAVE ALLOWED YOU TO LIVE, BECAUSE I ENJOY THE GAME AND WISH IT TO CONTINUE. BUT DO NOT PUSH ME TOO FAR.

The front door was ripped from its hinges and flung out into the street. The voice left with a wild rush of sucking any loose paper in the office out the open doorway.

Gordie was the first to speak. "You touched a raw nerve that time, Al."

"I didn't make any brownie points, that's for damn sure," he agreed.

The men began cleaning up the office. Sunny drove up, got out, and walked in through what was left of the doorway. She looked around. "My God, what happened?"

"Have a seat, Miss Lockwood," Gordie said, after introducing her all around. "Have a cup of coffee. Just as soon as we get this mess cleaned up, we'll tell you a story, and explain why I've ordered the town sealed off. Have you had anything to eat?"

She had not.

"Lee, call the Lodgepole and have them send over a platter of sandwiches."

Sunny tried a smile. "It's all so mysterious."

Gordie returned the smile. "Like they say, ma'am: you ain't heard nothin' yet."

Howie shut down his personal computer and rubbed his face. He had learned a few things about the voice; but not nearly enough. What he had uncovered had chilled the boy. He decided not to tell Angel just yet. He had time. But he wasn't sure how much time.

It had laid dormant for years—thirty years. It surfaced in the world every thirty years, creating somewhere hurricanes, typhoons, floods, wars. Then it rested, gathering strength, feeding on the energy of evil taken from the souls of the newly dead. It had no shape; it could take any shape. It could be small enough to fit in a box. It could be as large as ten supertankers.

It was thousands of years old.

It was not from hell. It had not been created by either God or Satan. It was evil. If evil could be pure, this then was ninety-nine point nine percent pure evil.

Like all things, it had a flaw, but no one it had ever encountered it in its thousands of years of existence had ever managed to best it. Nothing living, nothing dead residing on the other side of life.

Until now.

To have its efforts thwarted by a few smart-mouthed punks in leather jackets was infuriating enough. But for them to stand in the way of what it was created for, that was mind-boggling.

The Fury had never met an idealist yet that it could not reduce to a mass of quivering, quaking fearful jelly in a matter of seconds.

Some had even willingly chosen hell to get away from it.

Until now.

Sand had yawned at the Fury. Joey had made some smart-aleck comment about how ugly it was. And Morg had said that if he had a saddle, he'd strap it on and ride the howling mass.

And that had been during their first encounter.

Damned insolent punks! The Fury knew they could leave; go to their place in the hereafter. They were just hanging around to cause aggravation.

In time as measured in the firmament, only a blink of an eye. In time as measured on Earth: thirty long years. The Fury had been battling Sand for thirty years. Disgusting having to expel precious energy against a damn rebel who didn't know when to quit and to take his place with the other dead.

But now the Fury was all-powerful again, and it was time for a showdown.

Its thirty-year rest period was nearly over, and it was time to play games. The Fury loved games. Death games.

For years, the Fury could not understand how Sand and his friends came to be, but now it did, and knew how to best Sand. Now the Fury had the edge. It thought. But it had to separate Sand and his bunch from the Force. The Fury's archenemy had found another friend. And to make

102

matters even worse, Sand had made friends with that damned old mercenary, Michael. And if that unspeakable being that Michael served could ever be convinced to turn Michael loose . . .

The Fury shuddered at that thought.

And the Fury couldn't let Sand out of his sight for any length of time, for Sand had found the door—the way out.

The goddamned inquisitive, poking, prying, meddling, arrogant, insulting punk!

So the Fury would have to take it slow and easy with the town. At least for a few more days. Sand couldn't stop humans from killing other humans; at least he hadn't found a way to do it yet.

The Fury had never before met people like Sand and those who followed him. Sand was not especially religious; did not race about willy-nilly, mouthing heavenly utterances and boring everyone who came in contact with him. Actually, as far as the Fury was concerned, Sand had been nothing more than a thug during his short span on earth. Yet . . . even He liked Sand. Probably due in no small part to Michael, who was nothing more than a damned thug himself. He was not yet ready to fully accept Sand into His home, but the Fury knew all the signs. And He would. Eventually.

Disgusting.

It was almost enough to make one lose their faith and go straight.

And that really was a disgusting thought!

Sunny had listened to Gordie and Watts explain what had taken place over the past twenty-four hours.

It was mind-boggling.

"Your turn, Miss Lockwood," Gordie said. "We've leveled with you, now you level with us—deal?"

"Deal. But I don't know anything about what's been happening in this town. What can I tell you that would be of any importance?"

103

"Tell us about your day with the Jennings."

She looked nervously around her. "What if that . . . thing is listening?"

"I'm sure it is listening, but we can't do anything about that."

Sunny told them everything she could remember. The Jennings' strange behavior. The musty smell in the house. The dated magazines, newspapers, and medicines. Of her not having a reflection in the mirror. The funeral-home smell of the house. Her sensation of time-travel. She told them of the car Richard kept in his shed. Of being so close to Sand, she felt as though she could have touched him.

Gordie finished his sandwich and drained his cup of coffee. "Do you have a firm grip on your chair, Miss Lockwood?"

She tried a laugh that didn't work. "I guess so."

Gordie nodded at Watts.

Watts took a deep breath and said, "Miss Lockwood, Richard and Linda Jennings both died in a house fire . . ."

Sunny felt her world began to spin.

" . . . They were positively identified by their dental work and by their personal physician, who still had X rays of broken bones. The pictures were taken when they were both involved in an auto accident. They died ten years ago, almost to the date."

Sunny fainted.

She regained consciousness slowly, swimming slowly through a fog of jumbled memories of the events of that day. She opened her eyes and looked up at a man she did not know. He smiled at her.

"I'm Dr. Anderson, Miss Lockwood. Don't worry. All your vital signs are strong and steady. You fainted, that's all."

She sat up, blinked a couple of times, and felt her strength returning. "You . . ." It came out as a croak and she cleared her throat. "You know what is going on in this town, Doctor?"

"I know what. I don't know why."

"Could I have some water? My throat is awfully dry. Oh, hell, I know where the water fountain is. I saw it on the way in. There's nothing wrong with me."

Anderson helped her up and escorted her into the main room of the office. There were some half a dozen new people that she did not know.

And she was not at all surprised to learn that they were military.

"Some sort of top-secret government hoo-doo that went haywire—as usual—causing all this?" she asked sarcastically.

"Don't be stupid!" Lt. Smith snapped at her. She had been told who Sunny was and what she was doing in town. "Goddamn press people are all the same. Blame everything on the military before you even bother to gather up all the facts."

"Ladies," Maj. Jackson said, stepping between them. He was not fearful for Kathy; she could take care of herself and had, several times. Kathy was no hair-puller. She'd just haul off and knock the crap out of somebody. What the major didn't want was to see this reporter bounced around the room like a loose basketball. He looked at Sunny. "For your information, Miss, we are an advance team, in here to act as liaison between the townspeople and a base that will soon be completed in this area. Sheriff Rivera asked us to assist him in this, ah, matter, and we agreed. I gather you're feeling better?"

"Much better, thank you." Sunny had lost a brother in Vietnam. She had no use for career military types.

The phone rang and dispatch answered. "It's the governor, Sheriff. Returning your call."

"I didn't call the governor."

"He said you called and told his secretary it was top priority. A matter of life and death."

"What the hell?" Gordie muttered, taking the phone. Then it came to him. The damn voice had called. "Sheriff Rivera here, Governor."

"What's the problem in Blanco County, Sheriff?"

"Well, sir, we do have a problem, but I did not call your office."

"Is that a fact? Well, somebody claiming to be you called. He told my secretary that I was a lard-assed dickhead, and then told her some damned perverted acts he'd like her to do with him."

"I'm sorry about that, sir. But I did not call you."

OF COURSE, HE DIDN'T CALL YOU, the voice boomed. THIS SHANTY IRISH HALF-SPIC DOESN'T HAVE THE SENSE TO DIAL A PHONE. I CALLED YOU.

Not punch out the numbers, Gordie noticed. Touch-tone phones were not around thirty years ago.

"What in the hell is that, Rivera?"

"Part of the problem, sir. Or I should say, all of the problem."

GET IT RIGHT, TACO-BREATH. I DON'T WANT TO SHARE THE GLORY WITH ANYONE.

"You'd better identify yourself!" Governor Siatos shouted.

FOR WANT OF A NAIL, THE SHOE WAS LOST
FOR WANT OF A SHOE, THE HORSE WAS LOST
FOR WANT OF A HORSE, THE RIDER WAS LOST . . .
OH, HELL, YOU KNOW THE REST, YOU IGNORANT GREEK TURD.

Gordie listened as the governor let the profane hammer down and let it down hard. For about a full minute.

When he had wound down, Gordie asked, "You all through, sir?"

"Yeah!" Siatos panted. "Sheriff, what in the hell is going on there?"

"No press on this, sir. Please?"

"You have my word on it."

As quickly and succinctly as he could, Gordie explained.

"It's a flying saucer!" Siatos shouted. "Jesus, Mary, and Joseph. We got us a flying saucer landed in Colorado."

Gordie covered the cup with one hand and said to Watts,

106

"He thinks it's a flying saucer."

Watts grimaced. "He would." Governor Siatos was a very liberal Democrat, and Watts was a very conservative Republican.

"Hello, hello!" Siatos shouted.

"I'm right here, Governor."

"Have you found the ship?"

"Governor . . ."

"Do they look anything like E.T.?"

"Governor, goddamnit, will you stop babbling and listen to me?" Gordie shouted.

Silence on the other end, followed by heavy angry breathing. "You had best keep in mind just who you're talking to, *Sheriff* Rivera!"

"Oh, I am perfectly aware of whom I'm attempting to converse with," Gordie snapped back. "I'm trying to talk some sense into a pompous, overbearing, excitable fool, who somehow managed to get himself elected governor of this state by the smallest margin in the history of Colorado politics. Now, goddamn you, either you calm down and listen to me, and stop babbling about little green men, or I'll call every wire service in the nation, and lay this entire damn mess slap in your lap! Now, how's it going to be, Siatos?"

Sunny started viewing the sheriff with a totally different perspective.

The governor cleared his throat. "Perhaps I did become a bit overwrought, Sheriff. Of course, you have my full attention and cooperation. Sheriff, what is that . . . *thing* over there in Blanco?"

"Governor, we don't have the foggiest notion. What it has done is killed about ten people. Maybe more. We don't know for sure. But what we don't want is press attention at this time. Perhaps we can contain it right here. That is my wish, my hope."

"And you want me to . . .?" Siatos left that open.

"Seal off the town."

"Drastic step, Sheriff. And a brave one on your part, I

might add. But let me ask you this: do you have the approval of the people in the town."

"That's just the point, Governor," Gordie explained again. "The thing won't let me evac the town. So I don't want anyone else in here."

"Ahh! Yes. I see. Good move, Sheriff."

"Thank you." Gordie had turned on the speaker so all could hear, and he smiled at Al. The old cop was shaking his head in disgust.

"I hate politicians," Watts muttered.

"What about food and other necessities?" Siatos asked.

"Drive the trucks right up to the barricades and off-load there. But I don't think that's going to be a problem. I think this . . . creature is going to tire of this game long before we run out of food."

"Well, my goodness, Sheriff. What's it going to do then?"

"Well, goddamn, Governor. It'll kill us all." He slammed the phone down, breaking the connection. "Idiot!"

WE AGREE ON SOMETHING, GREASEBALL. WHERE IS THAT GOOD-LOOKING NIGGER DEPUTY OF YOURS?

Judy.

"Out in a unit. Why?"

YOU SURE HAVE A MIXED BAG AROUND HERE. JEWS AND SPICS AND WOPS AND NIGGERS. WHAT ARE YOU TRYING TO DO, WIN THE NOBEL PRIZE?

"No. Dr. King has already done that."

WHO?

"Never mind. Is there anything else you want?"

NO. NOT AT THE MOMENT. I JUST WANTED TO LET YOU KNOW THAT I WAS LISTENING.

"Don't you have something better to do?"

WHAT A SOREHEAD.

And as before, all knew when the thing had left them. Where it went was anybody's guess.

Gordie studied the report taken from the college kids. He

was looking for some common demoninator; something that would link them all together. They had all remained pretty much the same throughout the period since the first murders, unlike many in the town, including the mayor, his secretary, Hubbard, and the town council.

There had to be something.

But Gordie couldn't find it.

He wrote his thoughts on a pad and passed it around. All agreed that he was on the right track, but no one could add anything.

Rich Dawson came in for a break, and reported that a lot of wild parties were breaking out all over the town. Heavy drinking, folks running around half-naked, and worse.

"Breaking under the stress?" Sunny asked, tossing the question out to anyone willing to pick it up.

"I don't think so," Watts said. "It would be my guess that this . . . thing has taken control of them."

"Why would you think they weren't breaking?" Maj. Jackson asked.

"This has always been a tough little town. I don't mean in the sense of law-breakers; just filled with independent folks. This is cattle, farming, and mining country. It would take more than a few murders and a little stress to break most of these folks."

"I wouldn't bet on the press staying out of this for very long," Norris said.

Sunny kept her mouth shut about that.

"Twenty-four to thirty-six hours," Gordie said. "Tops. Less, if our bodiless voice has its way."

"I don't follow, Sheriff," Sgt. Dixon said.

"It *wants* publicity. At least that's the impression I get. Whatever it is, it wants a lot of attention. Think about it. It could have killed us all at the outset. It didn't. It's deliberately dragging this out. Hell, it called the governor's office pretending to be me. Why would it do that except for attention?"

"Then we've got some time." There was a hopeful note in Bergman's voice.

"Until it wearies of the game," Watts dropped a damper on any rising spirits.

"And then?" Sunny asked.

"Unless we can come up with some method of fighting it," Gordie told her. "It will kill us all."

PURPLE PLUMS THAT HANG SO HIGH,
I SHALL EAT YOU ALL, BY AND BY.
DO BOP DE DO BOP DE DO BOP, DE DO.

Chapter Eight

Pam was not at home when Gordie got to his house, and he did not expect her to be. The breakup of the childless marriage was not all one-sided . . . it almost never is. Gordie was well aware that he could make more money doing something else, and that Pam had never liked his being a cop. First a cop in Denver, then joining the sheriff's department in Blanco County. His success had been swift.

And Pam had hated every minute of it.

Her retaliation had been to attempt to screw her way through the entire male population of the county. And so far, she'd made a better than average dent in that goal.

Gordie took a long, very hot and soapy shower, shaved carefully, and went to bed. He did not expect to get much sleep.

The next thing he knew, he opened his eyes, looked at the clock radio, and was pleased to see it was six-thirty in the morning.

Without getting out of bed, he called his office.

"Everything was reasonably calm last night," he was informed. "Lots of parties around town, but nobody was murdered that we know of. The state patrol rolled in about two o'clock. We're sealed off."

"Pull half of our people off the blockades, and put them back on patrol," Gordie ordered.

He walked into his office thirty minutes later, and was surprised to find Sunny there.

"I thought you'd be at the Jennings' house."

"Hell, no! Those people are *dead*."

111

"They didn't hurt you, did they?"

"Well . . . no."

"Sunny, you have to go back there. You're our only link with . . . the other side. You've got to help us find out what this thing is, and if—I don't know how to say this; it sounds so stupid—if someone, well . . ."

He shook his head and took a sweet roll from a sack.

"You want me to determine if a ghost can help us?" Sunny asked.

Even though he felt like an idiot saying it, Gordie said it. "Yes. That's about the size of it."

"The Force is on our side. Whatever it is."

"Yes. Try to find out more about that. Believe me, we need all the help we can get."

He sat down across the table from her. A real looker, he thought. Short brown hair, green eyes. Five-five, he guessed her height. Great figure.

She was appraising him while he was checking her out. She noticed the wedding band. "Kids?"

"No."

"Your wife a career woman?"

Gordie smiled. "That would be one way of putting it. Yesterday the voice told me she was spending the afternoon screwing somebody named Chuck. Chuckie-baby, it said. I know him. Ex-college jock who busted out of the pro's. He's from over Monte Rio way. Serves him right if he's trapped in here."

"Why'd you two marry?"

"Oh, love. We loved each other. We didn't like each other worth a damn, but we loved each other. Took me awhile to learn that like is a lot more important in a relationship than love."

Sunny was easy to talk with, Gordie quickly found out, and it surprised him to find that he wanted to know more about this big-city reporter/writer. Over the past couple of years, Gordie had substituted work for sex. Not that he hadn't had plenty of offers—he had. But with the threat of AIDS, anybody who engaged in casual sex was a fool in Gor-

112

die's opinion.

Now he felt some stirrings. He smiled, looking down at his coffee cup. Hell of a time for that to rear up, he thought, amused at the silent play on words.

Sunny noticed the smile. "You find something amusing in all this?"

"I don't think you'd see the humor in it."

She returned his smile as she stood up. "Richard told me to be there early. So I guess I'd better be going. Conversations with a ghost." She put a hand on Gordie's shoulder. "It's not real to me, yet. This situation, I mean. It's like a bad dream. I keep thinking that I'll wake up at any moment. I just can't, won't, accept that we're all . . . trapped in here, just waiting to die."

"Keep that defense up, Sunny. And don't give up hope."

OH, MY, HOW TOUCHING. PANCHO AND SUNNY. HAS A NICE RING TO IT, DOESN'T IT?

Sunny turned to leave.

HEY, BITCH! DON'T TURN YOUR ASS TO ME. SET IT BACK DOWN IN THE CHAIR.

Gordie nodded his head and pushed out a chair. Sunny sat down.

YOU KNOW WHY I DON'T JUST KILL YOU NOW, BITCH?

"No," Sunny whispered.

I'M NOT GOING TO KILL YOU. IF YOU DO WHAT I TELL YOU TO DO.

Sunny's eyes widened.

"It wants its story told," Gordie said, putting together another piece of the puzzle. "Everybody has a damn story to tell around here."

THAT IS VERY, VERY GOOD, COWBOY. YOU'RE SMARTER THAN I THOUGHT. I'LL HAVE TO KEEP THAT IN MIND. YOU'RE RIGHT. I THINK MY LIFE'S STORY WOULD BE A BEST-SELLER.

"What are you?" Sunny asked.

WHAT AM I? EVERYTHING. ALL THINGS. TOUGH AS A BOOT AND BIG AS ALL OUTDOORS. The voice

113

laughed.

Sunny said, "How can I interview you and write your life's story, if I don't know what you are?"

UMMM. YOU DO HAVE A POINT. ARE YOU SAYING THAT YOU WOULD LIKE TO VISIT ME?

"Not necessarily. But it's rather awkward interviewing you this way."

Sunny screamed, and Gordie almost lost his just eaten sweet roll as the mangled and crushed body of Hubbard the hardware man was suddenly plopped down in a chair at the table. Hubbard's misshapen jaw began working up and down in a grotesque mockery of speech.

INTERVIEW ME, TWINKLE-TWAT.

Hubbard fell over on Sunny, one bloody hand on her breast. Sunny almost fell out of her chair. Gordie caught her just in time. She had fainted.

"Sheriff!" dispatch called. "It's the governor on the phone."

"He has great timing," Watts spoke from the doorway. "You talk to him. I'll take care of Miss Lockwood."

"Somebody toss a blanket over Hubbard," Gordie said, walking to the phone. He realized just how powerful the voice was. Hubbard had been stored in a locked and sealed cooler across town in the morgue. "Yes, Governor."

"I had a visitor last night, Sheriff." Siatos' voice was filled with fear, very shaky. "At first I thought I was dreaming; having a nightmare. I wish it had been."

Gordie waited. He didn't like the governor. Had not voted for him; would never vote for the liberal son of a bitch. Siatos didn't like cops, believed in all sorts of gun control, was against the death penalty, and was totally soft on criminals. Piss on him.

"Are you there, Sheriff Rivera?"

"Right here, sir."

"Sheriff?"

"Yes, Governor?"

"Who in the hell is Sand?"

114

Howie and Angel had slipped out of their house, using the window in Angel's bedroom. They didn't take time to pack anything. Howie had watched his parents changing, and knew he and his sister had to get out of there.

This time Angel didn't argue. She just pointed toward the window, and they split.

"We couldn't get out last night, Howie," Angel reminded her brother. "So now what are we going to do?"

"We go to the sheriff's department, Angel. It's all I can think of."

"Reed Saunders, Governor?"

"That's the one. Yeah. That's the . . . thing that appeared in my bedroom last night, and . . . scared the beJesus out of me."

Perhaps it was because Gordie was under such a mental strain, that something had to break to bring him some relief. Gordie thought the sight of the governor cowering on his bed while Sand hovered about him, or whatever it was that Sand had done, hysterically amusing. He busted out laughing.

"You think this is funny, you asshole!" Siatos yelled. "My wife and I were . . . well . . . involved when that apparition showed up!"

The thought of Sand catching the governor in mid-stroke broke Gordie up even more.

Watts had a what-the-hell? look on his face.

Choking back laughter and wiping his eyes with the back of his hand, Gordie managed to ask, "What, ah, did Sand want, Governor?"

"To clear his name!" Siatos hollered. "Clear his name? I never even heard of him. What'd he do?"

"Killed a bunch of people, back in fifty-eight I think it was. Colonel Watts is the one who punched Sand's ticket." Gordie smiled and looked at Al. "Would you like to speak to Al Watts, Governor?"

"Yes, I sure would."

Watts was waving his arms and shaking his head.

Gordie held out the phone, and with a sigh, Watts got up and walked over, taking the phone.

"Thanks a lot, Gordie."

"Think nothing of it, buddy." Gordie was entering the coffee room when he heard Watts say, "He wasn't a punk, Governor . . ."

Gordie knelt down beside the couch just as Sunny was opening her eyes.

"I promise you, I am not the fainting type. I had never fainted before until yesterday." She tried to sit up, and Gordie gently pushed her back down.

"You rest for a time. Richard and Linda Jennings can wait. They have nothing but time."

She pushed his hand away and sat up. "Richard says that is the one thing they *don't* have. And I think you know what he means by that."

Gordie helped her up. She was steady. "All right, Sunny. I'll have a deputy escort you over there. See if you can find out what we're up against."

"I'll meet you back here late this afternoon."

He touched her face with his fingertips and smiled at her. "I'll be here."

Deputy Alan Hibler looked across the barricaded no-man's-land at the trooper.

"Real pisser, huh?" the state patrolman asked.

Alan nodded his head. He had been ordered by Sheriff Rivera not to say a word about the real situation in town. And Gordie Rivera was not a man you wanted to jack around with.

"It's bad," Alan finally said.

"Governor Siatos didn't tell us what was going down."

The deputies had been ordered to say, "Killer on the loose." And that's what Alan said.

"We figured it was something like that. Well, it's a damn cinch he can't get out of the valley. Not unless he can fly.

We've got all the roads and trails covered; Siatos really poured us in here. I know you can't talk about it. I'm just rattling to break the monotony."

"I know. We're trying to keep the press out of it."

"I heard that. But they'll find out, and when they do, they'll be in here like maggots on a dead body."

"We got those, too."

"Can you say how many? You know it's not going any further."

Alan thought about that. He reckoned he could. "At least fifteen."

"Damn! You got a grizzly loose in there?"

"Worse. With a bigger appetite."

The deputy watched as Sunny turned into the driveway. Only the slab remained, showing where the house had once stood. He watched her get out of the car, carefully lock it, and walk toward the slab. She dissolved into a mass of multicolored sparkles and disappeared.

"Holy Mother of God," the deputy muttered. He put his unit in gear and got gone.

"You're late," Richard admonished her.

"It couldn't be helped." Sunny looked at the two of them. Robin was not in the room. The man and woman seemed so normal. "There is no further need for pretense. I know that you're both dead."

"We know. But for this . . . period of time, Robin doesn't. So she will be sleeping most of the time."

"How? How can that be possible? She has to know you are dead. I'm sure she went to the funeral."

"I'll try to explain. She knew of our demise in our previous life. Not in this one." He smiled at the expression on her face. "You see, Sunny, we borrowed time from the future for this mission. That is allowed where we are; but only for very special needs."

They walked into the den, with Sunny being very careful not to touch either of them. "Let's talk about Robin," she said, after being seated and turning on her tape recorder. "How long can you protect her from that . . . thing?"

"Not much longer. She may have to rejoin you on the outside. And take her chances," he added.

"Why didn't you get her away from here before it was started?"

"That is not allowed. There are limits as to what we can do. We cannot alter history, and we cannot prevent natural happenings from occurring."

"You said not much longer. Why? Is there trouble where you . . . live?" In paradise? she also added.

"It isn't paradise, Sunny. But it isn't too bad. Yes, I can read your thoughts. Where we are is indescribable—to you. There is no way either of us could make you understand."

"All right. I won't pursue it. Sand."

"Yes. We must hurry. The Fury is gaining strength."

"The Fury?"

"The evil you face."

"What it is?"

"It's an entity. A being, if you like, that has existed since the beginnings of time. Our time, your time—Earth. It was not created by God. It was just there. There are some things that even we don't understand . . . where we are."

"Are there other inhabited worlds?"

"Thousands."

"All created by God?"

"Yes. This is not a safe subject, Sunny. Not for you."

She didn't understand that, but she accepted what he said. She was stepping lightly around dangerous territory, and did not want to misstep. "Are you both with Sand?"

"By choice. We don't have to be there."

"That's a lot of loyalty."

"Sand is a lot of man."

"Still?"

"Even more so. He's been fighting the Fury for years."

"How do we begin?"

"Close your eyes."

Thunder cracked.

118

"Al?" the governor pleaded. "How in the hell can I clear the guy's name? Jesus, man, he killed at least half a dozen people."

"Nevertheless, I think you'd better find a way. He's helping us, so to speak, and we owe him that much. We believe, that if it wasn't for him, you'd have seven thousand dead bodies on your hands right now."

"The entire town?"

"Yes."

"Colonel, I know you don't like me. You made that crystal clear during the campaign. But level with me: what is your assessment of the situation?"

"Lousy. But we have a person who is interviewing a couple of people who know Sand —"

"Who *knew* Sand," the governor corrected.

"No, Governor. I mean, who *know* Sand. They've been dead about ten years."

There was a long pause from the governor's end of the line. Siatos cleared his throat. "Ah, Al, you want to run that by me again?"

"Trust me on this, Governor. We might not know, yet, what we're facing, but we know an ally. And believe me, we need all the help we can get. Especially if they come from the other side."

"The other side of what?"

"The grave."

"Jesus, Mary, and Joseph." His sigh was audible. "What else can I do from here, Al?"

"You and the attorney general" — that liberal son of a bitch, Watts thought — "are old friends, aren't you?"

"Sure. We go way back."

Not far enough, Watts wanted to say. "Get him working, very quietly and very swiftly — like right now. I will have sent to you, by personal courier, my jacket on Sand —"

"What's your coat got to do with this?"

Watts sighed heavily. He suppressed an urge to tell the governor that anybody as stupid as Siatos appeared to be, should be institutionalized for the public good. He calmed himself. "His file, Governor. I have the complete file here with me."

"Oh. Right. Ah, how are you going to send it out by courier? You can't get out."

Watts took several deep breaths. "Well, governor, I'll probably use an officer from the state patrol, since we seem to be surrounded by them."

"Oh! Good thinking, Al."

"Thank you. Governor, find some way to exonerate Sand. New evidence—anything. Make something up, if you have to. Those punks he killed deserved what they got. And go public with the news, all right?"

Watts hung up the phone and walked over to Gordie's side. He pointed to the phone. "Gordie, are you aware of the fact that the man I just spoke with is so stupid, he'd have to use a compass to find his way off a merry-go-round?"

"Yes. But right now, he's the only thing we have working for us on the outside."

"God help us all."

The college kids walked into the office. They all looked rested, but still a little confused.

"Sheriff," Hillary said. "We'd all like to go home now."

"I'm sorry, Miss. But no one is allowed to leave."

"But you can't keep us here against our will," Leon said. "That's unconstitutional."

Watts sat down, muttering under his breath about the nation being constitutionalized into anarchy.

"People," Gordie faced the group of college kids. "I tried to tell you yesterday. Perhaps you were all too exhausted and scared to fully comprehend. That . . . thing out there," he waved his hand, "up there, wherever the hell it is, won't let anyone leave—"

I'LL LET DOYLE LEAVE, IF HE'LL GIVE THE OLD COPPER A BLOW JOB.

Doyle looked wildly around him.

Watts looked disgusted.

"No way!" Doyle yelled.

120

YOUR OPTION, POOPSIE.

The voice started singing "Love Me Tender" and gradually faded away.

"Everything is from the nineteen-fifties," a voice spoke from the doorway.

Howie and Angel stood there, scared looks on their faces, their clothing blood-splattered.

"Are you two all right?" Gordie asked, walking to them.

"We're all right," Angel told him. "Some kids threw the blood on us. They killed some poor little dog." She started crying.

Gordie waved for his secretary to get Angel, motioned for Mack to take Howie. "Get them cleaned up. Tell one of the trustees to wash and dry their clothing."

Watts walked over and whispered to Gordie: "Howie had a point about the fifties."

"Yeah, I know," Gordie returned the whisper. "I put that together yesterday. We'll talk about it."

A car slid to a stop outside the building, and a woman came rushing into the office, a shotgun in her hands. She pointed it at Deputy Ralph Minor and blew his head off.

121

Chapter Nine

Sunny opened her eyes. She was still in the chair, still looking at Richard. There was a worried look on his face.

"I can't get you through," he told her. "The Fury is too strong. It's growing on the evil, feeding on the evil in this town. Feeding and storing."

"Like a reactor?"

"Sort of. It stores evil. It usually feeds on the souls of the departed, just at or just after the moment of death, as the soul travels between worlds. It's like electricity."

"Then what some scientists claim is true, about the human body and the brain, especially?"

"Yes. To a degree. But that is not important now. I can't get you through to witness."

"Can't you just tell me?"

"Not enough of it. Some you will have to see through your own eyes. It's important, imperative, that you personally feel, to some degree, the pain and mental anguish. That's the only way you could possibly comprehend the grief and mental state of the accused and wrongly judged in this matter. That way you might be able to write the truth, and possibly alter the way our—your—judicial system works."

Sunny had to smile. Even in death, Sand was still fighting the system. "Now what do we do?"

"I don't know. I've got to get some instructions. No one thought the Fury would grow this strong this soon."

Sunny got up to leave.

"Sunny? Don't go back out there. I can give you some

122

protection here, nothing out there."

"I have to leave. The Fury wants its story told as well."

"I . . . see. That's odd."

"Why?"

"It wants to strike in a blaze of glory," Richard said softly. "That has to be it." Sunny had to strain to hear him. "It's never attacked a town of this size before—not in any civilized industrial nation—not and made its true self known."

"Tell me this: why hasn't this thing, the Fury, been reported before now? Mass killings are big news."

"Because it can disguise itself as anything. It can bring down planes, cause typhoons and earthquakes, stormy seas to sink ships. The Fury loves wars. It encourages them. More grist for the mill, so to speak. But it hasn't struck at home for more than a hundred years."

"What do you mean?"

"The old mining town of Thunder. The Fury hit there a hundred years ago."

"What about this blaze of glory you mentioned?"

"I'm not sure. I'd guess the Fury plans something much larger in scale. Bear in mind that it has a monumental ego."

"It's fooled us all for years, Richard," Linda said. "It led us to believe we were containing it. Anyway Sand thought he was. And maybe he was, to a degree. But all the time it was planning something much larger; evil on a scale the world has never seen."

"I think you're right," her husband agreed.

"What evil could it do that would encompass the world?" Sunny asked.

Richard looked at her. "You couldn't possibly comprehend the Fury, Sunny. It's a huge mass of energy. All of it evil. It's had eons to grow. Its size is enormous. Gargantuan."

"What does it want?" Sunny wanted to scream the words.

"And there isn't anything that could stop it, with the exception of God," Richard muttered. "Every man, woman, and child on the face of the earth could kneel and pray—

123

that wouldn't stop it."

"Then God will stop it," Sunny said firmly.

Richard's smile was sad. "You don't understand, Sunny. The Fury is evil. Pure evil. That's how it's grown so huge; by feeding on the earth's evil. Feeding on all the bad deeds and wicked thoughts and humans' lack of compassion for each other and for God's creatures."

Sunny began to comprehend. She felt weak and sick and dirty and scared and guilty. And she was just one human out of several billion on earth. She thought of that poor, scared, and wet puppy she had found on her back steps one time. She had shooed it away rather than take it in. A few days later, she found the little puppy dead, after a car had struck it. One of God's creatures that she had a hand in killing.

She thought of all the starving people around the world, and then thought of her closets packed with clothes and shoes . . . much of which she never wore. She just bought.

She thought of the homeless and the abused and the mentally ill. She thought of all the mean little cuts and slights she had uttered and, yes, written over the years, knowing that her words would scar.

"And you are just one really very decent person," Richard said, reading her thoughts.

He was misty through the tears in her eyes. "Are you telling me that God would not save us?"

"Why should He? Perhaps He is weary of the whole miserable business here on earth. He has much nicer and gentler worlds in His domain; worlds where humankind and animals live in peace and harmony. Read His word, Sunny. He gave it to you. Read Ecclesiastes, chapter 3, verse 19: 'For that which befall men also shall befall beasts; even one thing befall them: as the one dies, so dies the other; they have all one breath; so that a man hath no preeminence above a beast: for all is vanity.'

"He warned us, Sunny. He told us that He is a vengeful God. He gave us the Commandments and told us to follow them. Why should Willowdale fare any better than Sodom and Gomorrah, or the state or the world, for that matter?"

"Then He'll just let the earth be destroyed?"

"No. He'll just let it be turned into part of hell and turn His attentions to another world, where people are more prone to follow his teachings and the teachings of His son."

"But I can't change the world, Richard!" she cried.

"You can try."

Gordie, Watts, and two deputies fired at the shotgun-toting woman. Their slugs staggered her, knocking her back, but did not put her down. With blood pouring from her wounds, the woman lifted the autoloading shotgun and fired again, the buckshot striking a jail trustee in the chest and slapping him against a wall. He died on his feet, a very startled look on his face.

Watts leveled his .357 in a two-handed grip, and put one hollow-nosed round between the woman's eyes. She dropped the shotgun from dead hands. As it hit the floor, the shotgun fired, the buckshot blowing a hole in the side of the desk housing the dispatch equipment. Old Mack, showing surprising agility for a man his age, jumped flat-footed over one side and hit the floor on the other side, belly down.

"Secure the outside," Gordie yelled.

Watts stood over the dead woman. "Sue Horvit," he said to no one in particular. "Big worker in her church. And one of the biggest gossips in town. Mean-spirited woman."

"She won't gossip anymore," Gordie said, punching out his empty brass and reloading. "But why did she come in here blazing away with a shotgun."

MARY, MARY, QUITE CONTRARY,
HOW DOES YOUR GARDEN GROW?
WITH SILVER BELLS AND COCKLESHELLS,
AND PRETTY MAIDS ALL IN A ROW.

Gordie looked up. "Oh . . . fuck you!"

125

The room rocked with laughter. THAT'S IT, CHILI PEP-PER. SHOW SOME SPIRIT. LET EVERYONE KNOW YOU HAVE BIG COJONES. OH, BEFORE I GO . . . YOUR ADORING WIFE HAS RETURNED TO THAT RATHER HUMBLE ABODE YOU CALL HOME. WHY DON'T YOU RUN OVER THERE AND GIVE HER A GREAT BIG JUICY SMACK!

Those in the room could sense the entity was still with them.

Gordie looked at the bodies. "We're running out of room at the morgue. Lee, have Johnny pick them up and bag them."

The radio began cracking with deputies calling in, wanting to know what the shooting was all about.

"Ask them how they knew about the shooting?" Gordie said.

I TOLD THEM, CACTUS-HEAD.

Gordie ignored that and said, "Mack, once you get up off the floor, tell them that everything is under control and to continue with their assignments. I'll be at my house for about an hour." He walked out to his car.

"I really hope that crap-head is over at Gordie's," Watts said. "If he is, that ex-jock is about to find out that there are some tough ol' boys in this world who don't give a damn about past glories on the playing field."

"Hey!" Angel called from the hall. "I gotta have something to wear. I can't walk around in my panties!"

When Sunny left the Jennings' house—leaving Richard and Linda alone with their plans of breaking through to the other side and beyond—she looked back, and knew then that all pretense was over.

There was no house.

Just a charred foundation and several neatly stacked piles of bricks.

She felt like crying and screaming and jumping up and

126

down in frustration.

Instead, with a sigh, she put the car in gear and drove back to the sheriff's office.

"Funky," Sgt. Janet Dixon said, as she rode patrol with Deputy Hunt. "You feel it, Duane?"

"Yeah. Just look at those people all gathered on the yards and sidewalks. They're just standing there, staring at us."

"With no emotion on their faces. Their eyes look dead."

Duane radioed to other units. All units were reporting the same thing: the citizens of Willowdale, young and old, were all behaving very strangely.

Sheriff Gordie Rivera found that out when he walked into his house.

Chuck Golden was sprawled in a chair in the den, one big hand wrapped around a can of beer. He grinning arrogantly, knowingly, at Gordie.

"I helped myself to the beer, Gordie-baby. I figured you wouldn't mind."

Like a spring that had been wound too tight, Gordie suddenly relaxed. He grinned at the man. "You figured wrong, Chuckie-baby."

With fists balled, he stepped forward and gave Chuckie-baby five on the side of his jaw, knocking the man out of the chair and to his knees, on the carpeted floor. Which needed cleaning, Gordie noticed.

Gordie had grown up on the fringes of a tough neighborhood in Denver, learning early that there is no such thing as a fair fight. There is just a winner and a loser. The sheriff of Blanco County took another step and kicked Chuckie-baby in the mouth. Chuckie's pearlies bounced around the room, and he screamed in pain. He tried to crawl toward the door. One more boot to the side of his head, and he stopped screaming and crawling.

"Have you lost your goddamn mind!" Mrs. Rivera screamed from the archway leading from the hall to the den.

Gordie walked over and back-handed her. Not with all his strength, but hard enough to get her undivided attention for the first time in a long time.

The pop knocked her back against the hall wall, blood leaking from one corner of her mouth. Her eyes were very wide and very frightened. She knew she had pushed Gordie past the limit, for Gordie, she knew, had never struck a woman in his life . . . not even in the line of duty.

"Gordie, listen to me . . ." Her speech was slurred, and not from the blow she'd just received. She reeked of booze. And her body odor was enough to kill flies. She smelled like she hadn't bathed in days.

Chuckie-baby moaned and stirred on the floor. He managed to get to his hands and knees, blood dripping from his busted mouth. Gordie opened the front door, propping it open with the telephone stand. Then, with one hand firmly gripping the denim covering Chuckie-baby's ass, and the other hand on Chuckie-baby's dirty shirt collar, Gordie propelled the man out the front door. Chuckie landed on his face and belly in the yard. Which needed mowing, Gordie noted.

He turned to his wife . . . loosely speaking. "You have one minute to get your crap together and carry your ass."

"You're crazy!" she spat the words at him. "You've lost your mind."

"Fifty seconds and counting."

She ran past him and out the front door, screaming curses at him. She stood over her fallen hero; a lone cheerleader trying to resurrect that which never was.

When Gordie pulled his pistol from leather and jacked back the hammer, the cheerleading got really frantic. When Gordie put a round about a foot from her tootsies, that was all the incentive hero and ex-pom-pom girl needed.

Gordie watched them hightail it down the middle of the deserted street, hero running yards ahead of pom-pom and picking up speed.

Gordie felt an immense sense of relief at the sight of his

wife running away.

"Come back here, you son-of-a-bitch!" she squalled at Chuckie-baby. "All those press clippings you showed me said you were a hero. Some hero."

If Chuckie had a reply, Gordie didn't hear it.

Gordie shut the door and locked it, then took a shower. To his surprise, he found himself humming as he rub-a-dubbed. And thinking of Sunny.

Sunny drove Angel and Howie back to their house on the nice street in the upper income part of town.

"Don't leave," Angel said. "We'll just get some stuff, and be right back."

Just after they turned onto their street, Angel had said that neither of them wanted to stay at home. "What's the matter?" Sunny asked, pulling into the driveway.

Howard Ingram answered that question. He jerked open the front door and yelled, "Get your ass back in this house, Angel!"

"No way," the girl muttered.

"You goddamn little bitch!" the father yelled at her. "I'll tear your ass up; in more ways than one." He started off the porch.

Sunny quickly backed out of the drive. "Where is your mother, kids?"

"Drunk, the last time we saw her," Howie said.

"Maybe the pressure got to her," Sunny suggested.

"She partied all night with the teenage boy who lives next door," Angel said matter-of-factly.

"Your father?" Sunny felt a sick feeling in the pit of her stomach.

Angel was fighting back tears. "He spent the night with Carol. She's my age. We came down to the sheriff's office to tell Sheriff Rivera about our parents, and to ask him if we could stay with you all."

Sunny recalled some of Richard's words: *It feeds on evil.*

129

"You two stay with me until this is . . . over." She stumbled on the last bit.

"Whole neighborhood has gone crazy." Angel did not acknowledge Sunny's offer. Sunny didn't even know if the girl heard her. "People running around naked and stuff. Drunk." She shook her head. "It's like our minister was talking about last Sunday. The end of the world."

"Don't be silly," Sunny tried to keep her voice calm, but it was an effort. "This isn't the end of the world. We've just got a little problem in this town, that's all."

"Why didn't you leave then?" Howie spoke. When Sunny did not immediately reply, he smiled and said, "You can't, can you?"

"Why the smile, Howie?" she asked.

But he would only shake his head.

"Sheriff Rivera would like for everyone to stay close to their homes—that's all there is to it," Sunny said.

The kids exchanged glances, knowing looks. Angel said, "No, Sunny. That isn't all there is to it. I don't think you believe kids are dumb; but you do believe all kids should be protected from the truth, if the truth is dangerous. For their own good, of course."

Sunny kept her expression bland. Angel was right, of course.

Angel looked at her brother. Howie said, "Go ahead. You're doing fine."

"You see, Sunny, Howie and me, we slipped out of the house about midnight; trying to get away. We have an aunt in Boulder. We changed our minds about leaving when we saw what happened to a group of people who tried to slip out just ahead of us."

Sunny braked and pulled over to the curb. "What did happen to those people?"

"Something just reared up in front of them and then they were gone. It was like . . . well, it was like they were turned into sparklers."

"Sparklers?"

130

"Of course," Howie said. "It's no more difficult to comprehend than a simple math problem. It was the body's energy being taken. Theologians commonly refer to it as the soul."

"Theologians commonly refer to it as the soul," Gordie repeated, after talking with the kids at the office. "Spoken with no more emotion than asking for a peanut butter sandwich."

Sunny touched his arm. "Kids have to have a defense mechanism, too, Gordie." She looked around the busy office. "Where is Howie?"

"Mack took him on a tour, and Howie noticed several computers we had seized some time back. Over there in the gun room. He asked if he could plug them up and re-boot them. I didn't know what he was talking about, but I said yes."

"He's a brilliant boy."

"Yes. Sunny, about what Jennings told you. Richard really thinks God would just turn His back on us and let the Fury take over?"

"He said we brought it on ourselves. And I believe that, and I also believe that Richard is in a pretty good position to know."

Gordie nodded his agreement. "Yeah. You, ah, really did see the house when you pulled up in the driveway?"

"And from the road. But no more. After this morning's session, Richard knows there is no further use in pretense. When I looked back today, the house was not there."

Gordie could not hide a shudder.

Howie left the gun room and walked up to them. "Sheriff, is there a way you could open up a series of phone lines around the town?"

"I don't know what you mean, Howie?"

"It's just an idea I had. You know that computers can be connected by phone?"

131

"If you say so, Howie. I know nothing about computers."

The boy was busy writing on a legal pad. "Oh, well. It probably wouldn't work anyway. The Fury is too smart for us. I'll just go play a game on the computers."

He held out the legal pad. He had written: The Fury is energy. It feeds on evil energy taken from departing souls. Open phone lines around the town—all around the town. Bare the lines in small spots. The Fury has so much energy, I might be able to make contact with it, and thereby keep track of its movements without it knowing.

"I saw a number of games in the room. Games I can play with on the . . . television. Do you mind if I play with them?" The boy smiled and winked at Gordie.

"You go right ahead, Howie," Gordie said, catching on and writing on the pad: But won't you get a lot of interference from phone users?

"Thank you, Sheriff." Howie wrote: Go to the main switcher and disconnect all but emergency numbers. Besides, I don't know if it's even going to work.

"Sure, Howie. You have fun." I don't know much about phones, either, Gordie quickly wrote.

Capt. John Hishon leaned over and wrote: I do. One of my MOS's is communications. The boy might have a great idea. We don't have to scrape. I can tie in.

Gordie printed, in block letters: GO!

Hishon smiled at Howie and left the room, heading for the telephone equipment building down the street.

Watts took the pad and wrote: Howie, what are you going to say to the Fury if you do make contact?

Howie wrote: I'm not. That was just a ruse to throw the Fury off in case it was listening. I'm going to try to make contact with Sand.

Watts blinked; looked startled. He wrote: A phone call to purgatory???

Gordie wrote: You have any better ideas, Al?

Watts shook his head and walked off, muttering, "This should be interesting."

132

Howie went to the gun room and sat down behind a bank of computers that he had hooked up.

Sunny noticed that Gordie's right hand was slightly swollen. She touched his hand. "What happened?"

Gordie grinned. "You might say I just applied for a divorce."

Chapter Ten

Using the legal pad, Gordie instructed his people that any further communications with the outside would be done by the computer/teletype, and to alert the governor and the state patrol of that decision.

Hishon had roamed through the deserted telephone company warehouse for materials, and gave his people a quick lesson in pole climbing and what to do once on the wires—and which wires were which.

At the office, with all people there instructed to make small talk so the Fury would not become suspicious, Gordie wrote on a legal pad: Why us? Why are we not affected by the Fury's power?

He passed the pad around and got some interesting replies. But the one that made the most sense to him, at the time, came from Al Watts. The tough old ex-cop had written: How the hell should I know?

The tying in of the phone lines was completed by the middle of the afternoon. If the Fury noticed, the entity made no comment about it. It had been silent for several hours.

And that troubled Gordie.

Looking dazed and confused, Robin Jennings wandered into the sheriff's office. She asked, "What's going on in this town? I feel like I've been drugged."

She was immediately put to bed on a couch in the day room.

"That's it, then, I suppose," Sunny said. "Richard has

gone back to the other side."

"I wonder if he'll return?" Watts asked.

A question no mortal could answer.

"Lee," Gordie said. "Send a deputy to find Ricky. Bring him here."

There had been a teletype from the governor: the attorney general's office says the families of the murdered are going to raise hell about any exoneration of Saunders.

Quite unlike him, Gordie leaned over the operator and typed and sent: Screw the families. According to what I've read, the punks got what they deserved.

The governor replied: We must think of the image of the state.

Watts moved to the chair and said, "Let me tell that son of a bitch what he can do with the image of the state."

But before Watts could push the operator out of the chair, the screen flashed: Wait!

The words began racing onto the screen.

I did only what the courts would not do. I did what I believed was right and just. I still believe I did the right thing. I will never apologize for my actions.

No one spoke for a moment. Howie broke the silence. "Tell him to sign his communique."

Sand.

"Jesus God in heaven," Watts breathed. "He did it. The ageless rebel broke through from beyond the grave. He said he'd be back." Watts waved the operator away and sat down behind the computer, his fingers on the keys.

Al Watts here, Sand.

How you doin', Seymour?

Watts grimaced as Gordie laughed. "I always wondered what the S stood for, Al."

Watts typed: We're not doing so hot, Sand.

Yeah, I know. You folks have got a big problem.

Is it just Willowdale with the problem? Watts asked.

No. It could be the entire state. Perhaps the world.

135

Howie was watching the screen, a legal pad in his hands. He wrote: Ask him if the Fury knows what we are doing?

Watts typed it out, hunting and pecking.

The reply was quickly flashed on the screen. *No. The Fury knows practically nothing about computers. Its last visit for food—energy—was thirty years ago, in the form of a typhoon, thousands of miles from here.*

Howie impatiently waved Watts away from the computer terminal. With a smile, the man had relinquished the chair.

Howie typed: How is it that you know of computers?

Neither Joey nor I ever lost our interest in learning. And since we are not alone on this level—where we are—we talked with others and kept abreast of developments on earth. But the Fury is limited—or has been up to this point—only to what it can ingest through the energy of the dying. Because of its nature, it has been forced, in recent times, to use its destructive powers only on remote islands, a few ships at sea, and war-dead, usually in primitive parts of the world.

I see. Thank you, Sand.

You're welcome, Howie. You're on the right track in what you're doing, but be careful. Tell Sunny to start listening to the Fury's ramblings, perhaps recording it in preparation for a manuscript. That's what it wants. Attention. Get the Fury preoccupied in telling its story. Its ego is enormous.

Howie nodded in agreement and typed: OK, Sand. What can I be doing with my computers? I'm about ready to see if I can pick up any signals.

Play it by ear, Howie. I can talk to you on any of the computers in the office. Tell the Major to get in touch with his superiors and level with them. He's probably going to have to go all the way to Sugar Cube with this one.

Howie thought about that, then typed: What's Sugar Cube?

The White House. There's a lot of CIA types where I am.

All gathered around laughed at that.

Sand typed: *I think the Fury will probably make its move just as soon as it's finished telling its story. Or as much as that windbag can in five or six days.*

Why that length of time, Sand?

Because it is building and storing energy and knowledge very rapidly now. Feeding off the town.

I see. The more educated and enlightened the energy, the faster the Fury grows, and the more dangerous it becomes.

Very good, Howie. Yes. You are correct. The townspeople don't know it, but the Fury is slowly killing them; sucking them dry of all knowledge. It has removed all inhibitions from most of the people in town, so you all will have to be very careful.

They're going to attack us?

Probably.

Is the Fury going to turn the world into a hell?

That is its plan. It might be a bit grandiose, but it can certainly envelop the state. And if it hasn't been stopped by then, there will be no stopping it.

Is God going to intervene?

The screen remained wordless for a long time; so long that all gathered around began to stir with restless anticipation. Finally, very slowly, words began to appear on the screen.

If you were God, Howie, and you were witness to the birth and development of the human race, only to have them degenerate into hate, perversion, hypocrisy, pettiness, greed, callousness, cruelty to animals, total disregard for the environment, and starving homeless people, when it could all be prevented . . . would you save the world?

Gordie grunted. Judy was crying, as were several other people, men and women. Dr. Anderson shook his head.

137

The others stood in silence.

Howie typed: But there are those of us who do care about all those things you named.

Not enough of you. The vast majority pay lip service and nothing else.

Give me an example, Sand.

I'll give you several, and take it from someone who knows, this is from The Man. The gate receipts for one year's total sporting events would build shelters and create a job for every homeless person in America. Anybody want to volunteer, from spectator to player to team owner to TV networks to advertisers to the gamblers in off-track betting? I think not. Translate that into selfishness and pettiness. Humankind would not have to worry about the animals in the forests, if their natural predators were reintroduced and hunters kept out. Have you noticed any legislation to that effect? Translate that into callousness for God's other living beings and pure bloodlust. Humans are destroying the earth's environment. Translate that into greed. Various religious factions around your world are engaged in so-called holy wars. Translate that into hypocrisy. People are being judged by other people solely on skin color, and not by what is in their minds and hearts. Translate that into hate. Do you want me to continue, Howie?

Howie looked around him at all the adults. Most slowly shook their heads.

Howie's fingers touched the keys: No, Sand.

The words flashed in return: *Then you have your answer.*

Amen.

Did you print that, Sand? Howie asked.

No. That came from a much higher level.

Mack bowed his head, folded his hands, and began repeating the Twenty-third Psalm.

138

Robin and Ricky were sitting in the day room when the TV popped on by itself. The teenage boy called for someone to come look.

"That's an old fifties movie," Robin said.

"No, it isn't," Watts corrected. "Take a better look. That's the main street of Willowdale, back when I was a lieutenant on the state patrol. See Patterson's Drugs, right there? That building was completely destroyed by fire back in '61."

The scene changed.

"Man, look at those great old cars!" Bos said. "Those are custom street rods."

Sunny knew then what they were viewing. "That Mercury parked closest to the corner. That's Sand's car, isn't it, Colonel?"

"Yes," he said softly. "It is."

The computer keys in the gun room rattled impatiently. Howie ran to the room and sat down behind the screen. Gordie stood behind him.

The words flashed: *Videotape it all! Let the world see. Know my pain. Feel my loss. View the injustice. And tell my story!*

Is that you, Sand? Howie typed.

Yes!

"Lee," Gordie called. "Get one of those VCR's out of the evidence room and hook it up. There must be hundreds of tapes back there that we seized on that bootleg tape operation. Let's tape it all."

"You're going to need someone to change tapes," Hillary said. "The faster the tape speed the better the quality. We'll take turns doing that. It'll help take our mind off the . . . problem."

"Thank you," Gordie said with a smile. "You've got a job."

"Well, well," Old Mack said. "Would you just take a look at that young whippersnapper there."

All looked. Al Watts, thirty-odd years younger and

139

sporting a pencil-thin moustache, was talking with a young man.

"Uncle Sand!" Robin yelled.

"Wow!" Lynn said. "What a hunk."

"Thank you," Watts said with a smile, knowing full well the girl was not referring to him.

Lynn glanced at him and grinned.

Smiling, Gordie walked out of the room and to his unit. He drove off, thinking: Take one hell of a man to be dead thirty years and still evoke a reaction like that.

He drove through the town and found it deserted. Or deserted-appearing, he amended. He stopped at each checkpoint and told his people to be on the lookout for trouble from the townspeople. He did not tell them how he had gained that information. He knew that Sand could work around the Fury; how, he didn't know.

And fervently hoped he wouldn't find out for another forty years or so.

On the empty main street, he flagged down Bergman and Norris. "I'm going out to meet with the state patrol. Want to come along?"

They did.

The commander of this unit of patrolmen was standing at the roadblock by the state highway, and Gordie had only to look at him to know the man knew everything the governor did about the situation.

"Sheriff Rivera, if you need additional manpower —" he glanced at a female trooper. *"Peoplepower,* I can manage fifty volunteers in an hour."

All the patrolmen were dressed in urban-warfare cammies.

WHAT THE HELL DO THESE ASSHOLES THINK THEY'RE GOING TO BE ABLE TO DO WITH ME?

The state patrol — all veterans and many of them SWAT-trained and accustomed to just about anything life had to offer — could not contain their startled looks.

"Now you all know," Gordie said. "Just keep people out

of here."

OH, LET THEM IN, LET THEM IN. BY ALL MEANS. THE MORE THE MERRIER. It faded away, humming, DO BOP DE DO BOP DE DO BOP, DE DO.

"I've made contact!" Howie said, unable to keep the excitement out of his voice.

Sunny walked to the gun room, which had been cleaned out to make room for the four computers the boy had hooked up. Phone lines had been run into the room and a cot placed amid the computers, terminals, and tape recorders.

"I'm utilizing all the screens," Howie explained, as more people crowded around the door and into the already crowded room, looking at the mass of equipment. "I can use this screen for graphics. This one is to monitor the Fury's whereabouts. This one is bringing in all the various languages I'm picking up. This one is to communicate with Sand. And this one is hooked into that smaller console. It's for math work."

Sunny, like the others, felt awed by the mind of the ten-year-old. She pointed to one screen. "Why is that math screen all, well, blippy?"

"That is energy you're seeing. I'm storing it on hard disk, and then I'll try to break it down mathematically."

Useless! the word flashed on Sand's screen.

Why? Howie typed.

Because your present technology is not advanced enough to comprehend the composition of the Fury's makeup.

Is this Sand?

No. I'm Joey.

Nice to meet you.

Thank you. Would you like to meet Morg?

Yes.

Howdy, Slick.

Howie, the screen flashed. *This is Sand. Don't concern yourself with something that would only baffle your scientists. The Fury is pure evil energy. Bear that in mind. It is energy. Does that tell you anything, Howie?*

Howie stirred restlessly in the chair, an odd expression on his face.

"What is it, Howie?" Sunny asked.

But the boy would only shake his head and stare at the screen.

"I'm hungry!" Angel said, from just outside the gun room.

"Then go stuff your face!" Howie told her, an edge to his voice they all picked up.

Sunny took the girl's hand, and they wandered off in search of something to eat. "Howie can be a real nerd when he wants to be," Angel said.

Or just a very worried child, Sunny thought. With more knowledge in his head than a ten-year-old should have.

"Leave us alone," Howie said. The room cleared of people. Howie typed: Sand, are you telling me there is only one way to destroy this thing?

It is the only practical way.

And I know what it is, right?

You have it in your thoughts, yes.

Sand, that would destroy this part of the state.

Not necessarily. Your technology is sufficient in that area.

The sheriff can't order something of that magnitude.

I know. That is why I asked the military people to contact their superiors.

What about us . . . in here?

You definitely have a problem.

You're telling me! Howie's fingers flew over the keys. We're in here . . . you're out there. Wherever that is.

The computer emitted a musical sound and Howie looked down to see if he'd hit the wrong key. Then he

142

knew what was making the sound: Sand was laughing. Howie suddenly realized that he liked Sand.

Howie typed: You were just a young man when you died. Why did Mr. Watts kill you?

Don't blame Al. He had a job to do and he did it. It was a righteous kill. Just as mine were. Get Al in the room with you, Howie.

Howie called for Watts and motioned him to sit down behind the terminal.

Al! the word flashed on the screen. *Sand here. You're going to have to go all the way to the top on this thing.*

The governor?

Screw the governor.

Watts laughed and wrote: I know you're not in heaven, Sand.

You got that right. But, boy, did I come close to that other place. Singed my hair. I talked my way out of it.

You'll never change, Sand.

How right you are, Al. How right you are.

And Watts knew then the enormity of what he had just read on the screen. The vast endless eternity in those words.

It made his stomach knot up and his head swim for a few seconds. Watts typed: You didn't call me in here for chitchat, Sand. Let's get to it.

Be sure and store everything that will be exchanged, Al.

"I'll store it, sir," Howie said.

Go, Sand, Watts typed.

The words began flashing on the screen. Howie struggled to fight back tears. Watts felt as though he'd been slapped in the face.

When Sand was finished, Watts typed: Is there no other way, Sand?

Not from where I stand, Al. I'm sorry. The Force could block the Fury. But that would alter history to some degree. And that is not permitted.

I don't understand, Watts typed.

Time would stop for an instant. A door would open. You could exit that way, then time would once more resume. But you might end up in King Arthur's court with no way back.

Howie leaned over and typed: But we would be alive.

Yes.

Howie thought hard for a moment, then typed: But there are other reasons why you don't want the Force to interfere, right?

That is correct. It's more than just dangerous. When the living are near the Force, death is imminent. For an instant, just before death, those worthy of passing on to a higher level know all things, language becomes common—words become as one. There is no earth problem that cannot be solved in your mind. You see the danger?

Howie typed slowly: We could die, but if we did not, and somehow made it through the door, retaining all that knowledge . . . are you saying that we might all be insane?

There is a good possibility of that. Your brains are not yet advanced enough to allow you to cope with so much knowledge pushed on you so quickly. You have centuries to go before that would have been allowed to happen.

Would have been?

Past tense.

"It seems as though the Almighty has made up His mind to wash us out," Watts muttered.

"I have to think for a while," Howie said, getting up. "You talk to Sand."

The boy left the room and Watts sat down. He typed: The other alternative, Sand? There would be tremendous losses.

There will be losses, but Joey says they can be kept to a minimum if we plan carefully.

I presume you have a plan?

That ain't my department. I'm all muscle and kick-ass, Al.

144

You're a liar, boy.

*Thanks. But I really don't have any other plan. We're
. . . limited where we are.*

Ask your father-in-law.

Carl went on to a better place.

Watts smiled as a warm feeling swept over him. He and
Carl Lee had been the best of friends. Watts put his fingers on the keyboard: That's good to know. Sand, how
many people do you want to know of this . . . finality?

Any that you think can cope with it.

Okay, boy. I'll be back in touch. So to speak.

The computer chimed merrily, and the screen went dark
as Howie leaned over and stored the information.

"He was laughing, you know?" Howie said.

"Yeah." Watts gave the chair to the boy. "That would
be something he'd do."

"Did you like him, Mr. Watts?"

Watts stood for a time in silence. "Yes, I did, son. I
think toward the end, I began to love that boy as one of
my own."

"Yet you killed him," Howie said, with the honesty and
openness of the young.

"Yes, I did that. Howie, I had a dog one time. I loved
that dog more than I ever again loved an animal. And I'm
an animal-lover. Rascal went bad on me. Dogs can go
crazy just like humans. I had to have him destroyed. I was
seventeen years old, and I cried like a child. In both cases,
I think I put them out of their misery."

"I . . . believe I understand, sir."

Watts turned to leave and bumped into Sunny.

"I heard that last part, Al, and I wasn't eavesdropping.
I was bringing Howie a sandwich and a glass of milk."

"And you wonder why I would say such a thing?"

"In a way. I just saw on the TV where Sand seemed to
be a hardworking and quite honest young man."

"He was all of that and much more. He was honorable.
But he was out of time and out of place, and he knew it.

He tried to tell me that several times. I just let it slide by me. He should have been a mountain man or a gunslinger. What happened to Sand convinced me that people are born out of time and place."

"And Joey?"

"Same thing. Joey could—and I know this sounds foolish—he could see things that others couldn't. I didn't believe that for a long time. But I know now that it was true. Both of them foretold their destinies. Sand was a born leader. If you had just one ounce of rebel in you, you followed Sand. And even back in the fifties, it didn't make any difference to Sand if a person was black or white or Latin or Chinese or from Mars. Race or nationality didn't make any difference to him."

"Sounds to me that in some respects, he was ahead of his time."

"He knew what lay behind him, and what lay in front of him."

Sunny rubbed her arms. Goose bumps had suddenly appeared on her flesh. "And this Morg person? He looks like a cretin to me."

Watts laughed, openly and loud. "God, what a character. Drove a souped-up black hearse and wore a black silk top hat. Carried a damn coffin around in the back of that hearse. When he'd get sleepy on the road, he'd just pull over, crawl in that damn coffin, prop the lid open, and take him a snooze." Watts chuckled. "Morg was dumb in many respects, and crude, but a decent sort. Won the Congressional Medal of Honor for bravery in Korea."

"Was Morg married?"

"He married a beatnik girl from the Village in New York City. Jane. She wandered in here, hitchhiking across country. They got married toward the end. Jane died of cancer, just before the bottom dropped out for all of them."

Sunny shook her head. "It just seems like it was all, well, so tragic."

"It was, Sunny. And it was, without a doubt, the darkest period in my life. Up to this point. Those damn rich punks from over Monte Rio way rigged the brakes on Joey's street rod. Joey and his wife, Tuddie, were riding around up in the mountains when the brakes failed. Killed them both. Shortly after that, the same bunch killed Sand's wife. She was eight-months pregnant when they kicked her to death. Then Sand went off the deep end and turned murderous. So did his father-in-law, my best friend, Carl Lee. That was one dark and bloody night in this part of the country."

"How did it start, Colonel?"

Watts looked at the TV set and smiled sadly. He pointed. "Sand is showing you right now."

Chapter Eleven

A local drive-in cafe in Willowdale. Early spring. A few Pack members had enjoyed burgers and fries and Cokes and were gathering up their coats. Robin Lee was waiting by the front door. A group of young men from the town Monte Rio had decided to go slumming over in Willowdale. They had pulled up in their new Thunderbirds and Impalas — paid for by mommy and daddy, of course.

Robin pushed at the door. A grinning young man was blocking it from the outside with his foot. She pushed again. The young man whispered a vulgarity that Robin chose to ignore.

A waitress looked over the counter and saw what was going down. "Damn!" she muttered, and headed for the kitchen, putting a wall between herself and what she felt was sure to happen. She knew Sand.

The saying probably began in the Old West, but it will hold true as long as there are people who throw caution and common sense and good manners to the wind. The adage reads: Do not mess with the gunfighter's girlfriend.

The young man from Monte Rio pushed his face against the screen and made kissing sounds at Robin. "You're cute, baby."

"Get out of my way," Robin told him.

He grinned and rubbed his crotch, then repeated his earlier vulgar suggestion. This time it was said a little louder.

Sand heard it. His cold pale eyes did not change. But he smiled thinly.

Worldly people know that danger can be read in a person's eyes and body language. But if one cannot read *anything* in a person's eyes; if it appears that one is looking into the eyes of a rattlesnake—cold and unblinking and emotionless—a wise person will, if possible, and with all deliberate haste, get the hell away from that locale.

Sand walked to the door. "Move," he said softly but firmly.

"I don't take orders from you," the kid from Monte Rio replied.

Sand drove one big, flat-knuckled and work-hardened fist through the screen door. Fist connected with nose, and the young man with the vulgar mouth was propelled backward, landing on the hood of his Thunderbird, blood pouring from his busted beak.

The jukebox blared *Lawdy Miss Clawdy!* and the kids in the cafe became silent, watching the action.

"Now see here!" one of busted-beak's friends protested. "That was really unnecessary."

"Quite," another of flat-nose's friends declared.

Each group of young men wore the uniform of the day: the Monte Rio college freshmen all wore loafers, white socks, pressed, pegged pants, button-down shirts, sport jackets.

The hot-rodders wore jeans, boots, dark shirts, dark windbreakers.

Uniforms denoting just who belonged to what caste in this casteless society.

The Pack members were outnumbered, but they were all used to that.

"I demand an apology!" a sport-coat shouted. "Or by God, we'll fight."

"Oh, my heavens!" Joey put one hand over his heart and another hand to his forehead. "I'm actually flushed from fear." He could not contain his laughter. "I'm trembling from fright. The sight of such foreboding and physically overpowering adversaries fills me with terror. I have this

149

growing urgency within me to run screaming into the night."

Bill Marlson looked at Joey and flushed as the Pack members, male and female, laughed. "You got a real smart mouth, don't you, Jew-boy?"

Joey, with the musculature of a weight lifter, back-handed Marlson, knocking the young man on his butt and bloodying his mouth.

The fight was on, but it was a very short one. The Pack had learned early on that rules do not apply in fighting. They kicked, stomped, gouged, and almost always won.

The Pack members walked to their custom cars and drove off into the night, leaving a battered, bloody, and badly shaken group of young men, none of whom were accustomed to or expecting the type of savage gutter-fighting they had just received. All in all, the Marquess of Queensberry would have been appalled.

"Goddamn you!" Bill Marlson shouted, shaking his fists at the fading taillights. "We'll get you for this."

"Damn right," John Murry said, holding a bloody handkerchief to his busted nose. The words came out, "Am ite."

"Drop it," Nick Grables said. "It's over. We lost."

"You don't mean that," Ronnie Murphy said, one eye swelling closed, a dark bruise under it.

"I sure do mean it. I know Sand and Joey; you guys don't. Besides, you started it, John. They finished it. So it's over, as far as I'm concerned."

"Not for me," Charles Lenton sniffed, heading for his car and taking a pull at a bottle of sloe gin.

"I agree with Charles," Robert Center said. "Why, if word ever got around that we allowed this outrage to go unavenged, we'd be laughed off campus. We never will get any cunt." He hadn't had any yet. He never would.

The Monte Rio bunch left, regrouping outside of town, after picking up a couple of six-packs of beer.

Nick tried to explain things to his friends. "Look, guys,

150

just drop this thing. Sand is poison when he's stirred up, and Joey is just about as bad. John, you started this whole thing. You were out of line with Robin Lee."

"She's nothing but street trash," Wallace Branon said. "She'd have to be, to take up with a thug like Sand."

"We'll get them," George Alexander said. He chug-a-lugged what was left of his bottle of beer and belched manly.

"Damn right," John said.

"Sand started that," Bos said, as the TV screen darkened.

"You go right straight to hell!" Robin said, defending her long-dead Uncle Sand.

"Easy, Robin," Ricky said, putting his hands on her shoulders.

"Easy my butt!" Robin jerked free.

"I agree with Robin," Hillary said, looking at her boyfriend with considerable heat in her eyes. "You mean, Bos, that if some creep like that . . . whatever his name was, came up to me and asked me to fuck—like he did—you wouldn't do anything about it?"

"Well," Bos verbally back-pedaled. "Sure, I would. Of course. But Sand and his bunch didn't fight fair."

Watts chuckled. "Son, outside of the ring, there is no such thing as a fair fight."

WHAT ARE YOU TALKING ABOUT? WHAT IS GOING ON? WHAT ARE YOU DOING? WHY CAN'T I SEE WHAT IS HAPPENING?

"Sand is blocking him somehow," Howie whispered.

"Nothing is going on," Sunny stepped in. "I'm just gathering up materials for our interview. Are you ready?"

WHAT DO YOU HAVE IN MIND, DOLL FACE?

Sunny chose not to respond to that.

I SUPPOSE SINCE THAT PUNK RICHARD JENNINGS AND HIS WHORE WIFE WERE RECALLED,

YOU HAVE TIME FOR ME, HUH?

"Who are you callin' a whore, you cowardly son of a bitch!" Robin screamed at the voice.

WELL, NOW. WHAT HAVE WE HERE? OH, YES. YOU'RE THE ONE RICHARD WAS PROTECTING. WELL, HE CAN'T PROTECT YOU NOW, DUMPLING. I'LL HAVE SOME FUN WITH YOU.

Again, Sunny made it shift its attention. "Are you ready to begin telling me your life story?"

The room pulsed with silence for a moment. VERY WELL. JUST LET ME SLIP ON MY BLUE SUEDE SHOES AND I SHALL RETURN IN A SEC, BABY.

The Fury left them.

"The screen went crazy while the Fury was here," Howie called from his cramped quarters. "The disks are absorbing so much information, I'm going to have to prepare several hundred to be ready for it."

"I thought you could put a million words on each disk?" a deputy said.

"A million characters, on some of the hard disk drive machines," Howie told him.

Watts patted the boy on the shoulder. "Stay with it, Howie."

He walked over to Gordie and the two state investigators who had just entered the building. "Hadn't we better be laying in supplies and repairing the broken door and windows, Gordie?"

"For once, I'm ahead of you, Al," Gordie told him. "I've got some deputies doing just that right now."

A wild screaming began from upstairs, in the main cell block area.

"That's the kid," Gordie said, moving toward the gun rack.

"The kid?" Sunny looked up from the TV that had just clicked on.

"Eighteen-year-old being held on armed robbery charges," Mack told her. He looked at his monitor screens.

Everything appeared to be normal in all lock-down areas.

But something was definitely wrong.

Gordie had grabbed a shotgun on the way out of the room, running toward the elevator. Lee and Sid joined the sheriff, both of them armed with sawed-off riot guns.

Mack again checked his screens and felt his guts knot up.

"The cells are open, Sheriff!" he yelled. "The kid is being gang-shagged in his cell." He began frantically punching buttons. "I can't secure the cell blocks. Nothing works," he shouted. Mack cussed the modern, up-to-the-minute lock-down equipment. Back in his youth, when he had first hung on a badge, jails were a lot safer and much more secure. A man didn't have to depend on electronics. You locked the cells with a key and kept order with a club.

The screaming of the kid intensified as another inmate took his turn in the perversion.

Sid was the first off the elevator. He clubbed a rampaging inmate with the butt of his shotgun and drove the muzzle into the gut of another one, as Lee and Gordie went running down the hall.

Gordie cursed the sight that greeted him. It was not the first time he'd seen such a sight, but it always sickened and angered him. He did what a lot of people feel should be done in cases of male rape. Gordie threw procedure to the wind and lifted his shotgun, blowing the half-naked con away from the naked teenager. The kid fell to the floor, sobbing. The inmate who received the load of 00 ought buckshot had raped his last person. Part of his head was spread all over the cell wall.

DAVY DAVY DUMPLING, BOIL HIM IN A POT
SUGAR HIM AND BUTTER HIM AND EAT HIM WHILE HE'S HOT.
DO BOP DE DO BOP DE DO BOP, DE DO.

Doing his best to ignore the voice, Lee slammed the butt of his shotgun against a man's head, stepped over him, and butt-stroked another con. The man's eyes rolled back and he dropped to the floor, unconscious.

The other prisoners, seeing it was useless, jumped back into their cells and slammed the doors.

"Get the kid out of here and call the doctor," Gordie told Sid. "Lee, start cutting lengths of chain and get some padlocks." Taking a set of keys from the jailer, Gordie tried one in a lock.

They turned around and around. The locks had been rendered useless. He tried other cells, and got the same results as the cons laughed at him.

"Won't the Fury do the same with other locks?" Bergman asked.

"Probably. But we can't weld the door shut, so I don't know what else to do."

"Let us outta here, Sheriff!" a prisoner hollered. "We know what's goin' on. You ain't got no right to keep us locked up with that thing controllin' the town."

Gordie waved his people back, out of earshot of the prisoners. "He's got a point." Gordie took several deep breaths, calming himself after the brief flare-up. "But I can't justify turning loose many of these people. Some of them are nothing but scum."

OH, REALLY? WELL, LET'S PLAY A GAME THEN.

The sheriff and his deputies waited.

A prisoner was lifted off his feet and slammed into a concrete wall. Then, as if playing pop-the-whip, the man was whip-sawed back and forth in his cell. His arms were broken, the bones sticking out. His head was battered into mush. The dead inmate was dropped to the floor with a squishing sound.

The other prisoners began screaming in terror, shouting to be set free.

Downstairs, Leon was watching the monitors. "That is unfair to the prisoners. I demand you turn those people loose. They're human beings, you know."

Mack shifted his chaw and looked at the college kid.

"You demand, huh? You want to take responsibility for one of them? How about if we handcuffed you to one? Take Logan, there." He pointed to a man. "He's a real jewel. Rape, torture, murder, armed robbery. He's waiting to be transferred to the state pen to serve three life sentences." Mack spat into a cuspidor on the floor. "You don't want him? Too bad. Well, there's Bingham. He killed two people with an axe up in the mountains, and then cut them up into chunks with a chainsaw and fed them to the bears. Not him, huh? Well, there's always Diminno. He's another sentenced to life for murder. You gettin' the point, boy?"

Leon swallowed hard a couple of times. "Yes. But what are you going to do with them?"

"I don't know, boy. I ain't the sheriff, and I'm glad I'm not. But I'll tell you what Sheriff Rivera don't need right now is a bunch of smart-assed lip from a college kid."

Leon walked away, his back stiff. He was slightly miffed.

Doctors Anderson and Shriver walked in. Both of them wore grim expressions. Gordie was just sticking his shotgun back into the gun rack on the lower floor. The kid had been taken to a secure room. The dead prisoner had been dragged out of his cell and placed in a room at the rear of the jail. The cell was being hosed down.

"Homosexual rape, Gordie?" Anderson asked.

"Yeah." Gordie jerked his thumb toward a door. "He's in there."

"Let us outta here, you motherfucker!" a prisoner shouted.

"What are you going to do with the prisoners?" Shriver asked.

"I don't know!" Gordie snapped his reply. He shook his head. "Sorry. I didn't mean to be short with you. I just don't know."

"I understand, Sheriff. We're all operating under a strain."

But Gordie couldn't understand the tears that were run-

155

ning down the man's face. Why Shriver was silently weeping.

I AM READY TO BEGIN MY EPOCH.

Shriver jerked his head up, his eyes wide with fear.

Two nurses entered the building and walked over to the doctors.

"You two it?" Anderson asked.

"Yes, sir."

"What's going on?" Gordie asked.

I SAID I AM READY!

"This is all that showed up for the second shift at the hospital," Anderson explained.

"What about the patients?"

Anderson's expression hardened. "There are no patients, Sheriff."

"You want to clarify that?" Watts asked. "The hospital was nearly full a couple of days ago."

I AM READY TO PROCEED, GREASEBALL.

The nurses moved closer together, fear in their eyes and on their faces.

Sunny rose from her chair. "Where should I do this, Gordie?"

"Use my office. And close the door, please." He smiled at her.

She returned the smile and walked to his office, closing the door behind her.

All experienced the sensation as the Fury moved closer, and then a slight lessening, much like the sensation when a plane has achieved cruising speed. Gordie wondered what it was like in his office.

"The hospital has been turned into a slaughterhouse," Anderson said. "The scene is terrible, just . . . incredibly indescribable."

Shriver sat down at a table and began weeping.

"His wife was in the hospital for minor surgery," Anderson said. "You'd better go over there, Sheriff. And take a strong stomach with you."

I WAS CREATED EONS AGO, the voice boomed, smug and oily. AND WHILE IT MIGHT NOT APPEAR SO, I AM REALLY A SHY, MODEST, AND UNASSUMING BEING . . .

Gordie gave the voice the middle finger and walked out of the building.

Chapter Twelve

They found the first body on the front lawn of the small hospital.

Norris knelt down, careful not to touch the woman. He looked up at Gordie. "You know her?"

"Louise Farmer. She worked here."

"Not a mark on her," Bergman said. "But, God, look at her head. There's something wrong with it."

The head appeared to be smaller than Gordie remembered. He knelt down and thumped the head. A hollow sound emanated from the single thump.

"Sounds empty," Norris said.

"Yeah."

The men walked on. The second body was found on the entrance steps. A boy of about ten. The head appeared slightly shrunken. Bergman thumped it. The same hollow sound.

The men walked up the steps and entered the building. They could all hear the high single note of a machine that monitored life signs. It was signaling a straight line. Dead.

Just like the receptionist—dead. And the nurse sprawled grotesquely on the floor—dead. And the young intern—dead.

And all with that same peculiar indented-head look. The head, when thumped, sounding as hollow as a bass drum. *Thonk!*

Bergman was busy taking pictures.

Gordie looked in radiology. The operator was lying on the floor—dead. He walked on down the hall. The straight line wailing was getting louder. He looked in on the patient. The entire chest cavity was ripped open, organs flung around the room, the bed slick with blood.

Bergman took a picture of that.

Norris walked out of a lounge. "Slaughterhouse in there. Bodies literally ripped apart. If it can kill without tearing the people apart, why does it do so?"

Bergman took a picture of the lounge and its gory walls and floor. "Because it wants to," he said.

The monitoring machine in the blood-splattered room was turned off. After the shrillness of the beep, the silence was slightly unnerving.

The men walked on, their boot heels striking sharply on the polished tile floor. They looked into a few more rooms, and every room contained death, singularly and in bloody, mangled heaps.

"We've got to check every room," Gordie said. "But as God is my witness, I don't want to."

"Especially the nursery," Norris said, his voice low.

"Surely, it wouldn't!" Bergman protested, his voice filled with disgust.

AND WHY NOT?

Gordie never stopped walking. "I thought you were having your life story taken down for posterity?"

I HAD TO TAKE A BREAK. IT'S VERY EMBARRASSING HAVING TO BARE ONE'S SOUL. IN A MANNER OF SPEAKING.

They came to the nursery and looked in. The babies were dead—none of the men really expected to find them alive. But it was a very ugly and disgusting sight.

And like all the others, their little heads were indented, shrunken.

Standing in the doorway, their faces clearly showing their anger, Bergman asked, "But why kill the babies?"

"I would guess that's the only way the Fury can absorb

159

innocence," Gordie said. "Without some degree of innocence, I don't believe it could function. It would be nothing more than a wild, uncontrollable mass."

VERY, VERY GOOD, GREASEBALL. FOR A STUPID HALF-IRISH TORTILLA-HEAD, YOU'RE REALLY SHARP. THE BRATS WERE TASTY, TOO. BYE BYE.

They could all tell when the Fury left them. None could as yet tell when it made its appearance; not without Howie and his computers.

"I wonder what its real reason was for visiting us?" Norris asked.

Gordie led the way out of the nursery. "I like to think that Sand is worrying it."

"It'll be dark soon," Bergman said. "Let's check out the rest of this place and get gone."

Gordie read Sunny's notes and listened to the Fury's droning on the tape recorder. He could only listen for a few minutes before turning it off.

"It's the most disgusting thing I have ever heard," Sunny said. "He, it, speaks of destroying entire civilizations. Wiping out cultures."

"Here it comes!" Howie called from his tiny, cluttered space.

The screen used to monitor the Fury's movements went wild with blips at its approach.

ALL RISE! ALL HAIL FURY THE MAGNIFICENT!

No one moved.

WHAT A BUNCH OF SORE LOSERS.

"What do you want, you ugly thug?" Angel blurted, standing with her hands on her hips, a defiant look on her face.

The Fury pulsated in the room for a few seconds, and all knew it was studying the girl. HOW DO YOU KNOW WHAT I LOOK LIKE, BITCH?

160

"Because nobody could do the things you do and be very pretty."

YOU THINK I'M UGLY, LITTLE CHICKIE? JUST HANG YOUR PEEPERS ON THIS!

Chuckie-baby Golden was suddenly deposited into the room. A beer can had been jammed into his mouth—all the way in. The back of his neck was poked out from the force of the rammed-in can. He had been split from throat to groin. Some of his intestines were wrapped around his thick neck, then neatly tied in a bow behind his head. Both his legs had been broken in many places. They were twisted together like rubber bands.

NOW THAT'S UGLY!

Maj. Jackson had grabbed Angel and turned her face away from the sight, holding her to him. He had a little girl at home, about Angel's age. He wondered if he'd ever see her again? He had a hunch he would not.

What happened to Chuckie-baby had just happened. Blood was still leaking from his horrible wounds, and his guts were steaming from the coolness of late afternoon.

AND IF THAT ISN'T UGLY ENOUGH, TRY THIS!

The kid who had been gang-raped was flung from his cot and rolled along the hall, squalling in fright and pain, the doctors and nurses running after him. The door slammed open, depositing him in the big main room of the sheriff's office. He was jerked to his feet and shoved stumbling around the floor, his face wild with terror. Screams pushed from his throat, as his legs were forced to propel him along. He was rammed into the water fountain, his head jerked back. His face was slammed into the dispenser, the metal cone entering through the skull, ripping through and into his brain.

His screaming ended in a gurgle. The kid hung on the fountain, his arms slowly relaxing and falling to his side as death took him.

DO BOP DE DO BOP DE DO BOP, DE DO.

The kid fell off the fountain, plopping to the floor.

161

"Fury is gone," Howie called from his little room.

"Not far enough," Watts summed up the feelings of all in the room.

Dr. Shriver uttered a moan and passed out cold, Sgt. Preston catching the man before he could bust his head on the floor.

The college girls were clinging to one another, their eyes just a bit wild.

And because of a scene unfolding on the outskirts of town, the whole world was about thirty-six hours away from learning the plight of Willowdale.

"What do you mean I can't get into town? I live there, officer," the man said.

"I'm sorry, sir. But no one is allowed to enter the town."

"By whose orders?"

The state patrol officer then said what he had been instructed to say by his commander, who had been instructed by Governor Siatos. "Sheriff Gordie Rivera."

"But why?"

"I'm sorry, sir. I cannot divulge that information at this time."

"But, our," he waved a hand toward the town, "daughter is in there, officer."

"Name?"

"Carol Ann Russell."

The trooper consulted a list on a clipboard. "I'm very sorry to have to tell you this, sir, but your daughter was in an accident. She's dead."

"My . . . our . . . Carol, is *dead?*"

"Yes, sir. I'm sorry. There is no easy way to inform someone of a death."

"How did she . . . I mean . . ."

"Sir, I don't know."

And because of a slight screwup somewhere along the

162

chain of command, the state patrolman did not know *what* to tell anyone who was turned away about *where* they were supposed to go.

"Well, officer, where is the body? Where are we supposed to go for the night? Our home is in Willowdale; my business is there."

The trooper looked at the others around him. Looked at the deputy standing on the other side of the barricade. They all shrugged their shoulders. They couldn't help.

Just a slight screwup. Like the Fury said about the horse and the shoe and the rider and the war.

The man and woman, both numbed and close to tears, left, heading out of the valley. They drove to another town, about twenty-five miles away, and checked into a motel.

Mr. Russell asked the clerk, "What in the world is happening over in Willowdale?"

"Nothing that I know of, sir."

"Well, the whole town is sealed off by the state patrol. They won't let anybody in; and we *live* there!"

"They say our daughter is dead," Mrs. Russell said. "But we can't get in to see the body."

"That is odd. There hasn't been a thing on the news." She thought for a moment. "I have a friend in Willowdale. Let me give her a call."

She tried several times, getting the same results each time. "The system is down," she told the parents of Carol Ann. "I can't get through. All the operator says is that communications have been temporarily disrupted, and crews are working trying to repair it."

A city cop came in for supper, and the desk clerk waved him over. "What's going on in Willowdale?"

He shook his head. "I don't know. All departments in this area have been asked to use alternate frequencies and leave 31.7 open. And there are a lot of strange coded messages, that make absolutely no sense, being passed between the Blanco S.O. and the state patrol."

163

The owner/manager of the local radio station had stopped in for a drink, and paused to listen to the conversation at the front desk. A former network newsman who had left the big city rat race for a calmer existence, he quickly smelled a story.

"Pardon me," he said to the red-eyed mother. "You say the state police won't let you into Willowdale?"

"That's right. Our daughter was killed, and we can't even get in to see the body, or find out what happened or anything!"

"You're staying here tonight?"

"Until we can get back to our home," Mr. Russell said. "No telling when that will be. I'm gonna sue the damn state, by God. Somebody is gonna pick up the tab for our rooms and meals."

"I'll find out what's going on." He returned to his station and put in a call to his old network, Los Angeles bureau. "Mike Stapleton here, Tom. How you been? Good. Yeah. Me, too. Listen, what have you people got on this breaking story in Willowdale, Colorado?"

"What's a Willowdale, Mike?"

Mike spoke the magic words. "The state patrol is covering something up, Tom."

"Bring me up to date."

Mike told all that he knew.

"How far up do you think it goes?"

Mike took a chance. "I'd say all the way to the governor's mansion."

"You want to check it out for us?"

"Damn right."

"Go."

Willowdale was off the beaten path. The joke was that you couldn't get there from wherever you were; you had to go somewhere else and start. The nearest interstate was seventy-five miles away. No big towns in the area. But the two-lanes were in good shape, and Mike made good time. As he topped the ridge of mountains and looked down

164

into the valley, he felt his guts tighten up.

Red and blue flashing lights were showing up at various checkpoints around the town. Mike had spent twenty years with the network, covering hundreds of stories all around the world. He sensed he'd found a big one.

He pulled up to the checkpoint and got out, walking up to the line of cammie-clad troopers. "Mike Stapleton," he announced. Everybody knew Mike Stapleton, or so he thought. Big deal ex-reporter.

"So?" The lieutenant of state patrol looked at him.

"I'm handling this story for the network. What's going on in there." He looked toward the town. No smoke, no sounds of rioting, no gunfire.

"The Blanco County Sheriff's Department is hunting for a killer. We've sealed off the town."

From the ridge overlooking the valley, Mike had counted at least eight checkpoints, and he suspected there were more. Too many cops. And all state boys . . . and girls, he amended that, spotting several gun-toting women in urban cammies. And while they might indeed be hunting a killer, there was still something funky going on. What killer? There had been nothing on the news wire about any massive manhunt, or any killings in this area, for that matter.

"I'd like to get an official statement on the manhunt, officer."

"That would have to come from Sheriff Gordie Rivera."

"All right." Mike waited. None of the cops moved. "Are you going to get him for me?"

"He's busy."

"Well, how do I get in touch with him?" Mike was getting the runaround and knew it.

"Might try phoning."

"I've been told the system is down."

"Then you'll just have to wait until it's repaired, won't you?"

165

Mike stared at the patrolman. "I don't like your attitude, officer."

"That's your problem. Mine is this: I've been ordered to keep people out of Willowdale, and that is exactly what I intend to do."

"And that includes the press?"

"You're people, aren't you?"

Mike decided to switch tactics. "The public has a right to know what is going on."

"Yes, they sure do."

"Lieutenant, you cannot, by law, keep me from entering this town."

The man smiled. "You wanna bet?"

"I assure you, I will be back."

"When you return, bring me a ham and cheese on whole wheat, please."

Mightily pissed-off, Mike wheeled around, stalked back to his car, and drove off to find the nearest phone, which wasn't far.

"Won't be long now, Lieutenant," a trooper said.

"Yeah, I think all hell's about to break loose around here."

He was right, in more ways than one.

Mike stopped at the first phone he came to and called into L.A. "It's big—real big. I counted at least eight checkpoints manned by probably forty troopers. I think they're SWAT-trained and they're all wearing camouflage field clothes. All communications into and out of the town have been blocked. The crap they're handing out doesn't hold water. All official statements have to come from the sheriff, and he's made himself inaccessible. What do you think?"

"I think we've got a big one. I'm rolling Dean Hildreth right now. You brief him."

Mike gave the man instructions and directions on how

166

to get to Willowdale.

Jill Pierce, super-duper reporter from a rival network, just back from covering a story in Germany, was walking through the terminal at L.A. International when she spotted Dean Hildreth at a ticket counter. She stopped and watched. Dean was in a hurry, and he was excited. She'd known him for several years and sensed that something big was going on. She slipped into line, staying several people behind him, and listened.

"Willowdale is south and west of Denver, Mr. Hildreth," the ticket agent told him. "The only way I know that is because I'm from Leadville, and Willowdale is not too far away from there. You'll have to rent a car in Denver and drive over."

"No commuters?"

"No, sir."

Jill stepped out of line and walked to another airline ticket counter. "Denver," she said. "The first flight out you've got. And have my luggage transferred." She handed over her luggage stubs.

Ticket in hand, she went to a bank of phones and called in to her network.

"Willowdale?" the bureau chief questioned. "What the hell is a Willowdale?"

"It's a town, south and west of Denver. Something big is going down there. Dean Hildreth was foaming at the mouth, and he doesn't have rabies."

"I wouldn't be too sure of that. He might have bitten himself." Dean was a good reporter, but not loved by all. "You sure he isn't going on vacation? We have nothing to indicate that anything is going on in Willowdale."

"Trust me. From what I understand, Willowdale is in the middle of nowhere. Why would Dean be going there on vacation? He's the South of France or Aspen type."

"Okay. See what's going on. I'll have a crew in Denver in the morning."

"Have them meet me in Willowdale."

"You're going on alone?"

"Yes. I have a hunch it's that big."

"Play it your way, Jill."

She ran to catch her plane.

Chapter Thirteen

The sheriff's office was beginning to take on the aura of the defenders at the Alamo. Cases of food and bottled water were stacked around the rooms. Bedrolls and suitcases were piled around the place.

None of the staff at either motel had showed up for work that afternoon, and when the college kids had attempted to return to the motel for their toothbrushes—all they'd managed to bring down from Thunder—the girls had come close to being raped by some wild-eyed citizens.

OH, GO ON AND GIVE THEM SOME SNATCH! Fury had howled. I'D LIKE TO SEE SOME GOOD OLD-FASHIONED HUMPING.

Toothbrushes in hand, the kids beat it back to the sheriff's office.

At the S.O., the Fury was playing games. As soon as lengths of chain were secured and padlocked on the cell doors, the locks would suddenly pop open.

The prisoners thought it very funny.

Gordie failed to see the humor in it.

"How is the Fury doing it?" Robin asked. "Making bodies come hurling out of the air, unlocking padlocks, causing car wrecks? How?"

"With its mind—or minds," Howie called from his space. "What it has done is simply perfected the old spoon-bending and page-turning tricks that illusionists have done for centuries."

"Now how did he figure that out?" Maj. Jackson asked.

169

Howie laughed. "Joey told me!" he called.

Gordie posted guards with shotguns at the entrances to the cell blocks and let the prisoners have their limited freedom, with this warning, "The first one of you who sticks his head out a door, a deputy blows it off. You want to talk to one of us, you knock and then step back."

Gordie prowled the downstairs. He knew there was nothing any of them could do to protect themselves from the Fury, but there was plenty they could do to keep the townspeople from inflicting harm on them.

And some of the citizens were beginning to get openly hostile.

Gordie boarded up all the windows with three-quarter-inch CD plywood on the inside and the outside, the cavity between the boards filled with gravel. There was a ten-inch gap between top and bottom decking to use as gun slits, if it came to that. Any vehicles not in use were placed in the compound behind the office, and the gates locked and the fence electrified. The big generators were checked, and fuel brought in.

The teletype clacked out another message. "For Major Jackson," Mack said, tearing off the paper and handing it to him. Jackson had sent out a dozen messages that afternoon, all of them coded. Mack had typed out the gibberish, muttering under his breath as he did so.

Howie stepped from his enclosure and stretched, just as the Maj. was decoding the communique. "What computer would you like me to contact, Major?" the boy asked. "It would be better if we did it that way, and you know why."

The Fury did not understand computers.

"I'll give you the access code, Howie."

Howie handed the Major a pad. "Actually, you can just tell me. The Fury is not here. I have analytically correlated this afternoon's finding and built a graph. Let me show you."

As many as possible crowded into the room and around the door.

Howie brought it up onto the screen. "This graph, or outline is what it really is, is of the town. North, south, east, and west," he pointed out the directions. "You see the heaviest concentration of blips? That is the present location of the Fury. It's really very simple."

"Howie," Sunny said. "You're going to make a great scientist later on."

"Oh, no, ma'am!" the boy laughed. "I plan on becoming the person in charge of the computer section at the CIA."

Sunny looked horrified. Maj. Jackson grinned. Then they both realized that Howie was having a joke by putting them on and laughed with him.

"You're sure," Gordie asked, "that Fury won't be able to pick up on what you're sending or receiving?"

"There is no way—at the present time—that it can. I've tested it. I called that thing every ugly word I could think of. Even tried to break through and tell it of false escape plans going on. It just doesn't understand."

Captain Hishon said, "Howie, if that thing is over there," he pointed to the screen, "what would prevent us from slipping out the other side of town?"

Howie adjusted the screen's contrast; now they could all see a circle of tiny silver blips all around the perimeter of the town. "The Fury has the ability to break off parts of its mass, let's call it, and establish listening posts, or sentries, if you will. They are little thinking pockets of energy— that's my theory on it. But they are sufficiently powerful enough to kill. I've seen them do just that. So has Angel. And the mass of the Fury can move with blinding speed. It can go from one end of town to another in less than a second. Maybe that's our way out?" he mused.

"What do you mean, Howie?" Hillary asked.

"Everybody scatter out and tire it. Make it use its strength chasing us."

No! the single word flashed on Sand's screen. *That won't work.*

Why not? Howie typed.

171

The sentries are pockets of mass. They don't tire. And the Fury has enough energy stored—at this time—to prevent it from overtaxing itself. Good try, Howie.

Thanks, Sand, Howie typed.

Watch it. Here comes old fart-voice. See you.

The screen went dark. On another screen, the blips became more concentrated.

The crowd broke up, wandering away from the computer room.

THINGS ARE BEGINNING TO PICK UP, BOYS AND GIRLS. TOMORROW IS GOING TO BE A VERY INTERESTING DAY.

"You mean you'll be leaving?" Gordie fired a verbal shot at the Fury.

The room pulsed silently for a moment, a slow beating throb of anger. I'M GOING TO ENJOY WATCHING YOU DIE, SPIC. I HAVE PLANS FOR YOU.

"I'm sure you do."

Howie had left his cramped space and was sitting in a chair, listening.

I DON'T TRUST ANY OF YOU PEOPLE. YOU'RE ALL UP TO SOMETHING.

The TV set that was playing Sand's short life history began to wobble back and forth. The air was filled with curses, all of them directed at Sand.

BAH!

All felt the Fury leave.

Howie went back to his computer room.

The college kids once more gathered around the TV set.

Outside, someone began screaming.

At dawn, Jill Pierce was standing at a police blockade, arguing with a trooper.

She had been delighted to find that Dean Hildreth had not, as yet, arrived.

"I want to speak to the sheriff, Lieutenant."

"The sheriff is not here, Miss Pierce."

"I can see that!" she said acidly. "So why don't you just get him for me?"

"I'm not your personal servant," the trooper said, then turned his back to her and walked away, before he lost his temper and said something he knew he would later regret. And it was going to get much worse, just as soon as the camera crews arrived and started putting the whole god-damn scenario on film.

Jill prowled the outside of the barricade, set up on the main road leading into town. She questioned each trooper she encountered. When they answered at all, it was in monosyllables.

To Jill, it was irritating as hell.

Back to the lieutenant. "Do you mean, Lieutenant," she said, "that you or one of your people would shoot me, if I tried to enter Willowdale?"

"No, ma'am. I don't mean that at all, and neither I nor any of my people have threatened to do that."

"Then get out of my way, for I am going into this town."

The trooper stared at her. "Ma'am, can't you understand that we are under orders? Personally, I don't give a damn what happens to you, or to any reporters like you. But you're pushing me, and I strongly recommend that you stop."

Jill stuck out her chin and her chest and scowled at the man.

Nice set of hooters, the trooper observed.

"More newspeople, Lieutenant," a trooper called.

Dean Hildreth and his camera crew got out of one car, Jill's camera crew stepped out of the other vehicle.

"Get shots of all this," Jill shouted, pointing to the line of camouflaged and heavily armed state police.

Dean told his people to do the same. He walked to Jill's side. "What's up?"

"I don't really know. All they'll say is that there is a killer on the loose in town. Supercop over there," she pointed to

173

the lieutenant, "won't let anybody past those barricades."

"We'll just, by God, see about that." Dean walked to the lieutenant as the camera recorded it all. "Lieutenant, you know that as members of the press, we take chances many times doing our jobs."

"I am fully aware of that, sir. But I have my orders, my job to do. And my orders are that no one is allowed inside Willowdale."

"How do you propose to stop us? Shoot us down like the police do in South Africa?"

The lieutenant noticed that the sound man recorded Dean's combative remark and he resisted a nearly overpowering desire to tell the reporter to get fucked. "No, sir," he replied. "But we shall overwhelm you with sheer numbers, and then place you under arrest on a variety of charges."

Dean knew he had pushed enough. "I . . . see. Well then, do you mind if we just wait around on this side of the barricade?"

"Not at all. Just as long as you stay out of our way."

Dean walked back to Jill. He spoke only two words: "It's big."

The Blanco County sheriff's deputies inside the barricades had gone to their tach frequency. "The press is gathering at the blockade on 80, Sheriff," Deputy Hunt radioed. "I used binoculars to watch them. They're top guns. It's Jill Pierce and Dean Hildreth."

"Top guns is right," Sunny said, drying her hair with a towel after a quick shower. "They're both million-dollar-a-year broadcast journalists, and just as talented as they are pretty."

"You know either one of them?" Watts asked.

"I'm on speaking terms with Jill."

"What's that mean?" Gordie asked.

"It means that we're not close friends, but neither are we enemies."

"Would she listen to you?"

"Maybe."

"Let's give it a shot. Come on, we'll talk about what you can and can't say."

Jill and Dean watched as the sheriff's car pulled up and stopped, a man and woman getting out. Gordie and Sunny stood for a moment by the car.

"Sunny Lockwood," Jill murmured. "The plot thickens, as they say."

"What do you mean?" Dean asked, his eyes appraising the woman as the pair walked toward the barricades. He liked what he saw of Sunny.

"Trade talk is that some major New York house approached Sunny to do a book on some renegade punk who was killed in this part of the country years ago. Sunny is a very good writer."

"So what does that have to do with this lockout?"

"Beats me." Jill smiled as Sunny approached. "Sunny. Looks like you got in, and we're out in the cold. What's going on in there?"

"How are you, Jill."

She was introduced to Dean, then Sunny introduced Gordie all around.

The cameras began to roll, moving in close.

"Sheriff Rivera, what is going on in Willowdale?" Jill asked, shoving a microphone under Gordie's nose.

Gordie took a deep breath and verbally jumped in. "For the moment, all I can say is that we have a very bad situation in town. We have had a dozen brutal murders over the past few days." He couldn't even remember when it all started. The days and nights were getting blurry. "But we have the guilty party or parties contained within the perimeters of the town. That's the reason for the blockades. To admit others would only add to the confusion."

Jill and Dean looked at each other. Both felt the sheriff

was lying.

Gordie noticed the quick look that passed between the reporters. It's all going wrong, he thought. They're not buying any of it.

Jill studied the sheriff. A handsome man; but he looked haggard. She could not see his eyes behind the very dark sunglasses.

"Can you tell us how the people were murdered, Sheriff?" Dean asked, sticking another microphone under Gordie's nose.

"Brutally."

The wind picked up and then shifted, bringing with it the smell of death. The small morgue was filled to overflowing. The hospital had been locked up, the bodies left where they were. There was nothing else Gordie could do until the shipment of spot-embalming fluid and bodybags arrived. And it was going to be gruesome work after that.

Gordie lifted his eyes, and the cameras recorded his expression and the mikes picked up his sigh. Two eighteen-wheelers were coming down the grade from the pass. Gordie knew right then that all further pretense was useless. They could be the trucks he'd asked for yesterday. Filled with spot-embalming fluid and bodybags and medical supplies and various other equipment that Howie and the military had requested.

Gordie wondered why the Fury was remaining silent. It wasn't like the creature . . . whatever it was . . . to pass up an opportunity like this.

The drivers of the trucks parked and got out, walking up to the barricades, the men holding clipboards in their hands.

"We got some stuff here for Sheriff Rivera and for a Major Jackson," a driver said.

"Major?" Jill jumped on that. "Is the military involved in this, Sheriff?"

"To a degree."

"Why?" Dean asked.

176

"They were inside the town when the . . . incidents occurred. They received permission to assist the sheriff's department."

"Where do you want this stuff?" a driver asked.

Gordie sighed. He had to say it. "Unload on your side of the barricades. We'll take care of it after that."

Jill and Dean were silent, listening to the unusual orders.

"Be easier if we just drove to where you want this stuff, Sheriff," the second driver said. "Cuts down on handling."

"I want it where I told you to put it," Gordie said.

"Do it," the lieutenant of state patrol told him.

"Yes, sir," the drivers said. "Whatever you say." They walked back to their trucks.

And, as Gordie had feared, many of the first crates out came straight from the military and were clearly stamped: BODY BAGS.

Thankfully, most of the other crates bore numbers instead of letters.

"You must have a lot of bodies in there, Sheriff," Dean asked, as innocently as possible.

"Quite a few," Gordie acknowledged.

"And expecting more?" Jill asked. "Possibly."

"Wouldn't it be simpler to just move the bodies to a larger facility, Sheriff?" Dean asked.

"We prefer to do the autopsies here."

"Oh. I see. What is that awful smell, Sheriff?" Jill asked. "It seems to be coming from town."

"Cattle back there," Gordie said, waving his hand as the lies came easier. But the reporters weren't buying any of it. "A large herd got into poison feed. That's another reason the town is sealed off. Health hazards."

"A killer on the loose. Mass murders. Dead cattle," Dean said. "You've had your share of problems, Sheriff."

"More than our share." Gordie tried a smile that didn't quite make it.

"Sheriff Rivera?" Jill said.

"Yes, Miss Pierce?"

177

"Why are you lying to us?"

Gordie was conscious of the cameras rolling, pointing at him. All of a sudden he had it up to his neck with reporters. To hell with the both of them. He put his hand on the wooden barricade in front of him and pulled it open. "You people just have to push, don't you? Well, that's just fine with me, folks. You want a story, Miss Pierce, Mr. Hildreth?"

"That's why we're here, Sheriff," Dean said.

"Certainly, we want a story, Sheriff," Jill told him.

"And if I don't let you in, you're going to run those tapes and try to make me look like either a fool or a villain or both, right?"

His question was answered by stony stares and silence.

"All right. Fine. If you people come in here, I have to inform you, in front of witnesses, all of you, that none of you will be allowed to leave until our situation is cleared up. Once in here, if you attempt to leave, or to go past the barricades, I will not be responsible for your lives. Is that understood?"

"Aren't you being a bit melodramatic, Sheriff?" Dean asked with a smile, or a smirk—with him it was hard to tell.

Gordie ignored that and turned to the state patrol lieutenant. "If they try to pass film, confiscate it."

"Right, Sheriff."

"Now, see here!" Dean opened his mouth.

Gordie stuck a big finger in the man's face, at this point not giving a damn whether it was being filmed or taped or whatever the camera crews was using. "No, *you* see here. Do you accept the terms, or don't you? And I want to hear everybody say it aloud, for the sound man's benefit."

The crews said it, and it was recorded.

"Whatever you say, Sheriff," Dean said with a smile.

"Miss Pierce? Once you're in here, I don't want to hear a bunch of bitching and complaining."

"I agree with your terms, Sheriff," Jill said, then pushed past him and into the town limits. Gordie closed the barricades.

Sunny whispered to Jill, "I hope you've given your heart to God, Jill."

"Whatever do you mean?"

" 'Cause you just lost your ass!"

Chapter Fourteen

Gordie waved for a deputy to transport the camera crews and their equipment. A trooper handed the luggage over the barricades.

"We'll park their vehicles off to one side, Sheriff."

"Good deal."

When he joined the group, Dean glanced at first the growing mound of supplies, then at Gordie. "Judging by the amount of supplies, you must think we're going to be in here for sometime, Sheriff?"

"Until it's over. You've all been exposed now. You can't leave. It won't let you."

"It?" Jill said, pulling up short. "Are you telling us that you have deliberately exposed us to some deadly virus?"

"I didn't ask you to come in here, lady. I'm sure the state patrol told you repeatedly not to come in. If you choose to ignore well-meaning warnings, that's your problem."

"Then you were lying to us?" Jill glared at him.

"To a degree," Gordie admitted. "We do have a killer in here, and we are all confined within the perimeters of this town. Why do you think none of us tried to pass the barricades?"

She wrinkled her nose. "Phew! What is that horrible smell, Sheriff?"

"Death." Gordie's reply was very blunt. He walked away, seeing to the loading of the supplies into pickup trucks.

"Sunny, we were both in Lebanon," Jill said, turning to her. "It takes a lot of bodies to produce that smell. I . . ."

She stopped as she watched a middle-aged man walk toward the curb. He stood there, grinning like a mindless fool.

Then he unzipped his trousers, took out his penis, and shook it at Jill.

"How about gettin' some lipstick on my dipstick, baby?" he called.

"Why . . . why . . . that *bastard!*" Jill said. She looked at the sheriff. He was behaving as if perverted acts like the one she had just witnessed went on all the time. She looked at the troopers. The lieutenant merely shrugged his shoulders in a I-told-you-so gesture.

Gordie rejoined them. "The man is not responsible for the things he does, Jill. His mind is being slowly drained. Get in the car, please."

The man was wiggling his tongue at Jill, a rapid in and out snakelike motion. "How about me goin' to work on you, baby?" he yelled.

"Jesus!" Jill muttered, quickly getting into the car.

Gordie cranked up and pulled out, the camera crews behind him.

"What kind of sorry-ass town are you running here, Sheriff?" Jill demanded, considerable heat in her voice. She ignored the mind-draining bit. All bullshit, she thought.

Dean had been strangely silent. Gordie cut his eyes at the man, riding in the front seat next to him.

Dean felt the look and said, "Remember that line about discretion being the better part of valor, Sheriff?"

"Yes. *Henry the Fourth,* I think."

Dean smiled faintly without a trace of a smirk. "I think Miss Pierce and I just blew that line."

"Yes, Mr. Hildreth, I believe you did."

"Is that man drunk over there, Sheriff?" Jill asked, pulling herself up close to him and pointing.

Gordie noticed that she wore a very expensive-smelling perfume. Very subtle and pleasant. He cut the wheel and pulled over to the man who was sprawled face down in the gutter. Gordie noticed the man's head.

"No, Jill. He's dead. You're going to see a lot of that. Come on, get out. Tell your camera crews to start rolling, or whatever the expression is. I want to show you something."

Kneeling down, Gordie thumped the man's head. It had a hollow sound, just like thumping a dry gourd.

Dean knelt down. Looked at Gordie. "What in God's name is going on around here, Sheriff?"

Gordie ignored that and returned to his car, calling in. "Mack? We have another dead one. Corner of Aspen and Sixth."

"Ten-four, Sheriff. But I can't raise Mark. He's disappeared."

Gordie rehooked the mike. He had a pretty good idea what had happened to the funeral home director. "Back in the cars, folks." He slid in under the wheel. Sunny had not gotten out of the back seat.

"Are you just going to leave the man here?" Jill's question was very nearly a shrill shout.

"What do you want me to do, Jill?" Gordie asked. "Stuff him in the trunk? Get in."

I BELIEVE THAT NEW BROAD HAS THE GREATEST-LOOKING ASS I HAVE EVER SEEN.

Jill was so startled by the booming voice out of nowhere that she banged her head on the car as she jerked back. She looked around. "Who said that?"

GREAT BALLS OF FIRE! JUST TAKE A LOOK AT THOSE TITS!

Dean was visibly shaken. His eyes locked onto the gaze of the sheriff. Gordie smiled at him. "You were all warned. Now get in the car."

GOING TO TAKE THEM ON THE GRAND TOUR, PANCHO?

"I thought I might."

I'LL TRY TO ARRANGE A WELCOMING-IN CERE-

MONY FOR THEM AT THE HOSPITAL.

"I can hardly wait."

FUCKING SPIC. NO SENSE OF HUMOR AT ALL. NO GRATITUDE, EITHER. BOORISH OAF.

"That's me, Fury." Gordie got in the car and rolled out.

Gordie noticed that Dean's hands were shaking so badly he had to shove them under his thighs to control the trembling.

Jill's face was chalk white, her eyes wide and unbelieving. She found her voice. "What in the hell was that voice? Where . . . I mean, yes, where was it coming from?"

"It's coming from all around us, Jill," Sunny told her.

"You called it Fury, Sheriff." She met his eyes in the rearview.

"Sand told us that was its name."

"Sand?"

"Yes. He's been dead about thirty years, I believe. You'll meet the man who killed him."

Dean cleared his throat. "How, ah, do you know that is what Sand calls him?"

"Sand told us."

Dean closed his eyes for a moment.

"A dead man told you?" Jill's voice was small from the back seat.

"That's right. You'll see."

The reporters were silent as Gordie turned into the parking lot of the hospital. All could clearly see the dark row of buzzards perched atop the building, waiting with a million years of built-in patience.

"I had a chance to take an anchor," Dean muttered. "Chauffeured limo to and from work. New York City. But no, I wanted the field for one more year." He sighed. "Well, I sure got it."

Gordie parked and got out. The others, including Sunny, reluctantly followed. Sunny knew about the hospital, but had not expressed any flaming desire to view the carnage firsthand.

183

Even to those standing outside, several hundred yards from the building, the odor was not pleasant.

"Fit everyone with masks, Duane," Gordie ordered.

Part of the equipment Gordie had requested from the military, with the help of Maj. Jackson.

The masks on and tested, Gordie waved his little group forward. The masks had built-in mikes and receivers, and that was a pleasant surprise, since Gordie had not requested that.

"People moving around in there, Sheriff," Duane spoke.

"Yeah. I see them."

"What is so unusual about that?" Jill asked. "It is a hospital."

"It's very unusual, Miss Pierce. Since I checked out this place yesterday afternoon, and everybody in there was dead."

She gasped.

Gordie did not respond to the gasp. He felt like gasping himself.

DO BOP DE DO BOP DE DO BOP, DE DO. HOW'S THAT FOR A ONE-MAN BAND, RIVERA?

"Absolutely takes my breath away, Fury. I can truthfully say that I have never heard anything to compare with it."

WOULD YOU LIKE TO HEAR SOME MORE? PERHAPS A LITTLE BIT OF BE BOP A LULA?

"Frankly, no."

GODDAMN TIN EAR.

Gordie ignored that. Truthfully, he was tone-deaf. His singing in the shower had been known to drive dogs and cats out of the yard.

The front doors to the hospital were slowly opening.

Dean shook his head at the sight. "Who is opening the doors?"

"Call it black magic," Gordie said.

BLACK MAGIC, MY ASS, YOU HICKTOWN GUNSLINGER. HERE I GO OUT OF MY WAY TO DO SOMETHING TO ENTERTAIN YOUR GUESTS, AND

184

ALL YOU CAN DO IS INSULT ME.

"I shudder to think what the smell would be like if we didn't have these masks on," Sunny said.

WHEN ARE YOU GOING TO STRAP SOME OF THAT PUSSY ON THE SPIC, BABY? I'D LIKE TO WATCH.

"Neither one of us have been in the mood lately," she popped back.

Jill could but walk on in fearful bewilderment.

The group walked up the steps, past the dead bodies, and entered the gloom of the hospital. Past the reception area, the lights suddenly popped on. Dean took a look at the blood-splattered walls, and the human carnage lying stiffened and bloated on the floor. He ripped off his mask and ran from the building. He just made it past the open front doors when he tossed his cookies.

Jill fought back sickness and won. But it was with an effort.

Gordie had wondered what had happened to Mark. Now he knew. Mark lay sprawled in death on the floor, beside the bloated body of the receptionist. The mortician had been sliced open, from throat to groin, the organs and intestines tossed to one side.

"Now we know," Duane said.

"Yeah," Gordie replied.

Mark suddenly sat up and opened his eyelids. He had no eyes, only dark empty holes. "Hello, Sheriff," he said, then toppled back to the floor.

That's when Jill started screaming, forcing them all to cut down the volume controls on their masks.

The camera crews had stood their ground, filming it all.

Dean walked back into the slaughterhouse, his mask back in place. Gordie turned up his volume.

"What'd I miss?" Dean asked.

"Mark just greeted me."

"That's Mark on the floor?"

"Yes."

185

The reporter had absolutely nothing to add to that.

COME ON, COME ON! Fury boomed. I HAVE SUCH A FANTASTIC ENTERTAINMENT PROGRAM LINED UP FOR YOU ALL.

"Can't you just keep it simple?" Gordie asked.

ABSOLUTELY NOT. NOTHING BUT THE BEST FOR THE GALLANT PERSONNEL OF THE LIGHT BRIGADE.

"You like Tennyson, eh?"

ONE OF MY FAVORITES. TELL ME IF THIS IS NOT APROPOS:

DEAR AS REMEMBER'D KISSES AFTER DEATH,
AND SWEET AS THOSE BY HOPELESS FANCY FEIGN'D
ON LIPS THAT ARE FOR OTHERS; DEEP AS LOVE,
DEEP AS FIRST LOVE, AND WILD WITH ALL REGRET;
OH, DEATH IN LIFE, THE DAYS THAT ARE NO MORE.

"That's great, Fury," Gordie told him. "I'm almost moved to tears."

YOU'RE AN ASSHOLE, SPIC. BUT I DO ADMIRE YOUR COURAGE. TELL THE TRUTH, I RATHER LIKE YOU. SO . . . I'LL MAKE YOU A PROPOSAL.

"You have a captive audience, Fury."

OH, THAT'S GOOD, GORDIE. VERY GOOD. HERE IT IS: GO BACK TO YOUR OFFICE AND KILL THE BRATS, HOWIE AND ANGEL. DO THAT, AND I'LL LET YOU AND YOUR SWEET PETUNIA WALK OUT OF HERE. YOU HAVE MY WORD ON THAT.

"No deal," Gordie said.

OKAY, HOW'S THIS: SCREW THE LITTLE BRAT. LET ME HEAR HER SCREAM. THEN YOU AND

YOUR CORN MUFFIN CAN LEAVE.

"You know better than that, Fury."

OH, COME ON! JUST POP IT TO THE LITTLE AN-
GEL FOR A FEW MINUTES, AND THEN YOU AND
POOPSIE CAN LIVE.

"No deal."

THEN WALK ON, STUPID.

"Was he, it, whatever, serious with that offer?" Jill
asked.

"Probably. Fury?"

RIGHT HERE.

"I have a deal for you."

ROLL THE DICE, PONCHO.

"You let Howie and Angel leave, and then we'll talk.
How about that?"

YOU JUST THREW SNAKE EYES, PEPPER-
BREATH.

"It was worth a shot."

Fury had no reply to that.

They walked on, deeper into the building—it could no
longer be called a hospital.

"What do you want me to do about Mark, Sheriff?"
Duane asked.

"Nothing. Since he was the only certified mortician in
town, I guess we'll have to handle all the dead ourselves. I
know how to use that stuff. You body-bag them, and then
pour it on. Zip up the bag, and you're through."

"I'll help," Dean said. "I've seen it done, too."

"You're on," Gordie told him. "And thanks."

Then they all heard the sounds of music and wild laughter.

"Everybody brace yourselves," Gordie told them. "The
Fury has a strange sense of humor."

A fat, headless, and very bloody and naked man appeared in the hall. He rose up on his toes and slowly pirou-
etted on the tile, then danced slowly past the men and
women; their eyes, behind the bulbous plastic eyes of the

187

masks, watched in undisguised horror as the fat man waltzed on down the hall and gracefully turned the corner.

"Did you get it all?" Jill asked her cameraman.

"I got it," he said.

They walked on, toward the sounds of music and laughter; a party was in full swing.

BRING ON THE DANCING GIRLS! Fury howled.

A line of women, their bodies ripped and torn and mangled, formed in the hall. They were naked, each woman holding her drooping intestines in her hands. They began to slowly sway back and forth, then began a ragged dance step, twirling their guts in time with the beat. They sang in dead voices to the tune of *Old Gray Bonnet:*

"Put on your brand new bustle,
Get your ass out and hustle,
Tomorrow the room rent comes due.
Lay it down in the clover,
Let the boys look it over.
If you can't get five, take two!"

Then they all giggled like young schoolgirls and shuffled back into a room, closing the door.

"Dear God in heaven!" Dean whispered.

AND THAT'S ONLY THE BEGINNING. I'VE SO MUCH MORE TO SHOW YOU. PARTY TIME, PARTY TIME.

"Let's get out of here," Gordie said.

OH, NO, DONKEY FACE. YOU'RE GOING TO A PARTY. ALL OF YOU.

"Shit on you," Gordie said. "Let's go, people."

They turned around.

The long corridor was blocked; blocked by grotesquely mangled men. The men held clubs and broken bottles in their bloody hands. They stood with evil grins on their faces, staring at Gordie and the others.

Gordie recognized them all. There was Simmons, the attorney. Matthews, the grocer. Garrett, the carpenter. Some of them had broken limbs; how they could stand was a mystery to Gordie.

"Now what?" a cameraman said.

"We'll ram through them using these gurneys. Duane, you and me will take the lead. Dean and the rest, follow us and stay close. We're going to be moving fast."

"I hope," a cameraman said.

WHAT ARE YOU WHISPERING ABOUT? WHAT ARE YOU PLANING? ANSWER ME, DAMN YOU.

"Now!" Gordie yelled, grabbing the gurney and running toward the line of living dead.

Duane grabbed the other gurney and they charged, the men running as fast as they could on the slick, bloody, and body-parts-littered tile floor.

They crashed into the line of naked, bloody, and bloated standing dead, the force of their charge knocking half a dozen bodies sprawling. The rest of the group, bunched right behind the lawmen, charged through the hole in the line.

GET THEM! GET THEM! MAKE THEM STAY FOR THE PARTY!

The glass doors loomed bright with sunshine before them.

Gordie hit the doors hard and bounced back, bruising his shoulder. The doors had been locked.

"Gordie, open the doors!" Sunny yelled.

Behind them, the line of death-swollen and head-shrunken nakedness was lumbering closer, strange and inhuman sounds coming from their mouths. Those that still had heads, that is.

Gordie jerked out his Mag and blew the cylinder lock out of the metal. He kicked the doors open.

A naked and bloody man grabbed Jill from behind and rode her to the floor, just inside the doors. He had a huge erection. He tore at her clothing and, grunting and hunching, tried to spread her legs. Dean turned around and kicked the hideousness in the face, knocking him off of and away from Jill. Dean jerked her to her feet and shoved her in front of him, out the door.

The line of living dead gathered at the doors, but did not attempt to follow.

Buzzards had gathered all around the bodies sprawled in the front of the hospital and were busy dining on the rotting human flesh, tearing great chunks of meat from the dead and waddling around, some of them already so bloated they could not fly.

Gordie emptied his Mag into the air, to frighten off the carrion birds and to clear a path for them to get to the vehicles.

The hard and evil laughter of the Fury echoed all around them.

The group made it to the cars and roared off, just as Jill said, "I swear to God, I think I'm going to faint for the first time in my life."

Then she promptly passed out.

When she opened her eyes, she was lying on a cot in the sheriff's office, Howie standing over her, looking down at her through very serious eyes.

She licked very dry lips. "Where am I?" she asked.

"Hell," the boy said.

Book Two

Chapter One

The urge to kill, like the urge to beget, is blind and
sinister. Its craving is set
Today on the flesh of a hare: tomorrow it can
Howl the same way for the flesh of a man.

Voznesensky

Dean and Jill and their camera crews sat numbly in the
main room of the S.Ö. They had all been briefed as to the
situation.

All had taken it calmly enough. They had all seen enough
of the power of the Fury to know that they were solely in the
hands of the Fury, and solely at the mercy of its evil whims.

Jill had changed into fresh jeans, tossing away her torn
ones. With a sigh, she rose from her chair and walked over
to the group of college students who were gathered around a
TV set.

Jill looked at all the old cars displayed on the screen. "A
fifties movie? I don't think I'm familiar with this one."

Doyle looked up at her and motioned toward a chair. Jill
sat down.

"No movie, Miss Pierce," he said, as Dean wandered over
and took a chair. "Somehow, Sand is showing us the truth of
what happened, thirty years ago."

Jill had been raised a Catholic. But she had not been to
mass or confession in years. Without thinking, she crossed
herself.

Bos and Hillary had seen the gesture. "The local priest is dead, Miss Pierce," Bos said. "The deputies found his body this morning. He'd been stripped naked and nailed up to a wall in the church. And then mutilated," he added with a grimace.

"The . . . Fury?"

Hillary shook her head. "No. The townspeople did it to him."

"Why?" Dean asked.

The young people shrugged.

"Tell me about this Sand," Jill said.

She was brought up to date.

"Sand's just had the hell beat out of him by the cops over in Monte Rio," Lynn finished it. "Dan Thompson's father paid them to do it."

"Dan Thompson?" Dean looked at the girl. "The journalist who is MIA in Southeast Asia?"

"He's dead, Dean," Sunny said, walking up. "Richard Jennings told me."

"The . . . dead man you interviewed?"

"Yes."

Dean stuffed his pipe and lit it. "The greatest news story of the century unfolding all around us, and we can't get the film out."

WHO SAYS YOU CAN'T? DID YOU HEAR THAT FROM ME? NO, YOU DID NOT. AS A MATTER OF FACT, I INSIST THAT MY STORY BE TOLD IN AS MANY WAYS AS POSSIBLE. GREASEBALL AND THE OLD COPPER OVER THERE ARE THE ONES WHO DON'T WANT THE PEOPLE OUTSIDE OF THIS HOG-PEN TO BE INFORMED OF MY GREATNESS.

Neither Jill nor Dean said it aloud, but they both understood Gordie's reasoning behind the secrecy. Now. And they agreed with the sheriff.

BAH! the Fury faded away.

"He's gone," Howie called.

"How does he know that?" a cameraman asked.

194

Sunny explained that the boy was a computer genius. She looked at Jill. The reporter seemed captivated by the events unfolding on the screen.

"It's being recorded, right?"

"Yes," Sunny told her. "Sand wants me to do his story in book form."

"He told you that?"

"Richard did." She pointed to the screen. "Richard told me that Sand was living a hundred years out of his time period. And he knew that for a fact . . . after he died. Sand was truly born out of time and place. As was Joey. Fate—and he said to believe very strongly in that—was not kind to Sand. He said that Sand could no more change, or alter what he was, than a bear or lion or wolf."

"My God!" Jill pointed to the screen. "Who in the world is that? Or what in the world it is?"

Watts passed by and stopped. He laughed aloud at the familiar figure in a silk top hat. "That, folks, is Morg. Turn up the volume. My men were tailing him right after Sand was leaned on by the cops over in Monte Rio. I've always thought this is where they made their decision to band together and fight."

"I've missed something," Gordie said. "Why did they have to band together at all, Al?"

"You want to run the tape back, sir?" Bos asked Watts.

Watts shook his head. "No. I can fill you all in. That'll save time; since we don't know how much time we have before Fury kills us all. Or tries. There was a young man who lived over in Monte Rio. I can't remember his name. Anyway, he saw the writing on the wall, so to speak. He had a meeting with Sand and they agreed to cool the rumble—to use the vernacular of the nineteen fifties. They agreed to a truce. There had been several bad fights between the Pack and those rich shits over in Monte Rio. The kid from Monte Rio who had succeeded in doing what no one else had—that is, arranging a truce—was killed that same night.

"Well, the blame was laid on Sand's head. I personally led

the investigating team, and was convinced that Sand had nothing to do with the boy's death. About a week after the accident . . ."

"Fury is coming!" Howie called.

"Screw the Fury," Watts said. "We found the guy who really killed the boy. It was a young man all popped up on bennies. But by that time, conditions had deteriorated past the point of no return. Young Dan Thompson . . ." He looked at Sunny. ". . . the friend of your friend, had discovered his father had paid to have Sand leaned on by those assholes with badges over in Monte Rio. Young Dan left home and went to live with his great aunt, one Julie von Mehren." Watts paused, smiling, knowing he had just dropped a small bomb in the room.

And it shook everybody up. Gordie was the first to speak. "The huge mansion up in the mountains."

"That's the one. At that time, Julie was the richest woman on the face of the earth. And she was crazy about Sand. Julie died several years before you came here, Gordie. Lived to be in her late nineties." Watts was lost in memory. "She finally told me," he continued, "that on the night I . . . killed Sand, she was awakened out of a sound sleep. She didn't, at first, know what woke her up. She said the sky that night was so bright, so star-filled, it was almost like day. And it was. I remember how eerie it felt. She said . . . . some *thing* began circling around her bed. And the thunder that night, my God, it rumbled and raged. I had never heard anything like it; before or since.

"Julie told me that on that night, she stood shivering on her balcony, and watched the souls meet. She said something came down from the heavens to join something that the heavens rejected."

Everyone in the room had gathered around and was listening. "What did she mean, sir?" Sandy Dennis asked.

When he spoke again, Watts's voice was husky with emotion. "Robin, Tuddie, Jane, Joey. They came out of heaven to join Sand and Morg. And Julie said there was a tiny, mist-like object that followed the larger bursts downward. I think that was Sand's son, following his mother."

Sunny glanced up. "I wasn't aware that Sand and Robin had a son."

Robin Jennings said, "Yes. My aunt was eight-months pregnant when those crapheads from over Monte Rio kicked her to death. The baby died. That's when Uncle Sand snapped."

Watts rubbed his temples with his fingertips. "Yes, that is what happened. That was one bloody awful night. For all concerned."

OH, WHAT ROT AND DRIVEL. HOW NAUSEATING. IT MAKES ME WANT TO PUKE.

"What do you want?" Gordie asked.

I HAVE RETURNED TO RESUME THE RELATING OF MY GLORIOUS LIFE, CACTUS-HEAD.

Sunny rose and walked toward the office.

The others turned their attention to the TV.

The screen showed Sand sitting on the edge of a steel bunk. He was dripping wet with water from a high pressure hose. He was looking at a half-dozen cops. These cops hired and paid by the rich folks of Monte Rio, to keep the non-rich out. Sand knew he was in the basement of the Monte Rio jail. He'd heard horror stories about this place.

Sand knew he was about to get the shit beat out of him. No doubt about it.

"Am I entitled to a phone call?" he asked.

The cops thought that was very funny. Sand didn't see the humor in it.

"Who do you wanna call, punk?"

Someday, Sand silently vowed — and those watching from the future could read his thoughts — I will change your looks, bastard. "My girl — so she won't worry."

Sand looked down at his bare feet. No boots, no belt.

Never give a sucker an even break.

197

"She won't have to worry long, punk," a cop told him. "Just 'til your funeral. Then she can find someone else to fuck."

Sand came off the bunk and hit the cop, driving him back against a wall.

Then the other cops were all over him.

Those watching the events of thirty years past could actually smell the dew-covered grass as it filled Sand's head. Sand tried to open his eyes. He could not. For one panic-filled moment, he thought he was blind. Then he discovered his eyelids were caked shut with dried blood. He could not make his hands understand that they should rise up to his face and clear his vision. Finally, the bruised muscles in his arms responded, and his fingers dug away the hardened blood.

His vision cleared, faded, then sharpened as his eyes began adjusting. He coughed, and pain exploded all over his body.

His boots were on his feet and his belt was threaded through the loops. Nice and neat, he thought. No boots or belt would have been a dead give away.

Using brute strength, he pulled himself out of a ditch, coming to his car. The Mercury was nosed into a gully, the front fenders and hood crunched, the radiator still steaming, the windshield knocked out.

"I had a wreck," Sand muttered through swollen and smashed lips. "And I was killed. Almost nice and neat, boys. But you left some loose ends."

He crawled on, rage making him strong, forcing him on. "But you should have made sure I was dead, boys. You should have made sure. There will be a payback for this. That's a promise."

Watts walked to the TV and turned the volume down. His face was ugly and hard with anger. "I *knew* that's what happened! I knew it. I tried to get Sand to let me take care of it. He never would admit the cops leaned on him."

"Would the cops who did that have been beaten as bad as

198

Sand was beaten?" Howie asked.

"The law doesn't work that way, Howie," Watts told him. "And you know it."

"It should," Angel said.

The brother and sister walked back into the computer room.

"I know from reading old reports, that the cops who beat Sand were badly beaten themselves later on," Gordie said. "And no one was ever caught or charged for it. Sand?"

"Sure," Watts told them all, fitting another piece of the old puzzle together. "But I never could catch Sand. Julie's money put up quite a wall, believe me it did. That woman just flat-out told me, that if I wanted to remain with the state patrol, I better not ever charge Sand for doing what the courts wouldn't do. She told me that if I thought a billion dollars couldn't buy a lot of grief, just try her and see."

Gordie chuckled. "I just can't imagine you backing down from anything, Al."

"I didn't back down from a damn thing! I just couldn't pin it on him. Every time one of those jackleg cops would get hammered on — and brother, they got hammered on — Sand would have an alibi no DA would even dream of disputing. Carl Lee, Robin's father, one of the most respected men in this community, and he would always step up and say Sand had been with him."

"Carl Lee. CL Enterprises?" Gordie questioned.

"That's him. He owned a large chunk of this town, not to mention about a third of the county. A good, decent, honorable man, and my best friend. But Carl saw himself in Sand. He knew Sand was getting the raw end of law enforcement and stood by him. Right up to and including the end."

"Did Sand whip the cops that bad?" Paul asked.

"Oh, boy, did he! He whipped them all with a tire iron. He gave them double and triple what they'd dished out to him. Three of them were crippled so badly they could never work again."

"They got what was coming to them," Hillary said.

"Yes," Watts said. "That's what makes a good cop's job so difficult. I know they did." He turned and walked out of the room.

"Three hours of listening to that pompous windbag is three hours and fifteen minutes too long," Sunny said, when the session was over.

"Where are you now?" Gordie asked, pouring her a cup of coffee.

"About ten thousand B.C.," she said, disgust in her voice. "But I shouldn't complain. It's buying us more time, isn't it?"

"Howie, are we clear?" Gordie called.

"Yes, sir. Fury is nowhere around us."

Gordie sat down, after looking at and receiving a nod from Maj. Jackson. "Gather around, people. I've got to level with you all."

The crowded room fell silent.

"Major Jackson has informed, ah, certain parties in government as to our dilemma. And those people have agreed with . . . Sand and Joey's suggestion about how we might stop the Fury."

"We're still clear, Sheriff," Howie called. "I'll let you know when or if the Fury approaches."

"Good boy. Now, people, I don't know why we have been spared; why that . . . thing has not or cannot take control of us the way it's managed to do the majority of the people in this town. I think that right now, that's beside the point."

"What is the point, Sheriff?" Jill asked.

"How to keep the Fury contained, and how to destroy it."

"And the answer to that is . . . ?" Dean questioned.

Gordie told them.

Those he had not already taken into his confidence sat with shocked and unbelieving looks on their faces. Stunned. Dr. Anderson could practically feel the blood pressure going up in the room.

Lee Evans was the first to break the spell of gloom and impending doom. "Thirty or so of us as compared to millions is a small price to pay, I suppose. I don't have to like it, but I can see why it has to be."

A couple of the college girls began to cry. Angel leaned against the wall, close to her brother in the computer room, and said nothing. She really wasn't sure exactly what dying meant. Except you weren't around anymore.

"What are the odds of us getting out?" Dr. Anderson asked. "Or at least some of us making it?"

Gordie looked at Maj. Jackson.

Jackson stood up. "Some of us will probably make it out. The people who project casualties are saying less than half will make it. That's with the information we have so far been able to feed them."

"You mean, there is some hope that more might make it out of here?" Bos asked, a hopeful look on his face.

"Sure. The more we find out about Fury's weak spots—if it has any, and everything does—the better our chances of making it out."

"May I say something?" Howie asked. He stood in the door to the tiny, cluttered room that housed his computers, keeping an eye on the screens.

"Of course, Howie."

"Sunny has to keep the Fury talking; keep it occupied. But I would like for her to do that away from this office. With it occupied, away from here, in another part of town, we can get a lot of messages out of here. The longer she— and preferably Miss Pierce and Mr. Hildreth with her, for the Fury has a tremendous ego—can keep it talking, the better our chances of finding a weak spot in its defenses."

Dean looked at Jill. She shrugged. "Let's go for it," she said.

"Watch it!" Howie called. "Here it comes."

The Fury came with such a rush, all could feel its presence as it entered the room.

PLOTTING AGAINST ME, EH? WELL, I EX-

PECTED THAT. I'D BE DISAPPOINTED IF YOU DIDN'T.

"Did you expect us to just sit here calmly and wait for death?" Watts asked. He, like the others, did not know how much the Fury knew of their plans.

OH, NO. OF COURSE NOT. BUT NONE OF YOU HAVE *DONE* ANYTHING. IT APPEARS TO ME THAT YOU'RE ALL JUST SITTING AROUND WITH ONE FINGER UP YOUR ASS AND ANOTHER FINGER IN YOUR MOUTH, WAITING FOR SOMEONE TO TELL YOU TO SWITCH. COME ON, THIS IS A GAME. PLAY THE GAME. TRY TO BEST ME. I CHALLENGE YOU ALL.

The Fury left them.

"It's gone," Howie called.

"Let's do it then," Angel said.

"Do what, girl?" Watts asked.

"Try to beat it at its own game. When it comes back, let's find out the rules."

Lt. Smith began walking around the room, deep in thought. "Yeah," she snapped her fingers. "Sure. Let's make a game of it. Each time we win, well, maybe one of us can leave. It might go for that."

"And if we lose?" Hillary dumped cold water on the suggestion.

No one said anything for a moment.

Finally Old Mack stood up. "What the hell? We're all dead anyway, aren't we? What do we have to lose by at least trying to beat it?"

In the back room, Dr. Shriver began screaming, not in agony, but in fear. The scream chilled them.

Chapter Two

The door to the corridor was kicked open. At first, all they could see was Shriver, his face pale. He had gone to the back to take Deputy Sid Rico some coffee. Shriver began moving in a jerky walk. Then the convicts could be seen behind him. The bulk of Logan could be seen, the muzzle of a gun pressed against Shriver's head. Bingham and Diminno were right behind Logan.

"That's Sid's gun," Rick said.

"How right you are, Deputy," Logan said with a smile. "But he won't be needin' it no more, so don't worry about it."

"Let's get some pussy 'fore we leave," Diminno spoke from the rear. "Let's take a couple of these cunts with us."

"You dumbass!" Logan snarled at him. "There's a whole town full of pussy outside. Snatch is snatch." He jacked the hammer back, pressing the muzzle harder against the doctor's head. "Clear a path for us, folks. Everybody to one side. That's good. Right over there. Anybody gets hinky, the good doc gets dead. Understood?"

"Just leave," Gordie told him. "We won't try to stop you."

Logan smiled, and for a few seconds, cut his eyes to the TV set. They widened in shock. "I know that guy. He whipped my ass once—long time ago when we was kids. That's Sand. What the hell is goin' on? Sand's been dead for thirty years. Well, I'll just be goddamned! That's ol' ugly Morg yonder. Only man I ever knew who wore a silk

203

top hat. Silly-lookin' bastard." He cut his eyes to Watts. "What kind of shit are you people tryin' to pull?"

"Do you want to watch TV or make your break?" Watts asked him.

"I oughtta kill you, Watts. You been hasslin' me ever since I was kid."

"Nobody hassled you, Logan. You're just a goddamned loser, that's all." Watts stared back at him, unintimidated. "You're walking proof that abortion should be legalized nationwide." Watts had been dealing with punks all his life and knew them for what they were, and to hell with what the courts and mumbling judges and sobbing lawyers thought. He knew they were trash and scum and ninety-nine percent would never change. Not that they couldn't—they wouldn't.

"You're still a mean old bastard, aren't you, Watts?"

"Lay that gun down, and I'll show you how mean I still am, Logan."

Logan laughed.

"Let's split," Bingham said. "To hell with these people."

"Yeah," Logan agreed. "We can deal with them later." He shoved Shriver toward the door.

Diminno jerked two shotguns from the rack and checked them, tossing one to Bingham. He stuffed his pockets full of shells. "Let's go."

They edged toward the door. Logan said, "If nobody gets cute, the doctor lives. We'll leave him across the street, on the corner. He looked at Angel and licked his lips. Bergman pulled her close to him and stared at the man.

Logan laughed and shoved Shriver out the door and into the night. They were gone.

Mack walked to a boarded-up window and looked out the gun slit. "They turned him loose. Doc's just standing there on the corner, looking scared. Those three hardcases are gone."

Duane reached for a shotgun. Gordie's voice stopped him. "Let them go, Duane. I'm not going to risk losing anybody else on account of that crud. They'll soon find out they jumped from the pan into the fire. Lee, get the doctor back in here. Alan, check on Sid."

Sid was dead. His neck broken. He was body-bagged and stored in the rear.

Gordie looked at his chief deputy. "Lee, take a partner and prowl from Main east to the barricades. I'll take Major Jackson and work the other sector. The rest of you try to get some rest. I have a feeling this night is going to be a dandy."

It took only a few blocks for the men to realize just what a bind they were all in . . . in more ways than one. As they drove, they observed men and women and kids all milling around like . . .

"Zombies," Jackson broke into Gordie's thoughts.

"Yeah. Exactly what I was thinking. But this is only a small percentage of the town's population. If the rest were dead, we wouldn't be able to stand the smell. So where are they, and more importantly, *what* are they?"

"Look out!" Jackson yelled, as a man hurled himself onto the hood of the car.

The citizen crawled up to the windshield and pressed his face and mouth against the glass. Drool leaked from his mouth. His eyes were red and wild-looking. He clawed at the glass with his finger; even tried to bite the glass like a crazed animal.

Gordie braked and came to a stop in the middle of the street.

Other men and women began gathering around the car, rocking it back and forth. They mumbled and slobbered and cursed.

"They're going to try to turn it over," Jackson said.

Gordie looked to his left and saw several men gathering up rocks and sticks; other men joined them with heavy clubs and two-by-fours in their hands. He made up his mind.

Gordie didn't want to do it. He had known many of these

205

people for a long time.

But neither did he want to die.

"Kill them! Kill them! Kill them!" they began to chant.

Gordie dropped the unit in gear and stepped on the gas, running over anyone who was unlucky enough to be standing in front of the cruiser. Screams of pain came to the men as they drove off into the night.

Maj. Jackson turned in his seat, looking back at the sight. Several men were flopping and rolling around in the street, with smashed arms and legs.

He looked at Gordie. "Better them than us, Sheriff. You've got to believe that."

"I do," Gordie said. "And I believe something else, too." His cut his eyes at the Major. "I believe that it's going to get a hell of a lot worse."

LONDON BRIDGE IS FALLING DOWN, FALLING DOWN, FALLING DOWN. LONDON BRIDGE IS FALLING DOWN.

MY FAIR LADY!

DO BOP DE DO BOP DE DO BOP, DE DO.

"Now what the hell does that mean?" Jackson asked.

"I know what the my fair lady bit means," Gordie told him, pointing across the street. "Look over there."

A naked woman was bent over the hood of a restored MG midget, being serviced by a man with his pants around his ankles. She grinned and waved as Gordie drove by.

"You know that woman, Gordie?"

"Yep. That's my wife."

Washington, D.C.

"I am totally amazed that this . . . situation unfolding in Colorado has not been plastered all over the TV and the papers," the president said.

"It's going into its third day," an advisor said. "It's got to leak out."

The president looked at him. "And then?"

"John," Martin Tobias, the president's chief of staff said. "You don't really believe this story, do you? Some invisible cloud of evil energy controlling the town?"

The president smiled and pushed the latest communiques from the Pentagon, the CIA, the NSA, the FBI, and Army intelligence toward his longtime friend. The chief of staff read them, his expression growing more and more worried the further along he went. He got to the last page and jumped to his feet.

"A neutron bomb! Jesus Christ, John. We can't detonate a neutron bomb aboveground in Colorado. For God's sake, John!"

"Yes, Martin," the president said, his face serious. "That's it exactly: for God's sake."

Martin flushed and threw the papers on the desk. "Whatever that is out there, John, it is not, repeat, it is *not* something evil sent to us by the devil. This is not a holy war, John. The devil is not taking over the earth. God-damn, John—he wouldn't start in Willowdale, Colorado!"

"Why not? It's as good a place as any, I suppose."

"John, be reasonable. This is not like you. Look, do you realize what this would entail? You'd have to talk with the Russians—"

President John Marshall waved his friend silent. "Calm yourself, Martin. Calm down. I know all that. And since the Russian philosophy is that God does not exist, they would think it some sort of trick on our part. I've thought about that, too. Believe me, I have."

The other members of the president's inner circle sat quietly, listening to the old friends have a go at one another.

Martin put both hands on the president's desk and leaned forward. "You're really serious, aren't you? You're really going to go ahead with this . . . this . . . *insanity!*" He banged his fist on the scattered communiques.

The president stood up and laid it on the line. "I'll give you twenty-four hours to come up with an alternative plan,

207

Martin. Thirty-six hours at the maximum. Martin, the Joint Chiefs agree with me. NSC agrees. The Agency agrees. NSA agrees. The top scientists in this nation have studied printouts taken from planes from NASA . . ."

"Who the hell sent them in?"

"I did, goddamnit!" the president roared at his friend.

Martin stepped back, and the two men glared at each other for a moment. "I'd like to read those graphs."

"Hell, Martin. Your degrees are in history and political science. You wouldn't know what you were looking at."

"Did you?"

"Hell, no!" the president admitted. "Looked like a bunch of dots on the paper to me. But," he held up a warning finger. "The dots were only over Willowdale. Nowhere else. Now listen to me, Martin. Something very large and very strong and very . . . well, dangerous, is hovering over that little community. Take a couple of your nonbelievers out there with you. Go there. A plane is waiting. I anticipated this reaction from you. But do not go inside the barricades."

"Is that an order, John?"

The president shook his head. "No. I won't make it an order. You're one of the most intelligent men I have ever known, Martin. You're going to have to make that decision yourself. And while you're out there, try to find out what you can about a young man called Sand."

"Who?"

"That's a nickname. His name is Saunders."

"What's he got to do with this?"

"He's sort of, well, directing operations from the other side."

"The other side of the barricades?"

"No. The other side of the grave. He's been dead for thirty years."

Martin Tobias sat down. Heavily. He stared at the president. He cleared his throat. Shook his head and sighed. "Mr. President, sir. Old friend. With all due respect and ad-

208

miration, sir, have you lost your fucking mind?"

The others in the room braced for a storm from the president. John Marshall smiled, not taking umbrage at the remark. "I hope not, Martin. The plane is waiting at Andrews. A helicopter is waiting in Denver. Call me from Willowdale."

Martin stood up. "Oh, I shall, sir. I shall certainly do that. By all means. Yes." He looked at an aide. "Get Megan and Larry. Tell them to be ready to go in one hour. A car will pick them up."

The aide nodded and left the room.

Martin looked at the president for a moment, shook his head, and left the room. In the hallway, he paused for a moment. "Dead for thirty years and directing operations from the other side of the grave. Mysterious forces and evil voices. Zombies. I have never heard of anything so ridiculous in all my life!" He snorted and walked toward the elevator.

Outside the S.O. in Willowdale, the crowds of babbling, slobbering, mumbling, and seemingly mindless citizens of the town had gathered. They rattled at the newly installed security doors and shouted obscenities at those inside.

Many of the men urinated on the outside doors; both men and women squatted like animals and defecated on the sidewalks.

Then, in full view of those watching from the gun slits inside the office, the men and women began coupling under the bright moon and starlit skies, as often as not, men with men and women with women.

"If they start using young kids," Lt. Smith said, "I'll stop it with lead."

"Your option," Gordie told her. "I sure won't interfere."

"Fury has left the area," Howie called. "The sentries are still in place, but the Fury is gone."

Gordie and as many others as possible crowded into the

small room.

"Gone where?" the sheriff asked.

Howie shook his head. "I don't know. But it is definitely gone."

"Why'd it leave is what I'd like to know," Watts said.

The words popped onto the screen: *It's growing stronger and stronger. Stronger than it's ever been. It's checking out the valley.*

Sand? Howie typed.

Yes.

What do we do?

The townspeople, many of them, at least, are now no more than walking dead. They're mindless. Fury did this deliberately. It wants you all to kill in defense of your lives. It wants you all because you are the strongest ones.

A sudden very bright blip appeared on another screen for an instant, then was gone.

Howie typed: What was that?

The cops who were manning that particular barricade are no more. Fury is spreading its territory.

"I'll get on the horn," Watts said. "Tell the troopers to pull back." He looked at Howie. "Ask Sand how far back."

Howie asked.

A half-mile each twenty-four hours.

Howie asked: Is that good for us; Fury spreading itself out?

Maybe, the word appeared on the screen. *It's too soon to tell. Don't use your radio to warn the cops. Howie, you'll have to hack into the state police computer.*

No problem, Howie typed as he grinned.

"Do it," Gordie ordered.

Talk to you later, Sand's words appeared.

The screen went dark.

Howie went to work.

Martin Tobias and his people were boarding a plane at Andrews Air Force Base.

In the Oval Office, the president picked up a phone, hesitated, then—bypassing the White House operator—punched out the numbers.

At a top secret listening post, deep in the Rocky Mountains, a CIA staffer sat behind his huge bank of computers and watched as Howie hacked his way into the Colorado State Patrol's computers.

The CIA man smiled. "The kid is good. Damn good. We need to start talking to him as soon as this is over," he said to Gen. Brasher.

"Isn't ten years old a bit young?" the general said, the sarcasm thick.

"Naw. Just right. Colleges give football players money, cars, and pussy to play stupid games. We'll give the kid a new computer. Everything balances out in the end, General."

Brasher shook his head at the man's logic. But it was just logical enough to stall any argument. "Can you talk to the boy?"

"Oh, yeah. When the time comes." The CIA man was not military. *Yes, sirs* and *No, sirs* were rare from his lips.

At the White House, after completing his phone call, the president took a mild sleeping tablet before retiring. He knew he had to get at least a few hours' sleep.

In Los Angeles, the bureau chiefs of two major networks were rapidly working themselves into a blue funk over the abrupt disappearances of their reporters and crews. They could get nothing from Willowdale. For once, they were cooperating with each other, talking on the phone.

"If I don't hear from Jill by dawn, I'm going out there myself," one said. "You want to come with me?"

"Something big and funky and ugly is going down, Bob. Our man in Washington reports some strange goings-on in and around the White House."

"Andy? What the hell does Willowdale, Colorado have to do with the White House?"

"I don't know. You really want to wait until the morning to leave?"

211

"Hell, no. Match you to see whose Lear we use?"

"Come with me. I'll meet you at the airport in an hour."

The prime minister of Canada was awakened by the ringing of his telephone. The United States secretary of state was on the other end. The PM listened for a moment, spoke a few words, then hung up.

He sat up in bed and rubbed his face. "Holy Mother of God," he muttered. "A neutron bomb!"

Chapter Three

"Sand said the Fury wants us," Gordie mused aloud. "Because we are the strongest. Does it think that if we kill in defense of our lives, that will weaken us?"

"It kills and grows stronger, because it feeds on evil energy from souls," Watts picked it up. "Sure. Wait a minute! What does it do with the . . . well, compassionate souls it consumes? What I'm thinking doesn't say much for the human race as a whole."

"Perhaps," Sunny said, "that is why the only Being that could have prevented this, is doing nothing."

"I can't believe that," Jill said. "Babies are innocent."

"They are also insured a place in Heaven," she was reminded by Hillary. "But Jesus said: suffer little children, and forbid them not to come unto me; for of such is the kingdom of Heaven."

Those in the room became silent, each with their own thoughts.

Norris finally broke the silence. "I don't know whether it's in the Bible or not, but there is that bit about God helping those who help themselves."

"Aesop," Bergman said. "The gods help them that help themselves."

"While we're on the subject," Dr. Anderson said, "there is a fable about the eagle who was stricken with a dart. And when the eagle saw the fashion of the shaft, said, 'With our own feathers, not by others, are we now smitten.'"

Angel thought about that for a moment, then said, "God

is giving us a way out."

All looked at her. Dean said, "Go ahead, Angel. Finish it."

"Ourselves," the girl said. "But I don't think that's all of it. I think He sent Sand to help us."

"Or Michael," Watts said with a smile. "The mercenary. God's bodyguard. And it would be like Sand to buddy up to him."

"Kick ass and take names!" Howie yelled from his room. "That sounds like Sand."

Watts grinned and shook his head. "Sand's made another convert. Even dead, people still rally to him. In all my years, I never met a man like him."

"I cannot believe," Shriver said, "that in this entire town, we are the only ones He would choose to save. What's so special about us?"

Someone rattled at the door, and cursing filled the air. Somewhere close, a man screamed in pain and a woman laughed.

"I don't think God picked us at all," Howie called. "I think we all chose to save ourselves. We might not have known exactly what we were doing at the time . . . from a religious point of view. But it worked out that way."

"The priest was a man of God," Hillary pointed out. "Yet he died horribly."

"Perhaps he was not what he seemed," Sunny told them. "Or perhaps that was his fate. Richard stressed fate several times when I spoke with him."

"I've listened to a part of those tapes you made with Richard," Gordie said. "There's something in there that puzzles me. At one point, he said something like, 'Don't be afraid when this is over, for if you survive, you might see that it all happened in the blink of an eye.' "

"There's lots about this I don't understand," Mack grumbled.

"Fury is coming!" Howie yelled.

They all felt the Fury's presence. Stronger than ever. The

air seemed charged with static.

I JUST HAD A LITTLE SNACK. IT WAS QUITE DE-LICIOUS. It burped and shotguns and pistols and ammunition clattered to the floor. Several badges shone amid the pile of weapons. THE INTELLIGENCE OF COPS HAS GREATLY IMPROVED SINCE MY LAST VISIT, I AM HAPPY TO REPORT.

"Why do you say that?" Watts asked. He had gotten over feeling like a fool for talking to empty air.

HOW QUICKLY THEY RESPONDED AFTER I DINED ON ONE OUTPOST, THAT'S WHAT I MEAN. COPS USED TO BE THE DUMBEST FUCKERS IN THE UNIVERSE.

Naturally, no one had anything to say to that. But all breathed a sigh of relief at the knowledge that the Fury did not know who had tipped the state patrol.

HOWIE, MY BOY, WHAT ARE YOU AND YOUR SISTER DOING ALL COOPED UP IN THAT LITTLE ROOM?

"Playing space games, sir," Howie said.

ISN'T THAT SWEET? SHOOTING DOWN ALL THE BAD GUYS WITH YOUR LITTLE FLASH GORDON RAY GUNS. OH, I JUST LOVE IT. WELL, BYE ALL!

Howie stepped out, after checking to make sure the Fury had really left them. "It knows nothing of the advancement and technology over the past thirty years. Nothing at all. It would have said Luke Skywalker or Darth Vader or Captain Kirk or Spock. But it's locked into the fifties." He walked back into his computer room and sat down behind his terminals, typing.

Sand. What does all this mean? How can that knowledge help us?

The screen quickly flashed: *That is something I cannot tell you, Howie. You have figured out why you survived thus far; it's up to you to put the rest together.*

You won't help us?

I can't.

215

I understand.

"I don't," Gordie spoke from behind the boy. "What do you mean, Howie—you understand?"

"Obviously, he is forbidden."

The screen flashed, and words appeared. *This could well be not the end, Howie, but the beginning.*

Howie typed: Now I don't understand.

Go forth.

The screen went dark, as if waiting.

"And spread the word," Gordie whispered, and Howie typed.

One word appeared on the screen: Amen.

Megan LeMasters and Larry Adams had been briefed on the flight from Andrews to Stapleton Field in Denver. Since Megan professed to be an agnostic, and Larry an avowed atheist, both thought the situation—whatever it really was—amusing, as did Martin Tobias.

All three had a good laugh.

They stopped laughing over the matter, when they got to Willowdale and found the state patrol barricades had been moved even further out from the town.

"Why?" Martin asked.

"We lost six people to that . . . thing last night, sir," a captain of state patrol told him. "Sheriff Rivera ordered us to pull back a half a mile."

"What happened to your people, Captain?"

"They were dissolved, sir."

Martin arched one eyeball in visible skepticism. Before he could pursue the dissolved bit, their conversation was halted by the arrival of news reporters, camera crews, and several bureau chiefs, from both coasts.

A microphone was stuck under the nose of Martin Tobias. "What is going on in Willowdale, Mr. Tobias? And why is the White House involved? And how?"

From behind the barricades, Gordie and Maj. Jackson,

along with Norris and Bergman, leaned up against cars and watched and listened.

"We're in for it now," Bergman said. "And they're playing right into the hands of the Fury."

"Yeah," Gordie glumly agreed. "That's what the Fury wanted all along: modern knowledge. And that is something we cannot allow it to have."

Gordie walked to the barricades, a riot gun in his hands. He faced the gathering crowd. "I'll be very brief, ladies and gentlemen. My name is Sheriff Gordie Rivera, and I will personally shoot anybody who tries to cross these barricades."

Martin turned to face the sheriff. "Do you know who I am, young man?"

"Yeah, I know who you are. And I don't particularly give a damn. Captain," he spoke to the patrolman. "Keep these people on your side of the barricades."

"Gordie, I can't shoot the president's chief of staff, for Christ's sake!"

"If you don't shoot him, I will."

"Why don't you want us in there, Sheriff?" Megan asked.

"Get those reporters away from here, Captain," Gordie said, ignoring Megan.

"Gordie, how?" the captain pleaded. "It's a free country."

Gordie turned to the men behind him, motioning them up to the barricades. "Gentlemen, you all know the situation. I wish to speak to the president's man in private."

He waited for the Fury to speak. When it did not, Gordie knew it would not—not yet. This was what it wanted: for him to look like a fool. It was not going to tip its hand to the outside world. Not yet.

"Shoot the first reporter that follows us along the barricades," Gordie ordered his men. Bergman, Norris, and Jackson raised their shotguns. Reluctantly, very reluctantly, the state patrolmen followed suit.

"You wouldn't dare!" a bureau chief hollered.

217

"The hell I won't," Bergman warned.

Cameras were recording it all.

"This is an outrage!" a reporter yelled. "I'll see you in court for this, Sheriff."

Gordie smiled, and Martin made a mental note of the smile. "For a fact, buddy, we are looking at some judgement."

"You damn right."

Martin walked away from the crowded barricades, motioning Gordie to follow him. Away from the others and with the barricades between them, Martin said, "Would you like to bring me up-to-date, Sheriff?"

"You'll report to the president of the United States and not to the press?"

"That is correct. You have my word. I shall have nothing of substance to say to the press. I will have to make some sort of statement, certainly, but I am sure you are aware of any government officials' ability to utilize double-talk."

Gordie smiled at the man. "Oh, yes. I've used a bit of that myself, from time to time."

"No doubt." Martin's remark was offered drily, but softened with a returning smile.

Gordie spoke for several minutes, speaking quickly and as succinctly as possible, leveling totally with the president's man.

Martin Tobias did not change expression, so Gordie did not know if the man believed what he was hearing, or thought him to be a raving nut.

When Gordie finished, Martin asked, "How many dead do you have, Sheriff?"

"At last count, over three hundred."

"I knew it had to be a great many. The odor is, ah, pungent."

"Very."

"And you are convinced that this . . . problem is something supernatural?"

"Yes. I am fully convinced of that, sir. I was not at first.

But when some invisible force picks you up, personally, and tosses you around a room. Well . . ."

"Yes. I get your point. That might convince me as well. And you really think that you are in contact with a dead man? This Sand person?"

"I know we are."

"Very well. I see your dilemma, Sheriff. I really do. I'm not saying I believe all that you've told me. But I can see why you don't want this story to be spread all over the world."

"And . . . ?"

"I don't know yet, Sheriff."

"That's an honest reply. Mr. Tobias, while we are talking over here, and have the attention of the press, one of my people has passed a box of videotapes of Sand's story, several boxes of computer disks containing Howie's work, and all the transmissions that have passed between . . . one world and the other, to a trooper. They have just been put in your car. Go back to your motel room and review them, sir. Then make up your mind."

"Sheriff, even if they prove everything you've said to be true, that still leaves us with one hell of a big problem, doesn't it?"

"Go on."

Martin waved Megan and Larry over and very quickly laid out the problem. "Suggestions, people?" he asked. "And make it quick."

"You're buying this fairytale, sir?" Megan asked.

Gordie just about lost his cool. He just about reached over the barricades and slapped the piss out of her. He controlled himself with a visible effort, an effort that did not slip by Megan.

"Sheriff," she quickly said. "I am not implying that you are lying. Not at all. I'm sorry, if you took it that way. What I am saying is, that you must be under a great deal of stress."

"You can say that again, lady. If I wasn't so concerned

219

about your safety, and the safety and survival of the world, I'd ask you to bring your uppity ass in here and see for yourself."

Martin's smile was tiny. It vanished when Megan said, "I'd like that, Sheriff."

"You're a damn fool, lady," Gordie told her.

"I should like to accompany her, sir," Larry offered.

Martin looked at Gordie. "Sheriff?"

Gordie gripped the barricades. "Haven't any of you been listening? Once you're in here, you can't get out! And this is what the Fury wants. He, it, whatever that thing is, must have more modern day knowledge before it makes its big move. That's a guess. Guess or not, I'm trying to prevent that."

"When is your term of office up, Sheriff?" Larry asked.

Gordie sighed, knowing what the man was implying. "I was elected by an overwhelming majority. I have good reason to believe I will be, or would be, unopposed in the next election. So that won't hold water. People, listen to me: don't you think Maj. Jackson and his team would leave if they could? Can't you smell the stink of the dead? We're going to have a major health hazard in here pretty damn quick. Do you think I'd risk the lives of Angel and Howie for personal gain? My God, what kind of a man do you think I am?"

Larry flushed and opened his mouth. "Sheriff, I did not mean to . . ."

"Shut your goddamn mouth, pretty boy!" Gordie's frayed temper broke. "Now you all listen to me. We've got to get the Fury, all of the Fury, in one spot, and it's going to have to be coordinated right down to the last degree, and then it has to be destroyed. I've told you what will destroy it." He placed several sheets of paper on the barricade. "That is the list of everyone in town—as far as we now know—still possessing their facilities; the adults and the two kids. Everything else is spelled out on those pages."

"Gordie!" Bergman called out after a walkie-talkie

crackled. "Fury is near."

"What the hell is a fury?" a reporter shouted.

Martin Tobias had not taken his eyes off the sheriff. Gordie's expression did not change at the shout. Martin thought: the man is either a pathological liar, or the coolest person under pressure I have ever seen.

"I demand to know what a fury is?" another reporter yelled. "The public has a right to know."

"Assholes," Gordie muttered, cutting his eyes to the man.

"Some of them are that, naturally," Martin said. "But most of them are sincere in their beliefs."

"It's backed off," Bergman called.

"What's backed off?" a reporter yelled. "Damnit, somebody better start giving us some answers."

"This . . . thing called fury," Megan said. "It's gone?"

"Not far," Gordie told her. "But we can talk. Howie seems to think, from computations he's done, that last night's foray stretched it pretty thin. Howie thinks it's going to take it twenty-four hours to get back to full strength. Then it will expand further."

Martin had tentatively, hesitantly, picked up the sheets of paper and placed them in the inside pocket of his suit coat. "And these papers?"

"I just told you. They explain, as briefly as possible, what our situation is. They also outline our knowledge of what will happen to us if . . . the ultimate decision is reached."

"You are all willing to die?" Larry spoke the words softly.

"That is correct. But I wish the kids could be saved."

"Get that gun out of my face!" a reporter yelled at a trooper.

"Back your ass off, buddy," the trooper told him.

The reporter backed off.

Martin sighed audibly. "I came out here fully prepared to face a nut, Sheriff. My mind was made up, and that is something I rarely do without having all the facts going in. I have to conclude that you people in there are awfully brave. I salute you, Sheriff. All of you."

Before anyone could stop her, Megan pushed open the barricade and stepped inside, standing beside Gordie. She closed the wooden barricade.

"Someone from the White House has to be inside, Martin," she said, her voice calm. "I am an authority in quantum physics. You know that. If the decision is made, you're going to need someone in here directing the operations." She smiled. "On this side of the . . . grave." She stumbled on the last bit. "I just nominated myself and seconded the motion."

"You young fool!" Martin snapped at her.

"You are a very brave person, Megan," Larry said stiffly.

Megan forced another smile. "On the contrary, Larry. I am so scared I'm about to pee my pants!"

Chapter Four

"My suggestion is this, Sheriff," Megan said, out of earshot of the reporters at the barricades. "It isn't very original, but it's the best I can come up with on the spur of the moment."

"I'm damn sure open for suggestions." They walked on, further away from the crowded barricades.

"Plague. On the order of bubonic. You have a doctor still alive in here?"

"Two of them. Anderson and Shriver. And two RN's. Shriver is not . . . stable, but he's getting better. Go on, Megan."

"The plague has been codenamed Fury. For want of a better word. See where I'm going?"

"Yes. I like it."

STUPID CUNT. THAT ISN'T GOING TO FOOL ANYONE FOR VERY LONG.

"Fury," Gordie said. "Meet Megan."

Megan was openly, visibly, startled. Her mouth dropped open.

YOU OUGHT TO STICK A DICK IN THERE, GREASEBALL.

Megan closed her mouth.

GREAT SET OF JUGS ON THAT BROAD.

"I thought you were getting your life story recorded, Fury?"

I TOOK A BREAK. HAVE TO CHECK OUT THE NEW PUSSY.

Gordie looked at Megan. Her face was flushed, but she had a mean look in her eyes. She was rapidly regaining her composure.

She'll do, Gordie thought.

SHE'S NOT BAD. BUT HER ASS ISN'T AS GREAT AS JILL'S.

Their hair crackled slightly as the Fury left them.

"Pure energy, Megan?"

"I don't know. It certainly contains a great deal of electricity."

"That's energy, isn't it?"

Megan smiled. "Well, Sheriff, how much do you know about physics?"

"About as much as I do about plumbing."

"And that is . . . ?"

"Shit runs downhill, and you get paid on Friday."

Megan laughed aloud. She found herself liking Sheriff Rivera. "You're keeping your sense of humor, Sheriff. That's good."

"Call me Gordie. Let's get in the car and get away from that gang of reporters."

Driving away from the barricades, back toward the office, Bergman and Norris following in another vehicle, Megan said, "Energy is one of the two fundamental concepts of physical science. Energy, Sheriff, is defined as the capacity for doing work. It's a very intimate relationship. You see, no work is possible without energy stored up, unless work has been done with the body. You with me?"

"How in the hell did you ever get into politics? Or better yet, why?"

"Don't change the subject. It's important that you understand this. There are two kinds of energy: potential and kinetic."

"Which one is the Fury?"

"Be quiet."

"Yes, ma' am."

"Potential energy is when the position of a body is such

224

as to make work possible. Kinetic is when the body is capable of doing work as a result of its motion. You with me, Sheriff?"

"Megan, the Fury is comprised, composed — made up — of the souls of the dead. That's what Sand says and I think he's in a damn good position to know."

"I'm not disputing that, Sheriff."

"Gordie. Call me Gordie."

"Gordie. All right. Now this is important. Listen."

"Wait. My head is starting to hurt. I'm a cop, not a scientist. You and Howie get together."

The others listened as Megan and Howie talked. When Megan had reached the point she had made with Gordie, Howie said, "I understand that, Megan. Kinetic energy, due to its motion, is a gradually diminishing one as the velocity falls off, till the extreme height is reached, when the kinetic energy becomes zero."

"That's true, Howie. As the body rises, it gains in potential energy, or energy of position, till at its highest point this energy is at its maximum."

"I know all that, Megan. And that there is an exact theoretical equivalence between K at the bottom and P at the top; and that at any point in the path, the sum of the energies is equal to that same number."

"What in the name of God are they talking about?" Watts whispered to Gordie.

"Hell, don't ask me."

Sunny looked at him. "That's just basic knowledge, Gordie. They're just feeling each other out. That change of energy they just discussed is a simple textbook case, pointing out one of the fundamental laws of physical science known as the conservation of energy."

Gordie and Watts looked at her as if she had suddenly grown horns and a tail.

Megan and Howie heard her. "Hey, that's great, Sunny!"

225

Howie said. "Yeah, you're right."

The computer keys in the gun vault rattled.

"Sand," Howie said, leading the way. The others gathered around him.

Howie sat down and typed: Sand?

The screen flashed: *Joey.*

And Morg. Tell the kid I'm here, too.

You just did, Morg. Now be quiet.

"They must be doing that with their minds," Megan breathed. "My God! I'm actually conversing with the dead."

Howie typed: Hi, Morg.

Hiya, short-stuff. Look, don't sweat this gig too much. We're gonna help you.

Howie grinned and typed: Okay, Morg. That's good.

Morg, will you stop mucking about? We've got work to do.

I swear, Joey. I thought once we got here, you might start actin' more civil. You just as bad as ever.

"What the hell?" Gordie asked.

Watts grinned. "Joey and Morg are at it again. You'll see."

Howie typed: What is going on, Joey?

Morg is pouting. He'll get over it. He doesn't have choice in the matter. Not where we are. Howie, listen. Work on this: the total amount of energy in any body may be neither increased nor diminished without outside influence, but it may be transformed without absolute loss into any of the forms of energy to which it is susceptible. That

The screen suddenly went blank, and then dark, as if all power had been lost on the other side.

Howie frantically typed: Joey? What happened?

The screen remained dark and void of any words of reply.

"What's going on?" Maj. Jackson asked.

"I don't even know what they're talking about," Gordie bitched.

"Well, that's basic," Megan said. "What he, it, Joey just said. That law of universal application. I don't understand what he's trying to tell us."

"I don't either," Sunny said.

"Damn sure makes it unanimous," Watts muttered.

"Howie, would you print out all that Joey has told you?" Gordie asked. "Including the last conversation. I want to look at it."

"Sure, Sheriff."

"What are you thinking?" Sunny asked.

"I don't know." Gordie read and reread. "Just exactly what is a neutron, anyway?"

"One of the elementary particles of an atom," Howie told him. He was keeping one eye on another screen, watching for the Fury.

"They are also readily absorbed," Megan picked it up. "They are uncharged, with approximately the same mass as protons. A few neutrons decay into a proton, an electron, and a neutrino. Has a half-life of about thirteen minutes. That's one of the reasons a neutron bomb is better, if that is the correct usage, than your conventional atomic weapons."

"But it's still a thermonuclear device?"

"Oh, yes."

"I see. Sort of. Alright. Was Joey trying to tell us that we don't have to destroy the Fury? That we could instead contain it, maybe?"

"How?" Megan asked.

"I don't know. I'm asking you." He held up the printout. "I don't understand any of this. Was he saying that we, as a people, could harness the force of the Fury?"

"I see what you're getting at," Megan said. "But, no, it's a good thought, but no. That would be impossible; our technology is not that advanced."

"It came from outer space, didn't it?" Angel asked, leaning up against the doorjamb, eating a peanut butter and jelly sandwich.

Howie gave her a dirty look, then abruptly his look changed to one of confusion. "Well, maybe that's not all that far off the mark."

"What do you mean, Howie?" Megan asked the boy.

"Well, we really don't know where it came from." He looked at Sunny. "Has it told you?"

She shook her head. "No. And I have asked it several times."

"Scientists hypothesize that certain heavenly objects are, in fact, collapsed stars," Megan said. "They consist of immense numbers of densely packed neutrons."

"That's it!" Howie shouted, startling them all. "That's how it's so powerful. It's a neutron star. Listen, the surface gravity of a neutron star is something like one-hundred-billion times stronger than the surface of Earth. Let me back up. It was a neutron star. It evolved over the centuries into something evil. Megan?"

"Yes. Perhaps. Howie, you and Sunny hear this: pulsar. A pulsar star, a stellar remnant, pulses off and on at the rate of thirty times a second. From its magnetic poles, the pulsar radiates beams of energy that span most of the electromagnetic spectrum, *including,* the radio and visible wavelengths."

Sunny said, "The Fury has, over the centuries, evolved into a thinking mass, and has also learned to refine the radio pulsations it still contains from its original . . . well, shall we say, place in the scheme of things."

"Yes," Megan said. "Let's start from that. Let's assume, until proven otherwise, that the Fury is a stellar remnant. That meet with everybody's approval?"

Gordie looked at Watts. Both men shrugged. "Call it Harry, the Hairy Ape, if you want to," Watts said. "Does this get us any closer to killing the damn thing?"

"Maybe, sir," Howie said. "If we may continue with this

228

theorization, I would pose this question to those older than I: Why has this town, the county seat, never been able to keep a radio station on the air? Isn't the town large enough to support one?"

Watts walked to a boarded-up window and looked out of the gun slit. "That radio station was first put on the air back in '54, I think. Maybe '53. It never was worth a damn. Had a dozen owners over the years. No one was ever able to make a go of it."

"Why?" Megan asked.

Watts scratched the side of his face. "Technical problems. No one could keep the damn thing on the air. You'd be listening to one record, and all of a sudden another turntable would start, that record overriding the one that was playing . . . no matter what the disc jockey did with the control board. Weird things happened out there, too. Disc jockeys reported things levitating, ghostly sounds, all sorts of weird stuff. The FCC even agreed, due to the mountains surrounding the valley, to give it more power. That's about a six-hundred-foot antenna out there . . ."

Watts paused and faced the group. "The antenna?"

"It certainly could play a part in this matter," Megan said. "Where is the antenna located?"

Watts smiled, but it was not a pleasant smile. "It's located up near the old ghost town of Thunder."

Howie turned as the computer keys clattered. One word was printed on the screen.

Bingo!

Martin Tobias and Larry Adams sat in the motel room and reviewed everything they had found in their car. Neither man had spoken for over an hour. Finally, removing his glasses and rubbing his eyes, Martin broke the silence. "Mind-boggling!"

They then watched the dubs of the videotaping. Both closely inspected the young men called Sand and Joey.

229

Martin backed the tape up several times. It was depressing. He did not like to see such obvious talent and intelligence—such as that possessed by Sand and Joey—go to waste.

Martin was also slightly amused at the expressions on Larry's face. Larry was from an old blueblood New England family; everything right by the book. In Larry's upbringing, there was a correct way to do everything, and that is the way it must be done. One simply did not fly in the face of accepted mores.

There was no place for rebels.

And Sand was a rebel.

Larry had been appalled by the method of fighting used by Sand's Pack members.

Larry's idea of fighting—if one simply must engage in that barbarous practice—was to have seconds, put on the gloves, with a referee in the ring and refreshments ready when time was called, and fight like gentlemen.

Sand's method of fighting included no such niceties. Kick your enemy in the balls, and then stomp his damn face in was Sand's philosophy.

Larry finally rose from his chair and stretched. "How?" he asked. "Could such a person possibly meet with God's approval?"

Martin smiled. "Why, Larry! I thought you were an atheist?"

"That's assuming there is a God," Larry quickly covered his verbal tracks.

"Of course. Now, back to the business at hand; if we ever left it. Suggestions?"

"What to tell the president?"

"Yes."

"I think the president should call in our secretary of state, and the ambassadors from Canada, England, Mexico, and Russia, and level with them."

"Totally?"

"Totally."

Martin nodded his head. "See that these computer printouts and video tapes are in the president's hands today, Larry. Advise the motel manager that we are taking over this entire wing. Arrange for tight, very tight, security. I want a computer team in here fifteen minutes ago, with lines covering all bases, especially that boy's computers. Go, Larry."

Larry paused at the door, a serious expression on his face. "You know when it's really going to get interesting, Martin?"

The older man waited.

"When the preachers get word of this."

Martin suppressed a shudder. "You're right. I hadn't thought of that. My God, they'll be pouring in here by the busload."

"Yes. With many of them speaking in tongues and whooping and hollering and laying on of hands and snake-handling, and turning the entire matter into a carnival."

"Perhaps we could get one of them to heal the Fury?" Martin suggested with a straight face.

Larry was startled for a moment. Then he smiled. "Of course, Martin. Surely we must ask."

Martin was on the phone to the president before the door had closed.

"Look," Hillary said, pointing to the TV. "Sand all bandaged up in bed."

"I thought we saw that yesterday?" Bos questioned. "I know we did."

"He's asleep," Pat said. "He's dreaming."

"My God!" Leon breathed. "I can see the dream!"

Sand was standing on the crest of a small hill overlooking a cemetery, watching a funeral service. Two graves had been dug, one smaller than the other. Rain ripped earthward in near blinding sheets, miniature silver shrouds from a blackened sky. A dog howled in the distance. Morg squatted about fifty yards behind Sand.

"What is that . . . thing swirling around Sand?" Megan asked. "It's almost human in form."

"Maybe that's the Force Richard talked about," Sunny said. "He said that when death is imminent, the Force is almost visible."

"And that the Force could probably stop the Fury," Howie added, walking up to look at the screen.

"Yes. But probably won't this time."

The dream sequence faded. The TV screen darkened of its own volition.

Watts shivered and wiped his sweaty face with a handkerchief.

"What's the matter, Al?" Gordie asked.

"I was at Robin's funeral. And that," he pointed to the TV set, "was exactly the way it was. Sand knew his destiny, and the destinies of his friends, long before they were played out. It's eerie."

"Sit down, Al," Dr. Anderson said. "You don't look well."

Watts sat.

"What Sand was telling us, Howie," Megan said, "about the antenna on the mountain. Was he referring to the antenna—or the mountain?"

"Or both?" Sunny added. "And why was Joey cut off the way he was? Did the Fury do it?"

"No," the boy replied. "I think a much higher power did that."

"God?" Jackson asked. The boy shrugged.

"Perhaps there are some things they—Sand and the others—are not permitted to divulge," Megan offered.

"That would be my guess," the boy said. "Sand and the others, those that followed him, were chance-takers, so I've concluded. They tried to go over the limits placed on them—where they are—and got caught." The keys to a computer rattled. Howie ran to the computer room, the others behind him.

The words on Sand's screen read: *You are correct in your*

assumption. We do have limits.

Howie typed: Can you help us further?

Perhaps.

How are you monitored?

The screen was wordless for a few seconds, then: *That would be unexplainable to you. But does an eagle understand the winds that sigh around the mountain and any object that might be there?*

Howie laughed. "He's still taking chances. It's both the mountain and the antenna." He typed: What is the Fury doing?

Resting. Its strength was taxed by the enlarging of territory.

Watts said, "Ask him if Robin and Tuddie and Jane are there with him?"

Yes, the word flashed on the screen. *All as well as could be expected. Forever. Talk to you later.*

Megan shuddered. "The endless enormity of it all is unnerving."

"Yes," Watts said. "Those were my thoughts, too."

"At least we know there is life after death," Bos said.

"And we're much closer to experiencing it than I would prefer to be," Gordie added.

Chapter Five

The motel had filled up rapidly, with reporters taking one entire wing and government personnel taking another wing. It made the motel manager very happy when he discovered his motel would be filled to capacity indefinitely.

It made him nervous when dark-suited men with suspicious bulges in their jackets started filling up rooms on the government side of the building.

"FBI?" he asked one man.

The man smiled. "If that's what you want me to be."

"Secret Service?"

"If it makes you happy."

"Forget I asked."

Martin Tobias walked to the newly set up computer room. "Have you established a link with the boy yet?"

"I'm ready to go whenever you are."

"Contact him."

Howie read the simple message and typed: You may be free and open with your messages. The Fury does not understand computers. It has absolutely no understanding of the concept.

"This is a ten-year-old boy?" the computer operator asked.

"So I'm told. Ask him how things went last night."

It was very quiet. Sand says the Fury is very tired and probably won't regain its full strength for another ten to twelve hours.

"Who is Sand, Mister Tobias?"

"A dead man. Been dead for thirty years. He's directing operations from the other side of the grave."

The computer expert from NSA twisted in his chair and stared at the chief of staff for a long moment. "Are you sure this isn't a CIA operation?"

"Positive. Ask the boy if they need anything."

Out, Howie typed.

Martin smiled. "That's a very brave little boy in there, Hank. Tell him we're trying."

The teletype in the room began clattering. Martin walked over to it and read, a grimace on his face.

"Trouble?" Hank asked.

"In a manner of speaking. Willowdale was the lead story on every network's morning news program."

"We're in for it now."

WHERE IS MY SWEET CHICKIE BABY?

"If you're referring to Sunny, she's resting," Gordie said.

GET HER ASS UP. I WISH TO CONTINUE WITH MY LIFE STORY.

"Your wish is my command, your majesty."

SARCASTIC SPIC. I DON'T KNOW WHY I CONTINUE PUTTING UP WITH YOU.

"Perhaps it's because you're really very fond of me?"

Gordie was slapped out of his chair by an invisible hand. With the taste of blood in his mouth, he stared up into the air.

THAT'S HOW FOND I AM OF YOU, MUCHACHO. NOW GET ON YOUR DONKEY AND GET SUNNY OUT HERE.

"I'm here," Sunny said. "Am I going to be bothered walking up the street to the newspaper office?"

OF COURSE NOT. NOT AS LONG AS YOU DON'T DISPLEASE ME.

It had been Sunny's idea to use the newspaper offices for further interviews with Fury. The being had not objected to

235

the change in locale. It had said that was a good idea, since it preferred being alone with Sunny.

Sunny walked through the litter toward the newspaper offices, one block away. Bodies lay bloated in the street. Jill and Dean walked with her. All of them carried small tape recorders and notepads. And all of them tried to ignore the sights and smells of the dead.

"We're clear," Howie called.

Gordie thanked him and looked over at Watts. Watts waggled a finger at him, and Gordie walked over.

"We can't be alone in this thing, Gordie. There have to be others in the town like us. Perhaps they're hiding."

"Maybe. What do you suggest?"

"While Fury is occupied, why don't we have a look around. House-to-house in a designated area."

"All right. We can use gathering up the bodies and bagging them as a cover."

"All the military have volunteered. You were sleeping when this idea came to me."

"Jackson needs to stay here to decode all the messages that are coming in. The rest can come along with the deputies."

"You ready?"

"As I'll ever be."

They filled up the beds of pickup trucks with body bags and moved out, a stake-bed bob truck moving out with them to haul away the bodies.

It was to be a gruesome day for all concerned, in more ways than one.

The men and women who were assigned to the body-bagging detail were forced to wear gas masks. In many cases they had to shoot carrion birds to get at the bodies, the big birds protecting their meals savagely. Against talons that could rip flesh like tissue paper, the body-baggers had no choice but to shoot any they could not shoo away. The bodies had to be cleared; it was now a major health hazard.

Watts, Lt. Kathy Smith, Chief Deputy Lee Evans, and

Gordie started a house-to-house search along one block.

Gordie and Kathy did not have to enter the first house. They could smell death from the front door. Kathy moved to a window on the front porch and looked in. She shook her head.

"Slaughterhouse in there," she said. "People literally ripped apart."

Gordie lifted his handy walkie-talkie. Then he slowly lowered it, an odd look on his face.

"What's the matter?" Kathy asked.

"I was going to order the power cut to any house that's empty. But maybe that's not a good idea." His smile was a grim curving of the lips.

"What do you mean?"

He lifted the walkie-talkie. "Mack, ask the whiz kid if we're clear."

Howie had grinned when he was codenamed that the day before.

"You're clear, One."

"When we decide to make our break, Kathy, say several hours before we do—if we do—we move out and turn on every gas and electric stove and heater in every house in this town. But we don't light the gas."

She smiled, catching on. "Lots of explosions and a lot of fires with heavy smoke, right, Sheriff?"

"You got it."

"I like it."

"Senior to One," Gordie's walkie-talkie popped.

"Come on, Senior."

Watts said, "Found a young couple. They seem to be all right. Just scared."

"Meet you on the corner."

"Gene and Donna Harvey," Lee told him. "He's a mechanic down at the Ford place; she teaches school."

"Get us out of here!" Donna's plea was almost a scream.

"We can't leave, Miss Harvey. The Fury won't let us."

"The Fury?" Gene asked.

237

"It's a long story. Lee, take them back to the station, and brief them on the way."

When they had pulled away in Lee's unit, Kathy said, "They look in pretty good shape to me."

"Yeah," Gordie said. "Too good a shape, for my way of thinking." He lifted his communicator and called in on tach, hoping that Lee would not switch over.

"Mack, keep an eye on the pair that Lee is bringing in."

"That's ten-four, One."

They moved on to the next house, the three of them staying together. Another slaughter-pen inside.

"Whiz kid says to watch it, One!" Mack's voice crackled from the speaker.

AND WHAT MAY I ASK ARE YOU DOING, RIVERA?

"Bagging up the dead, Fury. Do you object to our doing that?"

I SUPPOSE NOT. IF YOU INSIST UPON BEING SO FASTIDIOUS. WHERE ARE YOUR BAGS?

"In that truck right over there." Gordie pointed.

The Fury sighed. YOU ARE SO TRUTHFUL YOU MAKE ME SICK, RIVERA. AREN'T YOU PEOPLE GOING TO FIGHT ME?

"Well, goddamnit, *how!*" Gordie yelled. "Yeah. You put yourself in human form, and I'll kick your stupid ass all over this town, you turd!"

Howling with laughter, the Fury left them.

"You took a chance," Watts told him.

"Pissed me off," Gordie said. "Come on, let's start bagging up the bodies, and look busy, in case that bastard decides to return."

"I wonder how things are going on the outside?" Kathy asked.

"Not as bad as in here, that's for sure."

The Rev. Willie Magee had traveled long and hard from

238

Louisiana. He had set up his post under a shade tree, and with Bible in hand, and a few of his faithful flock gathered around, Magee went about drawing a crowd.

"Oh, Lord!" he cried to the heavens (and any reporter that might be listening). "There is evil in that there town yonder." He pointed toward Willowdale. "Evil, I say! And it must be cut out like a cancer from the flesh!"

"Amen, Brother!" his flock called.

"When the roll is called up yonder," Sister Adele sang sweetly.

Willie cut a good eye toward Sister Adele. Woman had a great ass on her, and could give a blow job that would put a vacuum cleaner to shame.

"When the roll is called up yonder, I'll be there," Sister Adele finished.

"Thank you, Sister," Willie said. "We ain't gettin' no action here, gang. I think we picked us a bad spot. That damn preacher from Mississippi is drawin' all the crowds."

The Rev. Silas Marrner was working up a sweat, really putting on a show for the folks, and quite a few had gathered around.

Silas was jumping around on the ground like a man possessed. Speaking in tongues, as he sought to purge the town of Willowdale from whatever evil had befallen it.

Further down the barricades, Preacher Harold Jewelweed had traveled night and day from West Virginia to get to Willowdale. Along with some of his faithful flock and two crates of rattlesnakes.

Fortunately for Mister Jewelweed, the troopers did not know, yet, what was in the crates.

All that was about to change . . . among other things.

"My faithful flock," Jewelweed cranked up. "We are facin' Armageddon here. The beast is upon us, ah haw. But we know how to frighten the beast away, don't we?"

"Amen!" his faithful called.

Jewelweed held up a much-used Bible. "Says so right here in the good book, don't it, ah haw?'"

"Amen!" the flock intoned.

"This might be where he grabs 'em," Willie said. "I've seen this act before. It always gets 'em."

"What's he gonna do, Brother Willie?" Sister Adele asked.

"Watch."

"Be not afraid to face your sins!" Jewelweed hollered.

"Amen!" his flock called.

"Be not afraid to pick up the serpent!"

"Amen!"

Jewelweed reached down, flipped open the lid on a crate, and hauled out a rattlesnake about five feet long.

"Behold!" he cried, holding up the writhing snake. "And fear not the beast."

The crowd gasped, and the reporters told their camera crews to get it on tape.

The nearest Colorado State Patrol members had jerked iron and were preparing to blow the snake—and Jewelweed too, if he didn't put that ugly fucker away—right straight to hell.

Jewelweed looped the snake around his neck and marched up to the line of troopers. The rattlesnake looked all around, its forked tongue testing the air.

A sergeant pointed a finger at Jewelweed, the other hand on the butt of his pistol. "You take one more step toward me with that ugly bastard around your neck, and you're gonna be in Colorado for eternity."

"The snake represents your sins, my son, ah haw," Jewelweed told the man.

"I got a bullet that looks like your ass, too," the sergeant told him. "Back up."

Jewelweed backed up, muttering about heathens and Philistines.

"As if we don't have enough problems," Martin Tobias said to Larry, as they watched from a distance.

"Yes, and here comes more," Larry pointed out, as the press corps spotted them and came at a run.

240

"You ready for this, Larry?"

"No. But it has to be."

Martin held up a hand, and the rampaging gang of newspeople came to a stop.

"Right over there," he said, pointing to a spot where aides were setting up a rostrum. "Set your mikes up there, and I'll give you a statement as soon as you're ready."

"Mr. Tobias!" a reporter called. "What is going on inside the barricades?"

"If you cannot comprehend simple English, young man," Martin told him. "I might suggest that you seek other types of employment. Right over there is where I will take questions. And nowhere else."

The White House chief of staff turned his back to the crowd and walked toward the rostrum, Larry with him.

"How to win friends and influence people?" Larry asked with a smile.

"They have a job to do, but so do we, Larry. It can all be done with some degree of protocol—or not at all."

When everyone was ready, Martin stepped to the rostrum and nodded his head at a reporter.

"What is going on inside those barricades, Mr. Tobias?"

"Plague. On the order of bubonic. It is an entirely new strain, and our people at CDC are working around the clock to find some sort of vaccine."

"It's called fury?"

"That is correct. That is what it was codenamed."

"How many lives has it claimed so far?"

"Five hundred at the latest count—and climbing."

"Why is the White House involved?"

Martin fixed him with a look guaranteed to melt ice cubes. "That is a totally asinine question. We are facing a plague of monumental proportions. Naturally, President Marshall wants to stay on top of matters. That is why I am here."

"It's the Russians!" Willie hollered. "The Russians done started a germ war."

"The Russians have done nothing," Martin said, raising his voice to be heard over the babbling of Willie, the speaking in tongues of Marrner, and the snake-waving and shouting of Jewelweed. "We don't know where the disease originated; but I can tell you in all honesty, that it did not come from any foreign country here on earth."

"Great God Almighty!" Willie shouted. "Hit's from outer space. The little green men's done invaded us!" He dropped to his knees. "Oh, Lord!" he cried. "Give us a sign. Tell us what to do?"

Jewelweed walked over to him and held out a snake. "Here, Willie, take this."

Willie recoiled backward. "Get that motherfucker away from me!"

"When the roll is called up yonder," Sister Adele sang sweetly.

"Do you have people in the town?" the question was tossed at Martin. "From the White House?"

"Yes, we do. Megan LeMasters volunteered to enter the town and assess the situation."

"And her report?"

"Grim."

"When will she come out?"

"She won't, until a vaccine is found, and the survivors have been inoculated. She is a very brave young lady."

"I don't feel very brave," Megan said, listening to the radio. The press briefing was being heard around the world. WHEN ARE YOU GOING TO LEVEL WITH THE PEOPLE, BABY?

In his computer room, Howie shook his head. The Fury was bigger and stronger than ever. And it could now move so fast he had very little time to warn anyone that it was coming.

"That's what you want, isn't it?" Megan tossed the question into the air. "You want publicity."

I WANT THE WORLD TO KNOW WHO I AM AND WHAT I AM. YES.

"It isn't time for that," Megan said, taking a chance. "You tip your hand now, and our scientists could very well find a way to destroy you. Think about that."

UMMM. PERHAPS YOU'RE RIGHT. BUT WHY WOULD YOU WARN ME OF THAT REMOTE POSSIBILITY?

"To give us more time to live."

YOU PEOPLE ARE SO DAMNED HONEST YOU MAKE ME WANT TO PUKE. WHAT A BUNCH OF BOY SCOUTS. BAH!

"It's gone," Howie called.

"Came up pretty fast this time, didn't it?" Maj. Jackson asked.

"So fast I couldn't warn any of you," Howie said. "That was quick thinking, Miss LeMasters."

"Desperate thinking, Howie. And I may have bought us an extra day or two."

Mack looked over at the newcomers, Gene and Donna Harvey. He had known the pair for years, and there was something about them now, that was all out of whack. Something just didn't ring true.

Gene felt the old deputy's eyes on him and turned his head, meeting Mack's gaze.

His eyes, Mack thought. That's what's wrong. His eyes are . . . dead, he found the word.

Mack forced himself to smile at the man, and Gene returned the smile.

"People running up the sidewalk," Judy called. "Eight or ten of them. They're not armed."

Those in the office could hear the people outside yelling. "Let us in! For the love of God, please help us."

"Let them in," Lee ordered. "But keep an eye on them."

Howie inserted a tape into a VCR that he had immediately requested when Gene and Donna entered the office. The sounds of a space battle drifted out to the main office.

243

Megan and Judy exchanged glances and smiles. Howie was one sharp little boy. In the event those new survivors were imposters, he had quickly arranged it so they could report back to the Fury that Howie was indeed playing space games with his Buck Rogers ray gun.

"Oh, boy," Judy said, cracking the door. "It's the sheriff's wife among them."

Chapter Six

Gordie and the others bagged up a hundred bodies and poured the fluid. The smell was gone as soon as the fluid hit bloated and maggot-covered flesh. Finally, the smell and the back-breaking work took its toll on them all, and they knocked off for the day.

I DON'T SUPPOSE YOU'D LIKE TO HAVE A PARTY TONIGHT, WOULD YOU, SHANTY IRISH-SPIC?

"I think I'll pass, Fury."

PITY. I'M IN UNUSUALLY FINE VOICE. WOULD YOU LIKE TO HEAR?

"Do I have a choice?"

NO. LISTEN: DO BOP DE DO BOP DE DO BOP, DE DO. DOESN'T THAT TAKE YOU BACK TO THE GLORIOUS DAYS OF THE FIFTIES?

"I don't remember anything about them, Fury."

THAT'S PROBABLY WHY YOU'RE SUCH A DICK-HEAD.

Fury left, but not before unzipping the last pile of body bags and dumping the bodies out onto the sidewalk.

"I wonder if that's it?" Watts questioned.

"What do you mean?" Kathy asked, just as a hand closed around her boot-covered ankle and the smell of the grave wafted to her nostrils.

She stifled a scream and twisted, trying to break free of the dead hand. The man grinned up at her and opened his mouth to laugh. Bloated blowflies and maggots

245

dropped out of the mouth. The tongue was blue black.

Watts picked up a heavy stick from the sidewalk and bashed the living dead corpse on the head. The head exploded like an overheated pressure cooker, showering those closest with brains and blood.

Kathy jerked out her Beretta 9mm and began methodically pulling the trigger, blowing the dead wrist apart and finally freeing her ankle.

The dead fingers clung to her boot as the shattered arm flopped on the sidewalk.

Gordie had to kneel down and pry the cold fingers from her ankles, first breaking the fingers, and then peeling them off as one would a leech.

"Jesus!" Kathy said, as the last finger was tossed to one side.

THAT WAS FUN, WASN'T IT? LET'S PLAY SOME MORE FUN GAMES.

The body bags began moving, rolling from side to side, with muffled screams coming from each bag.

"They're dead, people," Gordie said, as much for his own benefit as for the others. "Keep that in mind. They're all dead."

THERE ARE DEGREES OF DEATH, GORDIE ME BOY. LET ME SHOW YOU.

A body bag suddenly burst open, and a man lumbered to his blackened bare feet, turning slowly to face the sheriff.

Kathy had already ran to the car and grabbed up two shotguns, tossing one to Watts. She pumped a round of double ought buckshot into the chamber and leveled the muzzle. She put a round into the dead man's chest, and the second shot took off most of his face, knocking him down to the sidewalk.

GOOD SHOW, GANG. GOOD SHOW. NOW YOU'RE ALL GETTING INTO THE SPIRIT OF THINGS. NOW WE CAN HAVE SOME FUN. PARTY TIME.

* * *

Martin had returned from a newly installed mobile home close to the town, just in time to hear the shots booming out of town. He was immediately surrounded by reporters.

"What's all the shooting about, Mr. Tobias?" he was asked.

"I have no idea, people. But you will know just as soon as I do, I promise you that." He turned to Larry. "Find out what that was all about, Larry."

"Yes, sir."

"Why can't anybody call into the town, sir?" he was asked.

"All existing lines are being used for emergency use only. And I was told there was some damage to the telephone company's terminals in there. We can't risk any lives by sending people in to fix it."

"Sir, there is unusual activity around the Russian, Canadian, Mexican, French, and German embassies in Washington. Do you have a comment on that?"

"No, I do not. This situation here in Willowdale is my immediate concern. I have not been briefed on any unusual activity in Washington."

"Sir, why isn't the governor of the state of Colorado present?"

"The governor is not feeling well. He caught a cold doing some late season skiing, and it turned into a mild case of pneumonia. I'm on the phone with him a half-dozen times a day."

Actually, both leaders of the House and Senate—both Democrats—after being briefed by President Marshall—a Republican—had called Governor Siatos, and told him to get sick and maintain a very low profile until this matter was resolved. They did not want him blundering around, shooting off his mouth, and sticking his foot in it.

Larry returned after speaking with the trooper in

247

charge at the barricades. "Some prisoners tried to break out of the jail, sir," he lied with a straight face. "They didn't make it."

"Thank you, Larry," Martin said. "There will be another briefing at eight o'clock in the morning, people," he told the members of the press. "I'll see you then."

"This is all a bunch of shit," one reporter said to a small group of his peers. "First, there is some story about a mass murderer on the loose. Then all of a sudden we get this bubonic plague crap. And I was told by a waitress up the road that this all has something to do with a man called Sand."

"Sand?"

"Yeah. Some outlaw rebel that was killed by a Colorado state trooper some thirty years ago. Man by the name of Alvin Watts."

"Where do we find this Watts person?"

The reporter pointed toward Willowdale. "In there. And no way to get to him."

"I'm with you," another reporter said. "I'm not buying any of the crap the government is handing out."

"I got an idea," yet another reporter said.

They all looked at him.

"Let's find a way to get into the town."

Gordie and those with him fought their way through a line of bloated and stinking walking dead and made it back to their vehicles. Several of the newly risen climbed onto the bed of the trucks and hammered on the top of the cabs, grunting and howling and cursing.

One crawled onto the top of the cab, a brick in his hand, and smashed the windshield, sending shards of glass into the driver's face. The poor man spun the wheel, fighting it, trying to see through the blood pouring into his eyes from numerous cuts on his scalp and forehead.

Gordie thought the truck was right behind him. But the

248

truckload of bodies, dead and still and dead and risen, had headed the other way after the windshield was smashed—straight toward the barricades.

The walking dead leaned over and threw himself into the cab, smashing the brick into the deputy's face, knocking him unconscious.

With an insane grin on his rotted and bloated face, the dead shoved the deputy out of the way and got behind the wheel. He dropped the truck into gear and headed for the barricades.

HEE HEE HEE HEE, the Fury giggled, spreading the distance its voice would carry.

"What the hell was that?" a reporter asked.

"I don't know. But it came from the town."

Martin and Larry had heard the giggling from inside their mobile home and had stepped out.

The truck, swerving from side to side in the wide street, lurched toward the barricades. The reporters noticed the erratically driven vehicle and began gathering near the barricades, as did the preachers and the government personnel. Cameras were recording it all.

The truck stopped about a foot from the barricades, the dead driver grinning at the crowd through the broken windshield. He picked his nose, pulled out a maggot, and flipped it toward the crowd.

"Jesus!" a reporter said. "That's a maggot!"

The deputy managed to open the passenger-side door and fall out onto the concrete, blood pouring from head wounds.

The reporters and camera crews tried to push past the troopers. The troopers shoved them back, none too gently.

OH, LET THEM COME IN, BY ALL MEANS.

"Who said that?" a woman yelled. "Where is that voice coming from?"

DO BOP DE DO BOP DE DO BOP, DE DO.

"All pretense is thrown to the wind," Larry muttered.

"I'm afraid you're right," Martin agreed. "Back up, Larry." There was urgency in the man's voice. "Run, boy, run."

They ran.

Gordie squealed to a stop, the tires on his vehicle smoking from the sudden stop. He jumped out. "Get back!" he screamed. "All of you get back. Run, goddamnit, run!"

Most ran, including the troopers. A few reporters and camerapersons stayed. But not for long. The barricades remained intact. The vehicles parked close to it were not harmed.

The people standing on the outside of the barricades, close to the barriers, disappeared.

Screaming leaped out of the air, followed by a heavy crunching sound. A bent and useless minicam popped out of the air, falling to the roadway. Tape recorders and watches and belt buckles and lipstick tubes dropped to the concrete.

A large belch sprang out of the air.

OH, MY, the Fury said. NOW THIS IS INTEREST-ING. I'M STORING SOME DATA TOTALLY NEW TO ME. I MUST TRY TO UNDERSTAND WHAT I HAVE GATHERED. BYE, NOW.

Gordie had returned to his unit and radioed in. He had walked back to the barricades, a bullhorn in his hand. He lifted the bullhorn and triggered it. "You goddamned sons of bitches. You greedy, sorry, motherfuckers have condemned us. I asked you to leave. I pleaded with you. Now I'm going to do what I should have done from the first."

He looked around as two S.O. units drove up. Deputies got out, scoped high-powered rifles in their hands. The rifles were 7mm Magnums.

"I will shoot anyone who gets within five hundred yards of any barricade," Gordie spoke through the bullhorn. "And my orders are to shoot to kill."

One reporter tested Gordie's orders. His body lay still under the warm spring sunlight. When asked if the body could be retrieved, the reply was a terse, "No."

Governor Siatos had finally broke his silence. He issued an apology for the death of the reporter and ordered his state patrol out of the area immediately. President Marshall ordered a full company of Army Rangers to be flown in from Fort Lewis, Washington. The Rangers were in place by nightfall.

Gordie talked over the barricades, now moved back another half-mile from the town, with the CO of the Rangers.

"Do my deputies have to remain at all checkpoints, Captain?"

"No, sir," the Ranger told him. "We are under orders from the president of the United States to shoot to kill anyone who attempts to compromise our perimeters."

"You have someone in constant touch with Howie?"

"Yes, sir. We have established both a voice and computer link with the boy."

"Good luck to you and your men, Captain."

"Good luck to you and your people, sir. I don't envy you your position."

Gordie tried a smile that almost made it. "We've lasted this long. Maybe we can pull this thing off."

"Captain," a man called. "The boy says the Fury is resting. The thing is all tapped out from the recent extending of its territory."

"What exactly does that mean, Sheriff?"

"It means we can talk freely without the Fury suddenly popping up to listen without our knowing."

"My briefing was pretty sketchy, sir. What is this thing you're facing? And I have a top secret clearance, sir."

Martin Tobias had walked up, and walked up very softly. "You may tell the captain, Sheriff. After the incident with those . . . dead people this afternoon, and the gobbling up of half a dozen reporters, we're worldwide news. And before you brief the captain and myself," he smiled, "how is Megan?"

"She's fine, Mr. Tobias. Like the rest of us, coping."

"Continue with the briefing, Sheriff."

"The Fury is a collapsed, neutron star that somehow — we don't know how and probably never will — managed to evolve to become a thinking mass. But one that is nearly totally evil."

"I don't understand the nearly totally evil bit," the Ranger Captain said.

"No thinking being is totally evil for very long, Captain," Martin told him. "Not even mankind. It would destroy itself. All things have to have some, well, call it compassion, love, weakness. What does it want, Sheriff?"

"Its wonderful, magnificent life story told," Gordie said sarcastically.

Martin removed his glasses and wiped the lenses with a very white handkerchief. "Keep it talking," he finally said. "It will probably kill you all when it's finished."

"Yes," Gordie agreed. "Mr. Tobias, now that the press knows, well, that something more than bubonic plague is here, I have a request, since I am still the sheriff of this county."

"Name it."

"Evacuate everybody for twenty miles around."

"We've already evacuated for five miles. Do you think that is wise?"

"I don't know what you mean."

"I'm trying to keep you people alive in there, Sheriff. Let's don't make the Fury so angry that he, it, will kill you all in a rage."

"All right. I see your point. But each time it advances a half-mile, you people back up five."

"Done."

"We're going to need more people in here," the Ranger captain said. "It's one thing sealing off a town, another

252

sealing off fifty or sixty square miles in all directions."

Martin slowly nodded his agreement. "I have a full contingent of the 82nd Airborne standing by."

"Get them up here, sir."

"Done." He looked at Gordie in the moonlight. "Sheriff, I have a bomber standing by, ready to be armed with what you requested."

"Then our scientists have agreed with Sand's theory on destroying the Fury?"

"Yes. Unfortunately. But we've got to get you people out of there."

"Howie and Angel. Maybe a few of the younger kids. Robin Jennings and Ricky what's-his-name, her boyfriend. The college kids if we can. The rest of us?" He shrugged. "If we have to go up with the Fury, that's the way it has to be."

"Do you understand what is going to happen with a neutron bomb, Sheriff?"

"No."

"It will detonate at ground level. One huge mass of energy meeting another huge mass of energy. A much larger mass of energy, I might add. There will be tremendous firestorms, possibly the most savage lightning ever experienced here on earth—at least since man became more or less civilized. In all probability, there will be nothing left for several miles in any direction. One very large hole in the ground near the center of the explosion."

"Will this area be radioactive?"

"Our scientists don't know. It's doubtful, but that is the best they can do without further knowledge of the Fury's makeup."

"Have you leveled with the press?"

"Not yet. Tomorrow morning, the president is going to speak on a worldwide hookup."

The Ranger Captain grunted.

"What's the matter, Captain?" Martin asked.

"That's when the shit hitting the fan turns into a clus-

253

ter-fuck, sir."

Both Gordie and Martin laughed at the young captain's bluntness.

"I couldn't have said it better, son," Martin said, patting him on the arm.

Chapter Seven

When Gordie returned to the office, most of the people were gathered around the TV in the main room. The new additions, including Gordie's wife, had been housed in an old unused cell block in the basement.

"I don't trust any of them," Mack said. "Not a damn one of them."

"I see someone put a deputy next to their door."

"Lee."

"Good move. What's with the television?"

"Sand has really been throwing it at us fast. It's both fascinating and depressing. He really got screwed by the law, Gordie. Makes me ashamed. I'm surprised he held on to his sanity as long as he did."

"Jesus God, I remember this scene," Watts was saying, as they walked up to the TV.

"Bring me up-to-date," Gordie said.

"About a year before the bottom dropped out for Sand and his bunch, every time I'd get around Sand or Joey, I'd feel some sort of, well, strange sensation. It was like a, well, pressure, very slight, on me. Now I know what it was."

"This Force Sand and Richard spoke of?"

"Yes. I was lecturing Sand here, Gordie." Watts pointed to the screen. "Trying to get him to see he was screwing up his life. I thought my mind was beginning to play tricks on me. Now I know it wasn't. It was real."

They looked at the screen.

"Goddamnit, Sand!" Watts roared. "Sit your ass down in that chair and listen to me."

Sand sat and glared at the trooper.

"I just came from Julie von Mehren's mansion up in the mountains. She likes you, boy. Why, I don't know. But she does. She's heard, as I have heard, that all hell is about to break loose between you and those rich snots over in Monte Rio, and that one frat house that's aligned with them."

"Captain, I swear to you, this is news to me."

"Sand, I believe you. My own sources tell me that crap that Bill Marlson is spreading about you is all lies. But tempers are running hot and heavy. Back off, Sand."

"Captain, where do I back off to? I have no backing room left me."

"You could break up the Pack."

"Why should I? Name me one illegal act that any of us have ever done? Point out one time that any of us ever set out to start a fight. All we do is work and drive custom cars. Since when is that against the law?"

"Public support is most definitely not with you people."

"So what else is new?"

"If you continue this fight with those rich snots at Monte Rio, and with this one fraternity house—even if you people don't start a single fight—public opinion is going to harden against you. Sand, you can be anything you want to be. You're big, tough, handsome, fast on your feet, a born leader, and you're a genius—just like Joey. But all those fine qualities have been wasted on you. God, I wish you had been born a hundred years ago. You'd have been a gunfighter. I'd be reading books about you."

"I wish the same, Captain."

"I know you do. But you can't go back in time, son. You've got to conform; you've got to, Sand."

Sand blurred in his eyes; the young man seemed to be wearing buckskins, his hair shoulderlength. The wall behind him changed into a saloon scene from the Old West.

Watts shook his head. The vision seemed to clear, blurred again. Watts blinked his eyes. Sand wore a pirate's outfit, the wall behind him became the sea, and the air was thick with smoke from a battle at sea.

Thunder cracked in Watts's head. He could not keep his eyes open.

When he finally forced his eyes open, Sand was wearing a breastplate and he was mounted on a horse. A castle loomed in the background. Watts gripped the arms of his chair and fought the images.

"What the hell!" he whispered.

"Is something the matter?" Sand asked.

Watts's vision cleared. Sand was looking at him curiously.

Watts looked out his office window. The day was clear. "Did you hear thunder just then?"

"Thunder? No, sir."

"I've been working too hard. You're driving me nuts, Sand. I don't know what motivates you. I don't understand you. I don't know whether to offer you a job with the state patrol, or to petition to have you placed in a crazy house. And me along with you. Get out of here, Sand. I have work to do. And Sand? Stay out of trouble."

The picture on the TV set faded.

"What happened after that, Colonel?" Megan asked.

"The next week those crap-heads over at Monte Rio ambushed a Pack member. His name was Norris. His girlfriend, Gloria, was with him. Norris was badly beaten, and Gloria was raped—repeatedly. They continued to rape her even after they had beaten her into unconsciousness. A deputy sheriff who was patrolling the back roads found her crawling along the side of the road, naked, babbling in hysteria, blood dripping from her mouth, nose, and ears. She was brain-damaged. She was finally placed in an asylum. She's still there. Norris regained consciousness only once, long enough to tell a doctor who had done him in. The DA rejected the deathbed statement. Norris died, Gloria sat in her padded room and rocked her dolly, the punks who raped her and killed Norris walked free, and the war was on.

Sunny said, "Sand and his friends seemed to get the shaft everytime they turned around."

"Yes, they did," Watts said with a heavy sigh.

They all turned and walked toward the computer room at the sounds of Howie typing. He had typed: Sand? Were you all those people that Mr. Watts saw that day in his— office?

Yes, the reply quickly came.

Reincarnation?

Yes. The soul does not die, Howie. It lives forever. If one is strong enough, and persistent enough, they can find the door.

Watts said, "Tell him that the government is ready with a bomber."

Sand replied: *That was a good idea the sheriff had about the fire and smoke. It might work. Keep it in mind.*

Gordie grunted. "Ask him about my wife and the others who came in today. Can they be trusted?"

I cannot interfere in that. I have been warned.

The screen went dark.

"How would you read that reply, Howie?" Watts asked.

"That they can't be trusted," the boy replied.

"Look out!" Mack screamed the warning, just as the door to the basement burst open and a butcher knife was driven into the back of the deputy guarding the door.

Mack jerked his old .357 from leather and shot the knife-wielding man between the eyes. The bullet went all the way through the head and wanged off the steel door frame.

The man dropped to the floor, then opened his eyes and grinned at Mack, while slowly getting to his feet. Mack emptied his .357 into the man's chest, the slugs knocking him back. He would not die. But his weight was preventing the others in the basement from pushing open the door and flooding into the room. All on the ground level could hear them cursing and howling to be freed.

"Is there another way out of the basement?" Jill asked, as men moved furniture moved against the door, temporarily blocking any escape.

"One door. But it's steel, just like that door," Gordie said. "They'll not get out that way. Lee, get that welder's set from the evidence room. I know something about welding. We'll seal them off."

"I know a lot about welding," Sgt. Janet Dixon said. "My daddy is a welder. I'll seal that sucker shut."

"Gordie, honey," the sheriff's wife called from behind the door. "I'm not part of the Fury's plan. I love you, baby. Open the door and let me out."

Others behind the door picked up the call, pleading to be set free.

Judy quickly set up a PSE machine and began monitoring stress in the voices. "They're lying," she said. "Everyone that I've checked."

"Those things are not reliable," Leon said. "They're not admissible in a court of law."

Mack — his .357 fully loaded — looked at the boy and inwardly fought to keep from shooting him.

Watts had handcuffed the man who refused to die, and with the help of Rich and Capt. Hishon, dragged the man outside and tossed him into the street.

The screaming behind the door was a howling roar as Janet began welding the door to the steel frame. Those trapped pounded on the door and cursed.

NOW YOU'RE CATCHING ON, FOLKS. NOW YOU'RE PLAYING THE GAME. I LOVE IT.

No one chose to reply.

SINCE THE ENTIRE WORLD — STUPID PLACE THAT IT IS — WILL KNOW ALL ABOUT ME COME THE MORNING, I SHALL GIVE YOU ALL A TREAT. YOU MAY ROAM THE TOWN BETWEEN NOW AND THEN AND I WON'T HARM YOU. YOU HAVE MY

WORD. REMEMBER, I SAID I WON'T HARM YOU.
TA-TA.

DO BOP DE DO BOP DE DO BOP, DE DO.

"Meaning the people are out there waiting for us," Watts said.

"Yeah," Maj. Jackson said. "So bullets won't stop them, we know that. But I know something that will."

All looked at him.

"Fire," the major said.

Those trapped inside the sheriff's office spent the next hour scrounging up empty bottles and filling them with gasoline siphoned from vehicles in the impound area.

OH, MY. BUT THIS IS GOING TO BE SUCH FUN!

"You going to watch and not interfere?" Gordie asked.

I GAVE MY WORD, BURRITO-BREATH.

"So you did. All right. Let's see how much your word means."

The air inside the office grew heavy, and all could sense the Fury was very angry. I HAVE NEVER BROKEN MY WORD, PONCHO. I MIGHT TRICK YOU, DECEIVE YOU, SET TRAPS FOR YOU. BUT IF I GIVE MY WORD, IT'S A FIRM BOND. DON'T EVER ACCUSE ME OF BEING A WELSHER AGAIN.

"Sorry."

THAT'S BETTER. BY THE WAY, WHAT IS A MO-DEM?

"I don't have any idea," Gordie quickly responded. "What language is that?"

I'M NOT SURE. IT HAS SOMETHING TO DO WITH A MACRO AND A SYSTEM DISK.

"I'm afraid you're asking the wrong people, Fury. I'd guess that those are reporters' phrases of some kind."

YOU MIGHT BE RIGHT. IF YOU ARE, IT WILL PROBABLY BE THE FIRST TIME. HAVE FUN.

The people behind the welded-shut door had shouted

themselves hoarse and were silent. But all knew that anytime the Fury wanted the door open, it could open it.

Gordie hefted a Molotov cocktail, half-filled with gasoline with a rag stuck in the top.

"Let's go to work, people."

The night had turned cool, cooler than usual for early spring in the Rockies. The men and women stepped out of the sheriff's office and looked up and down the street. It was deserted, and very silent.

"They're waiting for us," Watts said. "I spent too many years as a cop not to sense a set-up."

Gordie could also feel the intangible eerieness that Watts was experiencing, and it was not something he enjoyed. And neither was he going to enjoy the assault against the townspeople. He knew and liked most of the people in Willowdale. It was important to keep in mind that those they would face were merely shells of what they had once been—now they were dangerous, the enemy. The camera crews that had stepped across the line into the town were filming the desolation and the silence. Jill and Dean were speaking softly into tape recorders.

Dean felt eyes on him and looked up, meeting Gordie's gaze. "Reporter to the end, Sheriff," he said with a smile.

"Let's hope this isn't the end," Gordie replied, then walked to his car, Sunny going with him.

The men and women went to their preassigned vehicles, got in and pulled out, driving into the unknown.

Watts rode with Gordie and Sunny, in the back seat. Gordie keyed his mike. "One to Whiz kid."

Mack took it. "Go, One."

"Where is the Coach?"

"Everywhere," came the terse reply.

"That's ten-four."

WHO IS THE COACH?

"The enemy," Gordie said truthfully.

AHH. THE TOWNSPEOPLE. YOU REALLY DIDN'T THINK YOU COULD FOOL ME FOR VERY LONG

DID YOU, GUNSLINGER?

"I wouldn't even try that, Fury. I'm just going to beat you, that's all."

THAT'S THE SPIRIT, GREASEBALL. WHAT IS MY CODENAME?

"We didn't name you. We didn't think it would do any good."

WISE DECISION. CARRY ON.

The electricity in the air left them.

"Sentries all around the perimeters," Mack said. "The main mass is located near the stadium."

They could feel the electricity as the Fury leaped from the football field to center around the car. SO I AM THE MAIN MASS, EH? THAT'S NOT A VERY FLATTERING NAME.

"I thought you were going to stay out of this, Fury? What's the matter, afraid we'll be successful this night?"

DON'T BE RIDICULOUS. OH, VERY WELL, THEN. YOU'RE ON YOUR OWN.

"You'll stay out of this, completely out, and we can speak freely, without your eavesdroping and snooping?"

YOU ASK A LOT.

"Not so much. You're stronger and smarter and braver than we are," Gordie stroked the Fury's ego.

THAT IS CERTAINLY TRUE.

"Well? How about it?"

UMMM. I WILL STRIKE A BARGAIN. I WILL WATCH, BUT NOT LISTEN. HOW ABOUT THAT?

"You said your word was your bond. I accept."

YOU'RE A TRUSTING FOOL. BUT VERY WELL, YOU HAVE MY WORD ON IT.

The electricity left them.

Gordie keyed his mike. "One to headquarters. Where is the conceited, lying, ugly son of a bitch?"

Mack almost swallowed his chewing tobacco at that. But the Fury was keeping his word. It was not listening. "Whiz kid says it's back at the stadium. Whiz kid says

262

some of the blips have diminished on the screen, so it's cut its power."

"That's ten-four."

"It's so sure it's going to win," Sunny said. "My heart almost stopped when you called it that, Gordie."

"I had to be sure." He turned a corner, and the hospital loomed in front of them.

"Oh, Lord!" Sunny breathed.

"Relax. We're not going back in there. I just wanted to check it out."

"Thank you very much."

Gordie stopped, and they all could see the faces, pale-white in death, looming at the windows of the hospital.

"This will be one of the first places to go up when we bust out of here," Gordie said, then waited to see if there was any response from the Fury.

Nothing.

"Did you have this in mind when all those crates of explosives were ordered?" Watts asked from the back seat.

"No. Jackson just thought it might be a good idea to have some heavy firepower around when — or if — the time ever came."

"What all came in those crates?"

"Rockets. Grenades. C-4." He keyed his mike and called in. "We still clear?"

"Still clear, One. Howie says Sand just told him that the thing is keeping its word this time, because it desperately needs to rest, and this is helping it do that."

"That's ten-four. Out." He hung up the mike and said, "I figured that thing had some reason for being so damned agreeable all of a sudden."

As he turned the unit around in the hospital parking lot, a thrown rock bounced off the side of the vehicle. Gordie used a spotlight to scan the darkness, but could spot no one lurking on the grounds.

"Behind those shrubs," Watts said.

"Yeah. Got to be." He continued on, rolling out of the

263

parking lot and back onto the street. "Fury has something up his sleeve for us tonight. But damned if I can figure out what it is."

"It does enjoy surprises," Sunny pointed out.

Every light in town suddenly went out.

Chapter Eight

"And that's all we know about it," President Marshall told the representatives from a dozen countries, meeting with him in the White House.

Surprisingly, the Russian ambassador was the first to agree to the method of destroying the Fury. "This mass cannot be allowed to grow and spread," he said. "Each time it devours beings, it grows that much more stronger, and that much more difficult to destroy. Also that much more intelligent. We cannot allow this mass to grow; it must be destroyed."

"I concur," the Canadian said.

The others in the room quickly agreed.

"And you have no plan on rescuing those trapped in the town?" the German ambassador asked.

"I'm afraid not," President Marshall replied. "We know they have some plan, but they're not talking about it because the Fury might intercept the messages."

"The little children trapped in there distress me," the French ambassador said. "Howie and Angel. They are the only young people not affected by the mass?"

"As far as we know."

"We must have those tapes the reporter is gathering from the mass," the English ambassador said. "They will give us an insight to our past that we might never again have."

"We're all in agreement on that."

The ambassador from Japan turned his head to once more gaze at the TV screen showing the videotapes. "We are actually viewing life after death. This is the most incredible moment of my life."

"It shall certainly get much more interesting," the Russian told him. "Especially if the Fury grows much stronger."

The big emergency generator at the sheriff's office kicked on automatically ten seconds after the power went out.

But the TV set showing the events of thirty years past never faltered or dimmed.

"How is that possible?" Hillary asked, pointing to the set.

"I'm not sure I even want to know," Leon said. "I just want out of here—in one piece."

Gordie had ordered all personnel back to the sheriff's office.

ALL BETS ARE OFF NOW, GUNFIGHTER.

"Why?" Gordie asked.

YOU CRAPPED OUT BY RETURNING.

"Fine with me. I prefer the daylight anyway."

WHAT A CHICKEN-SHIT.

The Fury left them.

"Gordie," Watts called, standing in front of the television. "Look at this. This is when and how Joey and Tuddie died."

Everyone gathered around.

The young couple in the custom car had just topped the crest of Pioneer Mountain and started the roll down, when Joey stepped on the brake pedal. Everyone watching the set could feel the mushiness of the pedal.

"Oh, God," Hillary whispered.

"Damn," Joey's voice came out of the speakers as he realized what was happening.

A heavy invisible force gripped the young couple in a cold grasp. Those watching thirty years in the present could feel the clammy touch.

"The Force?" Dean asked.

"Yes," Watts told him. "Death."

"It is time," a heavy voice sprang from the speakers.

"Joey!" the blonde said. "Did you hear that. What is that voice?"

"But I want to live!" Joey said.

"Who are you talking to, Joey?" Tuddie asked. "What's wrong with the car? Why are we going so fast?"

"Sorry," the Force said. "All this was decided long before you took your present shape."

"Joey!" Tuddie screamed. "I'm scared!"

"Then take me, and let her live!" Joey shouted.

"Sorry."

Forty-five miles per hour down one of the most dangerous grades in the Rockies. "Hang on, babe," Joey said. "I'm going to slide it into the rocks on your side and stop this thing."

"No, you're not," the Force said.

Joey fought the wheel, trying to ram one side into the embankment. They were going too fast.

"Why are you doing this?" Joey shouted.

"I'm not. Don't worry. Sand will join you very soon."

"Jesus Christ!" he muttered.

"He has nothing to do with this."

The Force had completely enveloped the young couple in a dark mist.

"Joey!" Tuddie cried. "What is that dark stuff all around us? I can't see anything, Joey."

"Hang on, honey."

Sixty-five miles an hour. Joey knew their time on earth was nearly through.

Seventy miles an hour. Joey knew the next curve would be the one to punch their tickets, for that long ride across that dark river.

"Did those damn rich punks from Monte Rio cut my brake cables?" Joey shouted.

"Yes, they did."

"Damn them all to hell!" Joey screamed.

"Oh, yes. Sand will see to that." The Force was gripping them both in a damp, heavy pressure. "Soon," it whispered.

"All right, God," Joey said. "Take me, but let her live."

"Sorry," the Force told him. "He has nothing to do with it either."

They left the road at eighty, going over the high side, sailing through hundreds of feet of nothing.

"I love you, Tuddie!" Joey shouted, a second before they impacted with earth.

The car did not explode when it hit the ground. Joey and Tuddie were holding hands when the searchers found the crushed and mangled bodies.

"There you are, Al," Gordie pointed out the much younger highway patrolman standing with Sand by his side.

"Look at Sand's eyes," Lynn said. "They're changing from gray to yellow. They're wolf eyes."

"I didn't notice," Watts said. "He had just about lost it by then, and I didn't notice."

"I don't think it would have made any difference," Howie said. "All that was planned by a higher power."

"But who?" Dean asked. "That . . . voice said that God had nothing to do with."

No one had an answer to that.

"Inspect the brakes," Sand said.

Watts ordered it done.

"They were tampered with," the patrolman told them.

Watts cussed as Sand began yelling out names. The same ones who had been at the drive-in.

The scene shifted. Those Sand had named were being questioned, and questioned hard, by Al Watts. They each alibied the others.

"Naturally," Sand said to Watts. The scenes were shifting very fast. The viewers thirty years later had to struggle to keep up.

The eight young men from Monte Rio were picked up and questioned again by Watts. He could not break their story.

"That's just about the way I figured it would be," Sand said to Watts.

"Certainly," the Force whispered. "Matters were settled long ago. It won't be much longer. Soon."

The young Watts looked all around his office. He was certain he had heard somebody whispering.

The screen went dark.

"I remember thinking at that time," Watts said, "that the case was odd from the outset. I felt then it was getting macabre. Little did I know."

Gordie woke up to the sounds of screaming. One of the college girls was standing at a boarded-up window, screaming and pointing out into the street. Gordie threw off his blankets and ran to her side, looking out the window.

He had to lean against the wall for a moment, recovering from the sight.

Many of the people he had helped to bag were now dancing naked in the street, under the brilliance of moonlight, waving their body bags gracefully. Others had one end of the bags tied around their necks, using them as capes.

"I can't take much more of this," the young woman said. "I just can't!"

"Steady, now," Gordie said, putting his arms around her. "Just hang on."

"We're never going to get out of here!" she wailed, all the pent-up fears she'd held back surfacing. "We're all going to die in here!"

WHY DON'T YOU LAY HER DOWN AND GIVE HER A GOOD OLD-FASHIONED FUCKING, GUN-FIGHTER? THAT'D MAKE YOU BOTH FEEL BETTER.

Gordie, holding the trembling girl in his arms, said,

269

"Why don't you kiss my ass, Fury?"

OH, THAT'S GOOD, THAT'S GOOD. I LIKE IT WHEN YOU GET YOUR GREASY DANDER UP. DO BOP DE DO BOP DE DO BOP, DE DO.

A bleary-eyed Howie had gotten out of his cot when the screaming started. He called from his computer room, "It's gone, Sheriff."

"Didn't take it as long to regain its strength this time, did it?" Hillary asked, walking over and gently taking Sandy's hand, pulling her away from Gordie.

"Unfortunately, no," Gordie said. "And it may be getting ready to enlarge its territory. Howie, warn the Rangers at the checkpoints; have them pull back a half mile immediately."

"Yes, sir."

Gordie turned back to the street. The naked, rotting dancers had disappeared.

"What next?" he muttered wearily.

The TV set clicked on and Watts, despite all that was going on around him, laughed out loud.

"Tell me," Gordie said, walking over. "I could use a good laugh right now."

"Right in the middle of all the fighting between the hot rodders and the rich shits, I had men everywhere. That's Morg," he said, pointing to the screen, "towing in one of my men's cars that had broken down on the highway."

"You can't see the trooper," Jackson said.

"No," Watts chuckled. "He's got his hat brim pulled down low and is hunkered down in the seat, so nobody can recognize him."

The scene shifted.

"Who's that with you, Al?" Mack asked. Then took a closer look. "Oh, hell. That's that fool Governor Bradford."

"Was he as stupid as Siatos, Al?" Gordie asked.

"Just about. I remember this meeting."

"What was it all about?"

270

"Bradford had called us all in, then ordered us to pull our men in. I told him it was a mistake. That the shit was about to hit the fan."

"Was this before the deaths of Joey and Tuddie?" Sunny asked.

"Yes. Several months before."

"Goddamnit, Al," Governor Bradford's voice came out of the speaker. "Forget about the hot rodders. They're all a bunch of yellow punks. Nothing is going to happen. Hell, the month of December passed without a single fight, didn't it?"

"Sand called a halt to it, Governor. He ordered his people not to gather, not to run the roads, and to ignore the shit-heads. If we pull out, and anything happens to any member of any club that is aligned with Sand and the Pack, all hell will break loose. Sir, you don't know Sand. He can be hell's own creation. I have a mental picture of a Viking berserker, and his face is Sand."

"You also have a very active imagination, Captain. Hell, toss the punk in jail."

"He hasn't done anything that we can charge him with."

"Then make up something and toss him in the jug," the governor said with a wink.

Watts did not return the wink; just stared at the state's highest executive with disgust in his eyes.

"Pull your men out and send them back to their regular duties, Captain Watts," the governor ordered.

The screen went dark.

"Why did Sand go back and show us this?" Gordie questioned. "Why did he pull something out of sequence?"

"To tell you that you were right in ordering the Army to pull back," Howie called. "Get it?"

Gordie smiled. "Yeah, Howie. I got it, and you're probably right." He turned his head and cocked it. "Listen."

They all heard it: the sounds of marching feet, growing louder.

HUP TWO THREE FOUR. GIMMIE YOUR LEFT,

271

RIGHT, LEFT. COUNT CADENCE, COUNT!

Grunts and yells and unearthly moaning sprang out of the mouths of the marching dead, as they counted cadence up the street.

COLUMN, HALT! LEFT FACE!

"Now what?" Jackson said, moving to the boarded windows and looking out. "Jesus God!" he muttered. "Grab something to defend yourselves with, people. I think they're going to rush us."

Gordie looked out through a gun slit. The street directly in front of the sheriff's office was jammed with men and women, some of them walking dead, grinning hideously through rotting lips. Others included people that Gordie hoped were in hiding from the Fury.

He realized, finally, that his little group was all that was left in the town unaffected by the Fury's macabre sense of humor.

"They'll overwhelm us," Bos said.

"Maybe not," Watts told him. "Gas won't affect those already dead, but it will turn back the living. How about it, Gordie?"

"Everybody into masks," the sheriff ordered. "Jackson, get your people ready with tear gas grenades. Lee, get the tear gas guns."

GOOD MOVE, GORD-HEAD. SOMETIMES YOU AND THE OLD COP AMAZE ME WITH YOUR ASTUTENESS.

When no one replied, Fury said, ARE YOU ALL READY TO HAVE SOME FUN?

"Give it your best shot, bastard!" Watts said.

Watts was slapped down to the floor by an invisible blow. He got to his knees, grabbed hold of the edge of a desk, and pulled himself to his feet, one side of his mouth leaking blood.

Angel ran to Watts's side. "You turd!" she screamed at the Fury, her voice muffled through the gas mask.

SNIPPY LITTLE BITCH.

272

"Coward!" Angel yelled.

CHARGE! the Fury roared, the force of its voice rattling windows along the street.

The mob surged forward.

Those outside the barricades just made it back in time. Scientists with monitoring equipment recorded the Fury's advance of another quarter of a mile.

"A quarter of a mile," Martin noted aloud. "Not a half as before. But a quarter. Is it tiring? Running out of steam?"

"No," a scientist told him. "You've got to take into consideration that it is advancing in a full circle; in all directions. The territory it now controls is huge. You've got to make the decision to drop the bomb now, sir. And we've got to back off, clear out of this valley. When those two masses meet, the firestorms will be unlike any that human eyes have ever witnessed. The destructive powers will be enormous. There won't be anything left in this valley. Nothing."

"The mountains around this valley," Martin said. "Will they contain the blast?"

The scientists looked at one another. Finally one admitted the truth: "We don't know."

"Landslides, for sure," another said.

"On both sides?" Larry asked.

"Yes."

"The people living on the other side of the mountains," Martin said. "How far back should they be moved?"

"Ten miles would not be an unreasonable distance."

"Sand implied that there was some relationship between the Fury and the old radio antenna on the mountain," Martin pointed out. "Have you ascertained just what the connection might be?"

"No," another scientist admitted. "It doesn't make sense to us. The Fury does not need an antenna to do anything . . . as far as we can tell."

"But the mountain might be its source of power," another said.

"How?"

The woman shrugged. "Uranium would be one guess."

"Or it could just be its home," another said. "Everything has a place, a starting point. But we can't destroy the mountain," he was quick to add.

"I understand that," Martin said.

Another scientist sighed. "There really is a God. There is life after death. There are levels of heaven and hell. Every textbook in the world will have to be rewritten. Theories tossed out the window. Avowed atheists will be flooding the churches. Religions will swell."

The rantings and ravings of Willie Magee, Silas Marrner, and Harold Jewelweed drifted to them.

Martin looked around in disgust. "Larry, order the immediate evacuation of all people inside the valley, and for ten miles outside the valley. Do it now, son."

"Shooting in the town," an aide told him.

Martin shook his head. "Those poor bastards. God help them."

Chapter Nine

Clouds of tear gas billowed through the streets, as the men and women in the sheriff's office fought for their lives. Those manning the gun slits used broken-off chair legs and billy clubs and the butts of rifles and shotguns to beat back the mob of walking dead unaffected by the choking gas.

"Fire axes!" Gordie yelled. "Get axes and hatchets—machetes, anything that will cut! Lop off their hands as they stick them through the slits. Then burn the hands to destroy them."

Lopped-off hands crawled around the floor like huge, pale, misshapen spiders. The college girls, along with Megan, Sunny, Jill, and Angel beat them into pulp with clubs, scooped them up with shovels, and tossed them into buckets. They carried the buckets into a back room, doused the contents with gasoline, and burned the smashed hands.

Still the onslaught from the outside continued.

A hand crawled up a desk, up on the lamp, and leaped at Judy, attaching itself to her throat. She fought the hand silently, unable to utter a sound. The dead fingers punctured her flesh and dug deeper into her throat, ripping and tearing veins and arteries. With each beat of her heart, long streams of blood shot from her ruined throat. She collapsed on the floor, dying. The hand jumped from the bloody mess, scurrying along the floor. Angel smashed it with a shovel and beat it flat as a pancake.

Those prisoners that were left overpowered the deputy guarding the door to the hallway and ran into the main room, eyes wild with madness and fear. Some grabbed for weapons, others grabbed at women, trying to pull them down to the floor, ripping at their clothes; one more violent rape before death claimed them.

And death claimed them. They were shot. There was nothing else Gordie and the others could do.

Howie sat at his bank of computers, monitoring the screens while chaos reigned around him.

I'm sorry, Howie, the words flashed on the screen. *There is nothing any of us can do to help you . . . at the present time.*

Sand?

Yes.

Why is God doing this to us?

God has nothing to do with it. He did not create the Fury. He did not create the Force. They were and they are. Robin has gone into shock. See to her. We'll talk more later.

Howie stepped from his computer room into a blood-splattered arena of violence. He ran to Dr. Anderson and pointed to the room where Robin was huddled in a corner, her eyes wild with fear, her face pale.

"Sand told me," the boy shouted.

The doctor nodded. "Go back to your room. I'll take care of her."

The shouting, screaming hordes outside the door broke off their attack and ran silently into the gas-filled night. Silence fell on those in the building.

NOW THAT WAS ENTERTAINING. OH, MY, YES. I HAVEN'T HAD SO MUCH FUN IN YEARS.

Gordie leaned against a wall, a bloody axe in his hand. His face mirrored his exhaustion. "I'm glad you enjoyed it, Fury. Personally, I didn't see the humor in it."

"It's gone," Howie called. "The main body of energy is centered around Thunder Mountain."

The government technicians had also noticed the Fury's move to the mountain.

"It must have some importance," a scientist said. "But

276

what?"

"The mountain has been studied from every possible angle," another scientist said. "It was mined out before the turn of the century. There are no minerals of any significant amounts in the mountain."

The men and women looked at each other and shrugged.

"Robin wasn't as bad as she appeared," Dr. Anderson told Gordie. "I've sedated her."

"What are the odds of her flipping out?"

Anderson grimaced at the nonprofessional term. "As long as we can keep her mildly sedated, I don't think that's going to happen. You have to bear in mind, she's been through one hell of an experience. She remembers meeting her dead mother and father. Really, she's a damn tough girl."

Gordie nodded and looked out a gun slit. It would be daylight in about an hour. In one way he was looking forward to it. He glanced around the big room, blood-splattered and body-littered. Come the daylight, they had to get rid of the bodies.

"Burn them," Gordie ordered. "Behind the impound area. There's no point in jacking around with body bags any longer."

Soon, black stinking smoke was rising up into the air.

YOU ARE A VICIOUS LITTLE MEX, AREN'T YOU, GUNFIGHTER?

"I do what has to be done."

ARE YOU AWARE THAT YOUR GOVERNMENT HAS SEALED OFF ALL ROADS LEADING INTO THIS AREA?

"No," Gordie lied. "I was not."

THEY'VE EVACUATED ALL THE PEOPLE FOR MILES AROUND. THAT DISPLEASES ME, GORDIE.

"There isn't a damn thing I can do about it, Fury. Not one thing."

THAT MAY OR MAY NOT BE THE TRUTH. BUT SOMEHOW I SUSPECT IT IS. THOSE ON THE OUTSIDE HAVE WASHED THEIR HANDS OF YOU POOR WRETCHES.

"Then we'll just have to fight you with what we have."

THAT'S THE SPIRIT, GREASEBALL. RAH RAH, SIS BOOM BAH.

"Shit on you," Gordie muttered. He walked back into the office and said, "I'm going for a ride. Anybody want to tag along."

To his surprise, Angel raised her hand.

"Angel, it's dangerous out there."

"I want to go to my house, just one more time. There are some things I want to get."

Gordie waited as Judy's body was wrapped in a blanket. Lee looked at the sheriff.

Gordie shook his head. "Burn it," he ordered. "She'd want her body to be rendered useless, rather than risk having it used against us."

Sunny took Angel's hand. "I'll go with you, Gordie."

"As will I," Bergman said, picking up an M-16 and tossing it to Gordie. He chose one for himself and moved toward the door.

"Wait," Gordie said, holding up a hand. "Angel, what if your parents are there?"

The child stood a little straighter. "They aren't my parents anymore, Sheriff. They belong to the Fury. I belong to God."

Gordie smiled. "All right, Angel. We'll take a trip to your house. And Angel, all of us here in this room belong to God. He hasn't forsaken us."

"No, sir. I don't think He has either. I think He sent Sand to help us."

Watts grunted. "God must surely like His warriors, then. As much as I liked the boy, I'd sooner have stuck my hand into a sack of rattlesnakes than cross him."

"Wanna come along, Al?" Gordie asked.

278

"No. I think I'll stay here and watch the TV. There are some pieces to the puzzle that I still haven't quite fitted together. I think Sand will get around to it. I don't want to miss any of it."

"That's why we're taping it, sir," Bos reminded the man.

Watts looked at the college student and smiled. "I hope you make it out of here, son. But I won't."

Everybody still in the room looked at the tall, straight, ex-head of Colorado state police. "What do you mean, sir?" Dean asked.

"Fury isn't here, sir," Howie called. "We can talk freely."

"Gordie has the start of a pretty good plan for a bustout, when the time comes. Somebody has to keep the home fires burning, so to speak. I volunteered myself. I'm no hero, but I've lived a full life. And I won't be alone. Another person here has volunteered."

"You just had to go and flap your mouth, didn't you, Al?" Mack spoke from behind the console.

"I don't think we have much time left to us, Mack. I think it's down to hours now. We'd best start gathering up materials, and getting Major Jackson and his people to give us short courses on these plastic explosives." He held up a hand. "And I don't want to hear any weeping and moaning about our decision. It's firm, so keep your comments to yourselves. You ready to conduct a class, Major?"

Jackson nodded his head. "I'll get the materials."

"Gordie, honey," the voice of a woman came from behind the welded door. "Please let us out. I love you, baby."

Gordie took Angel's hand, and together they walked out the door. Behind the steel door, his wife started cussing him.

The television clicked on. Watts took a seat. "I remember this," he said. "Joey and Tuddie's funeral."

The others gathered around the set. "He's doing it again," Mack said. "Pulling events out of sequence. Why?"

"I think I know," Watts said. "Watch."

Joey and Tuddie were buried side by side. Joey's parents—who had disowned him, his mother burning a yarzheit candle—did not attend the funeral. Robin was in shock and heavily sedated all the way through the ordeal. She went to stay with her parents.

Watts was at the funeral, in civilian clothes. After the ceremony, he walked a short distance with Sand. "What are your feelings at this time, Sand?"

"I don't have any feelings. My guts are cold."

Watts glanced up at Morg, sitting on a small knoll above the hallowed ground.

"What's Morg doing, Sand?"

"Waiting."

The Force chuckled darkly. The sky rumbled with thunder. But there was not a cloud in sight.

"Why did you just chuckle, Sand?"

"I didn't."

"All right. What is Morg waiting for?"

"For me."

"Then what are the two of you waiting for?"

Sand stopped and looked at the cop. Darkness leaped from his eyes. The gaze gripped Watts, chilling him. "You wouldn't understand, Captain."

"Probably not," Watts said after a sigh. He felt strange, as if someone else were listening.

"Oh, yes," a voice spoke.

"Damnit, Sand!" Watts said, exasperated. "Who's doing that?"

"We're almost out of time, Captain. When you shoot, please shoot straight."

"What in the *hell* are you talking about, Sand?"

Sand walked away. Watts looked up at the knoll. Morg was gone. So was Bruno, Sand's big quarter-breed wolf. Bruno howled. Watts shivered.

"Eerie," Watts said.

"Oh, yes," a voice whispered. "Quite."

Watts looked quickly around him. There was not a living soul in sight.

A living soul.

Watts walked out of the graveyard. He resisted with all his might the urge to whistle.

The TV screen went dark.

"So what's he telling us, Al?" Mack asked.

"The Force is going to help us, I think."

Howie called from his room. "Come in here, people. This just popped up on Sand's screen."

They all gathered around and looked. The one word gave them all new hope.

Sand had typed: *Yes.*

Chapter Ten

Gordie pulled up in the driveway and gave the place a visual once-over. It had been a strange drive from the office. Not one person had been on the streets of the town. One *living* person that is. The streets were littered with the bodies of the newly dead.

Angel had looked at the bloating bodies through young eyes, that had already seen far too much of the darker side of life.

"Watch my back," Gordie said to Bergman, as the men got out of the car.

Gordie walked to the front door and knocked. He could hear nothing from inside the house. He tried the door and found it unlocked. He turned the knob and pushed open the door, his .357 in his right hand, hammer back.

No odor of death struck him. The house appeared to be empty. "I'm checking it out," he called to Bergman.

The house was void of living or dead.

Gordie checked the fenced-in backyard. Nothing. He looked in the basement. Nothing. He walked back to the front door and waved Angel in. "Stay with the car," he told Bergman. "This may be a set-up."

Angel went to her bedroom and retrieved a few articles of clothing and some pictures. She did the same in Howie's room. Gordie noticed that none of the pictures were of her parents. He asked about that.

"It's Howie's opinion that the Fury killed most of the good people first. It was not our fate to die. The Fury is using the weak people. If my parents are that weak — or bad, as the case may be — I don't want to remember them. Maybe you and Sunny can take care of us once this is over?"

Gordie smiled, mildly astonished at the astuteness of the young.

"I can tell by the way you look at each other that you care for each other. Howie can sometimes be a pain in the butt, but I'm not much trouble," she said with a hint of a smile.

Sunny put an arm around the child's shoulders. "That's a good idea, Angel. We'll leave it up to Gordie." Woman and child looked at him.

Gordie stepped forward and put his arms around the both of them. "Why not?" he said.

Outside, in the bright sunlight, they quickly joined Bergman in the car and drove away.

"I hope I never see that house again," Angel said. "I want this to be over."

"It will be," Gordie told her. Sooner than we both think, he mentally added.

"It's heading your way," the speaker crackled.

The car suddenly stopped in the street, the motor dead.

OUT FOR A PLEASANT LITTLE DRIVE, RIVERA?

"Yeah. I planned a picnic, but we couldn't find a suitable spot."

MY DEAL STILL STANDS, GUNFIGHTER. HUMP THE KID AND YOU CAN WALK FREE.

"Hang it up, Fury," Gordie told him.

YOUR ASS, GREASEBALL.

"It's gone," the words came out of the speaker.

The car's engine roared into life.

"Why doesn't it just go ahead and kill us and take our knowledge?" Bergman asked. "Is this just a game to the Fury, or is it somehow prevented from killing the stronger — if that is indeed what we are?"

A cold, very clammy feeling enveloped them all. And all knew what it was from viewing the reruns of Sand's life.

The Force.

"Listen to me," the heavy voice tingled their ears. It was so heavy it was almost painful. "I will help you through Sand. The door is close, but the way is dangerous. Once you enter the door, there is no turning back. You might exit in another time frame. If you do, remember this: you cannot alter history. I will contact you again when you are very nearly out of time."

"Wait!" Gordie called.

"I am waiting. I am always waiting when death is imminent."

"If we do make it clear, the press will be all over us. What do we tell them?"

"The truth. Always the truth."

"As we perceive it?" Bergman asked.

The Force chuckled darkly. "Even the very ignorant know when they are lying to themselves. Anything else is a myth, conceived in the minds of those who must justify what they do on your miserable planet."

"Why us?" Angel asked. "Why are you helping us?"

The pressure throbbed for a moment. "Sand is a very convincing speaker."

The pressure left them. Gordie put the car in gear and rolled on up the street. Back at the office, he told the others what the Force had said.

"I don't care if we end up in the middle of Apache country in the 1870s," Norris said. "At least we'll be alive."

"I'll advise Martin," Megan said. "Let him decide how much, if any, is released to the press."

"It's here!" Howie called.

PLANNING AND SCHEMING, EH? GOOD. I LIKE THAT. KEEPS ME ON MY TOES, SO TO SPEAK. ALTHOUGH ME ON MY TOES WOULD BE A RIDICULOUS SIGHT TO SEE.

Capt. Hishon took a chance. "I'd like to see you," he said.

WOULD YOU NOW? I THINK NOT, TIN SOLDIER.

284

PERSONALLY, I CONSIDER MYSELF TO BE A HANDSOME BEING. OTHERS, HOWEVER, DO NOT. BUT WHEN THE END COMES, I MIGHT GRANT YOU YOUR WISH. IT WOULD BE AMUSING TO SEE YOU GO MAD.

It left with such a rush, it crackled the hair of everyone in the room.

"Where is it, Howie?" Gordie asked.

"Thunder Mountain. It keeps returning there."

Troops had been brought in from Fort Carson. They closed all the roads within a twenty-five-mile radius of Willowdale, and sealed off the area.

Martin Tobias could not, legally, run the preachers out of the valley, anymore than he could run the press out, but he did order the rattlesnakes of Harold Jewelweed confiscated.

"You done violated my constitutional rights, ah haw!" Harold puffed up.

"Please remind me to apologize . . . at some future date."

Motels as far away as Denver were jammed full of reporters, diplomats, government officials, and the curious; schools and civic centers and gyms were packed with those evacuated.

Fury enlarged its territory again, spreading itself out another quarter-mile in all directions. But this time, Gordie was ready for it.

"It's moved back to the mountain, Sheriff," Howie called.

"Let's go, people!" Gordie shouted the words as he hit the door, the military and Mack and Watts right behind him.

They fanned out, planting explosives all over the town. Lee and several others were gathering up all the old tires they could find—oftentimes taking them off vehicles parked alongside the street. Anything that would produce a thick smoke.

"We can detonate many of these electronically," Maj. Jackson said. "But the majority of them will have to be hand set."

"That's where Mack and me come in," Watts said. "We'll go through the drill one more time, Major. Just before you people pull out."

"Bump Howie, Jane," Gordie said. "Let's see if we're still clear."

"Clear, Sheriff," the deputy said.

"Tell him to notify Martin Tobias that we're making our break at eight o'clock tomorrow evening. It'll be full dark. That gives us—and those outside the Fury's perimeter— thirty-four hours. Let's get back to work, people."

President Marshall looked at the chairman of the Joint Chiefs of Staff. He glanced at his watch. "We drop in thirty-three hours, forty-seven minutes. Eight-thirty tomorrow evening. Alert the crew."

"Yes, sir." The general left the room.

The president turned his gaze to the secretary of state. "The secrecy lid still on tight?"

"As tight as I've ever seen it."

"I am absolutely amazed that we haven't had worldwide panic. Astounded by it."

"We've had a lot of speculation. Martin is to be commended for the fine job he's done."

"You're going to be late for your press conference," the president was reminded.

President Marshall shook his head. "There won't be any press conferences until this . . . incident is over."

"The press isn't going to like that."

"I don't particularly care what the press likes; not at this juncture. What have you been able to come up with on this Saunders person?" That was directed at the at-

286

torney general.

"He got the shaft, legally speaking," the attorney general replied. "But that didn't give him the right to go out and kill half a dozen people and castrate another young man."

"What did these people do to bring down the wrath of this young man?"

"Killed his pregnant wife. The baby was stillborn."

The president grunted. True justice did out in this case. "Can he be exonerated?"

"No. That's impossible. He was never tried. But he is, somehow, showing his side of the story to those trapped in Willowdale. They're videotaping it. We'll have to go that route."

"Is he agreeable with that?"

"Jesus Christ, sir. The man is dead! What can he do about it?"

The president pointed a finger at the attorney general. "You just make damn sure his side of the story gets told. We'll leave the rest up to the people who see it."

"Yes, sir. Whatever you say, sir."

Night, the shadow of light,
And life, the shadow of death.
                    Swinburne

Those survivors had agreed not to venture out until unless they absolutely had to. Howie announced that only the sentries were still in place. The Fury was resting on Thunder Mountain.

The television clicked on and Watts said, "Here it is. Now maybe I'll know for sure what happened."

The others gathered around the set, standing, sitting in chairs, sitting on the floor. The sound of a phone ringing came out of the set's speakers. Sand was alone in the den.

Sand reached for the phone. The Force gripped him. "Be strong," it whispered. "For I am now more of you than you

287

are of me."

Music began in Sand's head. Softly, only a faint melody in the back of his mind. It would soon build to a thunderous crescendo.

Robin's mother said, "Sand, let me speak to Robin."

"She isn't here, Mrs. Lee. I thought she was at your house."

"She left here hours ago!" the woman's voice became very high-pitched. "Sand, where *is* she?"

"I don't know, Mrs. Lee." Someone was knocking at the front door. "Hang on for a second. Calm down."

He ran to the door, jerking it open. Watts stood on the front porch, a grim expression on his face. The Force became more a part of the young man as Sand spun in a whirlwind ride, a lonely maddening spin; an invisible calliope played a jumble of melodies, an angry roaring in his head. Mussorgsky, Beethoven, Wagner. *Night on Bald Mountain. Lenore. Götterdämmerung.*

Sand fought the thundering until the sounds faded.

"Robin," Sand found his voice.

"Yes," Watts replied, his voice sounding very distant to the young man. It was distant. A dark river lay between them. "There's been an . . . accident, Sand. About ten miles outside of town. It's bad, son. She's . . ."

"Dead." Sand said flatly, filling in the blanks of life's complicated crossword puzzle. His last puzzle. Only a few more squares needed to be filled.

"I am truly sorry," Watts said, thinking: what a stupid, totally inadequate phrase.

Sand pointed to the phone. "Mrs. Lee's on the line. You tell her the news."

"Now is the time," the Force spoke.

Watts looked around him, certain he had heard a voice. He walked to the phone like a man stepping through a mine field. Sand slipped into a jacket and ran to his car.

A dozen or more cars were parked around the base of a hill. Red lights gave the night a carnival atmosphere. Bobbing flashlights and dark figures moved about. Sand noticed Robin's Olds in a ditch, both left wheels stuck in the mud, the door to the driver's side open, the interior light burning dimly as the battery wore down. He could not make the connection between his wife's death and her car stuck in the mud. And where was his breed, Bruno? Robin never went anywhere without the quarter-breed wolf. He was very protective of her.

The roaring music began in his head, all mixed in with that strange pressure that seemed to constantly grip him of late. Then . . . silence. Loud in the absence of noise. He felt cold, detached from reality. And alone.

"You are not alone," the Force told him. "We are now as one."

An ambulance moaned and wailed in the background, the red lights and the siren cutting a scar into the night.

Why hurry? Sand thought. She's gone.

"Wrong," the Force corrected. "She is merely waiting for you."

Sand walked slowly up the hill, to the first level of lights, stopping when he saw Morg, standing alone.

"You hadn't oughta go up there, Sand. Man, it's awful."

"Come on," Sand said. "Walk with me."

A state patrol officer stopped them a dozen yards from the brightest blaze of lights. "The captain is right behind you, Sand. Said for you to wait for him." He looked at Morg.

"I ran you out of here once."

"I come back."

Sand knew the trooper could not hear the muted roarings in his head, raging like a huge orchestra under the baton of a mad conductor.

"I'll take it from here," Watts spoke from the darkness behind the men. Robin's father, Carl, stood with the captain, his big hands clenched into fists of silent rage. Watts said, "Follow me and be careful where you walk. Don't step in any roped-off areas. We're still trying to unravel this one."

Sand walked ahead of the others, ignoring Watts's call to wait. He ran toward the blanket-covered, lifeless, almost shapeless lump on the cool ground. Sand's face seemed carved out of granite. All but his eyes; God, they ached.

The roaring in his head became louder, more crazed, less definable. Kneeling down, he lifted the blanket and looked into the face of death.

Robin was chalk-white, her lips a light blue. Sand felt a wetness soaking through the knees of his jeans. He was kneeling in a thick puddle of blood. He turned his head to one side and vomited.

There was a tiny object between Robin's legs, her maternity skirt hiked up around her waist. She had miscarried. Sand was kneeling in the midst of twin death.

Wiping his mouth with the back of his hand, Sand dropped the blanket over Robin. Watts and Carl and Morg stood a few yards away, out of respect for Sand. A cold, white hand protruded from under the blanket. It was clenched in a small fist. Prying open the fist, Sand discovered a fistful of hair, blood, and bits of flesh. He slipped that into his jacket pocket and stood up.

The police were not going to handle this one.

"Good," the Force said, becoming more and more a part of Sand. "This time, justice will truly prevail."

"I don't want to see her like this," Carl said. The big man had tears in his eyes.

The four of them walked back down the hill. Watts said, "I'm going to level with you, and tell you what we have so far: The Patrol got a call this evening, about seven-thirty. The caller refused to give her name. She said a car had gone off into the ditch at the Steeleville exit and six or seven young men were chasing a young woman up a hill. She said the young men were clearly drunk; laughing and shouting and having a good time. She said the young woman was screaming and crying.

"There are several Steeleville exits, so by the time my man

checked this one—with the help of the sheriff's department—it was almost eight-thirty. He found the Olds, lights on, motor running, in the ditch. Where it is now. He said as he walked up the hill, looking for the woman, there was a, ah, strong odor."

"Blood," Sand said.

Watts looked at him. That strong sensation of pressure that lingered around Sand was even stronger. Watts could not imagine what it might be. "Yes. The men found Robin. The doctor just gave me a preliminary cause of death. A combination of things killed her. From the bruises on her stomach, she was apparently kicked or struck with some object several times. She miscarried, and that, combined with internal injuries, shock, fright . . . all contributed to her death."

Watts sighed heavily. "Anyway, on the way back down the hill, my man literally stumbled over the second body."

All eyes clicked toward Watts, unblinking. Waiting.

"The young man's name is, was, John Murry. Student at State. His . . . throat is gone. Completely ripped out. Done by a large animal with very powerful jaws and long fangs."

"Bruno got one of the cocksuckers, anyway," Sand said. "But where did *he* go?"

Watts grimaced. "We don't know that Murry had anything to do with Robin's death, although that appears to be the case. As to that quarter-breed wolf of yours, the trooper found him. He had been hit on the head with a club. We have the club, the animal is gone. Obviously, he was only stunned. When he regained consciousness, according to tracks around the body, he inspected Robin, found her dead, and ran back into the mountains. Where," he looked squarely at Sand, "any wild animal belongs."

"*Visser vous,*" Sand told him.

"I won't even ask what that means."

"It means screw you."

Sand looked toward the mountains, looming dark all around him. He had found Bruno in the mountains, and

291

could almost feel the breed's eyes on him now. The breed had tasted the so-called civilization of man, and found it not to his liking. Sand knew the feeling. Bruno was again running wild and free. Where he would remain, unless some stupid redneck shot him.

Back at his car, Sand said to Carl, "I'll be at the funeral home." To Watts: "And I don't want any goddamned autopsy."

"Sand," Watts said, "We have to—"

"I'm with Sand," Carl said. "I mean it, Al. No knives on Robin. I'll fight you on this if I have to, and if I have to, I'll enlist the help of Julie von Mehren."

Watts looked pained at the mention of the rich old lady. "I'll speak to the DA, Carl."

Sand did not leave the funeral home that night. He sat alone in the waiting room, drinking a dozen cups of bitter coffee—and waiting, listening to the music in his head.

It was full dawn when the attendant wheeled in the casket, and left Sand alone with his dead dreams.

He walked to the casket and looked down. Robin was lovely. But she was dead. Cold. Behind the veil. Standing on the Stygian shore.

"She is waiting," the Force spoke, and the voice was Sand's.

Outside, Morg waited for his friend. He had sat on the curb all through the night. Waiting. Maintaining his lonely vigil. He knew that if the cops didn't find out who killed Robin, and do it damn quick, Sand would find out and kill them. Morg would be there to help his friend. Since Jane's death, Morg had wandered around in a fog of loneliness. But now he had something he could do. And if both he and Sand died—and Morg was sure they would—doing the deed, or after it . . . who was left to care?

You take a life through injustice, you give a life.

Morg waited.

The director of the funeral home walked in to speak with Sand. "The boy was stillborn, Mr. Saunders. What do you want done?"

"Buried beside his mother. Fill in all the holes." His rage, his sense of loss, his frustrations, his hold on his temper, all lay just below the surface, ready to explode in a bloody rage. His head thundered with music. His voice shook with emotion.

The funeral director said, "It's just a . . . I mean, well, the casket cannot be opened."

"I know. Seal it."

"The boy's name?"

He and Robin had discussed it, and both had agreed. "Sand."

"I'll get right on it."

"Thank you. Lock the doors. I don't want anybody in here."

"I understand."

Sand sat on the carpet in front of Robin's casket. He prayed to God, to Thor, to Odin. But he could not cry. Someone rattled at the doors. Sand ignored them. The Force grew stronger until it was Sand.

"That's why the Force is helping us," Howie said, awed by what he had just seen on the screen. "The Force *is* Sand."

"Or at least a part of him," Megan said. "Although how that occurred is, and probably always will be, a mystery."

"Until we die," Watts added. He pointed to the screen. "There it is. The evidence Sand withheld from me."

Sand did not return to the funeral home after that long night and morning. He went to his now half-home. He showed Morg the dried blood, hair, and flesh.

"Somebody is gonna be tore up something bad," Morg said. "I got a buddy over in Monte Rio that can snoop around some, on the QT."

"We know this didn't belong to Murry. He was unmarked, except where Bruno ripped his throat. And we both know the others involved."

"And you want them all."

293

Sand smiled. His eyes were animal yellow. It was thundering out of a clear blue sky.

BAH! JUST LIKE A MORTAL BEING. PISSING AND MOANING OVER THE LOSS OF SOMETHING TOTALLY INSIGNIFICANT.

"You're jealous, aren't you?" Angel asked the Fury.

WHATEVER IN THE WORLD DO YOU MEAN, YOU LITTLE TWIT?

"You're very powerful, very strong, very intelligent. But you can never be like us. And because of that, you want to destroy us. But don't you see? If you destroy us, you destroy yourself. You can't live without us."

The Fury pulsed for a long moment. YOU WILL ALL BE MY SLAVES. I HAVE DECIDED TO LET YOU LIVE. MOST OF YOU. I WILL PLAY WITH YOU FOREVER. THINK ABOUT IT. I AM OFFERING YOU ETERNAL LIFE.

"We'll think about it," Howie said quickly. "But let us have some time to do that. That is a difficult decision to reach."

THAT IS CORRECT. YOU ARE WISE BEYOND YOUR YEARS. HOW MUCH TIME?

"Oh . . . I don't know," Howie said. "I should think perhaps a day and a night would not be too much to ask. If that's all right with you. If not, you set the time limits."

I AM GENEROUS TO A FAULT. I SHALL GIVE YOU TWO DAYS AND TWO NIGHTS OF YOUR TIME. FORTY-EIGHT OF YOUR HOURS. TA-TA, NOW.

"Smooth, Howie," Jill told the boy. "Very, very good."

Howie nodded and walked over to his computers, checking the screens. "It's returned to the mountain. When it starts to leave there, I want us all to gather in little groups and be engaged in serious debate."

The keys on his PC rattled. Sand wrote: *The door will be ready for you all at eight tomorrow night. Be quick and do everything I tell you to do.*

Howie typed: Are you the Force?

294

No. We are buddies.

But you are part of the Force?

In a manner of speaking. At the moment of death, the chosen are all a part of it. Talk to you later. I have to warn some friends of mine.

"I wonder what he means by that?" Howie muttered.

Gordie stood with a small group, looking out the gun slits. The street was devoid of life, or any other kind of movement.

Larry ran to Martin's trailer and jerked open the door. "Martin, come quickly. You've got to see this. It's an exodus of animals from the valley."

Martin ran outside and took the binoculars handed him by an Army officer. He adjusted the focus and looked up into the mountains.

"Dear God in heaven," he whispered.

Half a dozen gray wolves were leading the exodus out of the valley and over the mountains. The wolves were leading deer, elk, bear, cougar, and a parade of cats and dogs and horses and cattle and other livestock.

"Incredible," another government official said, looking at the scene through binoculars. "It's beautiful. But how do they know? How did they sense something was going to happen?"

"I suspect that somehow Sand told them," Martin said. "Until these animals can disperse and find new shelter, order a total ban on hunting in this area. I will prosecute to the fullest extent of the law any so-called sportsman," he spat out the word, "who pulls a trigger against any of those animals. See that that order goes out immediately, Larry."

"Yes, sir."

Martin walked to a heavily guarded trailer and was admitted inside. The trailer was packed with electronic equipment. "What's the latest word from inside the town, Hank?"

"The boy, Howie, struck a deal with the Fury. Fury gave them two days to make up their minds whether or not to accept eternal life as its slaves — or die."

"Everything else is still go?"

"So far."

"Keep me informed."

"Yes, sir."

Martin walked back to his trailer, ignoring the shouts from the press corps. The shouts now contained threats that the reporters' constitutional rights were being violated.

"Why are those animals leaving the area, Mr. Tobias?" the question was shouted.

"Ask the animals," Martin said. "I assure you that I cannot speak for them."

"What's going on in Willowdale now, sir?"

"It's very quiet in there."

"Are the convicts still loose?"

"Yes." Martin reached the door to his trailer.

"Were those really dead people we saw the other day at the barricades?"

"No," Martin turned to face the knot of reporters. "The disease had affected their skin, that's all."

"That's bullshit, Mr. Tobias," another said.

"End of questions," Martin said.

you. You got it."
"Very well. Lift your eyes upward."
Sand turned his head and looked. Room was standing a

Chapter Eleven

The smell from the town was very nearly overpowering to the survivors in the sheriff's office. Fans had been located and placed around the rooms in an attempt to push the stink out. It was not very effective.

"We can't take two more days of this," Gordie said. "All sorts of diseases are floating around out there. We're going to have to go out there, push the bodies together as best we can, and burn them. I won't order anyone to go with me."

"I can drive a front-loader," Dean said. "Let's go."

ARE YOUR MINDS MADE UP?

"Not yet, Fury," Gordie said. "But we're talking about it."

I DON'T TRUST YOU, SPIC. YOU OR THE BRATS. I THINK YOU'VE ALL GOT SOMETHING COOKING AGAINST ME. I WARN YOU NOW, IF YOU TRY THING FUNNY, ALL DEALS ARE OFF.

"Right now, Fury," Gordie told him. "All we're interested in is clearing away these stinking bodies You want us alive, don't you?"

UMMM. OH, ALL RIGHT. GO AHEAD. BUT I'LL BE WATCHING YOU.

"Watch all you want, Fury. Tell you what, why don't you sing to us while we work? It'll make the work go faster."

FINALLY RECOGNIZING MY TALENTS, EH? GOOD. HOW ABOUT THIS?

The Fury launched into *Shake, Rattle, and Roll.* Its voice was so thunderous it rattled the windows of the town and carried for miles.

The reporters all gathered as close to the line of troops as

297

they could, and listened.

"What the hell is that?" one asked.

"That's no singer that I've ever heard before."

"There isn't an amplification system anywhere in the world that good," another said.

The singing abruptly stopped. A voice sprang out of the sky. THAT'S RIGHT, ASSHOLE.

Martin stepped out of his trailer. Fury was about to make its move, and pretense was out the window.

The convicts Logan, Bingham, and Diminno were hurled over the barricades. They slopped wetly on the ground in front of the reporters and the camera crews. All the skin had been stripped from them. They were alive, but just barely.

The reporters got to them first.

"What's going on in that town?" the question was asked of the dying men. "Where did you come from?"

"A thing from space," Bingham gasped, the words coming hard through his intense pain. "It's called Fury. You're all doomed. All of you. Run. Run. Get away."

He laid his head down on the ground and died, just as the military doctors reached the bloody men.

Martin walked back into his trailer and picked up the phone. "Get me the White House," he told the Secret Service agent at the switchboard.

"And so far, we have it contained," President Marshall told the lie as he attempted to end the hurriedly called press conference.

But that was not to be.

"Where did this thing come from, Mr. President?"

"We don't know."

"Why Willowdale, Colorado?"

"We don't know that either."

"What are you doing about it, sir?"

"We are attempting to negotiate with it, trying to find out what it wants."

"What does it want, sir?"

"We don't know."

"And you're firm in your decision not to allow anymore reporters into the area?"

"No one is allowed in the area we have cordoned off. This mass has killed nearly everyone in the town of Willowdale. Only a few survivors remain."

"Is there a rescue operation planned, sir?"

"No. Not at this time."

"Why not, Mr. President?"

"Unworkable. Our technology is not far enough advanced to match that of the Fury. All we would do is lose more people." The president had been briefed to say that, knowing that in all probability, the Fury was somehow listening.

"Do the people inside the town know they are expendable?"

"They are aware of that. They've accepted it."

"Why didn't they get out when they could?"

"They never had a chance to escape. The Fury moved that fast."

The president tapped a finger on the side of the rostrum, and an aide came out at the signal and whispered in his ear.

"Ladies and gentlemen, I have a call I must take. There will be another briefing tomorrow." He left the podium without taking another question.

Whenever possible, the teams working the body detail removed identification before burning the corpse. That I.D. was taken back to Howie who transmitted it out by computer. Gordie knew, however, they had not encountered a living being this day.

"That's good," Maj. Jackson said in a whisper. "In a way. It means the Fury will be used to lots of smoke. We can work right up to bug-out time."

"Better yet," Gordie whispered without lifting his head from his work, "we can put some of the young people through the door, while the rest of us continue working."

299

Jackson grinned. "I like it."

Lee straightened up with a grunt. "I'm about ready to call it a day, boys."

Gordie checked his watch. Nearly five o'clock. "I'm with you. Let's hit the showers. We all smell like the bodies we've burned."

NOT SO FAST, GORDIE-BABY. YOU QUIT WORK WHEN I TELL YOU TO QUIT, AND NOT BEFORE. I KNOW YOU PEOPLE ARE UP TO SOMETHING, SO I'M GOING TO WORK YOUR ASSES UNTIL YOU DROP.

"Whatever you say, Fury. None of us have lied to you before, why would we start now?"

WORK. I SHALL SING WHILE YOU WORK. DO BOP DE DO BOP DE DO BOP, DE DO.

They worked until after dark, and when Gordie checked his watch, he was pleased to see darkness would fall sometime before their scheduled breakout. Now if their luck held out.

Luck has nothing to do with it, the voice sprang into his head.

Sand. It startled Gordie. He can read my thoughts.

You are all very close to death. Everything about you is transparent now . . . to those of us on the other side. We won't have to use the computer from this point on. Just think what you want me to know.

How about Fury?

It cannot read your thoughts. It knows only what it has learned from the souls of beings.

YOU MAY QUIT NOW. RETURN TO THE OFFICE AND HAVE YOUR SUPPER. IT MIGHT BE YOUR LAST ONE. HEE HEE HEE. GET IT? LAST SUPPER? SOMETIMES I CAN BE SO HUMOROUS.

Asshole, Gordie thought.

Right, Sand projected.

THE LAST DREAM

There had been nothing heard from those behind the door that had been welded shut. Dr. Anderson felt they were dead. Gordie merely grunted at the opinion.

Everyone was too tired to even think about using the jail's kitchen to fix dinner. They dined on military MREs.

Megan LeMasters almost spilled her cup of coffee when Sand's thoughts entered her head.

The president is on my side. Be sure to take all the video tapes you have made to him. He wants to view them.

All right, she projected. Bos will carry them through the door in a knapsack.

Everybody listen to me!

All heads jerked up.

The door is moving into position. When you step through, you will enter a world that is strange to you. Don't be afraid. I won't let anything happen to you, but you must do exactly what I say. Stay on the path I point out. Do not step off of it. Al?

Watts looked up.

My story is almost finished. We won't be able to talk, because you won't be coming here. You'll move to a better place. You and Mack. So don't be afraid of death. Think of it as a new beginning. Now go to the television set.

"Fury is on the mountain," Howie called, turning in his chair so he could see the TV.

The group gathered around.

"That's the old cemetery just outside of town," Gordie said. The cemetery of Sand's dreams.

Sand stood alone atop a knoll, looking down on the knot of people gathered around the two boxlike holes in the earth. Sand had avoided all contact with Robin's parents. Her mother was under heavy sedation, and the doctors were worried she was close to a nervous breakdown . . . or worse.

Sand was apart from what had been his kind, mourning his losses alone; the only way his mind could now cope. Morg squatted a few yards behind Sand, to his right, his top hat in his hands. They both had dreamed their last dreams, and now waited for time to run out.

Sand had not seen the face of Robin since that day at the funeral home. He did not want that face in his memory. His mind was already crowded with the memories of those he loved shrouded in Stygian darkness. Sand wanted to remember Robin alive . . . in the time he had left.

The minister who had married Sand and Robin, now spoke the burial words over mother and son.

As Sand stood on the hill, he felt the wind pick up, great dark clouds rolling above the cemetery, thunder rumbling in heavy waves. Midway through the graveside services, the skies opened, and the angels cried. Those who brought umbrellas quickly opened them, and placed their sad expressions back on their faces, as is required by all who attend such public barbarisms. Occasionally, Robin's father would glance up at the tall young man, standing alone on the hill.

But Sand was not alone. The Force was in him.

Just as the minister was intoning his final pleas for whatever he felt stretched beyond the grave—Sand already knew—his words muted in the rain, Sand caught the faint but unmistakable sounds of howling. His dream was now complete. He would not dream it again. He searched the dim light of the stormy afternoon for the source of the howling, knowing it was his quarter-breed, Bruno. The animal was sitting on a hill, his head thrown back, face to the sky, voicing his displeasure to his own ancient gods. Only the theory that man is superior to beasts prevented Sand from joining the breed in the petition.

The howling from the quarter-breed wolf stirred something deep in Sand; something dark and archaic and Druidlike. The stirrings screamed for justice, justice in the form of revenge. A monster roamed within the young man, hairy and fanged. Sand allowed the grotesqueness to come close to the surface, before pushing it back.

"Wait," the Force whispered. "Wait."

The roaring became a whimper, the cloaked monster squatted in Sand's mind, picking at itself, momentarily calmed and silent, but still a part of him.

Bruno's howling ceased, the rain dripped off Sand's face,

the downfall coming harder, in thick sheets of silver, until it finally drove off the last of the curious. Only then did Sand walk down to the gravesites.

"Get out of here," Sand told the workmen.

They dropped their shovels and got.

Lightning split the heavens as the wind raged and thunder rolled, the wind ripping the tent over the graves, sending the canvas flapping through the air, the ends popping and cracking like a giant bullwhip.

Sand did not notice. He worked through the cruel afternoon, filling in the holes of his past nightmares, shoveling wet dirt over what was once life and love, hopes and young dreams, laughter and pain, birth and death.

Sensing someone behind him, Sand turned to look at Robin's father.

He turned away, resuming his shoveling, filling in all the holes of his nightmares. Then the tears came, filling Sand's eyes. When the muddy earth was patted into place, forming two earthen mounds, Sand collapsed on the ground between the twin earth mansions of eternal quietude. The steel wall of his emotions clanged open. On his knees, he put his muddy hands to his face and wept.

Robin's father walked away. His own eyes were streaming rivers of tears.

On the hill overlooking Willowdale's most prestigious cemetery, Morg squatted in the downpour, waiting. He had the information that Sand needed, but a man should have the time to grieve his losses. Then, together, they would do the deed.

Somehow Morg knew they had just enough time left to do that. And no more.

It was dusk when Sand rose and walked to his car. Watts was waiting at his house when he got there. The highway patrolman waited until Sand showered, then Watts handed him a cup of coffee.

"You're not going to like this," Watts said. "But I may as well give it to you straight, no matter how it rubs you the wrong way.

"You may fire when ready, Gridley." Music raged in Sand's head.

"Marlson and the others who run with him came to see me early this morning. They are all clear in this matter, Sand. They saw Robin's car parked by the side of the road and stopped to help. To see if anything was wrong."

"Of course, they did," Sand said with a smile. "Being the type of concerned citizens that they are." *Clair de Lune* played softly in his head.

"The polygraph tests were inconclusive, Sand. But the operator thinks that they are telling the truth."

"Compulsive liars can pass polygraph tests, Captain."

"I know that, Sand. Damnit, I know that. I'm not going to drop this thing, boy. You have my word on that."

"Wonderful. What else did these concerned citizens have to say?"

"They said Robin was already dead. When they got too close to her, the breed jumped Murry and the rest of them panicked. They got themselves together and finally came to see me."

The Force that was Sand chuckled darkly. "Why did they wait two days?" The *Tragic Overture* rudely pushed *Clair de Lune* out to sea.

"They'd been in a fight — so they said. They were afraid I'd think they'd been fighting with some of your bunch. Truthfully, Sand, they had been in a small scrape. I checked it personally. One boy was cut up, scratched on the face and neck."

Sand smiled and said nothing.

"It works, Sand. It's fitting together. But I won't drop it. I promise you that. If they did it, I'll find out. And they'll be punished."

"If they did it, and if you find out, will they die?"

"Goddamnit, Sand, the law doesn't work that way, and you know it."

"How unfortunate for the innocent."

"Sand, you told me a few days ago that you and Robin were planning on leaving this area. Are you leaving alone?"

304

"To be sure. I shall be gone within twenty-four hours. Probably sooner than that. I will probably never . . . well, shall we say, *personally* bother you again. Not in the flesh."

"That is a damn strange remark, son."

"And this maiden she lived with no other thought than to love and be loved by me."

"I'm familiar with Poe, Sand. Boy, you are taking this very calmly. That worries me."

Brahms played in Sand's head. Lovely. Bits of Alice's Adventure in Wonderland came to him: I'll be the judge, I'll be the jury. I'll try the whole cause and condemn you to death.

Sand laughed just as the phone rang. Watts was suddenly aware of that strange sensation filling the room. Heavier, stronger than he had ever felt it. It was not evil, Watts thought, then thought himself a fool for thinking it. But it was . . . dark, he finished in his thoughts.

Sand hung up the phone and slowly turned. "That was Carl Lee on the phone, Captain. Robin's mother went berserk. They have her in restraints at the hospital. She is to be transported to a private mental hospital."

"Dear God," Watts said.

The Force whispered to Sand. Sand smiled.

Watts heard the whisper. Dismissed it as the wind. The thought came to him: Nevermore.

He shook his head. "Where is your friend Morg?"

"Like me, waiting. We shall be . . . leaving together."

"Where are you two going?"

"After a time, to a place that is quiet. Sort of. It's not that far a journey. There, we might ponder the mysteries of cabbages and kings. And why the sea is boiling hot, and whether pigs have wings."

The Force laughed. Something very nearly tangible moved in the room. Sweat broke out on Watts's forehead.

"Is the house too warm, Captain?"

"Weird," Watts muttered. He sighed. "When are you two leaving, Sand?"

"Soon, Captain. But the time of our final departure will be up to you. I shall leave you with this bit of philosophy

305

from Baudelaire: There exists only three beings worthy of respect: the priest, the soldier, the poet. Do you understand that?"

"Not really."

"It's very simple. To know, to kill, to create." Sand smiled. "You will, I believe, Captain, soon experience all three."

Watts grimaced, shook his head, and walked from the house. He called over his shoulder, "Good-bye, Sand." He closed the door, strangely relieved to be out of Sand's presence.

"Very good," the Force spoke to Sand. "You are a very intelligent young man. Now we'll see to it that justice is truly served."

"I'm with you."

The room rocked and pulsed with heavy laughter.

Sand and the Force began speaking to each other, switching from one language to another. Morg came in through the back door. He stood for a time, wondering who his friend was talking to. Sand noticed him and fell silent.

"My man got it," Morg said.

Sand smiled. He pointed to something only he could see, and said, *"Il est toujours sur mon dos . . ."*

"Speak American, Sand. I can't understand a damn word you're sayin' "

"Yet," the Force said.

Morg looked around him.

"But your time is only minutes away."

"Buzz off!"

The Force chuckled.

Sand told Morg what Watts had said.

Morg waved his hand and cussed. "Them rich shits is lyin,' man. There wasn't no fight. That was a put-up job to get the heat off Marlson and his bunch. Marlson and them others stopped at a beer joint over the pass. They was pretty shook up. Talkin' about bein' in a fight and all that. 'Cept there wasn't no fight, nowhere, that night. It was all put-up, and that's firm."

"You have their names."

306

"You know them."

"Yeah. Marlson, Branon, Lenton, Jeffery, Murphy, Center, and Alexander. Bruno took care of Murry."

"Right. My pal says if you want to crack one open, it's Jeffery. He's a real fish, scared out of his gourd."

Morg stood for a moment, listening in amazement as Sand spoke in a language he could not understand, and to a . . . whatever the hell it was, that he could not see. Morg shivered as laughter rang out. But it did not come from Sand.

Then the Force spoke to Morg. "I have reviewed your future. You have none. You are now able to converse with us."

Morg looked wildly around him. "I know I ain't got no future. What's that got to do with the price of potatoes?"

The Force laughed. "I like you. You're crude, but I like you."

"Morg," Sand said. "Which one did Robin mark?"

"You talkin' to me or that . . . other thing?"

"You."

"She mauled Jeffery. Sand, you still got that spare piece?"

Sand found the .45 and handed it to Morg. "You know we're gonna get our tickets punched, don't you?"

"It don't make a shit to me no more, Sand. I'm . . . kinda like you now. Got no place to go, and no one to care about seein' me, if I got there." He smiled. "Well, one place, where *she* is."

"I know," Sand said gently.

Laughter echoed throughout the house as the hall clock chimed out the hour and then quit working, its mainspring broken.

Time had stopped for Sand and Morg.

Morg shoved the .45 auto behind his belt. Sand did the same with an identical .45. "You ready to go, Morg?"

"Oui, mon ami."

Sand smiled at Morg's startled look.

"Man, I don't know no Frog talk!"

"You do now," Sand said.

They started conversing in fluent French.

"All language is as one," the Force told them. "But French is such a refined and gentle language, don't you think?"

"That goddamned thing's gonna get on my nerves," Morg said.

"Au contraire," the Force spoke with a chuckle.

"Stick it in your ear," Morg told him.

The men stepped out into a star-filled, moon-hung night, the storm having blown past. They walked to Sand's Mercury and blasted through the night, an almost visible current sailing along with them.

Carl Lee had sent his remaining daughter, Linda, to stay with friends. He had spoken with Watts. Now he sat in the den of his home and knocked back straight shots of bourbon.

He stilled the ringing telephone, listened for a moment, and then broke the connection by tearing the cord apart. He hurled the phone across the room, shattering it against a wall.

That had been the hospital. His wife had just suffered a series of strokes, one right after the other. Extensive brain damage. Chances of recovery: none.

Carl drained the bottle, then went into his bedroom for his pistols.

Chapter Twelve

When the screen darkened, Watts stood up and walked to a boarded-up window, gazing out the gun slit. The others, sensing that he wished to be left alone, did not follow.

"What's with Colonel Watts?" Pat asked.

"He's preparing himself to die," Bos told her. The college jock had matured a great deal over the past few days, making himself a promise that once out of here, he would knuckle down to more serious college work.

"Gordie," Lee said, walking up to where the sheriff was sitting with Sunny, "what about the prisoners we have left in lock-down?"

"We're taking them with us. They're a worthless crew, but I can't just leave them here to die."

"Do we chain them?"

"No. We'll get them out at the last minute. We tell them nothing until we're at the door."

"What if they try to make a break for it?"

"That's their problem. If they step off that path Sand talked about . . ." He shrugged his shoulders and left it at that.

Lee nodded and walked off. Gordie waved Dr. Anderson over. "How is Robin?"

"She's much better. I told you she was a tough little girl."

"Howie? Where's the Fury?"

"On the mountain," the boy called.

The sheriff looked at his watch. "We've got about twenty-one hours left. Pass the word: before we leave in the morning, stash anything you want to take out in the knapsacks.

Do nothing out of the ordinary. Those that normally remain here, do so. I'll get word to them when it's time to bug-out."

Anderson nodded and walked away.

Sunny took Gordie's hand. "I'm more scared now than ever before," she said.

"Why?"

"Because I don't know what we're going to face, when we walk through that door."

"Think of it as freedom, Sunny, and don't dwell on it. Look, we might not have much time to talk tomorrow. So let's get some things said now — not necessarily in their order of importance. I've fallen in love with you, and the emotion came pretty damned fast. You think you could be happy with a hick-town sheriff?"

She smiled at him. "Oh, yes, Gordie. I think we could be very happy together."

"With Angel and Howie, we've got a built-in family."

"They're good kids. I'm looking forward to raising them."

"You're used to life in the fast lane, Sunny. Small towns can be very dull."

"I've got a lot of books to write, Gordie. I think it'll probably take me about fifty years to get them all completed."

He leaned over and kissed her. "You got a deal."

"We're going to be cutting it very close," Martin told the military commanders. "We've got to give those people in town every break we can afford. At seven o'clock tomorrow evening, we start evacuating out of here. And we do it with no fuss. Very quietly. Anyone who doesn't want to go, leave them."

"They'll die," it was pointed out by a three-star general.

"That is their problem. We're not here to hold their hands. Order them out one time, then walk off."

"You're a hard man, Mr. Tobias," the three-star said. "You ever think about running for president?"

"It has crossed my mind a time or two."

"You've got my vote."

Watts stood in front of the TV in the office. "Do it, Sand," he said. "We're running out of time."

I was born out of time, Al, the words popped into Watts's head.

"I know it. And I'm sorry for all the things I didn't do — back when."

There was nothing you could have done, Al. You'll understand that in a few hours.

Watts sat down in front of the set. "Bring me up to date, son."

VENDETTA

Allen Jeffery did not live on campus. He had a nice apartment off campus — compliments of mommy and daddy — in a secluded complex. When he looked up from his TV, he looked into the cold, hard eyes of Sand and the equally hard-looking Morg. Allen fainted.

When he awakened, he was in an old line shack deep in the mountains. Moonlight streamed in through the broken windows and the holes in the roof.

Jeffery pulled himself up, sitting with his back to a rotting wall. "You won't kill me, will you?" His voice shook with fear. He stank of fear. "I didn't do anything to your wife."

"You were there, weren't you?" Sand asked.

A sly look crept into the young man's eyes. "Why . . . no. As a matter of fact, I wasn't. I thought you knew that."

Sand hit him in the mouth with a gloved fist.

Jeffery screamed and spat out blood. "Yes, yes! I was there. But I didn't do anything. It wasn't my fault or my idea. I swear it!" His fright overwhelmed him. He soiled his underwear. The smell of him filled the shack.

"You tell me what happened," Sand said. "And you tell me the truth. Not that bullshit you people told Watts."

The Force whispered the thoughts that were in Sand's

head.

Sand replied in French.

"Yeah," Morg said. *"Se taire."* He laughed. "Man, this is wild."

Jeffery's eyes were wide and scared. "What was that other voice?" he shouted. "Oh, God help me. You people are with the devil!" he screamed his fear.

"Oh, for pity's sake," the Force said. "Why must I always be associated with that creature? No, no, young man. You are badly mistaken."

"Then who are you?" Jeffery screamed as he pissed his pants.

"Why," the Force breathed, "I am you. I am he. I am him. I am all things in all people. Even, regretfully, a part of such as you. I am many things to all people. I am old loves and old fears, old hates, and everything both good and bad. I am present in all people at all times. But especially vocal when death is imminent. You'd better tell all that you know of this matter. It would save you a great deal of pain."

Jeffery fainted.

The deep timber was silent as Morg slapped Jeffery back to his senses.

In the line shack, a dark form moved amid the shadows. It was almost human in shape. Almost.

"I'll tell all that I know, if you promise you won't hurt me," Jeffery spoke, his eyes darted from Sand to Morg to the flitting shape.

"Oh, my," the Force whispered. "I believe he wants to strike a bargain." The whisper became a howling roar.

Sand cursed Jeffery until he was breathless. A wild beast was uncaged within him. It leaped to the surface, crying out in an ancient tongue. Sand hit Jeffery in the mouth, slamming him against the rotted shack wall. The wall collapsed. Jeffery fell outside, Sand jumping after him. He picked the young man up and threw him back into the shack.

Sand stared at Jeffery. His eyes were not human. They seemed to glow. Even Morg backed off.

"I warned you," the Force said. His form was becoming

312

more definite to Jeffery.

"I know who you are now," Jeffery said.

"Yes, you do."

"All right," Jeffery moaned. "I'll tell you."

A wolf howled in the night. Sand smiled. The Force laughed darkly as thunder rumbled in the distance.

"Eight of us," Jeffery said, then named them. "We took a blood oath to get you, Sand. I mean literally cut ourselves and mixed the blood. We all tasted it. We were frat brothers, you know."

The Force snickered.

"We were rolling that afternoon, looking for girls and drinking beer and chasing it with whiskey. Two cars of us. We got drunk. Just as we were leaving Willowdale, we saw this souped-up Olds. Your car, somebody said. Somebody else said we ought to have some fun and scare your wife." Blood dropped from his lips, plopping onto the floor, amid the bird droppings and rat shit. "I didn't know she was going to have a baby."

"She was in her ninth month and in maternity clothes, you sorry bastard!" Sand yelled at him.

"But we were *drunk!*" Jeffery screamed.

"Stop trying to excuse what you did. Tell it!"

"By all means," the Force said. "And do pick it up a bit, please. So far, it's all been rather mundane."

Jeffery's eyes were wild as the Force became a recognizable shape. And it knew what it was.

Death.

"B . . . Bill Marlson was driving the car I was in. He was the drunkest of us all, and he gets mean when he gets drunk. He's never forgiven you for whipping him that night. He's tried to kill you before. Did you know that?"

"He ran down Boom Boom, too, didn't he?"

"Yes."

"Why? She never hurt anybody in her life."

"She was a friend of yours, that's why."

"You all knew about that?"

"Yes."

313

"And didn't going to the police ever enter your mind?"

"We belonged to the same fraternity," Jeffery said. "Brothers don't rat on each other."

"And these kind of assholes run the government and big business?" Morg questioned. "I'm glad to be leaving."

"Are you going somewhere?" Jeffery asked, anything to buy a little more time.

The Force chuckled. "Oh, yes. He is. And so are you."

"Go on, crap-head," Sand told him. "Tell it all."

"Bill and others . . . me, too, we fixed the brakes on that Jew-boy's car."

"You admit being a party to Joey's murder?"

Jeffery licked bloody lips. "Yes."

"Go on."

"Your wife panicked when Bill began tailgating her, bumping the rear end of her car. She took off out of town. We stayed right with her. About eight or nine miles out of town, she cut off the highway and down a gravel road. Her car began fishtailing, and she went into a ditch. She got stuck. We stopped about a hundred feet behind and got out, all of us yelling and whooping and laughing. But we didn't mean her any harm. Then she got out of her car with that . . . horrible animal!"

"Oh, my," the Force simpered. "I do believe he's about to have a snit!" The shack rocked with frenzied laughter.

When the laughter died away, Sand said, "Tell it."

"She stood by the car, crying, the dog snarling at us. It was getting late, but light enough for her to see what Bill and Wallace did. They exposed themselves to her—shook their peckers at her."

The music began in Sand's head. The beast within snarled and howled and roamed about. The Force sighed in disgust. Morg spat on the floor.

"We all exposed ourselves," Jeffery's voice firmed. "I know you're going to kill me, and I know what that other . . . thing is in the room with us. So I'm going to say what's on my mind. She'd been giving it to you and all the other hot-rodders for years. Everybody knows about the orgies

314

you people have. All the wild sex parties."

"I musta missed out on them," Morg said sarcastically. "You dumb little shit. You been seein' too many movies about hot-rodders and custom clubbers. Maybe some clubs do that, but none that I know of. You fuck with somebody else's old lady, you gonna get killed. That's the way it is, chump."

Jeffery looked sick. "She didn't have to run up that hill, just because we shook our cocks at her. We weren't going to hurt her."

"I ain't believin' this punk," Morg said. "No decent human bein' does something like that to a lady."

Jeffery shook his head. "I'm decent. I was just drunk, that's all. What difference does it make now?"

"None at all," the Force told him.

"When she got to the top of the hill, she tripped and fell down. She landed on a small stump, on her stomach. She rolled off, screaming. We . . . didn't pay her any attention. Didn't help her. Thought she was just doing that so we'd leave her alone. It was a game to us, that's all."

"A game," Morg whispered. He shook his head in disbelief.

"John Murry was the first to reach her. He began jumping up and down, acting a fool. You know, like in an initiation. John shouted ugly things at her. But we were drunk! You have to understand that."

"I been drunk lots of times," Morg said. "I never bothered no good woman. Least of all, not no *pregnant* woman. That's obscene."

"All that is truth," the Force said. "And it is being taken into consideration by those who judge."

"And what about *me?*" Jeffery shouted to the dark shape.

The Force made a spitting, vulgar sound. "Everyone has some control over their destiny. So putting it into words that you might comprehend: you blew it, blizzard-head!"

Jeffery began crying, the tears streaking his face. "John stepped toward your wife. He was screaming filth at her. The dog jumped. It was awful. All of a sudden, John didn't

315

have any throat.

"Charles picked up a big stick and hit the dog on the head. He walked over to your wife and began telling her what we were going to do to you . . . when we caught up with you. She was crying and screaming, saying the baby was coming.

"Marlson and the others laughed at her. Then he kicked her in the stomach —"

"Who kicked her!" Sand shouted the question.

"We . . . all did after Marlson did. She rolled over on her side. Blood was coming out of her mouth and nose. You have to understand, a court of law would, I'm sure. It was like . . . things weren't real. A dream; a play. I jumped around so much I fell down. That's when she clawed me. I never heard anybody scream the way she did. She grabbed at her chest and stomach. Her face turned blue. I saw my grandfather have a heart attack. I think your wife had a heart attack the same time the baby . . . came out. God, that was awful. I got sick. She was bleeding so badly. We ran down the hill and drove off."

"You just left her there to die?" Sand asked softly.

"Please!" Jeffery screamed. "Yes! I know it was wrong. But we were drunk and scared and . . . didn't know what to do."

"Good God," Morg said. "Robin never hurt nobody in her whole entire life."

"That is truth," the Force whispered. "She is good in heart and thought. She has been judged thusly."

Sand squatted in front of Jeffery. His only emotions were fire and ice and steel. The music began.

The Force whispered, "You know what you came to do."

Sand jacked back the hammer on the .45 auto and shot Alan Jeffery in the face, the slug hitting him just above the nose, tearing out the back of his skull. Jeffery fell through the shattered wall, one foot catching on a hole in the floor. He dangled headfirst.

"Excellent. Very good," the Force said. "Everything is on schedule."

"We're on a timetable?" Morg asked.

"Certainly. Everyone is. The list of names is very long. Every time some medical breakthrough occurs, it really throws us off."

Sand looked at Morg. "You ready?"

"Yeah. Jane's waitin' for me."

"Not . . . exactly," the Force said. "But it can all be worked out to everyone's satisfaction, I'm sure."

They headed for the frat house, the dark shape of the Force sitting in the back seat of the Mercury, complaining about the quality of the rock and roll music pushing out of the hi-fi speakers.

Only a handful of young men were in the frat house. They were herded to the basement. The walls were thick and windowless. Morg had cut the telephone wires from the outside.

Lenton, Murphy, Marlson, and Branon stood together. All of them were trembling from fear.

"Alexander and Center," Sand said. "Where are they?"

"They had dates in Willowdale. They were sleeping over." The young man's eyes were on the big .45 in Sand's hand.

"They better not run into Carl Lee," Sand told him.

"I know a secret," the whisper came, echoing around the basement.

Sand knew then that Carl had found Alexander and Center.

"My God!" a young man said. "What is that . . . that *shape* over there in the corner?"

"Only the Shadow knows," the Force whispered, then chuckled.

Sand's eyes touched all the young men, lingering on Marlson. "Allen Jeffery told me what happened. I didn't like the ending. I killed him about an hour ago. You boys tell me your version. I might like it better."

He looked at the frat brothers standing apart from Marlson and his bunch. "You're all liars. Everyone of you. You lied to protect Halsey after he killed Jesse last year. You lied to protect those who killed Reb and raped Gloria. And now I find you bastards lied to protect those who killed my wife. I should kill every goddamned one of you."

"No," the Force said. "That would be a mark against you. You do not need another."

"Sand!" a college student said. "Don't do this."

The room seemed to shift.

"You know, man," Morg said, leaning up against a wall. "I feel really weird. Like a part of me is gone from my body."

"Yes," Sand said. "I felt it leaving."

"That is truth," the Force spoke. "Your fate is settled. Your life's clock has stopped for you both." It chuckled. "Among others in this dingy room."

A frat boy fainted.

"No shit!" Morg said. "Outta sight."

"Bill, you said we wouldn't get caught!" Lenton cried.

"Shut up, you fool!" Marlson screamed.

Lenton pointed a shaking finger at Marlson. "It was all his idea. He did it all."

"Liar!" Marlson screamed. "You all helped me fix the brakes on the Jew-boy's car. You all took part in kicking Robin on that hill."

Sand leveled the .45. "Tell it all, Lenton."

He told it all in a shaking voice. With much more brevity than Jeffery. But it was as Jeffery had said.

"Sand," an older student said. "Don't do this. All right, we were wrong. I'll admit that to the police, and take whatever punishment the courts hand us. But don't do this."

"Fuck you, boy," Sand told him.

"For such an intelligent and usually grammatically correct young man," the whisper came, "you certainly do retreat to the gutters in times of stress."

"I suppose all that will change shortly?" Sand asked.

"We shall try."

Sand shot Lenton in the knee, knocking the young man off his bare feet. Calmly, he shifted the muzzle and shot Branon in the stomach. He allowed them both to thrash in agony on the floor before shooting them in the head. He pulled the trigger twice on Murphy, tearing great holes in his stomach.

The stench in the basement was foul.

Marlson slobbered down the front of his T-shirt.

"Jesus God, Sand!" a student cried. "This is barbaric. You don't want justice. You want revenge!"

Sand laughed at him; a bitter bark that was void of humor. "Revenge? You bet your silly asses I want revenge. You arrogant bastards — all of you — helped destroy everything I loved in this world. And you sons of bitches did it deliberately. You stripped me bare, and now you have the nerve to talk about justice? *Justice!* None of you know the meaning of the word. Courts of law? Shit! Would those guilty have suffered like my wife, like Reb, like Gloria or Boom Boom or Joey and Tuddie? No. And you all know that." He held up the .45. "This is justice."

He shoved the .45 behind his belt and took out a heavy knife from his jacket pocket. "And this is justice," he added, opening the blade. "Shoot anybody who moves, Morg."

"Gotcha, man."

Sand walked to Marlson and faced him. "Marlson, since you're so proud of your pecker, I'm going to give it to you. You can have your mother put it up in a Mason Jar."

"No!" Marlson screamed.

The whispering Force became a howling.

Sand knocked Marlson down and kicked him into moaning submission. He looked up at the knot of badly frightened frat boys . . . who only wanted justice.

"If you boys act quickly, Marlson will live. And I want him to live a long, long time. I want him to remember me for the rest of his miserable, worthless, lying life."

The beast within and without roared as Sand's knife flashed, dripping crimson.

Chapter Thirteen

The screen on the TV set went dark and Watts stood up. Sand, are you going to finish it this night? he projected.

No. I'll be away for a time. I must see if the path is clear. Warn the others that they will be pestered on their journey, but that no harm can come to them, as long as they do not step off the path.

Pestered?

You'll see. Talk to you later, Al.

"Pestered?" Megan questioned, after Watts had briefed them all. "What does he mean?"

"I don't know. I guess you people will find that out when you get there."

She touched his arm. You and Mack haven't changed your minds, Colonel?"

"No." He smiled at her. "You better get some sleep. Tomorrow is going to be a busy, busy day."

UP, UP, UP, PEOPLE! Fury woke them all at dawn. WE'VE GOT A LOT OF WORK TO DO. HUP TWO THREE FOUR. MARCH, MARCH, AROUND THE FLOOR. GET THAT BLOOD CIRCULATING.

"Do we get to eat breakfast before you start cracking the bullwhips?" Gordie asked.

THAT'S NOT A BAD IDEA, GUNFIGHTER. THIRTY LASHES MIGHT HELP STRAIGHTEN YOU RIGHT UP. OH, GO ON AND EAT. I WAS JUST HAVING SOME FUN.

"He's gone," Howie called. "Back to the mountain."

"Major," Gordie said. "Right after we eat, start planting

the rest of those explosives that you can detonate electronically. We can have that much done. Lee, start soaking
those piles of tires with kerosene. Al, you and Mack can
start placing fire bombs around some of the older houses.
The rest of us will be burning bodies."

They worked until noon, with Fury popping up every
now and then to inspect their work.

"You have any objections to us breaking for lunch?"
Gordie asked.

NOT A BIT, BOY SCOUT. ARE YOU GETTING ANY
CLOSER TO A DECISION?

"Yes, we are. We'll vote this evening after work. Are you
going to allow us a secret ballot, or will you be snooping
around?"

UMM. OH, VERY WELL. WHEN YOU KNOCK OFF
FROM WORK, I WILL LEAVE YOU ALONE FOR ONE
HALF HOUR TO EXERCISE YOUR DEMOCRATIC
PROCESS.

"We're almost finished with this sector. We'll probably
work late this evening. If that's all right with you."

THAT'S JUST PEACHY WITH ME. SINCE YOU
PEOPLE ARE GOING TO BE SPENDING HUN-
DREDS OF YEARS IN THIS PIGSTY—SERVING
ME—I WANT IT AS CLEAN AS POSSIBLE.

"You shall certainly have everything wiped clean, Fury. I
promise you a place befitting a being of your caliber."

Sunny looked up at that and could not hide her smile.

GOOD. YOU'RE LEARNING YOUR PLACE WELL.
SEE YOU LATER, ALLIGATOR. DO BOP DE DO BOP
DE DO BOP, DE DO.

"Insufferable asshole," Gordie muttered. "Let's break
for lunch, people."

The government people had already begun packing up
equipment and moving out, a few at a time. The preachers
continued to rant and rave, the reporters continued to ask
questions of anyone they could corner, and the police had

been forced to close down any roads leading into the area for as far out as fifty miles. The area simply could not sustain any more people.

"Leave these temporary quarters, Larry," Martin ordered. "Leave the portable toilets and anything else that might draw attention to our pulling out."

"The bomber is fully fueled, and the crew is awaiting orders to arm the weapon, sir."

"That's up to the president, Larry. That is his decision and his alone."

"Sir, do you believe President Marshall will really level with the people of the world about this matter?"

Martin sighed. Thought for a moment. "I don't know, Larry. "Like an attorney, he'll try to be as honest as he can be."

"That's an . . . interesting reply, sir."

"Quite."

President Marshall had canceled all appointments, clearing the day and night. At 2030 hours, the president knew his life would be forever changed, altered as surely as the valley where the neutron bomb would explode at near ground level.

He decided he would try to take a nap. There damn sure would be no sleep tonight.

"Megan," Howie said. "I've been doing some computations, and I'm not at all sure I like what I've found."

"Explain, Howie." She sat down beside him.

"We know that Fury thrives on the souls of the just-departed. We know that it's been doing that since the beginnings of time. What we don't know is what forms it ingested in other worlds, and in earlier times here on earth."

"I'm . . . not sure I'm following you, Howie."

"The neutron bomb will destroy the bulk of the energy

322

mass. It will not destroy it completely. And we don't know, none of us, in here and outside, not the smartest scientists in all the world, what changes these two clashes are going to produce. See what I'm getting at?"

"Are you talking about some metamorphosis; energy into . . . whatever?"

"Yes."

"My God, Howie. I haven't given that any thought."

"Neither did I, not until this morning. But it's frightening. The impact of two large energy masses—one an unknown factor—could spin off . . . " He shrugged his shoulders. "Anything."

"Are you suggesting," Megan spoke slowly, choosing her words carefully, "that since the Fury is made up of once-living souls, or still-living souls, the clash might produce some form of life that could exist . . . once more. I mean, like us?"

"Yes. It's possible, I think. And it would be quite a danger to us all."

"Have you discussed this theory with anyone?"

"My CIA contact up north of here."

"Your . . . CIA contact?"

"Yes. He's quite a nice fellow. Major Jackson okayed the link for me."

Megan left the computer room, shaking her head. The CIA never missed a bet.

The major and the others had returned from their work. Gordie walked over to him. "Everything go?"

"Ready to pop."

Watts said, "Joey just spoke to me. He's ready to wrap this up so we can store the final tapes. Gather around. But I warn you, it isn't pretty. I know. I was there."

OUT OF TIME

Captain Al Watts was at the state patrol barracks ten minutes after receiving the call. Some campers had heard the shot and had investigated, finding Alan Jeffery. They

323

had hiked out and called the state police.

Sand and Morg had been spotted, each in their own vehicle, driving aimlessly in the mountains.

"They're not driving aimlessly," Watts said, a grim expression on his face. "They're letting me have time to get ready. They'll head for Thunder Mountain."

"Why there, Captain?"

"Why not? They have nothing to lose now. Sand is telling us to come and get him. Goddamnit!" he cursed.

"Four college boys dead. Another with his privates cut off. God, what a bloody night."

"How is the Marlson punk?" Watts asked.

"He's going to live. But he doesn't have any equipment left."

"Good," Watts said. "The son of a bitch won't be able to sire any like him."

"We got more troubles," a trooper said, entering the room. "Carl Lee was spotted about one hour ago, getting gas. He had two German Lugers stuck in his belt. Then he was seen following two college boys pretty close. They looked scared. Carl looked grim."

"Names of the boys?" Watts asked, quickly putting it all together.

"We think they're Alexander and Center."

"Get some people on it," Watts ordered.

"Captain?" another trooper stuck his head into the room. "The hospital just called. Judge Wentworth and the D.A. were just admitted to the emergency room. Both men have been stomped and it was Carl Lee who did the stomping. I guess he's getting back at them for all the times they refused to indict and prosecute those Monte Rio shits. And for the times they hassled Sand. The judge is in bad shape."

"Goddamnit!" Watts hollered. "Where the hell is the sheriff?"

"The sheriff took off for Denver about two hours ago. His deputies have cleared out. They're running scared, now that Sand has flipped out."

"With good reason," Watts said. "All the times they applied a double standard of law enforcement. All right, roll every man." He walked to his office and got his rifle. "Are the roadblocks in place?"

"Yes, sir."

"All right, boys. Let's stop Sand and Morg."

"Shoot to kill, Captain?"

Watts gripped his .30-06. "Yes. I somehow always knew it would come to this; felt it would. Sand was a genius; Morg was a genuine national hero. Something . . . somebody, has to take part of the blame for what has happened, and will happen. But, I suppose as badge-toters it isn't our position to analyze or criticize the present mores of society, is it, Sergeant?"

The sergeant wasn't really sure what Watts was talking about. "Ah . . . I guess not, sir. Sir, you used the past tense talking about Sand and Morg."

Watts sighed heavily. He looked as though he had aged ten years in one hour. "Yes, I did. Sand told me just a few hours ago that I would soon Know, Kill, and Create. Very well. I *know* that much of what has occurred and will occur is not altogether the fault of Sand, I suppose that I will be the one to *kill* Sand. But what am I *creating?*"

The sergeant didn't know it at the time, but he was being very profound when he replied, "A legend, sir."

Sand took Morg back to his customized hearse, and they both headed for Thunder Mountain. Both now knew why that had to be. They took high risks when they discovered the roads were blocked off to traffic and that they were in no danger of killing some innocent. They laughed grimly at the gods of fate and chance. They took mountain curves at speeds no other hot-rodder had ever done— and lived to tell about it.

Morg pulled up alongside Sand and yelled over the rush of wind and roar of engines, "I'm goin' out first, Sand. See you, pal!"

Sand laughed with the now constant Force and lifted one gloved hand in a final salute.

Watts and his troopers intercepted the hot-rodders at a roadblock just inside Blue Smoke Valley. The hot-rodders went through the blockade at eighty miles per hour, sending troopers scattering for cover as the wooden sawhorses were splintered and tossed high into the air.

"Fire!" Watts yelled. The rifle slammed his shoulder and bucked in his hands.

The night rocked with muzzle blasts.

"I'm hit!" Morg yelled, losing control of his hearse. He went over the high side, shouting as he went down. Not a cry of fear, but a shout of defiance, directed at a world that does not care nor attempt to understand the nonconformist; to a society that decorates genuine heroes and then refuses to associate with them; to a society that would prefer a nation of clones, patterned after a very narrow concept of right and wrong, dress codes, social behavior, and arrogance.

The polished hearse sailed through the air, headlights blazing, spinning in crazy space as Morg held on, laughing as he experienced his last ride. The tank exploded on contact with the rocky canyon floor, and Morg got his wish: he met Jane.

Sand had slowed, spun around, and stopped, watching as his friend met what he had been born to meet. He got out of his car and watched the flames far below him. He could not see Watts raise his rifle.

"Are you ready?" The Force asked.

A line from Kipling came to Sand. "God help us," he spoke to the night. "For we knew the worst too young."

"Yes," the Force agreed. "But you also knew the best, and were able to see the middle ground and the flaws in what your world calls justice. And that is an accomplishment that few are able to achieve."

"Didn't help me much, did it?"

"Your contribution is still years away. Are you ready?"

"I'm ready."

326

Watts shot him twice, in the stomach and in the shoulder, knocking him down on the road. Sand staggered to his boots and reached his Mercury. He dropped it into gear and roared out, tires smoking. He floored the gas pedal, tearing through the night, heading for Thunder Mountain, climbing upward. The pain from his wounds sent brilliantly flashing lights through his head.

So this is how it feels to die.

He didn't care. Up the lower slopes of the mountain, faster and faster and higher and higher. He weaved from side to side in the gravel road.

"Do it!" the Force commanded.

Sand spun the wheel to the left and went over the side. The Mercury impacted with earth and sent him flying through the windshield. He landed on his chest and belly, one leg bent under him. He heard ribs crack and a leg pop as he hit the rocky ground. Sand lost consciousness for a few moments.

When the blackness lifted, he lay still for a moment, disoriented in his pain. His nose and mouth were smashed and bloody. He ran his tongue over broken stubs of teeth. He was so confused that for a moment he thought that he was on his honeymoon with Robin, in Key West. He called for her. Something began shimmering far above him; but only silence answered his summons. He could hear sirens below him.

Reality stuck him hard with hot agony. Fighting the pain, Sand began climbing and crawling toward the shimmering lights far up the mountain. He used the powerful muscles in his arms to pull himself upward.

After several minutes of painful climbing, he stopped and looked down the mountain. Men and lights moved below him. Death circled below him, death circled above him. The shimmering shapes were closer. Sand shivered, as if the icy finger of the reaper had lightly touched him.

"How prosaic," the Force whispered. "Come along, young man," it urged. "You still have some distance to go."

He dragged himself upward, higher and higher, mangling and bloodying his hands on sharp rocks. The pain in his chest became almost unbearable. He crawled on. He was almost to the shimmering, misty lights.

Then his strength failed him. He could go no further. For the first time in his life, the young man gave up.

"Oh, the hell with it," Sand muttered, blood from his lips staining the ground. He pressed his face against the coolness of mother earth. "What's the use?" he questioned the night. He laughed, a grotesque, blood-spraying vocalizing of dark humor. "You can tell everybody you were right, Dad. You said I'd never amount to a hill of beans."

"Your father was wrong," the Force told him. "Your father judged everything from a materalistic point of view. He was, and always will be, afraid to challenge the system. He is a narrow-minded, bigoted, cowardly little man. He is everything you were not. You know the value of beings, including God's lesser creatures. Someone had to do you harm before you would think ill. You did not expect more from an animal than you did from humankind. Every good and bad point is recorded."

Sand raised his head as all pain suddenly left his broken body. His world was very clear and bright. The lights of towns widely separated shone below him. "You couldn't break me," he spoke to society. "You never made me beg. And you couldn't make me conform."

"Was it worth it?" the Force asked.

"You bet your ass, it was."

The Force laughed.

A few hundred yards below Sand, Watts and Mack stopped as the sounds of the laughter reached them.

"What the hell is that?" Mack asked.

"I'm not even sure I want to know," Watts replied. "Come on. He might be still alive."

"What if he is, Al? What are you going to say to him?"

"I'm going to apologize."

The laughter of the Force faded into a chuckle. "Rebel to the end, right, Sand?"

"You got it."

"Very well. Lift your eyes upward."

Sand turned his head and looked. Robin was standing a few yards away. He smiled at her. "I love you, Robin," he spoke to the shimmering image before him.

She was so beautiful, so fresh-looking and lovely. She was peaceful, dressed in a garment of sparkling, misty colors. She seemed to be. . . he struggled for the word. Fluorescent. She returned his smile.

And she held their son. But the boy had grown, as if time had somehow hung suspended for Sand, and flown for them. The child laughed and waved at his father.

Joey was there, holding hands with Tuddie. Morg and Jane stood beside them. None of them appeared to be touching the ground; but instead seemed to drift slowly about, smoothly and effortlessly. Their movements fascinated Sand. He reached out to touch Robin.

She laughed and moved away. "Oh, no, Sand. Not yet. It is not yet permitted." The child laughed with its mother. Robin's voice was deeper than Sand remembered. Hollow, almost spiritual in tone. She seemed to be speaking from a great distance. "You have to make up your mind to join us, Sand. We've waited for such a long time. Finally, we got permission to come down to join you." She held out a small hand. "Come on, now, honey. It's time. You've run out of time, as you know it."

"Wait for me, Robin," he gasped. "Wait for me."

Morg said, "It ain't half-bad once you get used to it, man. It ain't that real good place; but it ain't that bad place either. You gonna have some talkin' to do, but you can do it. Come on, Sand. We got a lot of catchin' up to do."

"You've waited so long?" Sand whispered. "I don't understand."

"You will, my old friend," Joey said. "Come on over, Sand. You made your point. We all did. It's done."

"Not yet," Sand muttered.

Tuddie smiled at him, her blonde hair all sparkles and

329

multicolored hues. "You never were one to give up, Sand. But it's over where that small part of you still lives." She pointed. "There is the door, and there is the path. Take the door, and follow the path."

Sand looked at Jane. The beatnik girl said, "There is no need to fear death, Sand. For the word is a contradiction. You'll soon see that."

"I'm not afraid of anything," Sand managed to say. He could hear the footsteps coming up the mountain. And he knew it would be Al Watts. "Just give me a minute."

"He's talking to someone, Al," Mack said. "Jesus God, who is he talking to?"

But Watts chose not to reply to that.

"Just one more minute," Sand pleaded.

"Your time stopped hours ago," the Force whispered.

Sand looked into the distance and could see the lights of Willowdale and of Monte Rio. Painfully, he turned his face toward the twin cups of light shining through the night. Just before infinity took him winging into the unknown that humans fear and animals accept as a part of living, just before Sand joined his wife and son and friends, slipping through that misty curtain to stand on the shores of the dark river, the young man tried very hard to speak just two more words to the lights below him. The profanity would not form on his bloody lips.

He was at peace with all things.

He smiled, curving bloody lips. He thought: if You are doing this, would You just cool it for a minute, please?

"He is not," the Force told him. "But I will give you the necessary seconds for your final salute to the world that birthed you and killed you."

"Thanks," Sand said to the voice that only he could hear.

"I think," the Force added, "that you are going to turn into the proverbial pain in the butt."

"Probably," Sand agreed. Just as his mouth filled with blood, his lungs, punctured and torn, collapsed, just seconds before his heart stopped, Sand clenched his right hand into a bloody fist and extended his middle finger to the lights below.

"Fuck you," he said. His final hail and farewell to a world that had birthed him one too many times.

He looked up and saw Watts and Mack standing over him. He spoke to them, and hoped they understood.

The sighing winds on Thunder Mountain became a shrieking cry; the mist became a shroud for Sand. The clouds moved in, covering him. His legs trembled and jerked, the coldness now moving swiftly, touching each part of him, finally stilling the heart.

His last conscious thought as the electricity left him was: I just wanted to be me. I just . . .

Sand's physical body died on the mountain, his field of force that would never die moved from him to join his friends. The clouds swept away, presenting a velvet sky pocked with diamond stars—luminaries that seemed to play a silent symphony over the mountains and valleys. A dirge for the fearful, timid beings who are content with the ordinary and do not care what might lie beyond the next mountain. But it was a cantata of rebirth for those few, who are ever fewer in number.

The hall clock in the empty house began ticking, its mainspring repairing as time directed.

Julie von Mehren had awakened when a strange force began humming, circling her bed. She rose, to stand by her window, watching the sky over the mountains.

"So he's dead," the old lady muttered. "I'm sorry, Sand. I'm sorry."

Captain Watts and Mack stood over the broken, bloody body. Both of them heard the words he whispered; neither of them, then, knew what he meant.

Watts shook his head and smiled through his tears. Sand's right arm was raised, propped against a rock, the middle finger still erect.

To Know, To Kill, To Create.

"What a waste," Watts spoke to the night. He knelt down, opening the fist, erasing the obscene gesture. "You

331

made your point, Sand. And, by God, I agree with you."

Watts stood up just as something almost tangible moved in front of him. He would swear for years that whatever it was, was laughing. A victorious laugh, as if even in death, Sand had won.

The thunder began to roll.

"Captain?" the voice came from behind him.

Watts turned. "Yes, Gleeson?"

"Carl Lee killed two college boys about an hour ago. He just turned himself in."

Chapter Fourteen

"You have the tapes all packed up, Bos?" Gordie asked the burly college student. He had returned to the office for one more check.

"Yes, sir. They're secure."

He looked at his watch. It would be dark in about an hour.

"Is there anybody left alive out there, Sheriff?" Howie asked.

"No one, son. With the exception of us, it's a ghost town."

In more ways than one, Sand's thoughts popped into his head.

I bet you weren't a Boy Scout, Sand.

Oh, yes, I was, until I got kicked out.

Gordie chuckled. Why?

Stole a rubber raft and tried to make it down river to the Girl Scouts. Now listen, Sheriff: you and the others be in the alley between the pool hall and the grocery store at seven fifty-nine this evening—your time. I'll be there to guide you. Don't be afraid. You have two prisoners left in your custody. I would advise you not to bring them; but that, of course, is up to you.

I can't leave them to die, Sand.

I understand that. But if they try to bust out of the path, they will suffer a much more severe fate.

Can you tell me what?

No. That is forbidden.

I'll warn them.

333

Good. Go back to work. I'll see you all in about an hour.

Gordie explained what Sand had just told him, then looked at Dean. The reporter met his gaze. "Have Sunny and the kids in the alley several minutes before the deadline. Angel knows where it is."

The reporter nodded his head. "I'll have them there, Sheriff. And that's a promise."

"I know you will. Howie, where is Fury?"

"Still on the mountain, Sheriff."

Gordie walked over to Watts and Mack and stuck out his hand. "I wish you boys would change your minds about this."

Watts smiled and shook his head. "We talked it over, Gordie. We're staying and buying you people some extra time. Mack and me will be leaving now. No elaborate goodbyes for any of us, please. Just . . . good luck to you all."

Without another word, the two men picked up knapsacks and walked out the front door.

Several in the room were silently weeping, both men and women.

"I liked those men," Howie said, his voice husky. "I liked them both a lot."

The boy shut the door to his computer room.

President Marshall rose refreshed from his nap. He showered and carefully shaved with an electric razor, then dabbed on aftershave and dressed casually. He had sent his wife to their summer home for the duration of this . . . he smiled. What the hell to call it?

It would probably be referred to as an Incident.

He walked into his living quarters and rang for coffee. Along with his coffee, there was a sealed folder. When the porter had left, Marshall sugared and creamed his coffee, sipped, and then broke the seal, opening the folder.

He read it through and through, then read it again, becoming furious with each read. He hurled the folder across the room and swore, loud and long. He stopped swearing

334

when a knock came on his door.

"Come!"

The Chairman of the Joint Chiefs, the Secretary of State, DCI from CIA, the heads of Treasury, FBI, NSA, and a dozen more top level men and women.

The DCI spied the folder and retrieved it. "I gather you disapprove of the plan, sir?"

"You goddamn right I disapprove of it."

"It was not the CIA's idea, Mr. President," the man from State said. "It was mine."

"May we have some coffee, sir?" the Chairman of the JC's asked.

"Of course, you can. Ring for it."

The president sat in silence until the men and women were served coffee and the room was secure. "Why?" John Marshall asked the group. "Why must we lie to the people?"

"To retain the status quo," the Speaker of the House said.

"Now, what the hell does that mean?" the president snapped.

"If I may be so bold," the DCI said. "I think it means that there are many more ignorant people in the world than there are intelligent ones. I personally think the plan is a good one because our computers—since the Secretary informed me of this plan—have shown that the majority of the world's population simply would not, or could not, cope with this knowledge should it be made public."

"It would be even better if there were no survivors," a man spoke from just outside the main group seated around the president.

John Marshall looked at the man. The President of the United States said, "Fuck you."

"It was just a thought."

"Not a very good one," the president said. He cut his eyes to the secretary of state. "All right, tell me what the leaders of the countries we have brought into this matter think about your plan, and don't hand me any crap about your

335

not having spoken with them about it."

"They agree with it," he said simply. "It was unanimous, John."

The president exhaled softly. "We'll have a problem with that fool governor out in Colorado."

"No, we won't," the speaker assured him.

"There is a little matter of a deal we made with a dead man."

"Saunders," the attorney general. "I can clear his name without those tapes being made public."

John Marshall said, "Lies, deceit, half-truths."

"The economy would collapse, John," the secretary said.

"What?"

"People would stop smoking, drinking, behaving frivolously. They would stop spending money on hundreds of items—some of them big ticket. Think about it, John. With the absolute fact that a hereafter existed, with heaven and hell proven to be real, there wouldn't be a sinner left in the world . . ."

"Oh, bullshit!" the president said. "That's all crap and conjecture. I'm a Christian; I just said bullshit. I told that asshole," he pointed to the man who opted for no survivors from Willowdale, "to get fucked. I know now that heaven and hell are real. I still plan on taking a drink before dinner and swearing when I get mad. What's the matter with you people?"

"John, you're a very educated man. A reasonable, rational man. The majority of the people even in heavily industrialized nations are not that well educated, or informed. If you think the great unwashed is a thing of the past, you're badly mistaken."

The president looked at his watch. "The balloon goes up in about fifty minutes. You gentlemen better be a hell of a lot more convincing during that time than you have been so far."

The director of the FBI took a thick computer printout from his brief case. "I think we will be, Mr. President."

"All communications with the town are now down," Martin Tobias was informed. "They're on their own in there."

Martin glanced at the luminous hands of his watch. "Thirty minutes to drop. The Fury?"

"Still on the mountain."

"Let's get out of here. Tell the gawkers and preachers and the press we're backing up another mile."

The order was given to security, and the troops began clearing the area.

"Sir," Larry said.

Martin turned to face the younger man. He held a communique in his hands. His face was tight. "Yes, Larry?"

"Everything's been changed, sir. Orders of the president." He handed Martin the directive.

Martin read, a look of displeasure moving across his face. He resisted an impulse to rip the paper to shreds. "It won't work," he finally said, carefully folding the paper and slipping it into an inside pocket of his jacket. "I understand why they're doing it, but it won't work."

"I don't understand it at all," Larry admitted.

"Many things, son. The president's inner circle—of which I am a part, unconsulted on this matter, however—don't want the preachers of the world to have any more power than they already wield. If all this," he waved a hand toward Willowdale, "were to be made public—i.e., that is to say if the truth were told and the tapes made public—it would prove, beyond the shadow of a doubt, that God and heaven and hell really exist. The preachers would run the world. Ours is an hedonistic society, Larry. All that would change, and the economy couldn't take such an abrupt blow. Hundreds of thousands of people could conceivably be thrown out of work. And that's just in the United States. The impact worldwide would be staggering. See what I'm getting at, Larry?"

"I think so, sir. Preachers are very powerful and persuasive. Instead of money going toward personal pleasures, it

337

would instead flow into the coffers of the churches. Theoretically, places like Las Vegas, Reno, Atlantic City, to name a few, would be ghost towns. The beer, wine, and liquor industry could, again theoretically, be wiped out. People would rededicate their lives to Christ, and instead of using their money to see movies, sporting events, buying nonessential big ticket items, they would give their money to the churches, to charities . . ." he trailed that off. "But, sir, if that were to happen, that would be good. It would help the homeless, the elderly, the sick, the abandoned, the environment, the animals."

Martin's smile was a sad one. "But big government doesn't work that way, son. If there was peace on earth, what would happen to the millions and millions of men and women making a living in the armed forces? The men and women who earn their living in the defense industry? If all nations were at peace, the unemployment rate would bury the nation. Not just this nation, but all around the world."

"But, sir, if we do this thing, we're going to be lying to God!"

"Cling to the faint hope that God will understand, and is truly a forgiving God."

Gordie checked his watch, then lifted his walkie-talkie. "Now!" he said.

Maj. Jackson began detonating the explosives he and his team had planted around the town. Gordie and the others began lighting fires. In minutes, the entire town was covered in thick, black smoke.

The Fury swirled about, screaming. WHAT IS GOING ON HERE? WHAT IS TAKING PLACE? WHAT ARE YOU DOING, YOU GODDAMNED GREASEBALL?

"It's working!" Howie said, taking one last look at his computer screens. "The Fury can't see through the smoke! It can't see through the smoke!"

Dean literally jerked the boy out of his chair and shoved

338

him out the back door, Sunny and Angel and a few others ahead of them. They made it outside the building, just seconds before it exploded as the Fury unleashed its rage.

Watts lifted a bullhorn to his lips. "Over here, you pompous son of a bitch!" he shouted.

On the other side of town, Mack lifted a bullhorn and shouted, "No, over here, you great big ball of shit!"

The plane carrying the neutron bomb was right on schedule, minutes away from the target.

The Fury howled in rage, flashing its mass from one end of the town to the other. Maj. Jackson and his people were throwing smoke grenades, as fast as they could pull the pins and hurl them.

All began moving toward the alleyway and the door.

All except Mack and Al Watts.

Capt. John Hishon ran across the street, momentarily exposing himself in a area that was thin with smoke.

All that was left of the captain were the soles of his boots, blackened spots on the concrete.

A deputy ran from a burning house, and the Fury spotted her. She was ripped apart, arms and legs torn from her torso and flung hundreds of yards. She mercifully passed out moments before death took her, silencing the screaming.

The sheriff's secretary broke under the strain and ran hollering down the middle of the street, stumbling and screaming and crying through the smoke. She was picked up and hurled into the air. She impacted against the water tower. She oozed down the outside of one leg of the tower.

Beyond the barricades, many of the reporters refused to leave.

"What's going on in there?" the bureau chiefs from the West Coast yelled to a soldier running for the trucks. "By God, somebody better give me some answers."

A minicam operator handed his camera to Andy. "Here," he said. "Stick this up your ass, and see what kind of pictures you get. I'm leaving."

"You're fired, you bastard."

"But I'll be alive."

The cameraman jumped onto the bed of an army truck and left the area.

About half of the reporters left. Many, seeing the barricades unguarded, pushed them aside and entered the up-to-now restricted area. They ran toward the smoke.

They ran into hell.

Preacher Willie Magee and Sister Adele put their feet to work and managed to reach their car, pulling into position behind an army truck.

Preacher Harold Jewelweed, a snake in each hand, ran toward the town. When he passed the city limits sign, the snakes were torn from his grasp and shoved down his throat. He died very unpleasantly.

Preacher Silas Marrner missed the last truck and was loping up the road . . . away from town. "Come on, feet do your stuff!" he hollered, pulling up to the bed of a truck.

"Give me your hand," a soldier yelled at him, holding out a helping hand.

"Are you saved, brother?" Silas yelled.

"Do you want your silly ass out of here?" the soldier questioned.

Silas grabbed the hand and was pulled aboard.

Several of the reporters realized that they had made a serious blunder by running toward the town. They tried to turn back. They ran into an invisible wall. No matter where they turned, trying to escape, they found they were trapped.

They looked up, hope springing in them as Al Watts and Mack walked up. "Can you get us out of here?" one asked.

"Not a chance," Watts told him.

FOUND YOU, YOU GODDAMNED OLD MEDDLESOME COPS.

Watts and Mack ducked back into the smoke and disappeared.

"Who are you?" a reporter screamed the question.

MY MY. WHAT HAVE WE HERE?

"We're members of the press," a woman said, her voice ry shaky.

DO YOU LIKE MUSIC FROM THE FIFTIES?

"What?" she asked.

TRY THIS: DO BOP DE DO BOP DE DO BOP, DE O.

"What are you, some kind of a nut?" she asked.

She melted in front of the others.

They went running and screaming into the smoke.

"Step in here," the voice came out of a shimmering mist the alley. "Do it. Step in here. Quickly."

Taking a deep breath, Dean grabbed Howie's hand and epped into the mist, Sunny and Angel right behind them.

The head of a deputy—mouth open in a silent scream—unced off a wall and fell with a wet smack onto the dirty ey floor.

Lt. Kathy Smith, Sgt. Maj. Christensen, Sgt. Dixon, and t. Preston stepped into the mist and vanished.

Maj. Claude Jackson tossed one too many smoke gre-des. The Fury found him and tore him apart, scattering guts up and down Main Street and sticking his head p a light pole.

Megan LeMasters stepped into the mist.

"Where's Gordie?" Bergman yelled at his partner.

"Right behind you. Come on."

The two state investigators stepped through the mist and o the door, followed by the college kids and Robin and cky.

Lee Evans grabbed Jill Pierce by the hand, and together ey disappeared into the mist.

Two deputies, Alan Hibler and Duane Hunt, dragging two badly frightened convicts, walked through the st.

Gordie looked at his watch. They were running late. The mber would be dropping its payload in three minutes.

"I'm not going into the unknown!" Dr. Shriver shouted. o. I won't."

He turned and ran into the street.

341

"Come back here, you fool!" Anderson yelled, as h
pushed two nurses into the mist.

"Hurry!" Sand's voice sprang out of the world beyonc
"The door is about to close."

Anderson and Gordie stepped through, just as Shrive
was spun around like a mad top in the middle of the stree
The doctor was picked up and hurled through a departmer
store window; hurled all the way through the store, exitin
out the back door, headless, his torso dripping blood.

"Over target in one minute," the navigator radioed th
pilot of the bomber.

The bomb bay doors were opened.

Al Watts and Mack stood in the center of the smok
main street, each with an arm around the others' shoulders
They began singing.

"Onward Christian Soldiers! Marching as to war,
With the cross of Jesus, Going on before. Christ, the
royal master, Leads against the foe . . ."

"Bomb is clear," the navigator radioed. "Let's get out (
here."

". . . Forward into battle . . ."

SHUT UP, YOU GODDAMN BASTARDS!

". . . See his banners go!"

I'LL MAKE YOU BOTH MY SLAVES AND TOF
TURE YOU TO DEATH. I PROMISE YOU IT'LL TAK
CENTURIES.

"Like a mighty army, Moves the Church of God . . ."

STOP THAT SINGING. I COMMAND YOU BOTH T(
STOP THAT DRIVEL.

". . . Brothers we are treading, Where the Saints hav
trod . . ."

DO BOP DE DO BOP DE DO BOP, DE DO.

"We are not divided, All one body we, All in hop
and—"

The explosion tore the tops off of mountains twent
miles away. Fire leaped into the sky so high that residents o

342

enver, seventy-five miles away, could clearly see the ames. Thunder Mountain exploded, sending huge boulers flying for several miles in all directions. The electrical orm that followed the merging of the two energy masses nocked out power for fifty miles.

The lightning storm that came seconds after the twin exosions was unmatched by anything ever seen by human es. Pilots as far south as New Mexico, as far north as yoming, as far west as Utah, and as far east as Kansas— no had been bitching about being grounded without exanation—stood in awe and wonder, their mouths open, d watched the lightning that ripped the skies.

The mountains trembled, and avalanches rumbled down th sides of the mountains surrounding the valley of fire.

"Holy Mother of God," Martin Tobias muttered. He uld feel the heat from the blasts from his position more an thirty miles from the site.

Larry Adams, avowed nonbeliever, fell to his knees and gan praying. Not for any worldly possessions, but for the ength to hold onto God now that he had found Him.

Where Willowdale had once been, there was a very large e in the ground, more than five hundred feet deep and one mile across. At the bottom of the hole, objects e moving about, beginning their climb upward and out.

THE DOOR

The light on the path was so bright, it hurt the eyes of ose who had entered through the door. On both sides of e path, objects staggered about in a swirling gray fog. illions of voices babbled in a thousand dead languages. Sand stood at the head of the column and counted.

"Uncle Sand!" Robin called from the rear of the column.

He smiled and waved to her.

"Where are mother and daddy?" she called.

"Ahead of us, baby. Guarding the door with some hers. Come on, people. Remember, don't leave the path."

They began their walk, the sparkling mist that was Sand

343

leading them.

Fingers that looked like sparklers jabbed out of the fog and plucked at the sleeves of those who walked on the path

"What . . . who are these people?" Bos called.

"Lost souls," Sand told him. "Don't be afraid. They can' hurt you. They gather every time the door opens, even though they know they can't get out."

"Can they enter the path?" Howie called.

"No. That is forbidden."

"Where are they?" Angel yelled to be heard over the enormous din of voices.

"At a very low level."

"Hell?" one of the convicts yelled.

"No."

"Then that's for me," the second con yelled. Bot jumped off the path, into the swirling fog.

Their screaming was a hideous thing to hear.

"It doesn't work that way, partner," Sand said, looking t his right.

The screaming of the cons faded away.

"Where are they, Sand?" Jill asked the sparkling mass the head of the column.

"Ten billion miles in space, spinning through galaxi and past worlds that no human eye has ever seen, or ev will see."

"Dead?" Dean asked.

"No. You can't die in here. You live forever. They wi spin for all eternity."

"That makes my head hurt, just thinking about it," Ar gel said.

"That's right, Angel. This is no place to make a mistake.

"How long is this path?" Hillary called.

"In my world, thousands of miles. In your world, an you are still a part of that, not far."

"What has happened back . . . in our world?" Kath Smith asked.

"Willowdale is no more. But the merging of the energ masses has left some rather unpleasant visitors behind, I'r

344

afraid. You were right, Howie."

"Can you tell me what they are, and where they came from?" Gordie asked.

"No. I am not permitted to do that."

"I guess we'll find out soon enough."

"If the door has not moved, and you don't get deposited in the middle of Gettysburg during the Civil War."

Martin had asked for, and was receiving, a division of troops from Texas. They had touched down in Colorado just moments before the bomb was dropped.

The force of the explosion had torn the bomber into shreds, scattering the pieces for hundreds of miles around.

"When the additional troops arrive," Martin told the commanding general of the troops already in place, "have them completely encircle the blast area. People are going in now, to check radiation levels."

"Yes, sir. The president is going to speak in a few minutes, sir. Do you want to listen?"

"No," Martin said.

"End of the trail," Sand said. "People, meet my friends. Joey, Tuddie, Morg, Jane. Sunny, you have already met Richard and Linda Jennings. And this is my wife, Robin. Our son is being looked after in a more secure place."

"Our computations were correct, Sand," the misty sparkling figure that was Joey said. "The door is open to within thirty miles of Willowdale, and right to the second of Central Standard Time."

"When can they pass through?"

"In about three minutes."

"What will we remember of this, Sand?" Sunny asked.

"Everything."

"How much of it can we tell?"

"As much as you want. But your president, at the urgings of his advisors, is now speaking to the world, telling a pack

345

of lies about what happened. The story will be that there was a huge spaceship that landed in Willowdale. It's so absurd that most will believe it. The ship, from some far-off world, carried disease. That is what killed the citizens of Willowdale. The ship exploded, causing all the damage. The bomber was lost during a storm, and fell into the sea. It's a stupid story, but many Americans are very shallow and stupid people. The truth does not interest them. Foolish games and mindless pleasures interest them. They'll believe it. Then, after awhile, everyone will believe it. And that's the way history will write it."

Bos said, "These tapes of your story?"

"They will be taken from you by government agents. Give them up without a struggle. You all know the truth, and Sunny will write the truth about what happened. That is enough for me."

"Sand," Megan asked. "How much of the history we were taught in school is truth, and how much is fiction?"

"That I cannot tell you."

"Can't, or won't?" Howie asked.

"Can't."

"Two minutes," Joey said.

"When you step through the door," Sand told them, "you will be slightly disoriented for a moment. It will pass."

"Then you've done this before?" Howie asked.

"That I cannot tell you."

Howie laughed, and Sand joined in the laughter.

"What would happen to you if . . . God found out you were doing this?" Hillary asked.

"Oh, He knows. He knows everything. He knows the beating of a sparrow's heart before some kid kills it with a BB gun. He knows the pain of the homeless and the unwanted. He hears the cries of the innocent who are in prison. He knows the pain of the starving. The helplessness of the abused children. He knows it all."

"But He won't help stop it," Leon said.

"He helps. He gives you brains that could solve the problems. But few care that much. He gives you the intellect to know that to demand more from animals than you do from humans is folly. He gives you all compassion, but most lose it — willingly. He gives you a mind to absorb knowledge, but most stop learning at age twenty. The list is endless and depressing."

"He's giving us another chance, isn't He, Sand?" Howie said.

"Yes."

"And we'd better not blow it," Angel added.

Suddenly, Sand and the others were gone. The sky above the little group was clear and star-filled. Gordie looked into the very startled face of Martin Tobias.

FREEDOM

Gordie and the others had been hustled out of the area, surrounded by government agents and soldiers. They had been taken to Colorado Springs and put aboard a plane and flown to Andrews AFB just outside of Washington. There they had been given physical examinations, hot food, clean clothing, and a place to sleep for the night.

Late the next afternoon, all of them rested and finally able to cope with the knowledge that they were alive and safe, they were taken to a huge meeting room, where they were sat down at a long table, across from the president of the United States.

"You're certainly looking well, Megan," President Marshall said.

"Thank you, sir."

"Sheriff Rivera, members of the military, children, ladies and gentlemen, we have a problem," the president said.

"We sure do," Angel said. "I read in the newspaper all that crap you told the world the other night. You ought to be ashamed of yourself for telling lies, Mr. President."

The president chuckled while Howie gave his sister a disgusted look.

"You're quite right, Angel," the president said. "And I am ashamed for telling stories."

347

"Then why did you?" Angel pursued it with the honesty of the young.

"It's a long and very complicated matter, Angel. And I'm not trying to be evasive . . . sidestep your question."

"I know what evasive means, sir," she told him. "Just answer me this: do you believe in your heart that you did the right thing?"

The president was a long time in replying. Finally he nodded his head. "Yes, I do, Angel. When the plan was first presented to me, only an hour or so before the bomb was to be dropped, I didn't like it. Didn't like it at all. And I'm still not at all sure that God will forgive me for lying to the people. But, yes, considering all the circumstances, I believe I did the right thing."

"And you want us to be quiet about it?" Angel asked.

"Yes, I do, Angel."

She looked him squarely in the eyes. Finally she nodded her head. "Okay, sir. If you say to keep quiet about it, I will."

"Thank you, Angel."

She looked at her brother. "Won't we, Howie?"

"I had already deduced that would be requested of us, Angel," Howie said.

"He already had it figured out," Angel translated for the president.

"Thank you, Angel."

"You want us to leave?" she asked. "So the grownups can talk?"

"Do you mind?"

She shrugged her shoulders. "Not really."

"I would like to see the computer room here at the base," Howie said.

"That can certainly be arranged," the president said. He looked at an aide, and the woman took the brother and sister on a tour of Andrews.

"What about Governor Siatos?" Bergman asked, when the kids were gone.

"The governor has been briefed. He will do what we tell

him to do."

"Does the public know we are alive?" Dean asked.

"Oh, yes. You'll all be regarded as heroes . . . for a time. The public is very fickle about these matters. The attention and adulation won't last long."

"What can we write about our experiences?" Jill asked.

The president smiled. "Let's talk about that."

One year later. Monte Rio, Colorado.

"Are we planning a reunion, Gordie?" Sunny asked her husband, just elected to his second term as sheriff of the county. The man who ran against him received one hundred and twelve votes.

Gordie looked out the window beyond the valley, toward the mountains. Troops still patrolled the perimeters of the valley. It was sealed off tight. Radioactivity, the government said. Gordie knew that was bullshit.

"Not as far as I'm concerned," he said, turning to face her. "How about you?"

"I really don't have time. I'm wrapping up this book on Sand. A couple more months, and I'll be through." She came to stand by his side, looking out the window at the mountains. "Angel and Howie will be home from school in a few minutes."

"Yes."

"What's over in the valley, Gordie? And why have you been summoned to Washington?"

"I've been summoned to Washington to discuss those . . . things over there in the valley. I don't know what they are, Sunny. I know that the army patrols that have gone in there have never returned. The government has never reported that to the public. I'm sheriff of this county, and I can't even go in there."

All roads, trails, and paths leading to the huge valley had been closed. Of late, military patrols had been beefed up. Lawsuits from the relatives of those killed in Willowdale were still pending against the government, and would probably go on for years.

"Things, Gordie?"

"Things, Honey. Grotesque, dangerous things."

Dean Hildreth and Jill Pierce were married. To each other. They still worked at competing networks. Dean was the anchor for the evening news at his network.

"Spawned by the Fury." It was not a question.

"Yes. And they want out of the valley."

Hillary had suffered a nervous breakdown and was still hospitalized.

"What do they look like?" Sunny questioned. "Has anybody ever seen one?"

"Yes. And I was just informed of that news yesterday. One army patrol reported seeing pirates. Another reported seeing a group of people who looked like Vikings. Still another reported seeing what appeared to be cavepeople. Another patrol said they saw men dressed like Mau-Mau."

Bos Graham had changed his major. He was studying to be a minister.

"Mau-Mau?"

Lee Evans was still Gordie's chief deputy.

"Yes. All sorts of wild things are being reported sighted in the valley."

Paul and Sandy got married. Both dropped out of school.

"Howie was right, then. The Fury did not destroy all that it consumed. It managed to somehow . . . leave behind a part of itself."

"Yes. A very dangerous part."

Sgt. Janet Dixon married Sgt. Keith Preston.

"So it's not over, is it?"

"It's just beginning."

Larry Adams left government work and dedicated his life to helping the homeless.

Megan LeMasters was still on the staff of Martin Tobias.

Sgt. Maj. Gary Christensen retired from the military and moved to Alaska.

Sunny put her arms around Gordie. "What's the government going to do about it?"

"I guess I'll find that out tomorrow or the next day."

"When is your flight out?"

"Ten-forty-five tomorrow morning. I'll land at Dulles."

Norris and Bergman still worked for the state police. They both stopped by to see Gordie and Sunny often.

Leon moved away.

Lynn dropped out of school and got married.

"It's a beautiful day," Sunny commented, looking out at the blue of the cloudless sky.

Doyle and Pat were still in college.

Dr. Craig Anderson was now practicing in Monte Rio.

"Gorgeous day."

Lt. Kathy Smith was now Capt. Smith, stationed in Germany.

Maj. Claude Jackson received the Medal of Honor. Posthumously.

Sunny cocked her head to one side and listened. She opened the window and looked out at the clear, cloudless day. Cool breezes fanned them both.

"What is that sound, Gordie?"

"Thunder."